TOM CLANCY

SHADOW OF THE DRAGON

ALSO BY TOM CLANCY

TOM CLANCY

SHADOW OF THE DRAGON

★

MARC CAMERON

G. P. PUTNAM'S SONS
NEW YORK

PUTNAM
— EST. 1838 —

G. P. PUTNAM'S SONS
Publishers Since 1838
An imprint of Penguin Random House LLC
penguinrandomhouse.com

ISBN 9780593188095

Printed in the United States of America
3   5   7   9   10   8   6   4

Maps by Jeffrey L. Ward

Men who are accustomed to eat at tiny tables in howling gales have curiously neat and finished table-manners.

Rudyard Kipling

When two tigers fight, one is injured beyond repair . . . and the other one is dead.

Chinese proverb

PRINCIPAL CHARACTERS

UNITED STATES GOVERNMENT

Jack Ryan: President of the United States
Arnold "Arnie" van Damm: President Ryan's chief of staff
Mary Pat Foley: Director of national intelligence
Scott Adler: Secretary of state
Robert Burgess: Secretary of defense
Admiral John Talbot: Chief of naval operations
Gary Montgomery: Special agent, Secret Service Presidential
   Protection Detail
Jay Canfield: Director of the Central Intelligence Agency
Robbie Forestall: Commander of the United States Navy,
   adviser to President Ryan

THE CAMPUS

Gerry Hendley: Director of The Campus and Hendley
   Associates
John Clark: Director of operations
Domingo "Ding" Chavez: Assistant director of operations
Jack Ryan, Jr.: Operations officer/senior analyst
Dominic "Dom" Caruso: Operations officer
Adara Sherman: Operations officer
Bartosz "Midas" Jankowski: Operations officer

Gavin Biery: Director of information technology
Lisanne Robertson: Director of transportation

OTHER CHARACTERS

Dr. Caroline "Cathy" Ryan: First Lady of the United States
Adam Yao: CIA case officer (NOC)
Dr. Patti Moon: Scientist on light icebreaker R/V *Sikuliaq*
Kelli Symonds: First officer, R/V *Sikuliaq*
Chief Petty Officer Shad Barker: Sonar technician, USS *John Paul Jones*

China

Liu Wangshu: Engineering professor
Medina Tohti: Uyghur woman, fugitive from PRC authorities
Hala Tohti: Medina's daughter
Zulfira Azizi: Medina's sister; Hala's aunt
Timur Samedi: Kashgar contact
Yunus Samedi: Kashgar contact
Ren Shuren: Major, Xinjiang Production and Construction Corps
Ren Zhelan: Chinese assistant bureaucrat, Kashgar Medina
Mr. Suo: Chinese bureaucrat, Kashgar
Ma "Mamut" Jianyu: Leader of the Wuming movement; Uyghur mother, Han father
Zheng Guiying: PLAN admiral in charge of naval intelligence
Fu Bohai: Zheng's henchman and primary hunter of Medina
Qiu: Fu Bohai's assistant

PLAN Yuan-*class attack submarine* Expedition #771
  (Blue Dragon)

Sun Luoyang: Captain
Bai Jiahao: Commander, XO (Executive Officer)

PLAN Nuclear SSBN 880 (Long March)

Tian Ju: Captain
Wan Xiuying: Commander, XO (Executive Officer)

USS Indiana *(SSN 789)* Virginia-*class fast-attack submarine*

Cole Condiff: Captain
Lowdermilk: Lieutenant, officer of the deck
Markette: Petty officer, sonar technician
Ramirez: New crew member

Roosevelt "Rosey" Jackson: Captain, USS *Makin Island*;
  nephew of former POTUS Robert Jackson
Jay Rapoza: Captain, USCG icebreaker *Healy*

ELISE

Monica Hendricks: CIA operations officer in charge of
  ELISE
Peter Li: Retired USN admiral
David Wallace: FBI counterintelligence agent assigned to
  ELISE
Odette Miller: CIA counterintelligence officer
Tim Meyer: CIA case officer

Albania

Leigh Murphy: CIA case officer, Tirana
Fredrick Rask: CIA chief of station, Tirana
Vlora Cafaro: CIA case officer, Tirana

Joey Shoop: CIA officer, Tirana

Urkesh Beg: Uyghur refugee living in asylum in Albania

Terms

ELISE: Operation to find Chinese mole within U.S. intelligence

PLAN: People's Liberation Army Navy

Bingtuan: "The Corps," short for Xinjiang Production and Construction Corps

TOM CLANCY

SHADOW OF THE DRAGON

1

D r. Patti Moon sat bolt upright in her plastic deck chair, startled at the sudden noise coming across her headset. The biting wind blowing off the Chukchi Sea didn't realize it was spring and pinked her round cheeks and smallish nose. Apart from her hands, which she needed to work the Toughbook portable computer, her face was the only part of her not bundled in layers of wool or fleece. Dr. Moon leaned toward the folding table, situated on the afterdeck of the research vessel *Sikuliaq*, straining to hear the noise again. *Sikuliaq* was Inupiaq for *young ice*—appropriate for a science vessel capable of traveling through more than two feet of the stuff.

They were in open water now, taking advantage of a large lead, more than a mile wide, to set some research buoys before the wind blew the ice pack back in.

Moon touched a finger to her headset as if that would help her make more sense of the sudden burst of sound. A former sonar technician on a Navy destroyer, she'd listened to a lot of noises from the deep, but nothing like this.

She sat up again, shook away a chill, telling herself it was just the wind.

The scientist slouching beside her turned to look at her with sleepy eyes that dripped barely veiled contempt. She didn't take offense. He looked at everyone and everything on the boat that way. Steven "Snopes" Thorson had spent his entire adult life in the world of academia. He knew he was smart—and he liked to make sure everyone around him knew it, too, fact-checking everything anyone said—especially his colleague and fellow Ph.D., Patti Moon.

Her academic bona fides were stellar—but she'd also had the experience of a life growing up in the Arctic, which apparently burned Dr. Thorson worse than the bitter wind.

Moon spent her first seventeen years in the tiny coastal village of Point Hope, Alaska, just four hundred miles south of where the *Sikuliaq* now motored to stay hove-to against the wind. She'd been in Anchorage for a high school basketball tournament when the USS *Momsen*, an *Arleigh Burke*–class destroyer, stopped for a port call. A female sailor had come ashore with the skipper—and that changed her life. No one pressured her to enlist—they didn't have to. She'd grown up on the ocean, fishing and seal-hunting with her father. The sea was in her blood, and though she wasn't sure how she felt about the U.S. government, the beautiful gray warship off the coast of her home state was all the inducement she needed to sign on the dotted line as soon as she graduated. She served six years as a sonar technician.

Her test scores were through the roof, and though she had a reputation for believing most every conspiracy theory she heard or read online, her sea-daddies (and -moms) pushed her to go to school when her enlistment ended. The GI Bill put her through undergrad at the University of Alaska Fairbanks, after which she'd gone on to attain a first-class graduate degree, and her doctorate in physics from Oxford.

She was just as smart as Dr. Thorson. And frankly didn't give two shits if he judged her for being human and touching her headset in hopes that it would make her hear better. Something was down there. A sound that didn't belong.

And then it was gone, yielding to the other squeals and grunts and songs of the ocean as quickly as it had arisen.

A strand of black hair escaped her wool beanie and blew across Moon's wind-chapped cheek. The wind had shifted, coming from the northeast now—beyond the pack ice. She ignored the cold, focusing instead on the sound she'd heard for only an instant as the hydrophone descended beneath the *Sikuliaq*.

Ballpoint pens were iffy in the cold, so Dr. Moon used a pencil to record the depth and time in her notebook. She shot a quick glance at Snopes Thorson.

"You didn't hear that?"

Wind fanned the ash on the end of Thorson's cigarette, turning it bright orange—like a tiny forge. Bundled in layers of merino wool, fleece, and orange arctic bibs, it was difficult to tell much about him, except that he wasn't very tall, and was, perhaps, very well fed. He wielded his sideways glares like weapons when he was annoyed, or, more often, when he was about to annoy someone else by fact-checking every little detail of a conversation. Thorson relished the notion of calling everyone out on the slightest error. Patti Moon made it a point to speak as little as possible around the man—not an easy thing to do when their jobs overlapped and their office was a 261-foot boat in the middle of the Arctic Ocean.

Like Moon, Dr. Thorson was a science officer, managing the dispersal of five expendable buoys that would be sunk in the deep water six hundred miles north of the Bering Strait and eight hundred miles south of the North Pole. If there were any mysteries left on earth, they were in the sea, Moon thought. And some of the greatest mysteries of all lay here, in the Chukchi Borderland, where the relatively warmer and saltier Atlantic met the colder, fresher, and more nutrient-rich waters of the Pacific. Oh, the Navy had bathymetric charts of the seafloor, but she knew from experience that they were not entirely accurate. Hidden reefs and shoals appeared and disappeared. Some believed them to be thick clouds of sea life that rose from the depths fooling a ship's sonar techs into thinking they were in much shallower waters.

No matter where one stood on climate change, there was no denying that the Arctic Ocean was opening to more and more sea traffic during summer months, cutting the delivery time of fossil fuels from ports in Russia and the North Slope of Alaska to the rest of the world by as much as two-thirds. Polar nations like Russia, Canada, Denmark, and the United States were as busy as they had ever been collecting data on the Arctic. Even China had edged into the game, arguing that they were a near-polar nation and going so far as to plant a CCP flag beneath the ice on the seafloor. Other countries had laughed this off as a stunt, but everyone worked to enhance their own capabilities on and under the ice.

Where there were ships of commerce, there were also ships of war.

Dr. Moon noted the hydrophone's depth at the time she'd first heard the noise. Two hundred and fifteen feet, but descending rapidly as the buoy and her underwater mic dropped toward the seafloors on the Kevlar cable. She adjusted the gain the old-fashioned way—by turning a knob, attempting to pick up the burst again.

"A passing whale?" Thorson said, his cigarette bobbing between his lips. "Sound can travel 4.3 times faster in water. Whatever you heard could be miles from here."

"Maybe," Moon conceded, ignoring the elementary physics lesson. She was professional enough not to rule out anything without a process. But even as she said the word, she knew that this was no whale.

The noise had not faded, but winked out, as if a switch had been thrown—leaving the rest of the ocean chorus to continue in its absence.

The sea was dark and cold, but it was not a quiet place. When she was only five, Patti's father had let her come with him seal-hunting beyond the jutting spit of land that gave Point Hope its Inupiaq name of Tikigaq—forefinger. Her father had showed her how to put the handle of the wooden paddle to her ear and listen to the undersea songs of *uguruq*—the bearded seal—as they vibrated up from the blade he'd left submerged in the water. The wooden paddle made for a rudimentary listening device, but she was able to hear the occasional song of a bowhead whale, bearded seals, and the ever-moving pack ice that shrieked and squealed like a badly fitting lid on a Styrofoam cooler. Later, during her time in the Navy, she'd learned that fish grunted, croaked, farted, and ground their teeth.

"Pack ice?" Thorson offered. Sullen, but wanting to guess correctly before she did.

She shook her head. "I'd still be hearing it if it was ice. No . . . it's gone dark, whatever it is."

Moon listened to the relatively dull burble of water as the science buoy continued to plummet toward the seafloor, taking the hydrophone with it. She stretched, glancing out at the sea. Calm today for this part of the world, the Arctic churned and swirled, looking like blue Gatorade and crushed ice—the good stuff, the kind you get from a drive-in.

Sikuliaq used her twin Wartsila ICEPOD azimuth thrusters, each capable of rotating 360 degrees, to stay in place relative to the seafloor. The big ice—the dangerous stuff that could gut even a tough polar ship like *Sikuliaq*—was still a half-mile away, glinting like silver on the northeast horizon.

Moon turned down the speaker and adjusted the headset over her ears, studying sound graphs on the screen of a second laptop, which was also attached to her hydrophone. Her primary laptop received readings from the expendable research buoy that Snopes Thorson had lowered into the water minutes before. The three-foot can was designed to remain under the ice all winter, far below the massive, fast-moving keels that raked the frigid water as deep as thirty meters. Surface buoys were a no-go in such harshly kinetic environments. They would simply be ground to bits. UAVs—underwater autonomous vehicles—drones—were useful. But they were also expensive. Frigid water sapped battery life and made them prone to loss. The Arctic, and the mysteries that lay beneath her surface, still baffled—and ate—technology.

That's where the under-ice buoys came in. Three feet tall and eight inches in diameter, the metal cans were relatively cheap, though *expendable* seemed not quite the right word for something with a three-thousand-dollar price tag. Attached to a fourteen-hundred-pound anchor, the device would remain on the ocean floor for most of the year, recording measurements on currents, temperature, and salinity at depth. At a predetermined time, shortly before the surface ice was expected to melt, a mechanism would release the buoy from its anchoring tether, allowing it to float to the surface, collecting more data about flow and thickness and melt rates. When the ice melted and the buoy peeked above the surface, it would send a message to its handlers via short-burst data transmission over the Iridium satellite system.

Ice data was all well and good, Dr. Moon thought. It was, after all, what paid the bills for now, but her real interest was in underwater sounds. To that end, she had begged permission to attach the hydrophone to the deploying cable as the buoy went down. She kicked herself for not rigging a camera at the same time. Even a GoPro might have given her video of whatever had made the sound.

She checked both computer screens, and then looked at Thorson. He surely thought the thick collar of his wool turtleneck made him look like a Nordic fisherman. Patti thought he looked like a little boy wearing his daddy's sweater.

"My money is on bubbles," he said, folding his arms across his chest. He nodded toward his computer. "It's not on the charts, but the sonar's showing a tall ridge jutting up from the seafloor about fifty meters northwest of our position. It's likely you're hearing current burbling around the rocks."

It was Moon's turn to shake her head. "I don't think it's burbling bubbles . . ." She fiddled with the touchpad on her computer. "What depth are you showing now?"

He checked his computer, then leaned sideways, squinting at her screen.

"Same as you. Three-six-five feet."

She gave Thorson her best imploring look, going so far as to bat her eyes a little. "Think we could bring it up a hundred feet, see if I could get that sound again?"

The numbers on her screen kept climbing as the buoy went deeper.

"Sorry, kiddo," Thorson grunted. "Entanglement danger if we reverse the winch right now."

Damn him, but he was right.

Moon thought of begging him more, but *Sikuliaq*'s first officer, a thirtysomething woman named Symonds, trotted down the steps from the wheelhouse and strode over to them, her head bowed against the wind. She also wore a wool turtleneck under waterproof orange Grundens bibs, but she wore hers better than Thorson, like she'd been born in them. A shock of curly blond hair jutted from beneath a black wool watch cap. One of the handful of people on the boat who didn't hold a graduate degree in science or engineering, Kelli Symonds possessed more common sense than most of them put together.

"Low pressure toward Wrangel Island is sucking a knife ridge of heavy pack ice south and west, right on top of us," she said. "The first course looks to be about the size of a cruise ship, and there's city blocks of the stuff after that. The skipper wants us up and outta here in five minutes."

Faces glued to their screens, both scientists gave Symonds a thumbs-up.

Sikuliaq was a Polar Class 5 vessel, fully capable of operating year-round in two and a half feet of new ice, with a few chunks of the previous year's stuff mixed in. Even now, a slushy soup of seawater and baby ice rattled and *thunk*ed against the powder-blue hull.

". . . and . . . we have touchdown," Thorson said. "Can is stable. Detaching now. Cable's coming up."

Patti Moon hunched over her computer again, ready this time, focusing intently on her headset as the winch wound in the Kevlar cable, raising the hydrophone faster now that there was only the counterweight and not a half-ton of gear dangling on the end of it.

The azimuth thrusters under *Sikuliaq*'s hull had already begun pushing her south, away from the jagged teeth of oncoming ice.

And there it was—at least part of it.

The noise started again at two hundred and fifty feet, continuing for almost four seconds before going quiet.

Dr. Moon marked the position in her journal and looked aft, past the red cranes and over the transom at the wake *Sikuliaq* left in the churning blue-green water. She shivered, and not from the bitter wind. This could not be what she'd initially thought. That was impossible.

Banging metal.

Screams.

Human screams.

2

Today, the lesson was on field-expedient weapons, a subject with which John Clark was intimately familiar. Two-by-fours, pointy mop handles, socks full of sand, a handy magazine rolled into a tight tube if it came down to that—all of them could be useful in a pinch when an operative found him- or herself without a gun or a suitable knife. Campus director of transportation Lisanne Robertson was proving herself to be an able student as they walked through the teeming Ben Thanh Market.

Clark registered the sweating European man with his peripheral vision. Open cotton shirt, juking this way and that as he made his way through the crowd. This guy was up to something, leading Clark to believe that some kind of a weapon might come in handy in the not-too-distant future.

Clark estimated the European to be in his mid-thirties. Lean, fit, with the kind of ropy muscles that were difficult to keep hold of in a fight. A workingman's muscles, like he'd just come from hanging Sheetrock or swinging a hammer at a construction site. Dark hair hung in sweaty curls over the collar of his shirt. Glancing furtively, obviously searching for someone, the man attempted to move quickly, but was impeded by the mass of shoppers and sightseers who clogged the aisles between what, at first glance, appeared to be an endless line of T-shirt shops.

Clark had spent the morning braving the crowds of Ho Chi Minh City, wading through rivers of scooter traffic and pointing out the various items an operative might find useful if he or she had to suddenly go on the defensive. Lisanne was former law enforcement and no stranger to conflict, making her a quick learner. In point of fact, Clark was more interested in observing the way she handled herself on the street than he was in teaching any of the finer points of tradecraft. Operational teams like The Campus, an off-the-books intelligence agency set up by President Jack Ryan and Senator Gerry Hendley, needed a periodic inoculation of fresh perspective and talent. The backbone of the team had been around since the beginning. They'd lost a couple of dear friends along the way, and, considering the type of work they did, were bound to lose some more if they were not extremely careful . . . or even if they were. Hence, Clark's desire to see how the young woman comported herself in a foreign land.

The greasy European had popped up on Clark's radar when he'd stopped to talk to a woman at a stall selling chunks of bloody unidentifiable meat piled up beside baskets of live frogs.

Clark didn't mention anything to Lisanne. So far, he had nothing more than a gut feeling, a hunch.

It wasn't so much how the man moved as the way those around him reacted to his presence. The woman with the basket of frogs recoiled when he approached her stall, as if he smelled bad or was about to draw a knife.

The man didn't look particularly dangerous, at least not to John Clark. In truth, Clark had no idea of the man's nationality.

But he carried himself like a European, legs together when he stood, furtive, catlike, instead of doggedly like an American— so Clark began to think of him that way as they walked.

Though the rest of The Campus was off doing "real work," Lisanne Robertson embraced the training week, rattling off possible field-expedient weapons nearly as quickly as Clark while they walked. The nine million inhabitants of Ho Chi Minh City—formerly Saigon—provided all sorts of deadly detritus in the way of rakes, tire irons, and bamboo poles. The wet market, pungent and loud, made up a relatively small area off the diverse indoor Ben Thanh Market. What it lacked in size, it made up for with an original odor. To Clark, it was the smell of Asia, and it brought with it a flood of memories. It was a smorgasbord of meat cleavers and fillet knives, free for the snatching if the need arose.

A smallish man crossed in front of them as they walked. Clark paused a half-step when he caught the man's eye. The small man bowed slightly and walked on, disappearing into the crowd. Clark pointed down the aisle, motioning for Robertson to take the lead.

"He looked Chinese," Robertson noted as they walked, calling out her observations like a good student. "Do you know him?"

"Nah," Clark said. "He just reminded me of someone. A Chinese colonel."

"From back in the day?"

"Yep," Clark said.

"Sorry," Robertson said. "Must be tough."

Clark stopped. The people behind him parted, passing on either side of him and Lisanne. "The particular guy was a colonel who'd come to Vietnam to teach the Vietcong how to better kill us. Though I have to say they were already doing a pretty damned good job of it. Anyway, I watched that colonel for three days, learning his habits, what kind of beer he liked to drink, his preference in women. Got to know his face very well."

"You think that guy was him?"

Clark looked at her, shaking his head as if to clear it.

"What?"

"Do you think that guy was the colonel you met years ago?"

"Oh, no," Clark said, picturing the reticle of his Bushnell scope settling over the colonel's ear. "I'm not positive about much in this old world, but I can assure you this. That wasn't him."

"Ah," Robertson said. "Gotcha."

She was a former Marine, and no shrinking violet when it came to human conflict.

They kept walking, Robertson calling out weapons, and Clark kept an eye on the European.

Clark liked his people to be aware of everything around them, keeping their "quivers" full, so they could draw on what they needed when they needed it. Even if an operative had a gun, circumstances could make producing it take too much time.

Ingrained in Clark's DNA, these were good points for even the most seasoned operative to review.

Vendors barked out to them as they walked, calling Lisanne "Madam," looking stricken with grief when she didn't stop and buy a pair of "Adodis" sweatpants or a "Nortfaze" jacket. Their faces magically brightened again as they barked at the next customer once Lisanne passed by.

Clark and his friends had frequented the market during his

first trip to Saigon. U.S. Navy HQ had been only a few blocks away and Ben Thanh provided a good place to meet girls, grab a plate of shrimp dumplings, or maybe buy a couple of knock-off T-shirts to send to your kid brothers who were getting all their news about the war from Walter Cronkite or *The Huntley–Brinkley Report*. Saigon had been loud then, and crowded, too, though nothing like it was now.

Many of the old buildings were gone, gaudy new ones with higher rent having sprung up in their place. It was hard to say which were the flowers and which were the weeds—the old buildings or the new. Maybe it was a bit of both. The people seemed better off than they'd been when he was here before, but Clark supposed that was more a function of pushing the poorer folk to the outskirts of town.

Thousands of scooters, called *motos* in Vietnam, groaned and buzzed on the teeming street outside the market. Clark and Lisanne Robertson were merely two in tens of thousands of other bees moving en masse inside a hive. Clark was unarmed, and he'd long since moved his wallet into the front pocket of his loose chinos—not because Vietnamese people were inherently more likely to pick his pockets, but because they were people and the odds around so many people were that some of them were going to try and pick his pocket. And of all the species of animals on the planet, Clark mistrusted people the most.

The sizzle and smell of *banh xeo*, an especially delicious shrimp crepe, twined around Clark's memory and pulled him sideways toward the stall. The crowd moved on behind him as he stepped out of the flow. Clark spoke quickly to the stooped mama behind a wooden board she'd set over two upturned crates. He paid for two cardboard baskets of yellow tacolike *banh xeo,* one for him, and another for his trainee, and then waited while the mama dished up his order. Clark couldn't help but wonder what this woman cooking *banh xeo* had been up to when he was here the first time. Had she been cooking then, too? Had they passed on the street? In a club? Had she or one of her relatives shot at him, killed his friends? Had he killed any of hers? Whose side had she been on? Likely her own side, Clark thought, trying to stay alive when two unstoppable forces were bent on grinding everything between them into the greasy monsoon mud.

Clark closed his eyes for a quick moment, just long enough to take in the riot of odors and sounds—fish, black vinegar, and scooter exhaust. When the wind shifted just right, he could smell the Saigon River, mere blocks away.

Clark passed one order of crispy shrimp crepes to Lisanne—who'd snagged them a couple of seats at one of the half-dozen low plastic tables beside the food stall. It wobbled badly and looked like something the kids would be relegated to at Thanksgiving. Clark didn't care. They'd been on their feet all morning and it was good to sit down.

Lisanne tucked a lock of dark hair behind her ear, and leaned across the rickety plastic table toward Clark. She wore khaki shorts and, like Clark, a loose microfiber shirt with the long sleeves rolled up above her elbows. The deep olive complexion she'd inherited from her Lebanese mother helped her blend in a little better than Clark. Though, he had to admit, old men were invisible just about anywhere in the world. It was a fact he used to his advantage. Clark was still in better-than-average shape, jogging five miles every other day. He was admittedly not nearly as fast as he used to be. He'd kept up with his lifting, lower weight and higher reps. He could still bench his body weight, an ability he'd used as a sort of litmus test for his personal fitness. These days, he spent a good deal of time recovering between sets, staring up at the ceiling and thinking about his grandson—or whoever he happened to be training at the moment.

"Doesn't this bug you?" Lisanne asked, her eyes darting from face to face in the crowd of passersby. "I've never thought of you as a person who'd like to turn his back on anyone."

Clark smiled at that, resisting the urge to call his young acolyte Grasshopper.

"We're predators," he said, biting into one of the *banh xeo*. "Our eyes are set in the front of our heads, perfect for being a hunter. When we focus those eyes on someone in particular, we have to turn our back on someone else."

"Still," Lisanne said, scanning the crowd. "It creeps me out to have anyone get behind me."

"I agree," Clark said. "That's a good quality for you to have in our line of work." He nodded to the food. "Go ahead and eat. We won't sit here long."

"Glad to hear that," she said. Supremely feminine, she still knew how to shovel down food.

After the Marines, Lisanne was working as a patrol officer in Virginia when she'd pulled Hendley over on a traffic stop. He'd been extremely impressed with the way she'd handled herself and he'd eventually recruited her to be their director of transportation. She was fluent in Arabic and could get by in Spanish and Mandarin. As DT, she often acted in the same capacity as a one-person Phoenix Raven detail, guarding the Hendley Associates G550 when it was on the ground at various airfields around the world. Clark rolled her into defensive tactics and other scenario-based training exercises with other Campus operatives almost as soon as she'd come aboard. She'd wowed the rest of the team with her fighting skill right from the get-go. More than anything, Clark was impressed with her ability to think under pressure. She was a better-than-average shot on the range, but began to really shine when the Sim rounds came zinging her way. She'd been downrange before and knew all too well what it was like to get shot at.

"Would it make you feel better if you had a gun?" Clark asked.

Lisanne looked up over half a bite of crepe and raised an eyebrow. She was used to him quizzing her all the time. Often calling him Socrates when he only answered her questions with more questions.

"I think it would," she said. "A little. Though I guess I'd worry about someone bumping into it in a crowd like this and making a scene."

Clark gave a contemplative nod. He wiped his hands on a handkerchief he took from the hip pocket of his khakis. Few food vendors wanted to cut into their bottom line by providing napkins for free.

"Tell me what you have on you right now," he said.

"My everyday carry?" Lisanne grinned. "I always enjoy it when Ding has everyone pocket-dump their EDC on the plane."

"Everyday carry . . ." Clark shook his head, scoffing a little. "I get a kick out of all the shit people call their *everyday* carry. A person in downtown Paducah might be able to get away with carrying two knives, a survival bracelet, multitool, tacticool flashlight, escape and evasion tools, and a SIG 365 with an extra magazine. Most of the time, we lose a bunch of those luxuries when we travel to other areas of the world, even in a private jet like we do. Your everyday Joe or Jill can run the most prepared setup imaginable in their hometown, surrounded by friendlies, but as soon as they get on a plane for Aruba, they can forget about a pistol. Carry one of those cool metal punch cards with a flat lock-picking set and you're liable to get picked up as a spy in a good many countries. A pocketknife better look like a tool when you go overseas, or there's a good chance you'll get to know the inside of a Yourassisgrassistan prison."

"Agreed," Lisanne said, wiping her hands on the handkerchief she got from her own pocket.

Clark gave the white rectangle of cloth a nod. "*That* is everyday carry."

Lisanne grinned. "Something I can have with me when I'm overseas or in Paducah."

"Exactly," Clark said. "The stuff you carry every damned day, rain or shine, wherever you are . . . That's a fairly sparse list. There is *everyday* carry, there's *most* days carry, and then there's *mission* carry. You and I will often accept the risks of carrying a concealed firearm in a foreign land because the danger of not having one outweighs the chance of arrest."

Clark tapped the side of his head. "The things you put up here are a hell of a lot more important than what you have in your pocket. If you don't remember anything else we talk about, remember this: You are the weapon. Anything you carry in your pocket or pick up from your surroundings—gun, knife, mop handle, or broken brick—is nothing more than a tool."

Lisanne nodded, chewing on the counsel along with the last of her *banh xeo*. Her face remained impassive, but Clark picked up on a sudden change in her countenance, a subtle shift, as if she were about to stand.

"That guy you were watching," she said without moving her head. "He's back."

Clark thought of complimenting her for noticing the same European he had, but decided the ultimate compliment would be to let her assume that he knew she'd been up to speed all along. In truth, it didn't surprise him.

"His buddy on the motorcycle just dropped him off," she said. "Directly behind you . . . Looks like he's locked on to someone in the crowd . . ." Both hands on the table, she scanned, looking for the European's target. "Got her. Local girl, maybe fifteen, at your seven o'clock."

Clark was on his feet in an instant.

"They're heading this way," Lisanne said. Fifty feet out.

Clark turned, spotting the girl first. She moved quickly, not running, but clearly trying to make time. Apparently unaware that the European was closing in on her, she looked over her shoulder at every other step. She knew *somebody* was out there, hunting her. Her yellow T-shirt had seen better days. Sagging at the collar and torn in several places, it looked to have been used as a rag to wipe the girl's grimy face as much as an article of clothing. Filthy denim shorts were cut high, revealing a map of faded bruises on her thighs. She wore heavy eye makeup, but no shoes. A band of pale skin stood out starkly from the otherwise olive complexion of her wrist, where she'd once worn a watch.

"I'll go after her," Lisanne said, already walking, showing Clark a grim smile. "You're liable to scare her."

"Copy that," Clark said, moving to intercept the oncoming European. He was close, so it didn't take long.

Clark got a clear glimpse of a pair of flex-cuffs protruding from the European's pocket—and the black butterfly knife in the man's clenched fist. It was closed now, as the European made his way through the crowd, but with a flick of his wrist, he could flip it open in an instant. It was a wicked little weapon, devastatingly effective in the right hands. And not at all likely to be carried by any sort of law enforcement in the process of arresting a fleeing teenage girl.

Certain now that the European had nothing but bad intentions, Clark jostled him lightly as he went by. There were plenty of non-Asians in the crowd, and the European gave the gray-haired Clark no more than a passing grunt for getting in his way.

The man had just begun to push off with his trailing foot when Clark drove the heel of a boot straight into his Achilles tendon.

Cursing in Slovakian, the man sagged, instinctively moving to shield his injury. With all the weight now on the man's forward leg, Clark gave him a brutal side kick. Human knees were not designed for lateral movement, and the ligaments and cartilage fairly exploded. Clark snatched away the butterfly knife. It had all happened so quickly and the man was so immersed in pain that there was a good chance he wasn't completely sure Clark was the person responsible for his injuries.

The crowd closed in around him as he fell, and Clark, as was his habit, melted into the shadows. Lisanne was still out there, watching out for the fleeing girl.

Clark found them less than a hundred feet away, at the edge of the no-haggle area where blue-smocked salespeople charged fixed prices for their wares.

Clark pushed his way through a knot of concerned gawkers— local Vietnamese and assorted tourists—to find another European flat on his back, unconscious, blood weeping from the burst flesh above a bushy black eyebrow. This one was shorter than the partner Clark had dealt with, broader, with the flattened face of a boxer—for all the good it had done him.

Clark scanned for other threats, but no one stood out. A frumpy saleswoman in a sky-blue smock held up her phone and rattled off something in Vietnamese. Clark recognized the word for *police*.

A frail Vietnamese woman who looked to be in her fifties clucked her way through the crowd. She wore a nun's headscarf and a sincere but stern look that Clark knew all too well from his childhood. The frightened girl stepped from around Lisanne at the sight of the nun and rushed into her arms, tears and words pouring out of her. Clark caught part of it, but his Vietnamese language skills had grown worse than rusty after all these years. The sobbing didn't help.

He shot Lisanne a look and nodded toward the market. Both knew any contact with the local gendarmerie would gain them unwanted attention that they didn't need. The rest of The Campus would be working here for a week, and he and his new operative still had a lot of work to do.

The nun enveloped the girl with her arm, like the wing of a mother hen, and led her back the way she'd come, disappearing in the mass of humanity. Evidently, she didn't want to get involved with the police, either.

"She'd come to meet the sister," Clark said, tipping his head toward the nun.

"I only got to talk to her for a couple of seconds," Lisanne said. "But as I understand it, those guys were pimping her out at a couple of the local hotels. They'd brought her to meet a client across the street and she bailed on them . . . At least, that's what I think she said. Her English wasn't much better than my Vietnamese."

Clark walked beside her, turning down a narrow alley made of bolts of colorful cloth stacked nearly to the ceiling.

"You made short work of the hairy guy," Clark observed. "I'll be interested to hear how you did it."

"Sure," Lisanne said, smiling. "Remember that upright cement post where I was standing?"

"I do," Clark said, seeing where this was going.

"Like you told me," Lisanne said. "Sometimes you bounce a rock off the bad guy's head, sometimes you bounce the bad guy's head off the rock. I'm the weapon, I just choose how to use the tool."

Clark gave her a wink. "Young lady," he said, "I believe you will do." He took out his phone and punched in his son-in-law's number.

"You guys about done for the day?" he said when the man at the other end picked up.

3

People's Liberation Army Navy *Yuan*-class attack submarine *Yuanzheng #771* cruised twenty meters below the choppy brown surface of the Bering Sea, towing a tethered communication buoy. The *Yuanzheng* (Expedition) designation applied to all conventional diesel-electric submarines that were armed with ballistic or cruise missiles.

Expedition 771 carried ballistic missiles, but she was far from conventional.

The PLAN Submarine Force referred to each vessel by class and hull number, but *771*'s crew, the collective soul that made her alive, called her *Qinglong*—Blue Dragon—after the dull color of her rubberized anechoic hull. Captain Sun Luoyang thought it fitting. The blue-green Dragon of the East symbolized the Yuan Dynasty's great sea power, and the name gave the men immense pride in their vessel.

Sun was an effective leader who had his father's strong hands and his mother's rock-solid devotion to duty. Not quite five and a half feet tall, he'd also inherited his father's narrow shoulders and diminutive stature. His size had been a nuisance in school, and much more so later in military training, when every success seemed to hinge on one's ability to excel at sports.

But a keen intellect and sheer determination carried him to the submarine force, where his small frame would serve him well. With an array of torpedoes and ship-killing missiles at his disposal, it didn't matter one iota if he was good at football or boxing or table tennis.

He'd never married, but took seriously the responsibility of mentor if not father to the young people in his crew.

Now that he'd come shallow, three of them were suffering acute symptoms of seasickness.

Less than twenty-four hours earlier, Captain Sun and the crew of *771* had finally slipped free from a two-week exercise with the Russian Navy in the semiprotected waters near Anadyr, the administrative capital of Chukotka, Russia. There had been problems with two of his pumps, and he'd had to stay behind for the better part of a week after the others had returned south. Sun had remained on his submarine through the entire training evolution and repairs, never setting foot in the city. He surmised that like all frontier towns he'd visited, this one was filthy and full of itself for its perceived rugged independence.

Captain Sun had found the exercise interesting enough— docking, refit and repair at sea, submarine warfare theory. All well and good, necessary to sustain a formidable force. But PLAN superiors steadfastly refused to allow any vessels to take part in the "war" part of the war game. Though well accustomed to littoral defense and denial, in Sun's opinion, the PLAN's abilities in the open sea needed more severe testing. Beijing wanted them to drill, but they were not about to be embarrassed in front of the Kremlin. Moscow did not push the subject. To them, the exercise had been little more than a sales pitch. The Kremlin wanted to brag about their technology in order to sell more of it to Beijing. The less they had to work for it, the better. Moscow was vocal to the point of bombastic on news and social media about their success at modernizing the Russian Navy, but Captain Sun was astonished to see how clankingly aged most of the ships and submarines were. Chinese and Russian weapons alike often finessed American technology into tractorlike hardware, giving them the appearance of a well-designed sledgehammer.

They were, of course, far from defenseless. Sun had never personally seen it, but the Russian Typhoon-class submarine was said to be large enough to have its own sauna and pool. Sun laughed at the thought. With the flick of his hand, he could turn his entire boat into a sauna and have the crew swimming in their own sweat.

The exercise had not been a complete waste of time. Simply being at sea was good training for his youthful crew.

Finally away, the last to leave, *771* was heading southwest by south off the Russian coastline, still in relatively shallow waters. She had yet to pass the point of Navarin, where the depth dropped to many thousands of meters—deeper and calmer. Here, they were in the growling gut of the Bering Sea—famous to Americans because of the bourgeois television program about crab fishing. The Bering was the birthplace of many a violent gale, and at this depth, Captain Sun Luoyang felt the roll of a confused sea shudder through his boat.

The three sick crewmen were all younger than twenty. The cook's helper had it the worst, unable to keep down even a thin broth. The boy's record said he was nineteen, but Sun suspected fifteen was closer to the mark, perhaps even younger. For a time, Sun thought he might even be a girl, a modern Mulan who had somehow slipped through training, to try her hand at the submarine service. Sun's executive officer spoke to the chief, who spoke to the petty officers, who were quickly able to ascertain that, no, the cook's helper was indeed a boy, who badly missed his mother.

Steadying himself on the navigation table, the captain had the word passed to engineering to increase speed by two knots, straining the communication buoy tether, but hopefully smoothing out the ride. The odor on a submarine was an unpleasant one to begin with, but the ability to smell it disappeared within a few days. The three sick crewmen were adding new odors, making everyone, including the captain, fight the urge to gag a good deal of the time.

Seaman Wang, stationed at the communications booth, coughed quietly, hand to his mouth, as if he were about to vomit. He mumbled something unintelligible, large glasses illuminated, buglike, in the dull blue glow of his computer screen.

At nineteen years of age, and a recent graduate of the submariner academy in Qingdao, the boy was a worthy example of fortitude to be sure, but it would be problematic if he were to vomit all over the sensitive equipment.

Seasickness was bad enough on a surface vessel. Here, in this windowless metal tube that smelled of diesel fuel, sulfur, and flatulence, vertigo and nausea could be soul-crushing. The boat's doctor—in truth, a submariner with six months of extra medical training—had given all three sick crewmen promethazine suppositories. This had apparently done little to ease Wang's discomfort, but his perseverance was heartening. He was the very image of the submariners whom Captain Sun and the Motherland wanted to grow for their Red Star, Blue Water fleet. This stripling boy had set aside his roiling gut to man his station during the appointed time, no matter how sick he felt.

The boy's hand shot to his mouth and he mumbled something again.

The chief of the watch barked at the boy to speak up, but the captain gave a slight shake of his head. He ran a tight ship, but no amount of discipline would chase away seasickness. It simply had to pass.

Commander Bai Jiahao, Sun's executive officer, stepped closer to relay the incoming message.

"Communication buoy successfully deployed and operational," he said. "Priority incoming from Fleet."

Sun nodded. Both men knew that Fleet headed every message as *Priority*, so this notation did nothing to raise any alarms.

"Very well," Sun said, waiting for the message to spit out of the small printer.

Three hours earlier—at a much more comfortable one hundred and twenty meters, *771* had received instructions telling her to surface as soon as practical for further communications. Only four countries in the world had antenna arrays large enough to send messages via extremely low frequency: China, Russia, India, and the United States. It was a point of pride with Captain Sun that China's ELF array was the largest of them all. Almost as large as the American island of Manhattan, China's massive installation essentially used the earth itself as an antenna with which to send its signals. Even so, communication through hundreds of feet of salt water was beyond difficult. The *Blue Dragon* had to pull two kilometers of wire behind her to receive the signals. ELF messages were one-way (the submarine could not respond) and they came in maddeningly slowly, on the order of a few characters per minute. For the most part, incoming signals were all the same—*"Prepare to communicate."* Essentially, this meant *"We want to talk to you. Come shallow enough to deploy your antenna or communication buoy so that we may do so."*

When it was dark enough on the surface that Captain Sun felt the risk of his shadow being spotted via satellite was minimized, he instructed the officer of the deck to have the boat brought to thirty meters and deployed the communication buoy.

"Captain," the XO said, stepping closer to pass him the printed message. The sub rolled to starboard, then righted herself. The XO, too, had to steady himself on the chart table.

"We are to alter course, sir."

Sun snatched the flimsy paper away and scanned the characters.

He read the message again, more slowly this time, and then handed them to his XO, who barked new orders to retrieve the communication buoy and then turn the submarine around one hundred and eighty degrees.

With the order given, the XO lowered the paper so he could meet the captain's eye.

"Sir, the Americans may not yet know our position, since we had to remain behind the others to finish repairs, but they will certainly hear, and in all likelihood see, us when we pass to the north through the Bering Strait."

"Indeed," Sun said.

A natural choke point, the Bering Strait was little more than eighty kilometers wide at its narrowest point. With an average depth of fifty meters, some areas were far shallower, leaving submarines visible to surveillance satellites or prowling P-3

Orion sub hunters. The Americans generally thought of the PLAN as a coastal submarine force, rarely venturing farther than the straits of Taiwan. They would be all too happy to discover a Chinese Dragon heading not just to coastal Russian waters, but for the Arctic Ocean.

The United States had placed sensitive hydrophones and other sensors on the floor of the Bering as well as other choke points around the world to monitor Soviet traffic. If one was to believe American propaganda—which Captain Sun did not—the Sound Surveillance System, or SOSUS, had been greatly curtailed after the Cold War, with only three devices still in place. Surely powers like the United States were growing their surveillance presence all around the world, not curtailing it. And that didn't count the presence of Canadian or other listening devices.

The Americans would see them, but it could not be helped. PLAN Fleet Command knew what they were doing. They had issued the orders and Sun would comply with them.

"We will be apprised of our mission once we are well north of the strait," Sun said. "Until then, set a course for these grid coordinates."

The XO typed the latitude and longitude, laying in a series of plot-dots on the screen that would allow them to run as deep as possible, while navigating around obstacles like underwater mountains or the Diomede Islands that guarded the center of the Bering Strait. Finished, he tapped a spot on the chart off the coast of Alaska, a thousand kilometers north of the strait.

Captain Sun knew exactly what his right-hand man was thinking.

"Exactly," Sun said. "The Chukchi Borderland. We're going under the ice."

4

The two men in the second-story window across the street from Huludao Smile Swimwear Ltd's tiny office made no attempt to hide. Both wore long coats, as if they planned to step outside at any moment and brave the cold. Pei Ying could feel their eyes before she saw them. Rather than look up and meet their gaze, she went about her midday routine. She had not grown a successful business to squander all her money on propane to heat an empty office, and it had grown cold while she was away all morning visiting one of her factories. She lit the gas heater on the wall beside her cluttered desk, then dropped the blackened match into an ashtray with a nest of dozens of other burned stubs—the remnants of a long and bitter winter. The faint odor of gas made her think of her late husband and those early days of the company. She chuckled at that, despite the men lurking across the street. Anyone who looked at her office would surely believe her business was struggling. The tiny heater wouldn't actually warm the cramped space until mid-April, but the blue flames and glowing ceramic tiles took the worst of the edge off. And anyway, Pei did not mind the cold. She enjoyed wearing a down jacket and sipping hot tea all day—an irony indeed for the owner of a company that manufactured skimpy swimsuits.

The main offices were located at the primary plant, nearer to the wharf, but Pei kept a personal office here, for the moments when she wanted to be away from the clatter of machinery and buzzing employees. It had been her husband's office—and now it was hers. Just like the company.

Tucked into the ground floor, the office was in the same squat three-story building as her home. Everyone in the building called her Pei Ayi—Auntie Pei. Her apartment was upstairs—a short commute. She could have easily afforded a private villa—what people in the West called a single-family home. She had plenty of money if she'd wanted a high fence and her own yard, like the ones across the alley, but she preferred to roll her money back into the company. She was always at work, anyway. A larger house was only more for her to clean. Her son's wife had different notions, of course, and leaned on the boy to buy her a lavish apartment. The stupid girl gambled, too.

Perhaps the men across the street were here about Pei's daughter-in-law. That would not be so bad.

Auntie Pei sat down behind a pile of invoices at her desk and took a sip of tea from a chipped mug, shooting a quick glance at the window across the street. One of the men drew back dingy yellow curtains with an open hand, peering down with narrowed, accusing eyes, like a falcon planning an attack stoop. He was young—as everyone seemed to Auntie Pei—perhaps in his early thirties. His mussed hair was thick and long. A wide face screwed into a crooked frown, as if he were trying to twitch a fly off the end of his nose without using his hands. The second man stood a half-step back. This one was bald and clean-shaven. Heavy glasses with black rims provided the only relief to an otherwise featureless egg. He blinked a lot behind the glasses. Surely this one followed the lead of the one with the frown.

Auntie Pei's neck burned from their stares. Perhaps they had come for her.

Everyone in China knew they were being monitored, but there was safety in numbers. Herring swam in great schools to protect themselves from hunting tuna. But if that tuna zeroed in on a single fish, it was impossible to get lost, no matter how large the school. If Beijing—or even the local government— turned the scalding light of their attention on you, it was over. There was no point in pretending otherwise. Everyone had something to hide.

In Auntie Pei's case, it was her half-sister. That would be enough to sink her for good.

The men across the street stayed indoors for the moment because it was raining, not because they cared about being seen. The bald head of the one on the right shone like a torch through the grimy glass. The smug frown on the other one was as noticeable as a festering boil.

They had to be MSS. Pei Ying was certain of it. Operatives from the Ministry of State Security—similar to a combined American FBI and CIA—tended to carry themselves differently from local police. They were haughty, highborn, like they could not wait to clean the likes of you off the bottom of their boots. She'd met worse men, but not many.

Standing again beside her desk, Pei flipped through a file folder, hardly seeing the figures on the paper. What could they possibly want with her?

Her social credit score, the Chinese national system used to indicate the trustworthiness of citizens, should have been near perfect.

Smile Swimwear contributed much to the economy. A quarter of all the bosoms and buttocks in the world were swaddled in fashionable swimsuits manufactured right here in Huludao—and a good many of those suits were born on the machines in Auntie Pei's factories. Her late husband of twenty-three years had been a trade adviser to local Party officials. Auntie Pei served on the board of the yearly International Swimwear Show. She sat on a municipal planning committee for refuse recycling and donated blood every two months. She paid her bills on time, including her exorbitant taxes, and had no complaints to the police by her neighbors so far as she knew.

Could a rotten-egg sister in the family really ruin all of that?

Sadly, yes.

The men were gone from the window now. Auntie Pei considered stepping out the back door of her office, but there was no point. Running would only make her look guilty.

Across the street, the MSS men stepped out the door of the apartment building. The bald one held a folded newspaper over his head, though the rain had tailed off. The leader, seemingly oblivious, stopped to light a cigarette he'd jammed into the slanting gash of his frown. Smoke and vapor curled around his face in the chilly air. He sniffed, like a hunter, and then stepped into the street.

Pei swallowed hard. To this man, her having a half-sister like Jun would cause all manner of hardship.

Four years younger than Pei Ying, Jun had dabbled in the practice of Falun Gong ten years earlier. China was an avowed atheist country, but Beijing allowed five religions. Falun Gong was not one of them, and its practice could bring the foot of the government down quite literally on the neck of anyone caught taking part. Beijing went so far as to demand local jurisdictions prosecute—and persecute—those who continued the practice. Jun's block warden had denounced her to the head of the local 610 Office, fearful of punishment for violating the mandate. Men from the 610 Office—tasked with no other duty than to see to the eradication of Falun Gong—arrested Jun at a park, where she was walking her little dog. Her pet was left abandoned, and she was thrown in a white van, transported to a transformation-through-reeducation facility on the outskirts of Beijing. In many ways, Pei Ying felt sorry for Jun. She was interested in everything, flitting from one hobby to another. Cheap steel, their father had called the girl—easily sharpened but just as easily dulled.

She'd been caught up in the idea of Falun Gong, but had never been a devout follower. Official accounts said she'd fallen getting out of the van, but however it happened, both her feet were broken on the first day. By that night, she made a video statement that Falun Gong had been a horrible mistake and that it no longer interested her at all. She implored her friends to stay away. And they probably would—from her.

Auntie Pei felt sure the mindless woman would have made the same statement in return for a stick of chewing gum. There had been no need to break her feet.

She glanced through the window at the approaching men.

They barged in without knocking, as she knew they would. The bald one was older, somehow missing even his eyebrows, and smelled faintly of old socks. The younger wore his smug frown like an accessory, the way some men wore an expensive watch. Both were dressed in khaki slacks and striped, three-button polo shirts of slightly different patterns, though the younger one's clothes were newer and better tended. He was single, Pei thought, and still cared what girls might think of him. The stinky, browless one was comfortably married and beyond such trivialities as grooming and hygiene.

Mr. Frown did the talking.

"Professor Liu," he snapped, hooking a thumb over his shoulder toward the house across the alley from her office. The sneer perked into the slightest of smiles when Auntie Pei blanched at the sight of the black pistol as his shirttail rode up.

She put a hand on her desk to steady herself. "What?"

"Professor Liu Wangshu!" the man barked, louder this time. "When did you see him last?"

"Ah, ah." Pei clucked, struggling to control her breathing. They were not here for her after all, but for Liu, the university professor who lived in one of the villas across the alley. These were not the first men who had come to talk to him. Instead of waning, her sense of dread grew deeper, pressing at her chest, making it difficult to speak.

She swallowed, lifting the teacup in a remarkably steady hand. "It has been at least two weeks. Maybe three. I assumed he was away on a business trip. He travels someti—"

"We are quite aware of how often he travels," Mr. Frown said. The MSS man gestured over his shoulder again, this time for the benefit of his balding partner. "She is useless."

Both men wheeled and strode out the door without another word.

Auntie Pei gasped, awash with relief.

When it came to members of the Ministry of State Security, *useless* was a very good thing to be. Perhaps she would be able to keep herself from becoming embroiled in whatever this was. She opened the lap drawer of her desk and took out a slip of paper, reading the number out loud to steady herself as she entered it into her phone. The tall man who had left her the paper was from the government. He'd worn a hat, pulled low over his eyes, but had taken it off when he spoke to her, respectful, not like the bad-egg MSS officers. He'd understood Auntie Pei's standing in the community. Still, there had been danger to him. Not aimed at her, but to whomever he happened to be hunting. His instructions had been clear—couched as a polite request.

Should anyone come looking for Professor Liu, she was to call him immediately, day or night.

It was a simple favor, he'd said. Auntie Pei knew better.

Chau Feng hammered on the professor's door with the meat of his fist. He looked up at the camera mounted above the frame where the front wall met the eaves of the house. An empty paper wasps' nest hung in the corner, less than a foot from the plastic box.

Chau's bald partner stood behind him, like always, probably thinking about brewing his homemade beer instead of how much trouble they would be in if they could not locate Liu Wangshu.

The professor's bank account had not been accessed for almost a month. A preliminary glance into his activity online revealed he had not sent or received a single e-mail in fifteen days.

"I'm allergic to wasps," Lung said, apparently just noticing the empty nest.

"I'll keep that in mind," Chau said. Pity that it was too cold for wasps . . .

Chau shook his head. He had more important matters to think about than his partner being stung to death.

Professor Liu had effectively disappeared from the face of the earth. His secretary at Bohai Shipbuilding Vocational College had just had a baby, but as far as she knew, he'd not been at work for several weeks. He was her boss, so she'd not questioned him.

Chau Feng heard another nail being pounded into his coffin at every new piece of news. It would have been different if the men they babysat were spies—or at least scientists who made bioweapons, or nuclear bombs, or missile guidance systems.

Professor Liu Wangshu designed boats, nothing dangerous or even remotely exciting. Beijing was interested in him for some reason, though, and if they were interested in him, then Chau Feng was supposed to be interested in him as well.

Along with their other assignments, Chau and his partner were to check in with Professor Liu at least once a month, ascertain if anyone else had been chatting him up, document any lifestyle changes, report on his mood.

Chau was twenty-eight and should have been promoted at least one step by now. Jobs like this were more suited to men like Lung, who yammered on about the beer festival in Qingdao and didn't have the figs for the tough stuff.

At least three of Chau's cohort from the University of International Relations, the Ministry of State Security training facility in Haidian, were already assigned as intelligence liaisons to charm offensive groups, handing out money like candy for infrastructure programs in Africa and the South Pacific. Chau's former roommate now spent his days hosting cocktail parties in Canada, offering special consulting fees to engineers from around the world if they could just see their way to helping China with a few problems. At least one of his former classmates had been fortunate enough to bloody his hands capturing Uyghur separatists.

Chau knew that bungling this simple job meant he'd likely be the first one from his class booted from the Service—or worse.

He pounded on the door again, bowing it against the hinges.

Lung worked his way between some evergreen shrubs and the house, cupping his hand between the glass and the spot where his eyebrows should have been to peer through the window.

"I don't think he's home."

Chau shot him a sideways look but said nothing. The door was locked so he put a boot to it, making easy entry. He didn't care if the neighbors saw them breaking in. They knew better than to say anything. Two well-dressed men would be official, not common criminals. Local police would smell MSS and stay well clear unless they were called.

Lung gave a somber shrug as soon as they were inside.

"Like I said, not home."

Chau strode through the main room quickly, eyeing the empty kitchen as he went past, thinking he should probably draw his pistol as he neared the bedroom. He would have had he been alone, but Lung would probably think it a weakness and crow about it to others.

Perhaps they would find Liu dead in the bedroom. That would make things so much simpler. They would be blamed, of course, but probably not punished.

No such luck. The low bed was made. Brightly sequined slippers sat alongside on the Persian rug, ready for the professor's feet when he got up in the morning. A purple silk robe hung on the back of the door. They'd looked in on the professor enough over the past few months to know how he dressed, so none of the flashy jackets or brightly colored shirts in the closet surprised them.

Nothing appeared to be disturbed.

Chau knelt to look under the bed and found nothing but a vacant square in the dust where Liu had presumably kept some kind of box or case. He stood to find Lung rummaging through the dresser drawers.

"What do you hope to find among his underclothes?"

"I will not know until I find it," Lung said, his voice matter-of-fact. "There is no blood, no sign of struggle. Perhaps he had something to hide that made him susceptible to blackmail or coercion."

"Perhaps," Chau said.

"Perhaps he defected."

Chau blanched at the thought. "Do not say that."

The place was too clean for a single man's apartment. A function of Liu's engineer brain, Chau supposed. All this felt very wrong. No one disappeared, not in China. Cameras and facial recognition were everywhere.

He remembered the entry camera. It was wireless, uploading its images to a cloud-based server. He located the router attached to the wall on Liu's spotless kitchen counter. The PRC government required tech companies to provide backdoor access to every piece of software and hardware—even those shipped to other countries . . . especially those shipped to other countries. A quick call to a girlfriend with MSS Information Technology saw Chau logged in through the professor's router with his own mobile phone, with access to the last month of video surveillance.

Liu had departed for the office at roughly seven a.m. every

day and returned at six p.m. On the evenings he went out, he stayed out past midnight. Five times over the past two months he'd brought home women, all in their early twenties. They always left a few hours after they arrived, and Liu departed the next morning at seven, as if he'd not been up all night with a guest.

"Wait," Lung said, leaning over Chau's shoulder to watch the surveillance video on the mobile screen. "This one is Caucasian."

The time stamp read 12:07 a.m., two and a half weeks earlier.

Chau chewed on his bottom lip, deep in thought. The woman looked to be in her twenties, staggering a little, probably intoxicated. She wore a heavy coat with a fur collar that matched her chopped blond hair.

"She is Russian," Lung said, nodding with a certitude that dared Chau to argue.

Chau obliged him, working hard to keep from rolling his eyes. He could not keep from wagging his head. "And how do you know this?"

"Because someone gave her a black eye and she did not cover it with makeup," Lung said, as if it were all so simple.

Chau shrugged. "That means nothing."

"She thought to apply the rest of her makeup," Lung pointed out. "Look. Lipstick, heavy eyeliner, even some red to her cheekbones, but she leaves the purple moon under her eye visible for the world to see?" Lung gave a smug nod. "The American women I know would cover their black eye in shame. This one wears her injury proudly, like a badge of honor."

"How many American women do you know?"

"It does not matter," Lung said. "This woman is Russian, you will see."

The woman noticed the camera above the porch at about the same time Professor Liu unlocked his front door. Both looked directly up, as if she'd mentioned it. Chau took a screen-shot with his phone and then let the video play.

The woman left two hours after she'd arrived, still stagger-ing, but on her own. She walked toward the street and turned left before disappearing from view.

"All of the others were picked up by taxi," Chau said to himself.

"This one walked," Lung mused, scrolling through some-thing on his phone. "There is a Russian pastry shop three blocks from here." He nodded toward the front door. "The same direc-tion the girl walked."

Chau stayed focused on the video, his mind racing. Liu's allegiance to China seemed firm enough. But someone high up had thought him worthy of watching. They were all so para-noid about defectors . . . and yet, Liu had gone somewhere. That was a fact.

The morning after the blond girl left—Chau still refused to call her a Russian, even in his head—Liu Wangshu departed his house at 7:08 a.m., carrying only his briefcase. This was the last time Liu appeared in the footage. If he'd planned to go away, it wasn't for long.

The camera recorded no other visitors for two weeks—but the day before, a tall man with a felt fedora obscuring his face picked the lock and went inside without knocking. He'd known no one would be there. His face was obscured when he left as well.

Lung made a call to request a forensic examination of known IP addresses connected to Liu. Chau didn't expect to find anything. Liu's accounts were, of course, all flagged. That was standard MSS procedure with a babysitting job. Still, it had to be done.

The apartment failed to turn over anything but a few erotic magazines, some ladies' underwear, and a stack of ungraded physics examinations that may as well have been written in another language as far as Chau was concerned.

Lung stood by the bedroom door, swinging a pair of lace panties round and round on his gloved index finger.

Chau dropped the folder of exams back on the desk. "You believe he went to work for the Russians?"

"You and I may not know what he was working on," Lung pointed out, "but someone in the Zhongnanhai thought him valuable enough to assign us to watch him. That says something."

Chau gave a thoughtful nod. His browless partner did make sense. Maybe the professor was selling his knowledge to the highest bidder. "North Korea is just across the border."

"Could be Koreans," Lung said. "Those witless turtle eggs could use a good scientist or two . . . And yet, Liu's last female visitor would indicate—"

Chau cut him off. "I know. Russians."

"It makes sense."

"None of this makes sense," Chau said.

Lung held up the panties and used the elastic to shoot them like a rubber band.

Chau swatted them away. "You have a brain illness."

Lung nodded to the tiny scrap of silk on the floor. "Look inside."

"I don't wish to—"

"At the tag."

Chau pinched the underwear with a thumb and forefinger, feeling dirty even with his latex gloves on. Panties freshly peeled off a willing female was one thing, picking up a pair in some other man's bedroom made him bilious. He rolled the elastic over to expose the tag—which was written in Cyrillic.

Lung's eyes widened, certainly thinking himself a paragon of wisdom.

"Now are you ready to go talk to the Russians?"

5

C hau's first mistake at the pastry shop was to forget that he was dealing with Russians and not fellow Chinese.

"Hey, Igor," he said in Chinese to the man behind the register, showing a screenshot of the blond girl from the professor's door video. "Have you seen this girl before?"

The Russian was older, perhaps fifty, with a thick neck and a swollen nose that was mapped with tiny red veins from his nightly affair with vodka. Had Chau taken the time to notice, he would have seen a map of scars along the right side of the man's head, almost but not quite covered by his shaggy salt-and-pepper hair, and the tip of a blue star tattoo peeking out from the collar of his button-up shirt.

"My name is not Igor," the man said in perfect Mandarin. He wiped his hands on a rag. Remnants of flour and dried dough on a white apron said he'd been baking since early in the morning.

"Igor, Ivan, Boris," Chau said and sneered. "I do not give a shit what you call yourself. What I want to know . . . what I require that you tell me, is if you know this girl."

Chau's second mistake was getting too close.

The baker acted as if he were reaching across the glass case full of sweets to get a better look at the phone, but grabbed a handful of Chau's forelock instead. Chau was already leaning forward in an effort to intimidate, and the Russian had no trouble slamming his head into the counter, driving it straight through the glass case and into a platter of sugared teacakes.

The MSS man yowled in pain, freezing in place for fear of cutting his own throat on the shards of glass if he jerked away. The baker lifted him straight up, as if he, too, was aware of the dangerous teeth of glass so near Chau's neck. Instead of letting go, he slammed Chau's face against the wooden beam beside the till, roaring something in Russian that Chau couldn't have understood even if he wasn't getting his face bashed in.

The baker let go suddenly and stepped back, raising his hands.

Chau dabbed at his tattered face, feeling shards of glass. His left eye was swollen shut, but out of his right, he could make out bald-headed Lung pointing his Glock at the baker. A Chinese woman came through the front door, ringing a chime as she entered. She took one look at Chau's face, covered with blood and powdered sugar, and turned on her heels. A gruff voice carried from beyond a set of heavy curtains that divided the kitchen from the public area.

"Who else is here?" Lung demanded, prodding the air with the muzzle of his pistol.

Before he could answer, a blond man who looked to be a younger and stronger version of the baker shouldered through the curtains carrying a heavy wooden rolling pin like a weapon. A female face peeked out behind him—the girl from the video.

The younger man saw Lung's pistol and swung the rolling pin.

Lung was quicker than he looked and sidestepped, letting the heavy pin whistle by his head to glance off the shoulder of his non-gun side.

"I will shoot you!" he barked.

The girl pulled her head back from the curtain, vanishing.

"Get her!" Chau screamed.

The younger man dropped his rolling pin but stepped sideways, blocking Lung's access to the back room.

"State Security!" Lung shouted. He was smart enough to bring the pistol in close, tucked in next to his body so the Russian couldn't snatch it away.

The baker, seeing Chau's attention drawn toward the kitchen, lowered his hands and made to vault over the counter. Chau drew his pistol and put a single nine-millimeter round through the man's neck. The baker stopped cold, one hand still on the wooden support of the counter. His other hand shot to his throat in a vain attempt to stanch the flow of blood. He swayed there for a long moment, opening his mouth as if to speak, and then pitched forward, crashing through the same glass where he'd sent Chau's face.

The younger man's mouth fell open. He stared in horror at the dying man. "Papa . . ."

Chau moved quickly to lock the door and draw the blinds so passersby wouldn't see what had happened.

The astonished Russian moved to help his father, but Chau leveled the pistol. "Sit down on the floor and cross your legs at the ankles. Hands flat on your knees." He nodded to Lung. "I have him. Get the girl."

Lung disappeared behind the curtain.

Chau began to gingerly pick fragments of glass from his face, all the while covering the young Russian with his pistol.

"I thought you were trying to rob us," the Russian said.

"I seriously doubt that to be the case."

"What do you want with my sister?"

Chau prodded the air with his gun. "I will ask you the questions."

"Okay," the Russian said, all the fight having left him at the sight of his father's blood.

"What is your name?"

"Ruslan Petrovich," the Russian whispered. "My father is Peter Nimetov. He was . . ." His voice trailed off and he began to sniff back tears.

Chau clapped a bloody palm softly against the side of the hand holding the pistol, feigning applause. "You may spare us the performance. If you are not Sluzhba Vneshney Razvedki," he said, using the full name of Russia's foreign intelligence service, "then you at least work as their assets."

Ruslan Petrovich eyed the dead man and gave a slow shake of his head. His words, barely audible at first, grew louder as he spoke. "You are insane. But even if I were SVR, that was still my father you murdered—for nothing but trying to stop you from robbing him." His eyes locked with Chau, flaming with intensity. "You would be wise to kill me now."

Chau ignored the threat.

"How did you meet Professor Liu?"

Ruslan shook his head. "Who?"

Chau prodded the air again with his pistol, quickly losing his patience. "The woman you call your sister spent the night at his house two weeks ago. Do not lie. We have her on video."

Ruslan's brow shot up, the only indication that he was surprised by this revelation. He took a deep breath. "She is a grown woman. I do not—"

"It's me!" Lung called from the kitchen. "Do not shoot." He parted the curtain with an open hand and shoved the girl in ahead of him, pushing her to the ground behind her brother—or whoever he was.

Chau picked a thin shard of glass from the point of his chin and threw it at the girl to get her attention. "Where did you think you would go?"

"The police, I imagine," Ruslan said, sneering. "You come in our shop making demands without identifying yourself. What do you think we will—"

Chau drove the toe of his shoe into the hollow of Ruslan's hip.

The Russian yowled, falling sideways on top of the injury, protecting it from another blow.

"*Stoy!*" the girl screamed. *Stop!*

Chau reared back to kick Ruslan again, but was stopped by a banging at the door.

"Come back later!" Chau yelled.

"Help!" the wounded Russian cried in slurred Mandarin.

The girl joined in. "Robbers! Murderers!"

A stern voice demanded entry. Chau recognized it.

Chau nodded to Lung to make certain he covered the Russians with his pistol before letting in Deng Li Wan, a major and regional supervisor of counterintelligence for the Ministry of State Security. Unlike Chau's and Lung's casual slacks and sports shirts, Deng wore a dark suit and heavy black glasses. Close-cropped hair and a crisp white shirt made him look more like a Party functionary than one of the Ministry's top spy catchers.

Major Deng took one look at the dead Russian draped over the shattered glass display case and closed his eyes.

"What is all this?"

Both Chau and Lung snapped to attention.

"We believe these Russians took a scientist we were watching."

"Ah," Deng said. "The nautical engineer, what was his name?"

"Liu Wangshu," Lung said.

"That is the one," Deng said. "So, am I to understand that you lost him?"

Chau and Lung exchanged glances. The Russian on the floor grinned, despite his injury.

"We," Chau began, careful not to shoulder the blame alone, ". . . we are assigned to check on Liu once or twice each month— as needed. He was—"

Deng cut him off. "*As needed* are the key words on which you should focus. Would you not agree?"

Chau began to protest, but Deng raised his hand. "So you believe the Russians took him against his will? Or do you believe he defected of his own accord?"

Chau looked at Lung, who nodded.

"It doesn't matter," Deng said, growing tired of speaking to these underlings. "I will tell you this much. Whatever happened, the Russians were not involved."

"You are certain?" Chau asked. Had Deng not so severely outranked him, he would have pressed harder.

"Quite certain," Deng said. "While you were supposed to be watching Professor Liu Wangshu, my squad and I have had eyes on these SVR operatives."

Both the Russians looked up at the major.

Ruslan muttered: "We are not SVR. I told them that already."

Deng raised his hand again, shushing the prisoner. The

49

young Russian's head slumped to his chest, knowing, no doubt, how this was going to play out for him.

Lung ran a hand over his bald scalp, leaving it there for a long moment while he worked through an idea.

"Liu Wangshu's loyalties to the Party appear to be firm enough," he said. "He has made no recent withdrawal of funds. He is not living above his means." Lung raised his index finger, tapping the air as he thought. "The video showed he had only a briefcase when he left his home for the last time. He was not planning a trip."

"The North Koreans?" Chau mused, going back to an old thought.

Deng shook his head. "Naturally, they have operatives here. But we have people on them as well."

"Not the Koreans," Lung said, almost to himself, before looking down at Ruslan. "And your people do not have him?"

"*Nyet*," Ruslan said, despondent, knowing that he'd heard far too much for these men to let him live. "Perhaps, if your scientist was working on something very important . . ."

Chau and Lung both spoke at the same moment.

"*Meiguo!*" The Americans.

Major Deng gave a slow nod.

Chau's head snapped up at the scrape of a footfall in front of the shop. "Closed!" he managed to say as the door flew open. A tall man in a long wool coat stood with a pistol in his hand. A felt hat was pulled down low, over his brow, completely obscuring his face. Major Deng attempted to draw his sidearm, but the man shot him twice in the neck. Chau registered danger a hair too late, catching two rounds in his chest before he could will his hand to move toward his own weapon. The rounds were suppressed, loud enough to crack inside the small shop, but hardly loud enough to cause concern to anyone in neighboring shops or even on the street. The man in the hat continued to fire, taking down Lung with a head shot. The girl lunged through the curtain, running, while the newcomer dealt with the others. Chau had planned to shoot her himself only moments before, but now he hoped she got away. Mortally wounded, he lay on the floor. At first he thought the man in the felt hat was an SVR asset, but he shot the Russian as well, twice, as he did everyone in the room.

"Mmmm . . . eeem . . ." Chau coughed, blood covering his teeth and chin. A crushing weight pressed against his chest. He reached upward, his bloody hand opening and closing in the empty air. "Eeemmm . . . MS . . . S . . ."

The man in the coat shook his head, but did not speak.

"W-w-w-wait!" Chau blurted out in English.

Blood spilled from his wounds, mingling with the shattered glass on the floor around him. His heart raced, trying in vain to supply his brain. The room was fast closing in around him. He could tell the man was standing over him now, but his vision was too foggy to make out any facial features. "Pl . . . Please . . . wait," he said again.

He was vaguely aware of the dark form of the pistol before his vision failed him completely, sparing him the momentary sight of the flash that killed him. *It made sense*, he thought, a split second before the faceless man fired. *The CIA would take Professor Liu and come back to tie up loose ends.*

The Americans were everywhere.

6

President Jack Ryan was accustomed to nights with little sleep. Sometimes even less than usual when his wife was in the residence and didn't have to perform an early surgery the next morning. He could get by on four hours. Four and a half was normal. Five hours, though—five hours of sleep was sheer bliss—a warm blanket on a chilly night, the cool side of the pillow, the soft puff of Cathy's breathing against his neck.

Ryan opened one eye three minutes before his alarm went off, squinting enough to make out the numbers on the clock—5:27 a.m. He did the math. Slightly more than five hours.

Dinner the night before with the prime minister of New Zealand and her husband had gone late. Ryan didn't mind. The first gentleman was an avid fisherman, a subject that always reminded Ryan of his father. Unlike at many state functions, Ryan had been genuinely sorry to see these guests leave for the airport shortly after ten o'clock.

As usual, he'd settled down for a few minutes of evening reading while Cathy got ready for bed. Being President turned out to be a hell of a lot like cramming for a series of pop quizzes that had little in common with the stuff you thought you were going to be tested on and more to do with some nugget in an *Economist* or *Wall Street Journal* article from weeks or months before.

Jack Ryan's father had been a Baltimore homicide detective, a tough man with a deeply ingrained sense of duty and a nose-to-the-grindstone work ethic that he'd passed on to his son. He'd been a man who noticed small things, then tucked them away for later to solve big problems. Small keys, he often said, opened large doors. And you never knew where you might find one of those keys you'd need later. Ryan had spent over an hour poring over a briefing book from forensic analysts at Treasury outlining money laundering schemes used by Russian oligarchs operating in South America. Convoluted money trails and on-line banking schemes should have been enough to put him right to sleep, but a quirk of his nature made the intricacies of global finance hold his attention almost as much as fishing. It was midnight before he tiptoed into the bedroom from his private study.

W16, the Secret Service command post located below the Oval Office, kept tabs on his whereabouts in the White House using pressure-sensitive pads installed under the carpeting. They knew exactly what time he walked across the floor and climbed into bed.

They did not know that Cathy had also been reading and was still awake. Fortunately, that meant he didn't get to sleep for another twenty-five minutes . . .

He could have slept a little longer, but there was too much to do—and Gary Montgomery was meeting him early for a walk and talk around the White House grounds, before one of those inevitable pop quizzes that required Ryan's full attention. Montgomery was the special agent in charge of PPD—the Secret Service Presidential Protection Detail. Most days, he was the innermost layer of many concentric rings that stood between Ryan and any would-be attacker. If things went bad, Montgomery was the person who shoved the President into the waiting armored Cadillac known as The Beast so he could be whisked away to safety. If things got worse than bad, Gary Montgomery's body would be the last person they peeled off Ryan.

Both men knew it.

Montgomery was never maudlin, but he was not beyond pointing out the danger of certain endeavors Ryan was wont to drag his detail into. "I cannot protect you if you do that, sir," really meant, "I'm with you, Boss, but your plan may well get us both killed."

Along with being what Cathy called "linebacker large," Montgomery was smart and capable and loyal. Ryan had come to depend on him not just for security, but for counsel from someone other than the political operatives who surrounded him.

Ryan was slated to attend a conference of polar nations in Fairbanks, Alaska, in a few days.

White House Advance, the military liaison officer, and agents of the Secret Service had already made three trips to the venue. Alternate routes had been planned, motorcade parking squared away, hospital trauma centers scouted, and local law enforcement liaised. A presidential lift was a complicated dance under the best of circumstances. Fairbanks, Alaska, was isolated enough from the rest of the United States that it qualified as an overseas trip.

An early walk with Montgomery would give the two men time to discuss any security concerns while providing a quiet excuse for exercise that might go a long way toward lowering their collective blood pressure. The good Lord knew Ryan could use a little of that.

Cathy felt him reach for his glasses and she gave a long, feline yawn. "I have to do a retinal procedure at nine. I could really use another half an hour . . ."

Ryan swung his feet over the edge of the bed, searching for his slippers. "Of course, my dear," he said. His mind was wide awake, but his voice was still thick with sleep.

He brushed his teeth and then slipped into a gray jogging suit with the presidential seal on the jacket that he'd laid out the evening before.

"I had a dream about Ding's son," Cathy said through another yawn. "Patsy says he got a little homesick during Boot Camp, but he's doing well now."

Ryan looked up at the smooth curves of his wife under the sheets in the blue shadows of the bedroom and thought seriously about kicking off his sneakers instead of tying them.

"He's a good man," Ryan said. "And a fine Marine."

Ding and Patsy Chavez's son—and John Clark's grandson—had only recently graduated from the Marine Corps' Infantry Training Battalion after finishing Boot Camp at MCRD San Diego.

Cathy pulled the sheet up over her face. "Turn the light on if you need to."

"I'm fine," Ryan said.

"You think JP gets special treatment because his godfather is the President of the United States?"

Ryan scoffed. "I'm betting he keeps that little tidbit of information to himself if he doesn't want to get his ass kicked on a daily basis."

"I guess," Cathy said. "Poor kid's got too much to live up to. Hey, there's a little bag on the table in my dressing room. Could you get someone to drop it off at Carter's office? It's for their new baby."

Ryan chuckled. FLOTUS put together her own gift bags and gave POTUS honey-dos. His press secretary, Carter Bailey, had just returned from family leave. "I'll drop it off myself," he said. "It's what? Ten steps out of my way. Gary and I are doing a walk and talk this morning anyway." He leaned down to kiss her on the forehead, which was the only bit of skin exposed, until she lowered the sheet and puckered her lips, eyes closed.

"Thank you," she said. "Now go save the world."

He winked at her, then realized she didn't have her glasses on so she could barely see him anyway. Getting old was hell, but if he had to do it, he'd just as soon do it with Caroline Muller Ryan.

"You, too," he said.

Good morning, Mr. President," the Secret Service agent posted in the West Sitting Hall said when Ryan eased the bedroom door shut behind him.

"Morning, Pauline," he said, nodding crisply to the stocky brunette. He made it a point to learn a bit about everyone on his detail. Along with being a crack shot, Special Agent Pauline Dempsey had an Olympic silver medal in the eight-hundred-meter run.

He held up the pink floral gift bag he was delivering for Cathy. "I know what you're thinking," Ryan said. "This doesn't go with the tracksuit."

Dempsey smiled. "Not at all, Mr. President. Perfect accessory."

She'd been up all night and was just reaching the end of her shift, but her smile was genuine and without guile, like someone who was self-assured enough to be comfortable in her own skin around the President of the United States. She was there to protect him. She was good at her job, and she knew it.

Dempsey spoke quietly into the beige mic pinned to her lapel as he passed on his way across the hall.

"Crown, Dempsey, SWORDSMAN en route to the first floor."

She nodded at the response she got over the radio.

"Special Agent in Charge Montgomery will meet you downstairs, Mr. President."

Ryan thanked her and boarded the elevator across the sitting hall, adjacent to the old cloakroom.

Gary Montgomery stood waiting on the ground floor, quiet, unflappable, except when he was not, and God help the man who got in Montgomery's way when that happened. He and his wife had just bought a house in rural Anne Arundel County not far from Annapolis. The commute in was a relatively quick drive down Highway 50 at this hour, leading the wave of commuter traffic. His dark hair was still damp and slightly curled from a morning shower. He wore gray sweatpants and a dark blue University of Michigan football sweatshirt that, no doubt, covered the SIG Sauer pistol he was never without when he was near the President. While Cathy compared him to a linebacker, at six-three, two-forty, he'd actually played fullback for his beloved Wolverines during his undergraduate years in Ann Arbor.

"Top of the morning to you, Mr. President," Montgomery said.

Ryan returned the greeting, genuinely happy to see the man.

He held up the pink gift bag again. "Mind if we stop in at the press secretary's office before we go for our walk?"

The Secret Service agent gave a slight nod. "After you, sir."

Not friends, exactly, they were certainly more than President and protector. If anything, Montgomery had become an unofficial adviser, often sitting in on meetings as a Secret Service agent, and then offering his opinion when Ryan asked him, usually while they were in the gym.

When he was growing up, Ryan's father often pointed out that most people never knew what to do with their hands when they stood and waited. Some shoved them in their pockets, others nervously clenched and unclenched their fists, some rubbed them together like a housefly. Gary Montgomery let his hands hang by his sides. Relaxed. Ready. Emmet Ryan would have trusted him—and as far as Jack Ryan was concerned, that was about the highest praise that could be given.

Ryan led the way west, down the colonnade past the Press Room. Instead of keeping left to enter the Oval from the outside, he continued straight, bringing him and Montgomery into the West Wing off the end of the Cabinet Room, where it was a short walk around the corner to Carter Bailey's office.

He was surprised to see a young man wearing a wrinkled beige trench coat over a crumpled gray suit enter through the door off the Press Room. A woman followed him in. She was a bit older, shorter by a head, and, unlike him, she ironed her clothes. She wore a blue raincoat and a matching tam against the cold outside. Both nodded to the uniformed Secret Service officer posted at the desk inside the door, who noted their lanyard badges. They knew the drill, and signed in at her desk.

Ryan recognized them as CIA staff who often accompanied the director, Jay Canfield.

The woman was Gretchen something. Ryan could not for the life of him remember her last name. She'd been back from maternity leave only a few weeks—everybody seemed to be having babies these days. Drooping eyes said she'd probably not gotten much sleep the night—or weeks—before. Still, exhausted or not, her bright smile lit up an oval face between the high collar of her coat and the jaunty tam. She hung back a few steps from the young man. He was at least ten years younger and impetuous with youth, so he led the way. His sandy hair was slicked back straight from a high forehead, looking darker, and starker, than it would have looked had he let it fall naturally. The copper stubble of a new goatee was his way of trying to do something about it. Ryan gave him an A for effort, and a D-minus for the patchy goatee.

Ryan nodded as they approached. Gretchen's cheeks flushed as they got closer. The youngster remained nonchalant.

Pack. That was her name. Gretchen Pack.

"Getting an early start?" Ryan asked.

"Good morning, Mr. President," the kid said, stopping cold a few feet from Ryan and Gary Montgomery. The Secret Service agent had that effect on people. "We're here to assist with the meeting."

Ryan looked at his watch, and then at Montgomery.

"The meeting? With me?"

"I assume so, Mr. President," the kid said.

Ryan fished his cell phone from the pocket of his track jacket and dialed Mary Pat Foley's number as they walked.

"You're up," she said.

"What's this about a meeting?"

"I was just getting everyone together before we woke you," Foley said.

"Okay," Ryan said. "I'll call you from the Oval."

"I'm there now," she said. "I'll tell you in person."

Director of National Intelligence Foley; Ryan's chief of staff, Arnie van Damm; and Navy Commander Rob Forestall were waiting in the secretaries' suite outside the open door of the Oval.

"Looks like our walk and talk is going to have to wait," Ryan said to Montgomery.

"You know where to find me, Mr. President." He smiled, then left through the main door, presumably to go to his office in W16.

"Burgess and Adler are on their way," Foley said. She was in her sixties, close to Ryan's age, though she'd been a career intelligence officer, working the street during the iciest days of the Cold War while he was still in grad school. "I've looped in CIA and FBI as well."

Ryan looked at his watch, a Rolex GMT Cathy had given him years before, and motioned toward the twin couches in the Oval.

"Please sit. I'll see what I can do about rustling you up some coffee."

Robbie Forestall, in his khaki work uniform, took a half-step forward. "I'll take care of that, Mr. President. I took the liberty of putting the night steward on notice that you might be asking."

"Very well," Ryan said. "Looks like you all have me at something of a disadvantage." He shot a narrow eye at van Damm. "It's enough to call in the secretaries of state and defense along with the directors of CIA and FBI, but not enough to wake me?"

"My call," the chief of staff said. "Mary Pat and I talked it over."

Ryan took his customary seat in the Queen Anne chair beside the fireplace while Foley sat nearest him on the couch to his right. Van Damm took the couch opposite her. Forestall remained standing to meet the Navy steward when he came in with the coffee service.

Scott Adler, Bob Burgess, and the two directors arrived moments later. All of them knew that a call from van Damm *was* a call from the President and skipped whatever it was they had to skip to arrive as soon as humanly possible. Burgess still had a piece of tissue on his jaw he'd used to stanch a shaving cut.

The coffee arrived at about the same time as the FBI director. CIA director Jay Canfield brought up the rear.

As was his custom, Ryan poured the coffee for his guests. Mary Pat started her briefing while he worked.

"Mr. President, officers from the Chinese Ministry of State Security are actively looking for one of their top scientists. A man named Liu Wangshu has disappeared."

The group nodded with varying levels of recognition. D/CIA Canfield had been briefed nearly as much as Foley, but the others were just being made aware of the situation along with the President. Some did, however, know of Liu.

"Engineering professor in Huludao," Secretary of Defense Burgess said. "Where the Chinese are building some of their ballistic missile and fast-attack submarines."

SecState Adler tapped his crossed knee while he peered over the top of his coffee cup. "I feel like the Chinese ambassador introduced him to me at an embassy function last year. The whole thing seemed highly choreographed. The ambassador wanted to demonstrate to us what intelligent scientists they have working for them. Liu is kind of an eccentric guy, if I remember right."

Director Canfield nodded. "You could call him that."

Burgess scoffed. "A blue dress shirt could be considered outside the norm to the powers that be in Chinese politics. Liu wears blue jeans, rolls up the sleeves of his paisley shirts, and keeps his hair over his collar."

Adler nodded. "I distinctly remember thinking he was a Chinese Austin Powers."

"You're an apt judge of character," Foley continued. "He's made the news several times for dating much younger women. Behaviors that Beijing wouldn't put up with for a minute but for the fact that he's single-handedly responsible for the great leaps forward the PLAN has made in submarine technology over the past three years."

"What kind of tech?" Ryan said. Submarine technology had been a pet project of his for years, since—a very long time ago.

"Propulsion engineering, Mr. President," Canfield said. "Beyond that, we're not exactly certain. We know both Beijing and the PLA-Navy brass have given Professor Liu three separate awards. One of them is the Order of the Republic—the highest in the country for someone not in the military—similar to our Medal of Freedom."

The secretary of defense spoke up again. "China hasn't had what you could really call a fighting Navy since the fifteenth century. And frankly, Mr. President, I'm not sure they do now. President Zhao is loud and proud about his growing fleet of technologically advanced submarines, but many of the details have yet to be confirmed. Don't misunderstand me. I'm not saying we underestimate him. We should just take him with a grain of salt."

Ryan took a sip of his coffee—strong and black—and gave a contemplative nod. "We project our force with carrier groups. Beijing wants to rely on a weapon you can't see but know is out there somewhere, hiding . . ." He shook his head. Acid from the coffee and a healthy dose of the unknown churned in his empty stomach. "And we like our submarines, too. They make for a pretty damned fine deterrent."

"We know the Chi-Comms have a lot of diesels," Burgess said. "Some purchased from Russia, some of them developed themselves. And, I have to admit, quieter than I'd like them to be."

"Some of their sub pens are in Huludao," Ryan mused. "Where Professor Liu taught before he went missing. Do we suspect foul play?"

"The Chinese do," Foley said. She glanced around the room, as if to assure herself that no one had snuck in since she last checked. "It goes without saying that this is extremely sensitive information."

Ryan nodded for her to continue. In the end, he had to trust somebody, and if he could not trust the people around him now, all was lost anyway.

"Our sources tell us that one of the reasons Beijing is so proud of Professor Liu is that he is behind much of their engineering progress in the way of propulsion technology. By that I mean he designed it himself. So much of what they have, they've been given by the Russians or stolen from us and reverse-engineered. As Bob so bluntly pointed out, China's naval exploits have caused them to lose a lot of face in the past few hundred years. Professor Liu is not only a genius, he is *their* genius, and I cannot understate the importance they place on that fact.

"I believe everyone here is familiar with VICAR, our asset in Russia." Foley didn't go into detail, but Ryan knew VICAR was Erik Dovzhenko, an SVR officer who assisted members of The Campus in thwarting an Iranian missile attack. According to Foley, Jack Junior knew the man well and trusted him completely, but father and son never spoke of it.

Foley gave a nod to Canfield.

"Late last night," he said, "one of our case officers received a flash communication from VICAR. Apparently, MSS operatives first believed the professor had defected or was taken by the Russians. They confronted agents working for the SVR in a Huludao pastry shop near the professor's home. One of the male Russian agents was killed in the initial contact, while an adult female and her adult brother were taken prisoner. The MSS officers questioned them, but eventually ascertained the Russians didn't have the professor. According to the female Russian, the Chinese were still working out the details of their theory when a new man kicked in the door and started shooting. She thought he may have been a gangster, but he immediately shot one of the MSS operatives as soon as he burst in. She was just able to escape—"

Ryan raised his hand. "Hang on a minute. Someone other than the MSS officers was shooting?"

"That's correct, Mr. President. The newcomer. The female SVR agent described him as a tall Asian male with a long coat and a felt hat, a fedora, but she didn't stay around long enough to get a good look at his face. She told her SVR handler that she heard at least five more shots as she fled down the alley. Local news says three Chinese and two Russians were killed at a Huludao pastry shop in an apparent botched robbery. The SVR report eventually landed on VICAR's desk. In VICAR'S words: 'The Chinese know you have Liu Wangshu.'"

"And we're sure we don't?" Ryan asked. "One of your operatives doesn't have him on ice at some Busan safe house right now waiting for the heat to blow over?"

"That possibility did cross my mind," Foley said. "Liu Wangshu would be a good get, for whoever gets him. He's privy to all sorts of treasure regarding Chinese submarine technology. But I've been assured by station chiefs and DIA assets in that part of the world that we are in no way culpable for this."

Ryan finished off his coffee and set the mug on the side table, none too gently. "Okay. Then tell me who is culpable."

"We do not know, Mr. President," Foley said. "Not yet. There's a possibility that he's gone into hiding on his own, wanting to defect. The Chinese want him bad, which means he's likely holding timely intelligence. If he's getable, we should get him."

"Agreed," Ryan said.

He looked around the room. Everyone present appeared to know something he did not.

Yet.

"Let's have it," he said, eyeing Mary Pat.

"Though Professor Liu's disappearance is problematic, the remainder of VICAR's communication is far more troubling." She gave an exhausted sigh. "Sir, it appears we have a mole problem."

7

A mole?" Ryan whispered.

The revelation wasn't a surprise. Wise intelligence organizations operated under the assumption that there was always a mole in their midst. What startled Ryan was that the unflappable Mary Pat Foley, who'd been doing this job since the days of dead drops in Gorky Park and midnight rendezvous in East Berlin, thought the information important enough to bring to him. That meant she believed the mole was highly placed enough to be a real danger.

The KGB had run moles in the U.S. government and the U.S. government ran moles in the KGB. Colonel Mikhail Semyonovich Filatov, cryptonym CARDINAL, became personal friends with Ryan after Ryan had assisted in his extraction from the Soviet Union.

But for the names and faces, nothing had changed.

"According to VICAR's report, much of his information was verified by a Russian asset working within the Chinese Ministry of State Security. This Russian asset suggested to VICAR that the PRC was checking the depth of U.S. involvement regarding Professor Liu with a source they had embedded within the U.S. intelligence apparatus."

Ryan rubbed a hand over his hair and fought off a yawn. It was much too early for this.

"Let me get this straight," he said. "Our asset inside Russian intelligence tells us the Russians have an asset in the People's Republic of China, who let it slip that Beijing has an asset in our house?"

"That's correct, Mr. President," Foley said. "We even know what they call him—SURVEYOR."

Ryan scratched his chin, thinking that he needed to shave. The incredible irony of the situation was overshadowed by the danger a mole posed to the U.S. case officers and their agents. It didn't take much more than a hunch in some countries for suspected assets to "accidentally" fall out of a window.

"If SURVEYOR mistakenly believes we have Liu," Ryan said, "then maybe he's not that highly placed."

"Perhaps," Foley said. "But I get the impression MSS is still in the process of contacting him . . . or her, to confirm. Newly acquired intelligence sources are among our most compartmented reports. If the Chinese think SURVEYOR has access to that information, at the very least, China *believes* their mole is in a place to do them some real good. And I don't mind telling you, that scares me."

"Containment?" Ryan asked.

Foley nodded. "We've already started to subtly wall things off," she said. "Other than the people in this room, VICAR's most recent communication has only been shared with four individuals, and VICAR'S identity is extremely close-hold."

"So," Ryan said. "A mole hunt, then. The Bureau and Agency working in a coordinated effort?"

It wasn't really a question.

Both directors rushed to be the first out with: "Of course, Mr. President."

The FBI's drive to build a case for violation of the Espionage Act that would bring a conviction in federal court versus CIA's overarching desire to protect the intelligence apparatus and plug the leak sometimes brought the two agencies to loggerheads. Mary Pat's job as director of national intelligence was, among other things, to see that long-fought turf battles didn't get in the way of the end goal.

Ryan turned to Foley, making it clear that she would be his point of contact.

"Good to hear it. What's our next move?"

"According to the Russians' source in Beijing, the PRC is actively hunting a Uyghur woman with some as-yet-unknown connection to Professor Liu."

"Uyghur," he mused. Ryan had been a thorn in Beijing's side of late, taking a political stand against the Chinese surveillance state and the government's internment of ethnic Uyghur Chinese citizens. Beijing's official stance was that they were not after the beard or veil, but targeting people who posed a future risk of the "Three Evils": terrorism, separatism, or religious extremism. From Ryan's perspective, it was about the closest thing on the planet to a Philip K. Dick novel.

There had been attacks by separatist groups—bombings, knife attacks—but Beijing's reaction had been crushing and broad. Hundreds of thousands of men and women had been rounded up and held for weeks or months for purposes of re-education and assimilation into Han Chinese culture. Children, effectively orphaned while their parents were interned, were housed in state schools for indoctrination into a more "Chinese" way of thinking.

"Where's she from, this Uyghur woman?" Ryan asked.

Foley shot a glance at D/CIA.

"According to VICAR, her name is Medina Tohti," Director Canfield said. "She's originally from Kashgar. Her husband was arrested and taken to one of their reeducation camps outside Urumqi. Nothing in the report indicates if he's alive or dead. At this point, we do not know what her connection is with Professor Liu. As we've discussed, he's something of a playboy. There's a theory that they may have had an affair at some point. Perhaps when he visited western China."

"Where are they looking for her?" Ryan asked.

"Word is, she's joined a Uyghur separatist group," Foley said. "Something called Wuming. Beijing lists them as a terrorist organization."

Scott Adler scratched his forehead. "Sorry to interrupt, but you're sure it's *Wuming?*" The secretary of state was conversant in several languages, among them, passable Mandarin.

"That's right," D/CIA said.

"Wuming means 'nameless,'" Adler said. "It would be like us saying the terrorist group formerly known as al-Qaeda."

"Anonymous?" Foley asked.

"Yes," Adler said. "Sort of."

"That fits," the FBI director said. "Wuming is on our watch list as well. Beijing says they're responsible for no less than nine targeted assassinations in western China. They've never claimed responsibility or even called their group by name. Beijing links the attacks together because of the MO."

"And that is?"

"They don't blow up things indiscriminately or run through a crowded train station with knives. They hunt specific people, much like the Israelis have done."

"So Beijing gave them the name *Wuming*?" Ryan asked. "They don't use it themselves?"

"Appears so, sir," the FBI director continued. "No one seems to know where the Wuming operatives are based, but judging from the attacks they're believed to be responsible for, we think they have to be somewhere in western China between Urumqi and Afghanistan."

"What we do know," Foley said, "is that Beijing is pulling out all the stops to find Medina Tohti. Facial recognition, surveillance, interrogations of anyone who might be connected with her or the Wuming."

Bob Burgess spoke next. "What about other family?"

"VICAR mentions a ten-year-old daughter," Canfield said. "Hala. She's supposed to be staying with Tohti's sister in Kashgar—the girl's aunt. I'm sure they're up on the sister's cell phone and any social media. They're watching her, but so far, no sign of Medina."

Ryan finished his second cup of coffee and gave a slow shake of his head, thinking this all through. "The MSS has a long reach."

"I'm sorry, Mr. President," Canfield said. "I didn't make myself clear. The MSS isn't looking for Medina. The people hunting her appear to be military intelligence, specifically PLAN operatives. They've shut the MSS out of their investigation completely, apparently blaming them for the brouhaha with the Russians—and losing Professor Liu Wangshu in the first place."

"Navy intelligence," Ryan mused.

"That would be Vice Admiral Zheng's shop," Burgess said.

"He's a piece of work, that one. If half the stories about him are to be believed . . ."

"I believe more than half," Ryan said, changing the subject. "I'd like you all to hold off on anything to do with Professor Liu or this Uyghur woman, Medina Tohti. Focus all your efforts instead on finding the mole. The last thing we need is another PARLOR MAID," he said.

The FBI director blanched at the words. It hadn't been many years since MSS agent Katrina Leung had agreed to be an asset for the FBI and then doubled back to spy for China. She also happened to be romantically involved with two of her FBI handlers while working for China. The incident still gave Bureau bosses indigestion. It didn't go well with the coffee roiling in Ryan's gut, either.

He patted the side table with the flat of his hand, mulling over the details of what he knew.

"SURVEYOR, eh? That's an apt name for a spy in this Great Game we're playing with China. I'm sure you're all up on your Kipling."

Mary Pat smiled. Most everyone in the room, except for Commander Forestall, squirmed in their seats.

"The boy, Kim," Ryan said. "What was his job in the novel?"

The CIA director sighed with relief. He knew this. "A spy."

"Right," Ryan said, nodding slowly, like a teacher who was almost, but not quite, satisfied with the answer. "But his job had another name. A legend, if you will." The leader of the free world showed mercy and answered his riddle almost as soon as he'd asked it. "He was trained as a 'pundit'—a surveyor in the area north of British India to see what the Russians were up to. I wonder if the spymasters in Beijing see the connection to their code name?"

Foley scoffed. "We're talking about the Chinese, Mr. President. They are masters at little details like that. They just believe we're too ignorant to pick up on them."

The FBI director stared down at his coffee. "Some of us are . . ."

"Don't beat yourself up," Foley said, giving Ryan the side-eye. "The president reads *Kim* the way a preacher studies the Good Book. His version is probably cross-referenced and annotated."

"I'm a good Catholic boy," Ryan said, getting to his feet, prompting everyone else in the room to follow suit. "Don't test me on my Bible, either. I do admit to having several copies of *Kim*. They make good gifts." He nodded to van Damm. "I'd like frequent briefings on this, Arnie. Mary Pat, hang back a minute, please."

The chief of staff ushered the group out through the secretaries' suite. He'd rearrange Ryan's schedule, delegating the meetings and appointments he could. Presidential schedules were fluid at the best of times, lifting and shifting to meet the needs of the day. Van Damm ran Ryan's like a combination boxing coach, concerned physician, and overprotective father. Arnie van Damm was a pro, and Ryan yielded to his expertise almost as much as he pushed back—which was saying a great deal.

"I'm assuming you have the same gut feeling that I do, Jack," Mary Pat said once they were alone. They'd been friends long enough that she felt comfortable calling him by his first name in the Oval if there was no one else around.

"If your gut is telling you that you'd like to know more about what connection the Uyghur woman has to the missing professor, then you're absolutely right." He motioned to the couch again. This was not a spur-of-the-moment discussion one had on the way out the door.

"Exactly," Mary Pat said, returning to her customary seat. "And since the mole has some connection to the CIA's China desk, the issues overlap. Giving the Agency point on this could put Adam Yao, VICAR's handler, in danger, not to mention rendering any mission a failure before it even gets off the ground. Mr. President, I believe this would be a good time to utilize the services of our friends at The Campus."

It wasn't lost on Ryan that his friend had suddenly grown more formal. The Campus was an off-the-books quasi-government entity that performed contracted work under the guise of former Senator Gerry Hendley's financial arbitrage firm across the river in Virginia. Ryan and Hendley had formed it, years before, for missions such as this, that required a deft touch, without the layers of bureaucracy attendant to even the best government agency. Ryan's old friend John Clark ran the show under Hendley, serving as director of operations. An extremely capable man leading a talented team. Still, for the most part, they acted independently . . . a separation of powers, so to speak. Activating them personally was something Ryan never took lightly. Beyond that, sending in The Campus meant sending in his own son.

"It looks like we are indeed thinking the same thing," Ryan said. "Chinese intelligence is hunting for this Uyghur woman. Perhaps we should look in that same direction. Do we have a starting point to give Clark?"

Foley leaned back, folded her arms, and crossed her ankles, staring up at the ceiling. "Didn't this place feel larger when we used to have to venture over here from our little cubicles at Langley?"

Ryan waited. Mary Pat often took a beat or two to answer, while she thought things through.

"We know her ten-year-old daughter, Hala, is staying with Medina's sister in Kashgar. We have a tentative address, a newly renovated area not far from the Jiefang street market."

"Stands to reason that Medina Tohti will want to make contact with her daughter at some point," Ryan said. "Clark's started with less and gotten what he was after."

"Adam Yao's worked with The Campus before," Foley said. "I trust him completely. He can help them with logistics getting into China." She chuckled. "I've gotta say, this is the perfect job for Clark and his team—finding a woman who has likely aligned herself with a separatist group that is on our terrorist watch list and is actively being hunted by law enforcement. Then snatching this woman out from under the noses of not only the militant separatist, but Vice Admiral Zheng, the butcher's intelligence operatives in the midst of one of the most heavily surveilled locations on the planet."

"You're right," Ryan said. "Tailor-made for John Clark. Mind if I ask where they are?"

Mary Pat looked at her watch. "About now," she said, "I'd imagine they're in the air."

8

D omingo "Ding" Chavez tapped his cell phone to answer the call. The interior of the thirty-year-old Russian Mi-17 helicopter squealed and chattered as if voicing strong objections to being in the air. The oil company had purchased this one from the Cambodians in the late nineties, after the Dry Season Offensive when they'd used it to go after the Khmer Rouge. Chavez consoled himself with the fact that while most Russian aircraft were lacking in finesse, they were generally cloddishly overbuilt—and could be fixed with a hammer and a screwdriver. A puddle of oil along the bulkhead said this bird was likely overdue for such an appointment. Chavez was partial to the Bell UH-1H. Though not exactly cheap, surplus birds could be had for a quarter of a million. Still, he understood that folks around the former Saigon might still have a little aversion to Hueys thumping the air over their heads.

Chavez pushed the tiny boom mic away from his mouth as he spoke, using a natural voice, despite the racket in the chopper. Connected to his phone via Bluetooth, the Sonitus Molar Mic clipped to his back tooth easily picked up his end of the conversation while transmitting incoming sounds via his jawbone instead of his eardrum. The device was comfortable enough for Chavez to forget it was there—which is what sold him on it in the first place. It worked with the radio in his pocket as well, linked via the wire-loop necklace through the same near-field technology used with surveillance earbuds. More and more tech was moving to cell phones, but the radios worked virtually anywhere and allowed him to talk to the entire team at once.

"We've been operating inside the nine-dash line most of the day. I'm seeing a few Chinese patrols on the radar, but they're way off. Looks like one of our Navy ships is conducting a freedom of navigation cruise eleven miles east, not far from the Vanguard Bank. That should keep any Chinese patrols from pestering us. Pilot says we're less than five minutes out, with open seas between us but for a couple of fishing boats."

"No pressure," Clark said. "But I'm surprised you're still at it."

"Me, too. The first two rigs were squeaksville. Nada."

"I thought you only had two rigs on the menu today," Clark said.

"We did," Chavez said. "But a very helpful roustabout on the second rig said he'd seen a bunch of old computers stored on DK454. Thought we'd pay them a surprise visit. Gerry's friend was happy with us doing a last-minute audit, but it took a little longer than anticipated to get us set up with another chopper, such as it is." Chavez looked around the cabin as he spoke, noting the odor of oil and something that he thought might be overripe bananas. "Anyway, we shouldn't be more than two hours once we're boots on the ground at this last stop."

"Copy," Clark said. "Head on a swivel. No such thing as a routine job in the middle of the ocean, especially when that ocean is disputed real estate."

"Roger that," Chavez said.

All the offshore drilling rigs they were visiting that day were located well within their Exclusive Economic Zone, or EEZ. They were also inside what the Chinese called the nine-dash line, a bulbous hanging loop on their maps indicating Beijing's sovereignty over more than eighty percent of the South China Sea—including all the fish, shipping lanes, and, most important, the minerals beneath the seabed. Malaysia, Brunei, the Philippines, and Vietnam all took great umbrage with China's map, since the line cut well into each of their respective EEZs. A court of arbitration had ruled that the PRC had no claim to the territory, their nine dotted lines notwithstanding. For her part, Beijing didn't appear to give a rat's ass about the court's finding, and continued to build installations on the Paracel and Spratly Islands, dredging up the seafloor to build more islands and ramming vessels that got in their way. President Ryan strongly condemned this bullying behavior, which Ding thought was probably one of the reasons Gerry Hendley's friend with Lone Star Oil had been persuaded to become a silent partner in DK454. The twenty-six trillion dollars of unexploited hydrocarbons beneath the South China Sea might have had something to do with their decision as well.

A joint Vietnamese, Russian, and U.S. venture in waters claimed by a hostile foreign power, Chavez mused. *What could possibly go wrong?*

Evidently, Lonnie Taylor, the CEO of Lone Star Oil, smelled something rotten, and called his old buddy Gerry Hendley to see if some of his investigators might conduct a forensic audit, snooping for any signs of industrial espionage or outright theft.

Clark's voice came over the line again, buzzing against Chavez's back tooth.

"Has Junior found anything?"

Most of the team was going to the rig, but Jack Ryan, Jr., had drawn the short straw and was stuck in the main office in Ho Chi Minh City, combing through files while Clark continued Lisanne Robertson's training and the others got to load up for a scenic flight in this bucket of spinning bolts.

"A few anomalies," Chavez said. "Lots of traffic going back and forth between the Rosneft people on-site and some unknown IP addresses in Russia. He anticipates being done about the time we are."

"Okay." Clark gave a low grunt. "Like I said, head on a swivel."

Chavez stuffed the cell into the pocket of his slacks, reset the small boom mic from his headset so it brushed his lips, and double-checked with the pilot.

His ears told him they were beginning their descent.

The pilot, one of Lonnie Taylor's men from Texas, gave Chavez a quick sitrep.

"Copy," Chavez said, and then held up four fingers to confirm that the other three Campus operatives each knew they were four minutes from touchdown.

Directly across from Chavez, Dominic "Dom" Caruso gave him a thumbs-up and then turned to continue staring out the scratched window at the choppy waves a thousand feet below. Adara Sherman sat beside Caruso. The wiry blonde with a pixie cut leaned on Caruso's arm while she scrolled through her phone. This was the closest they ever got to a public display of affection, though it was no secret that they were making a life together.

Former Delta Force colonel Bartosz "Midas" Jankowski sat on the same row as Chavez, staring out the opposite window, scratching his dark beard in thought. Without looking, he raised four fingers to confirm he was up to speed.

Like Clark said, there were no routine missions at sea, but this one appeared to be about as close as it got.

Forensic accounting amid uncooperative people fell squarely into Hendley Associates' swim lanes.

Adara glanced up from her phone. "There's a pho place we should try when we're done," she said. "It's near the hotel."

Midas chuckled, still not taking his eyes off the waves. His voice crackled across the intercom on the headsets. "I'm betting there are five hundred pho places near the hotel. They ladle that shit here like we serve french fries."

Dom raised a brow at his girlfriend. "He's not wrong . . ."

"I'm thinking steak," Chavez said. "But let's keep our heads in the game. Adara and Dom, you chat up the crew once we land, make some new friends. Midas and I will take a look at the hard drives—"

The pilot's voice broke over the intercom, interrupting them.

"Looks like you have a welcoming . . ." He paused for a beat, then said, "That's not good. I'm seeing smoke . . . It looks like they're throwing out life rafts."

The Chinese MSS operative dressed as a fisherman stood upright in the small fishing boat, shielding his eyes from the sun, watching the Russian helicopter approach. He lowered the cell phone and glanced at his partner, an older man, also dressed in shorts and the stained cotton shirt of a fisherman.

"What shall we do?" the first man asked. "The smoke will convince most of the roustabouts to abandon the rig, but we have always known there could be Vietnamese losses. The inspectors on that helicopter are Americans. That will surely raise a stink."

The older man toyed with a sparse crop of chin whiskers as he watched the chopper descend toward the landing pad on the superstructure of the drilling rig. The noodles he'd eaten for lunch wriggled in his gut like so many snakes. He hated boats, and wanted this mission to be over so he could step back on firm ground.

"These idiots are not supposed to be here," he said. "Collateral damage cannot be avoided."

The younger man punched a number into the mobile phone with his thumb, and then looked up for final confirmation before hitting send.

The senior officer gave a curt nod.

"Do it."

G et us out of here!" Chavez barked as soon as he saw what was going on. A half-dozen workers had already taken the fifteen-meter plunge off the rig deck. Others worked their way down three sets of ladders to inflatable lifeboats bobbing in the chop below.

Still two hundred feet above the rig, the chopper pilot increased power and broke quickly to the right.

Adara leaned to get a better look out the window. "There's a fi—"

A blast wave slammed into the Mi-17's fuselage, lifting it suddenly skyward as if with a giant hand.

The explosive roar that accompanied the wave covered the pilot's impotent curse as he lost all control of the helicopter.

Ding's gut rose in his chest as the helicopter began to fall.

The pilot, still struggling to regain control, spoke over the intercom, his voice surreally calm now, considering that the aircraft was spinning wildly as it plummeted toward the sea.

"Not looking good, boys and girls!" He paused, seemed to regain partial control, and then another piece of the tail boom broke away. "Brace, brace, brace!"

9

Eleven miles away, the communication officer on the bridge of the USS *Makin Island* passed the word to the officer of the watch that he was receiving an emergency distress call from an offshore Vietnamese oil rig, noting that he'd heard the distinctly American voice of the pilot of an approaching chopper preparing to land almost simultaneously with the emergency call from the rig. The watch officer noted an inky black ball of smoke above the horizon to the west.

Makin Island's skipper, Captain Roosevelt "Rosey" Jackson, had been on the weather deck, watching the Marines practice their marksmanship off the fantail, when the call came in. The officer of the watch called him and the XO in immediately. He'd already notified the *Prebble*, their escort destroyer, to prepare to adjust course to steam in the direction of the explosion. They were guests of the Vietnamese, with standing orders to assist in deterring Chinese aggression with their presence. And Chinese aggression wasn't exactly in short supply in these waters. Every sailor's first thought when a distress call came in was that a PLA-Navy or Chinese Coast Guard ship had bullied a smaller vessel again, or even rammed it, putting lives in danger.

"Good job," Jackson said to the young lieutenant standing

watch in his absence, noting their course and speed as soon as he entered the bridge. Captain Jackson was known far and wide as a deckplate officer, a servant leader who mentored and encouraged even his most junior subordinates to show initiative. Toward apparent danger was the right direction to be moving. "What have we got?" he asked, addressing the sailor at the radio.

"Distress call came in four minutes ago, Captain," the twentysomething radar operator said, his eyes locked to the screen. "I'm picking up broken static that I believe to be someone transmitting from a handheld VHF. Could be people in the water."

"Very well," Jackson said. "Let's get both the Seahawks and the 53 in the air. They can drop rescue swimmers and life rafts, start rescuing any survivors while we're en route." He turned to the radar tech. "Anyone else coming to the party?"

"Negative, Captain. I have two PLAN frigates eight miles to the north. Chinese Coast Guard Cutter 3901 is fifteen miles to our east. None of them appear to be making a move toward the location of the distress call at this point."

"They're timing our response, no doubt," Jackson said. "Seeing how long it takes us to clean up whatever mess they've made. All ahead full." He turned to Laura Kelso, his executive officer, who repeated the order to the helm. On the *Makin Island*, the petty officer first class actually driving the ship was able to increase the ship's speed using throttle control from the bridge, rather than the traditional telegraph system, to make engineering aware of the captain's orders.

Jackson caught Kelso's eye. "XO, have the birds report back to us as soon as they have visual."

"Aye, aye, sir," Commander Kelso said, and went to work.

A *Wasp*-class Landing Helicopter Dock, or LHD, the USS *Makin Island* was easy to confuse with an aircraft carrier. At 843 feet long, she was not a small ship, but still a football field shorter than a *Nimitz*-class big deck. Designated LHD 8, she carried a variety of armament and aircraft, the type and number varying depending on their specific mission. Today, in addition to the CH-53 Sea Stallion and the two MH-60 Seahawk helicopters Captain Jackson had already sent ahead, LHD-8 had a complement of two SuperCobras, eight V-22 Osprey tilt rotors, and four Harrier Jump Jets. But even the Sparrow Missiles and MK-38 chain guns paled in capability compared to the eight-hundred-strong U.S. Marine Expeditionary Unit on board.

Sometimes called a Marine Uber, *Makin Island*'s purpose was to move this impressive fighting force to project American might. Line officers sometimes tended to look down their noses at officers in the Gator Navy—the men and women who, for all practical purposes, drove the Marines around. Captain Jackson loved his Marines, and he had no doubt they would do anything for him, even if that meant risking their lives to jump into the water and save a bunch of Vietnamese oil workers if he ordered them to.

"ETA twenty-two minutes," Commander Kelso said. Like Jackson, she was an Annapolis grad. She expected nothing extra for it, and kept her ring-knocking to a minimum, intuiting early on that with this skipper past accomplishments mattered far less than present duty. Everyone on the ship knew that Jackson's uncle had been President of the United States until he was assassinated. But Rosey Jackson never mentioned that part of his past. His father had taught him well. There was tremendous gravitas in the things a man left unsaid.

OIL RIG

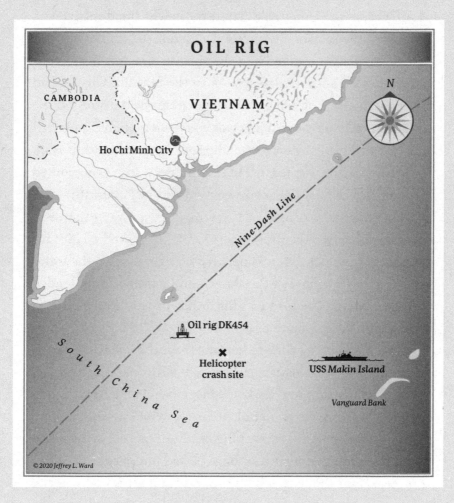

CAMBODIA

VIETNAM

N

Ho Chi Minh City

Nine-Dash Line

South China Sea

⚓ Oil rig DK454

✖
Helicopter
crash site

USS *Makin Island*

Vanguard Bank

©2020 Jeffrey L. Ward

———

Of all the training the U.S. government had afforded Ding Chavez, the thing he'd hated most was the dunker. At a nod from the sadistic instructor, the mock–helicopter cockpit slid down a rail, slammed into the surface pool like it was concrete, and then inverted as it sank to the bottom. Chavez had never been afraid of flying, or the water, but he'd dismissed the dunker as serious overkill. He was a ground pounder, an infantryman. If he went down in a chopper he would either walk away or his shit was toast. He saw no need in getting jerked around on a million-dollar government carnival ride with water up his nose and a couple of Navy divers waiting in the deep end, laughing into their regulators while they watched him try to figure out which way was up. Clark had mandated the training for every member of Rainbow, and Chavez had pretended to be on board. The man was his father-in-law, but he'd hated every sputtering minute of it.

Now, hanging by a nylon harness from the inverted floor of a rapidly sinking Russian helicopter, with his ass above his head, ears buzzing, and darkness fast closing in, Chavez found himself reliving every detail of his previous training. John Clark's adage of doing something not until one got it right, but until one didn't ever get it wrong, played out in spades. Without conscious thought, Chavez found the harness release and gave it a twist. Underwater, he didn't fall to the ceiling as he would have on dry land, but floated, trapped inside the body of the sinking chopper.

Chavez's first thoughts were for his teammates, and he found himself flooded with relief when a sweep to his left found an empty harness where Midas would have been. Chavez kicked forward, feeling in the darkness for the last place he'd seen Dom and Adara, his shoulder bumping into Midas as the former Delta officer performed the same search. Quickly running out of air, Chavez gave Midas a squeeze on the shoulder and pointed toward the cockpit. The pilot met them head-on, swimming his way aft to check on his passengers. With Adara and Dom apparently out, Chavez motioned toward the open door and followed the other two men out. He kicked toward the surface, feeling the searing pain of some unidentified injury in his neck. His lungs screamed for air. His ears chirped and whistled as the pressure against them dropped. Above him he could see light, legs dangling below the surface.

And fire.

Chavez broke the surface in a spot between the patches of burning oil and debris. He fought the pressing urge to breathe until he was reasonably sure he wasn't about to sear his lungs.

The flames looked worse from below than they did up top, with small patches of fuel and rafts of burning plastic bobbing between the waves. Midas had been right beside him, so Chavez scanned for him first, and found him immediately. He was helping Adara get a wounded Dom Caruso into a yellow rubber lifeboat with the aid of two Vietnamese roustabouts, one of whom looked badly burned himself. A strong swimmer, Chavez used adrenaline to help him battle the chop, and he reached the raft in seconds.

Caruso's left leg was bent unnaturally at the knee. His eyes gleamed with pain, but he was conscious. Looking outbound while Midas and Adara got him into the boat, he was the first to see Chavez in the water. "I'm good," he sputtered, wincing as he slithered over the side of the tube.

Midas patted Adara's shoulder, then turned, almost colliding with Ding.

"Holy shit, you're a sight for sore eyes." Midas sputtered, wiping water away from his beard. "I was just coming back to find you."

"I'm good to go," Ding said, bobbing and clinging to a line on the side of the raft. "You and Adara?"

"Banged up but otherwise intact."

Midas slipped over the side, and without another word, both men swam among the debris and began to drag survivors toward the bobbing rafts. They found their pilot first, alive, but one arm broken, the other burned, clinging to a piece of insulation foam. Injured on impact, the man's first inclination had been to see to his passengers. Chavez and Midas returned the favor and got him back to the raft with Adara and Dom.

Twelve minutes post-explosion, there were nine survivors in Adara's raft, and fifteen in a second that Chavez and Midas had lashed alongside the first. A third raft bobbed in the chop some two hundred meters away, and looked to contain at least a dozen men. The chopper pilot spoke Vietnamese well enough to learn that there had been fifty-six crewmen on the rig, which left over twenty still unaccounted for.

Chavez hauled himself into the raft, hoping the extra couple of feet in elevation above the chop would give him a better view. The water was warm, but exertion and the massive adrenaline dump of the explosion and crash left him and the others shaking violently, chilled to the core.

One of the Vietnamese drillers—with much younger eyes than Chavez's—was first to see the choppers on the horizon.

"Probably Chinese," the pilot said through chattering teeth.

Midas wallowed into a kneeling position on the rubber raft's trampoline floor and shielded his eyes to get a better look.

"Nope," he said. "Those are U.S. Navy birds."

The Seahawks arrived first, circling to approach from the west, then hovering close to the surface of the ocean as they dropped two rescue swimmers. Backlit by a low sun, the clouds of mist driven up by the churning rotors threw dazzling rainbows of color into the air below each gunmetal-gray bird.

Adara gave Chavez a good-natured punch in the shoulder with a shaky hand. "Bet you Army boys are happy to see the Navy now . . ."

The Navy swimmer broke the surface a few feet from the raft. He wore a black neoprene shorty and red helmet outfitted with a flashing strobe so the pilots could keep an eye on him. A black dive mask covered his youthful face.

"Petty Officer Third Class Aaron Ward," the swimmer said, as if he'd just sidled up to the bar instead of hanging on to the side of a raft with hurricane-force prop wash battering the ocean a few dozen yards away. "United States Navy. How you folks holding up?"

Petty Officer Ward's demeanor was relaxed—because calm was contagious—but he worked fast to triage the injured in the raft while the choppers scoured the surface for other survivors.

The helicopter pilot had it the worst, and Petty Officer Ward saw to him first, radioing his chopper with a situation report that would be passed on to his ship. It wasn't long before everyone on the rafts was wrapped in foil space blankets like so many shivering baked potatoes.

Inflatable runabouts deployed from *Makin Island*'s well-deck as she drew nearer, allowing the monstrous ship to stand off, protecting it from possible danger, and those in the water from its massive bulk. The runabouts made for an easier rescue than the helicopter hoist, letting the rescue swimmers get back in their respective birds and continue the search for survivors.

Chavez was last off the raft. He stayed out of the way as the coxswain ran the inflatable up the ramp of the *Makin Island*'s well-deck. Sailors and Marines were on hand to assist survivors as they climbed onto the ship. Ears half clogged with water and still shivering, Chavez was vaguely aware of a murmur among a small group of Marines.

One of them stepped away from the others.

Pausing mid-step as he climbed out, Chavez looked to his left. What he saw nearly sent him tumbling back into the runabout.

A slender lance corporal with green eyes administered an on-the-spot correction to a Marine PFC who he must have thought was being too rough bringing the Vietnamese roustabouts aboard. The correction was direct, colorful in its language, and over quickly.

Chavez, still dizzy and near hypothermia, squinted, turning his head slightly to be certain he wasn't seeing things. Satisfied, he chuckled to himself, suddenly much warmer than he had been.

"You kiss your mama with that mouth, Marine?"

The green-eyed lance corporal braced, wheeling to look directly at Chavez. His jaw dropped and his eyes flew wide.

"Dad?"

10

John Clark was almost finished with a call from Mary Pat Foley when his phone buzzed. He'd been expecting to hear from Ding, but this was an unknown number, so he let it go to voicemail. The same number called back twice more in rapid succession, prompting him to put the director of national intelligence on hold—something he was certain few people ever got to do.

It was Ding, calling on a borrowed phone.

Clark's helicopter touched down on the USS *Makin Island* an hour and a half later. By then, rescue operations had turned into body recovery and Lance Corporal Chavez had received permission to break away from his platoon. Captain Jackson cleared the wardroom so the boy could meet privately with his father and grandfather.

Clark had time to brief Chavez of the basics of Foley's call, but little else. The urgency of the situation in China drove him to want to return to the hotel immediately and formulate a plan, but the idea of spending a minute or two with his grandson made him step back and take a breath. Jack and Lisanne were already working logistics for a quick move and they were all waiting on direction from Adam Yao, anyway. He could spare a couple minutes.

Captain Jackson made certain everyone was comfortable in the wardroom and then, grinning, said, "Looks like the Marine has a question or two."

"That I do, sir," JP said. His nose was crooked now. Telltale scars above his right eyebrow and his lower lip had taken the brunt of what looked to have been a serious fight. Shoulder blades pinned, he stood so straight Clark thought his back might snap. Clark suppressed a smile, remembering the hundreds of times as a grandfather that he'd told the boy to stand up straight. As much of a Navy man as he was, he had to admit there wasn't any straight back like a Marine straight back.

Captain Jackson gave JP a soft nod. "Stand at ease, son. In fact, have a seat. Not sure how much your dad is going to tell you, but it'd probably be best if you were sitting down for whatever it is."

The younger Chavez moved mechanically, looking warily back and forth from his father to his grandfather and the captain as he sidled in on a chair at the long table.

Clark took a seat beside him, resting a hand on his grandson's shoulder. "What do you want to know?"

"I thought you and Dad were forensic investigators. I mean, I'm smart enough to figure out there was some security work involved, considering your backgrounds. I know you guys travel . . . but last I heard, Mom told me Dad was supposed to be on some business trip to Singapore. Now I run into him on his way out to an oil rig that gets bombed, and you're able to commandeer a helicopter on a moment's notice to my ship from Ho Chi Minh City . . . That's just . . ."

Clark laid his hands flat on the table and studied them for a moment, deciding whether or not to speak, then said, "The family business. That's what it is."

JP looked at his father. "Seriously? Are you guys mercs?"

"Hell, no," Ding said. "Far from it."

"We're more what you'd call contractors," Clark said.

Captain Jackson turned to leave. "I'll see myself out so you can read him in to whatever this is."

Clark gave a dry chuckle. "You're involved, Skipper. At least your family is."

Jackson nodded. "I thought as much. Jack Ryan was my uncle Robby's dearest friend. Ryan tapped him to be his vice president."

"That's true," Clark said. "But I was thinking of your other uncle. Tim."

Jackson cocked his head. "How's that?"

"Years ago—I hate to admit how many—I recruited our young Marine's daddy for a special mission. It remains classified, but what we were doing isn't important. Your uncle Tim was a platoon leader at Fort Ord and I sort of snatched Staff Sergeant Chavez out from under his nose. He got a pretty good ass-chewing for trying to find out what was going on, if I remember correctly."

Jackson laughed. "I remember hearing him talk about spooks invading his turf."

"Spooks . . ." JP Chavez stared into space, then turned to look directly at his father. "Does Mom know?"

"She does," Ding said.

JP's gaze shifted to Clark, who answered before he could ask. "Your grandma has known what I do since before I even really started doing it."

"I guess there's a lot you can't tell me."

Ding chuckled. "Quite a bit. But we're the good guys. That's the main thing you need to know."

"CIA?"

"For a while," Clark said. "Since we're getting it all out in the open."

JP looked down at his hands, folded on the wardroom table, and for just a moment Clark saw a bit of himself. "This is a lot to take in." He locked eyes with his dad. "You've been doing whatever this is since you were in the Army?"

"In one way or another," Ding said.

"Since you were about my age? Grandpa came to your unit and recruited you? So that could happen to me if it's the family business. Right?"

"First of all," Ding said, "I was a staff sergeant, not an E3." He looked imploringly at Clark. "Help me out here, Grandpa."

Clark put a hand on JP's shoulder again. "Let's just see where your career takes you. This kind of work has a way of finding the right person for the job. Let things happen in time."

"I thought you were going to help," Ding said. "That's not helping."

Clark gave his grandson a wink. "Like I said, it is the family business." He put both hands on the table, and gave Ding a warning side-eye. "As much as it kills me to cut this reunion short, we need to talk more about that call from the boss's boss."

JP got to his feet. Both Ding and Clark drew him in for back-slapping hugs.

"I always thought you guys were pretty cool," JP said. "But this is—"

"Between us," Clark said. "That's what it is. Secrecy is a burden, but it's a big part of that family business we talked about."

"Understood, sir," JP said. "I should get back to my platoon."

Clark gave him one more hug for the road, and then tousled what little hair there was on top of his regulation cut.

"Care to tell me how you got that broken nose?"

"Long story, sir," JP said. "For another time."

"But I should see the other guy. Right?"

JP laughed out loud. "You probably already have. He's my best friend in the platoon."

"Hmmm," Ding said. "I guess that is a long story . . ."

Captain Jackson followed him out the wardroom door. "Lance Corporal Chavez and I will leave you two to discuss your secret phone call. Can you stay for dinner?"

"Wish we could," Clark said. "But we'll have to take a rain check."

JP was shaking his head as he went out the door. "This is the most kickass thing I've ever even heard of . . ."

The Mi-17 pilot and Dom Caruso, who'd been sitting directly behind him, suffered burns from spilled fuel during the crash. The pilot went directly from the *Makin Island* to a hospital in Ho Chi Minh City. Caruso got some Silvadene ointment for his burns—and a splint for the severely damaged cartilage in his knee. The ship's doc agreed with Adara's assessment that he was going to need surgery—which would sideline him for the next several weeks at the very least. They gave him enough pain meds to get him back to the States and sent him on his way with Clark, Chavez, and Adara in one of the

Seahawks. Everyone in the city knew the U.S. Navy had assisted in the rescue after the oil rig explosion, so one of the matte-gray choppers dropping off some Americans didn't raise any eyebrows.

"Patsy's going to have my ass," Chavez said.

"The boy looks sharp, though," Clark said.

"I wonder about that fight," Ding said. "He took some kind of beating . . . and the dude and he are friends now . . ."

"And he's still standing," Clark said.

"Still . . ." Ding said, his mouth set in a tight line.

Clark patted him on the back. "We all got our secrets, son."

Clark got Foley back on the line as soon as he had the team convened in his hotel room.

Dom sat in a padded chair, his bad leg propped up on an ottoman under a bag of ice. Jack Junior barely contained his displeasure at having missed the action—even if that action was a helicopter crash. Frankly, Clark knew how he felt, but had seen enough action in his life that he didn't feel cheated.

Vietnam had good relations with the United States at the moment, but Clark had still taken time to sweep the room for listening devices. They'd drawn the curtains and set up white-noise "chirpers" by the door and each window to defeat laser mics anyone might be bouncing off the glass. Even so, they spoke in vague terms and coded names.

"Thanks, Chief," Clark said, when the DNI had finished her thumbnail brief. An enlisted sailor at heart, Clark used the title as a term of endearment, having generally reserved his top level of trust for the crusty old senior chiefs over most officers.

"So," Ding said, once Clark disconnected the call. "Two targets. Mother and daughter. We'll have to split up."

Midas lay on his back on top of Clark's bedspread, drawing imaginary circles in the air with the gimme hotel pen from the nightstand. "The kid should be a simple find. We're going to need something else to go on to find her mama besides 'hiding out with some terrorists somewhere in China.'"

"Yep," Clark said. "We'll get more from CROSSTIE anytime now." Everyone in the room knew CROSSTIE was CIA operations officer Adam Yao. They'd worked with him before, built that kind of rare trust that comes from spilling a lot of sweat and a substantial amount of blood together in the field.

"And they have a mole," Ding said, restating Mary Pat Foley's larger concern. "Will CROSSTIE's initial cables to his chain of command compromise him at all?"

"Remains to be seen," Clark said. "The boss believes his identity has been compartmented enough to keep him in the black. But we have to be careful. Without knowing the mole's identity and level of access, we can't be certain what he or she knows."

"Does it sound like she has any suspects?" Adara asked from her spot at Caruso's side. She'd been coddling him from the moment they got back to the hotel.

Clark gave her a knowing nod. "At this point, I imagine they suspect everyone."

11

Monica Hendricks stood barefoot on a padded office chair, her lips pursed around a mouthful of tenpenny nails. Like most of the bean counters in government buildings around the world, the powers that be at CIA paid an inordinate amount of attention to little things, like the tiny holes left by hanging framed plaques, certificates, and photographs on an employee's I-love-me wall. A certain type of hanger was mandated, or . . . Monica didn't exactly know the consequences, but she suspected it would entail either a firing squad or a flurry of e-mails from admin weenie bosses to operational bosses—who had, by virtue of their jobs, become admin weenies themselves. Hanging anything with something as large as a tenpenny nail was strictly verboten. Monica smiled, dabbing a bit of Colgate toothpaste into the tenpenny holes to cover her treachery. She was on her way out the door, anyway—the admin weenies would have to run fast if they wanted to catch her now.

Known for being a snappy dresser, Hendricks wore faded jeans and a Georgetown sweatshirt today. The Agency had a robust program to help see people through the transition to the private sector, help them understand that they are still relevant when they turn in their parking pass and building ID. It was a big step, leaving all this behind, and like most people who'd worked anywhere for as long as she had, she'd spent her last day reminiscing about her career, with colleagues and in her head. That reminiscing was doubly important now, because there was a lot she would never be able to talk about once she stepped out the door.

Fifty was young to be retiring from the CIA. Armed federal law enforcement agents had to pull the plug at fifty-seven. CIA officers didn't hit their sell-by date until they were sixty. Even then, they could come back as contractors to teach. By fifty you'd paid your dues. You'd just begun to untie the Gordian knot that was the Central Intelligence Agency. The best promotions came around fifty, when they still had ten good years to wring out of your soul. Everyone on the Asia desk thought she was making the biggest mistake of her life. She'd served in leadership positions in the headquarters and the field, including chief of station, and was on the short list for several plum promotions to the seventh floor. For the last three years, virtually every iota of intelligence regarding China had crossed her desk or the desks of those who worked for her. Some even thought she had a shot at deputy director if she played her cards right.

But she wasn't much of a cardplayer.

She missed the field to be sure, and lamented the "mom body" that came with sitting behind a desk—and her affinity for daily lattes from the Starbucks in the CIA food court. She wasn't particularly out of shape, but she wasn't in shape, either. Monica had never been the stereotypical slender female operator of the Hollywood spy genre. She'd been a bit on the chunky side when she was recruited. She was worried at first, but made it through The Farm fine, realizing quickly that a few extra pounds of fighting weight made defensive tactics easier to handle. She knew her way around firearms but rarely carried one, though her husband and two sons routinely chided her for not doing so for her own protection. Her adult sons had both known she was a CIA officer from the time they were in high school— old enough to keep a secret—and still they believed there was more gunplay in the life of an intelligence officer than there actually was. Both seemed to think that every CIA officer, including their mother, was a part of the ground branch—the paramilitary guys that the world equated with the CIA overseas. It made her smile. While the Russians, Chi-Comms, Iranians, and jihadis were all watching the bearded white guys who ate barbed wire for breakfast, the slightly chunky black woman slipped by unnoticed.

It was good work, but twenty-six years was enough. Now she was going to give back, to teach high school. Her friends with teenagers joked that she was leaving intelligence work to go into law enforcement.

Hendricks's family was accustomed to service. Her husband taught history at Georgetown. Her eldest son was an officer in the Army, in his final year of residency to become a trauma surgeon at Fort Sam Houston. Her youngest was in his second year with the Secret Service, stationed in the Seattle Field Office.

She'd grown up in a middle-class home outside Dallas, where her father was an engineer designing integrated circuits for Texas Instruments. She'd been a child at the end of the Civil Rights movement. Her parents kept themselves to themselves for the most part and were not politically active. She graduated high school in the late eighties with a handful of token minorities in her senior class—the doctor from India's kid, some Hispanic families. Monica had balked when her mother insisted she take a second language but found she had a knack for Spanish—the only language besides Latin offered by her high school. She took it all four years—and Latin, too, because the puzzles the languages provided seemed to fit well with the way her brain worked. She had plenty of kids to practice her Spanish with, but there were few kids like her. Reggie Good, the fastest wide receiver on the football team, was black, and in a Texas high school, football transcended color—up to a point. There were a few unwritten rules. She was a popular academic kid. Pretty, but not skinny enough to be a cheerleader. She could go out with virtually any boy in the school, no matter the color, so long as it was nothing serious. Reggie could date her, and possibly a couple of the Hispanic girls, but the line against him dating white girls was clearly drawn.

He wasn't *that* good at football.

There was never any violence as far as Monica knew, but there was an undercurrent, easy enough to feel when she was old enough to know what to look for. It bugged the hell out of her.

Monica left home at eighteen with a full-ride academic scholarship to the University of Texas at Austin and a righteous chip on her shoulder. She let her hair grow out into her natural Afro and became active in the Black Student Alliance as well as a Black Action Movement that modeled itself after the U of Michigan protests. But she was never so active as to fall behind on her studies. Her freshman Spanish professor bumped her to upper-level classes and hired her as his TA. She suspected he might have a thing for roundish black girls, but he turned out to be happily married, and was simply astounded at her ability with languages. One of her roommates was from Taiwan and spoke very little English. Monica made a deal that she'd help her with English if she'd teach her Mandarin. She majored in history but minored in languages and went on to pursue a master's with an added teaching certificate in history and social studies. She wanted to do something worthwhile. Something that could make a difference. Teaching seemed to fit that bill.

Then, near the end of her first year of grad school, a smiling brunette with piercing amber eyes sat down with her in the J2 food court across from Jesta' Pizza. She was a few years older, early thirties, maybe. At first Monica had thought she was a professor just looking for a place to sit. But there were plenty of empty tables.

"My name's Faye," she'd said.

Monica eyed her without looking up from her book. "Hey, Faye," she'd said.

The woman wasn't one to beat around the bush. "Maybe you've seen me around?"

"Nope."

"Here's the deal. I'm a recruiter for the CIA."

"No shit?" Monica looked up and smirked. Who was this lady? "Are you even allowed to tell me that out loud? I thought you guys were all secret squirrel and stuff."

Faye laughed and ate a french fry off Monica's paper plate. "It's cool. I'm wearing a disguise." She obviously wasn't. "Seriously, though, the Central Intelligence Agency is interested in people like you."

"People *like* me?" Monica said. "The CIA wants to hire me because I'm black?"

"Getting hired is a long way off," the woman who called herself Faye had said. "The CIA wants you to *apply*."

"Because I'm black?" Monica gave a smug nod, as sure of herself as any twenty-four-year-old empowered woman of color could be. "Got to raise those minority numbers and all, show your bosses you're doing your part for affirmative action."

Faye let her talk. Flashed those pretty amber eyes, then said, "You about done?"

Monica shrugged. "Sure."

"Good," Faye said, ignoring the affirmative action swipe. "As I was saying, the CIA would like you to apply because you are exceptionally smart." She went on to explain that the application process for a CIA security clearance was extremely rigorous. There would be "deep-dive" psychological evaluations, polygraphs, and a thorough background check where people she knew all the way back to junior high would be contacted about her loyalty and suitability. "It takes a good while to complete," Faye said. "You'll have time to finish grad school . . . It's better for us if you do finish."

Monica had just sat there, stunned, with the look on her face her daddy called poleaxed.

"The CIA?" she whispered, suddenly hyperaware of everyone else in the open food court. "You're interested in me? No kidding?"

Faye leaned forward, whispering across the table now, getting down to business. "No kidding."

Everything Monica knew about the CIA—which wasn't much—she'd gotten from spy books and James Bond movies. She had already come to grips with being a teacher, maybe a college professor, helping to shape young minds about the realities of the world. The notion of working for the government, much less working in intelligence, had never been so much as a tiny blip on her personal radar. She'd taken loads of placement tests over the years, and no guidance counselor had ever said, "Hey, Monica, have you ever thought about being a spy?"

Now, with Faye sitting there talking about how hard it would be, she found herself aching to get the job. No matter how rigorous the process, how deep the background, she *had* to have this job. She hardly even knew what it entailed, but suddenly, there was no other job for her in the world.

"I speak fluent Spanish," she'd all but blurted. "And can get by in Mandarin pretty well, too."

Faye, who still leaned over the table, ate another french fry and said, "We know."

And now it was over. Monica Hendricks was on her way out the door she'd come in, picking up where she'd left off, to become a teacher—as soon as she hid all the evidence from hanging her photos and plaques.

12

Reduced to eating nails?" Mary Pat Foley said, smiling as she poked her head in the door to Hendricks's office. The DNI wore a snazzy gray pantsuit in light wool, warm enough for the crisp spring weather and light enough to spend hours in the stuffy, artificial environment of her office at Liberty Crossing.

Hendricks dropped the nails into her hand and placed them on the corner of her desk. She knew Foley well. They'd worked together early in Monica's career, each earning the other's trust from living through dangerous times—dodging thugs, losing surveillance, and generally risking their lives in hostile environments. Poor Steve would never sleep again if he knew the half of what she'd done over the course of her career.

"Madam Director," Hendricks said. "This is a nice surprise. I'd shake your hand, but I just spit out those frame hangers . . ."

"Knock it off with the 'Madam Director' stuff, Mony," Foley said. "You and I have drunk too many grappas over the years for you to call me anything but Mary Pat. Anyway, I hear you're popping smoke, as they say, to what, teach high school?"

Hendricks moved a stack of frames off the chair so the DNI would have a place to sit. "That's correct. I know it's a necessary part of the job, but I'm just too tired of . . . well, the lying. You know?"

Foley chuckled. "Yeah, and high school kids don't lie."

"At least I won't have to. Seriously, ma'am . . . Mary Pat, it is nice of you to drop in and say good-bye."

Foley toyed with the frayed corner of the leather desk blotter with the tip of her manicured thumbnail. It was a marvel how far this woman had come from the days she'd broken her fingernails to the quick digging under rocks to retrieve an asset's message from some iced-over dead drop.

Foley glanced up, her hand lingering on the desk. "I didn't, actually," she said. "Come to say good-bye, that is. I came to ask you to stay."

Hendricks scoffed, thinking it was surely a joke. "Due respect, Mad . . . Mary Pat, but the director of national intelligence doesn't come down to Langley and ask a lowly CIA minion to hang around. My daddy told me the story of pulling the hand out of the bucket of water when I was a little girl. I'm self-aware enough to know my worth."

Foley smiled and shook her head. "I'm not sure you do, Monica. And I'm here to tell you, that's exactly what this DNI is doing. I need you to hang around."

Hendricks gave a little nothing-she-could-do-about-it shrug. "Sorry, ma'am. No can do. I have a teaching job lined up for the fall and I promised Steve we could do some traveling this summer."

Foley nodded, mulling this over, but obviously not taking *no can do* for an answer. "Remember that time you and I sat up for five days straight watching that safe house?"

"Outside Addis Ababa," Hendricks said and chuckled. "The

Soviets were up to their armpits in that place. I can still smell the curtains in that shitty apartment."

"I know," Foley said. "Mango-scented curtains . . . What was that all about? About three days in, you told me a story about how you wanted to stage a protest against people in your hometown when you were in high school."

"Right," Hendricks said. "Even the local ministers were against the state putting in a group home because of the so-called black troublemakers it would bring into the county."

"And your dad told you to stand up for what you believe in, but to be smart about it. He said—"

"He said that some causes were worth losing your life over, and some were like jumping off a cliff and screaming at the wind on the way down." Hendricks sighed, giving a solemn nod. "It was good advice. Served me well in picking my battles. That's why I'm quitting here to teach for a few years while I'm still young enough."

"I really do need you to stay," Foley said.

"Why?"

"Here's the funny part," Foley said. "I can't tell you that just yet. But I can promise you this. You won't be screaming against the wind. There's a good chance that what I'm going to ask you to do will keep friends of ours alive."

13

The rig bombing and chopper crash made everyone jumpy and reticent to speak openly in a foreign hotel room—not to mention all the talk of moles and counterintelligence operations. The CIA had few safe houses in Ho Chi Minh City, and even those were suspect. At this point, everything was suspect. The Hendley Associates Gulfstream made the perfect airborne secure compartmented information facility, or SCIF, in which Chavez and the rest of The Campus could discuss operational plans with Adam Yao. The Hendley pilots filed a flight plan to Hanoi and back, giving the group time to talk without having to worry about clearing customs anywhere until they hammered out the details of their mission—and direction of travel. Caruso came along, too. No way he was going on any op. He'd return to the States the following day, for an appointment with an orthopedic surgeon. Until then, he had a good mind for tactics. Chavez was glad to have him along, even if he was a little loopy on hydrocodone.

Chavez and Clark sat in aft-facing leather seats. Caruso sat in the very back on the sofa—Jack Junior's usual spot. Adara sat beside him. Midas and Jack faced forward across from

Chavez and Clark. Lisanne sat in one of the two vacant seats behind them.

"Now that we can speak in the black," Chavez said, "are you folks hearing any chatter on the rig bombing?"

Adam Yao's voice was crystal clear over the encrypted satellite link—which Mary Pat Foley assured everyone was secure, even from Langley and Fort Meade.

"I'm thinking it was a wrong place, wrong time type of thing. The Chinese make no bones about the fact that they lay claim to all waters inside their sacred little nine dashes." Yao's words dripped with derision. "Blowing up a state-owned oil rig isn't exactly a great leap forward from ramming Vietnamese or Philippine Navy vessels and drowning a bunch of sailors. These guys have no trouble throwing their substantial weight around to show the world who's boss in the South China Sea. Our Freedom of Navigation Patrols are pissing Beijing off something fierce. I know that much."

Dom groaned from his vantage point on the sofa in back, gazing out of one open eye. "Effective way to gather intel if you don't value human life," he said. "Blow the hell out of a rig to put some folks in the water, then sit back and see how long it takes for the United States Navy to respond."

"Or to see *if* they respond," Clark said. "It allows the Chinese to see what our rules of engagement are toward civilians."

"We're all intel folks," Adam Yao said, sounding very much like he was gritting his teeth. "And as such, we are responsible for submitting unbiased intelligence to Higher, so the analysts who often have the larger picture can do their jobs."

"True . . ." Clark looked around the Gulfstream's cabin to see if anyone else knew what Yao was getting at.

The CIA officer plowed ahead. "Honestly, guys, I've got to

tell you, it's getting awfully damned hard to be objective here. In order to do my job, I try to look at things through a Chinese lens. But that lens is getting pretty damned murky. I'm starting to think there aren't any lines—" Yao took a deep breath. "Sorry to go off like that. You'll see what I mean soon enough."

"Yeah, speaking of that," Chavez said, pencil stub poised over a small black notebook. "Still no line on this Medina Tohti woman?"

"Not yet," Yao said. "I have some hooks in the water. There's a guy I'm meeting with either tonight or tomorrow who may be able to point us in the right direction."

Clark spoke next. "The last couple of attacks attributed to the Wuming have been in and around Urumqi. She's hanging her hat with them now, so it stands to reason she's somewhere around that area."

"That's a good guess," Yao said. "But Urumqi is a city of three and a half million people. They have cameras like New York City has pigeons. I can guarantee you that right now, the place is crawling with People's Liberation Army Navy intelligence."

"Hang on." Caruso opened one eye again at the back of the plane. "It's PLA-Navy intelligence and not Ministry of State Security?"

"Oddly, yes," Yao said. "From what I'm hearing, Navy spooks reporting directly to Admiral Zheng are handling this one by themselves. The admiral wants the search kept low-key, but he also wants this woman bad, so they're leaving no stone unturned."

"And no idea why they want her?" Adara asked.

"Something to do with the missing professor," Yao said. "That's it so far."

"But too hot for us to go in without a better lock on Medina Tohti's location," Chavez said, nodding while he doodled in his notebook.

"It is for now," Yao said. "With any luck, my guy will give us a concrete place to focus on."

"Any chance Tohti will go to her daughter's?" Ryan asked.

"There's a chance," Yao said. "The girl's evidently some kind of gymnastics prodigy. The government had taken her to Beijing for training when Medina's husband was rounded up and killed. Sounds like Medina just lost it and ran off."

Adara gave a low whistle. "Makes sense when you think about it, wanting to join a group that's killing the people who have taken away her husband and her daughter. The poor woman's gotten the shitty end of the stick from her own government."

"We do know the daughter is in Kashgar," Yao said. "Staying with her aunt."

"The authorities are sure to be up on that address as well," Ryan said.

"Oh, yeah," Yao said. "Urumqi is bad, but surveillance in Kashgar is probably worse. Citizens in western China are surveilled more heavily than virtually any other city in the world. Cameras everywhere, facial-recognition software running full-tilt, checkpoints with magnetometers and X-ray screening all over the place. The place is crawling with Bingtuan."

"Bingtuan?" Chavez asked.

"The Corps. Short for Xinjiang Production and Construction Corps," Yao said. "Sounds a hell of a lot more benign than it is. The XPCC is a paramilitary government organization charged with protecting the frontier from invasion, but their primary focus is on tamping down any rebellion from the Uyghur population. They have their hands in everything—the farm quotas, education, healthcare, law enforcement—making sure everyone is being Chinese enough."

"I've read about them," Clark said. *"On one shoulder the rifle, on the other the hoe."*

"Or one boot on the neck of anyone who doesn't bend to Han Chinese will," Yao added. "They have a lock on Kashgar, that's for sure. Still, a mother's love and all. There's a good chance Medina Tohti will surface there at some point."

"You feel like we can get in?" Chavez asked.

"As tourists," Yao said. "Some professional eyes in case Medina Tohti does show up—or at least poke around and see what you can find out. I have a couple of assets there, but they lack training."

"Maybe Lisanne and I," Clark said. "While the rest of you get ready to head for parts yet unknown."

Robertson perked up.

Ding nodded in agreement. "If you think she's ready, Boss."

"I do," Clark said. "It'll be the perfect cover—an old man and his—"

"Nurse," Midas joked.

Clark gave one of his low and slow chuckles, the kind Chavez thought sounded particularly deadly. "I was going to say an old man and his lady friend."

Midas raised both hands as if in surrender. "You know I'm only kidding, Mr. C."

Clark's eyes narrowed. "Is that right . . ."

Yao's voice came across the speaker. "I suppose you and Ms. Robertson could be the ones to go. But I'm thinking Kashgar will be the easier place to provide workable cover legends.

Yeah, the XPCC goons are everywhere, but Beijing likes to show off how culturally sensitive China can be. Forget that they've rounded up over a million Uyghurs for 'reeducation.' They've got this whole Potemkin village vibe going in Kashgar, demonstrating to the world how China pulls its ethnic minorities out of the squalor they've been living in for centuries and provides them with modern housing and better living. They still welcome tourists there. I'll blend in wherever this mission takes us, but if the rest of you have to go into Urumqi hunting Tohti and the Wuming, two couples would draw less attention than a bunch of dudes."

"So," Clark said. "You're saying I should take one of the guys with me to Kashgar."

"I believe that dynamic would draw less attention there than in other parts of China," Yao said. "I could get you set up with Canadian passports and the necessary travel visas."

"Okay, then," Clark said. "Midas, you're with me. You get to be my nurse."

"Now, Mr. C.," Midas said. "No hard feelings, right?"

Clark gave him a narrow grin. "Time provides the sweetest revenge. You'll get old yourself one day, youngster—barring any unforeseen circumstances . . ."

"Well, shit," Midas said. "Nice knowing you guys . . ."

"How will you get us in?" Clark asked.

"I have a contact with Immigration and Visas in Beijing," Yao said. "A low-level functionary who helps me get visas on short notice. I never ask him for anything sensitive. He's an unwitting agent—has no idea he's helping out the evil American. As far as he knows, he's doing me a favor and acting as a middleman to help rich Canadians who want to tour China without all the red tape. I helped him out of a little jam involving some video of him and his boss's wife a few years ago, so he feels some amount of indebtedness toward me."

"Let me guess," Ryan said. "You're the one who took the video in the first place?"

"I'll leave the honey traps to the Chinese," Yao said. "But I may have taken advantage of a situation that my asset got himself into on his own—"

"Canadian tourists," Midas said. "So what's our cover?"

"You'll go in separately," Yao said. "John will be retired, out seeing the world. Midas, I'll set you up as a former Canadian Forces officer, since you have that military bearing anyway. Easier to explain if it's in the open. Your girlfriend is a doctor."

"Girlfriend?" Midas said.

"She was supposed to meet you in Kashgar," Yao said. "But she got called away at the last minute and wasn't able to make it. I'll have tickets for her as well, to backstop the story in the unlikely event anyone checks. Your rich girlfriend is paying for the trip anyway, so you figure you'll just take advantage of the vacay and see the sights."

"A kept man with a sugar mama," Clark said, a little smugly. "I can see that."

Midas groaned. "So this is how it's gonna go. I make one little joke . . ."

"Wherever we all end up," Chavez said, bringing everyone back on track, "we're likely going in slick. Traveling with a weapon once we're inside the PRC is one thing, smuggling one in on short notice is almost impossible."

Yao spoke again. "Depending on where we go, I should be able to outfit us up with some light weapons once we're in. John, one of my contacts can set you and Midas up as well."

"There'll be plenty of weapons lying around Kashgar," Clark said.

"A lot of Silk Road influence," Midas noted. "Cleavers and long butcher knives . . ."

"Pretty sure my contact can do a little better than a meat cleaver," Yao said. "I've seen to it that she has a number of useful items in her arsenal in the event any of my friends happen to stop by with the right introduction."

"And we'll have the odd Chinese pistol," Clark said. "Probably used by old Chiang Kai-shek himself, and maybe a Kalashnikov or two we can commandeer if the need presents itself. The way I hear it, Kashgar is going to be big fun—like Indiana Jones, except with People's Armed Police and XPCC goons instead of Nazis."

"That's on the nose, John," Adam Yao said. "Remember what I said about the boot on the neck of their people. According to my contacts on the ground, there are a couple of things going on with Medina Tohti's sister that you should know."

14

Ten-year-old Hala Tohti chewed on the embroidered collar of her loose cotton shirt while she chopped onions with the oversized cleaver as if her life depended on it. The cleaver was four times as big as her small hand, but she was used to the work and wielded it like an expert. Her uncle had always kept the cleaver razor sharp, before he'd been hauled away by the Bingtuan bastards, and he'd not been gone long enough for it to lose its edge. Everyone knew the Bingtuan. Teachers, police, farm superintendents: Anyone with power was part of the Bingtuan—even the man who ran the petrol station where Hala's aunt filled up her scooter. Hala was not sure what a bastard was, but her aunt had used it to describe the two men from Kashgar City government who'd visited her home every week for over a month, so it must have meant something ugly.

Hala had chewed on her collar when she was nervous for as long as she could remember. Now, since her father was dead and her mother had run away, the only time she stopped chewing was when her aunt gave her a swat.

Zulfira was only twelve years older, barely twenty-two. To Hala, she felt more like an older sister than an aunt. Zulfira's husband had been taken away two months earlier, to the same place they'd taken Hala's father. No one had heard from him since that night. The fat Bingtuan bureaucrat named Mr. Suo told Zulfira that her husband had been detained and sent for reeducation because of something the authorities had found on his phone. One of the Three Evils—terrorism, separatism, and religious extremism—but they never said which one.

Hala's uncle had been a quiet man who kept to himself. He paid his taxes without complaint, and was not overly religious. Even at ten, Hala knew the only "evil" he'd committed was being married to a pretty woman who fat Suo, the bureaucrat pig, wanted for himself.

Mr. Suo's assistant was not much older than Zulfira, with sickeningly red lips and eyes that drooped as if he smoked hashish— or was simply bored with everything going on around him.

Suo and his assistant had surprised Hala and her aunt earlier that morning, before daybreak. Hala recognized the electronic beep when Suo's assistant used his handheld machine to scan the barcode beside Zulfira's photograph and trustworthiness rating posted beside the front door. Zulfira said the men had to make a record to prove to someone higher than them in the government that they had checked on all the Uyghur homes in their area.

They'd come unannounced six times in as many weeks after Zulfira's husband was taken, always on some pretense— plastering the barcode on the door or checking the water quality from the kitchen tap—smelling, but not actually tasting it—and finally checking the structure of the house. The water often came out of the tap brown, and there were many cracks in the wall plaster, but Suo and his assistant ignored all those problems. The Bingtuan had condemned Zulfira and her husband's comfortable old home in an old section of Kashgar and promptly bulldozed it to the ground.

The visits were always a surprise. Each time they'd come, fat Mr. Suo had stood on the front step with his hands behind him and asked if he and his companion could come inside. This morning, the men simply scanned the door code and barged in as if it were their home.

They looked surprised and disappointed that Zulfira and Hala were already out of bed and up working. Fat Suo said he needed to look at the walls again, paying special attention to the bedroom, picking up Zulfira's blankets and putting them to his nose when he thought no one was looking. The younger man licked his freakish lips and looked oddly at Hala.

Suo turned suddenly, leaving the house without a word. The assistant had made a note in his small book and told Zulfira that he and his boss would return that evening. She would be well advised to have a hot meal prepared. She was, he said, to treat them as family, for that is what they were to be. The young man barked when he spoke, like someone who worked for the person in charge and thought that made him in charge as well. He never introduced himself, but Hala had heard the fat bureaucrat call him by name.

Ren.

Ren the bastard, Zulfira said, though Hala still did not quite know what that meant.

Hala wished she were bigger, stronger, so she could do something to help her aunt.

Zulfira must have read her mind, for she glared at her niece with narrow eyes as she expertly spun and pulled a skein of well-oiled noodles. "You will pretend you are invisible tonight," she said. "Do not speak with these men. Not a word."

"They are swine," Hala said. "I wish I could—"

"Well, you cannot!" Zulfira slammed the noodles against the countertop over and over. "I am not your mother, but your mother has run away and left you in my charge. There is nothing either of us can do about that. We will feed these men and treat them kindly, and I will not hear another word from you about the matter."

"That is not fair," Hala said, tears of anger welling in her eyes, her face flushing hot. She chopped harder at her onions, narrowly missing her thumb. "I cannot believe what you are saying. The Bingtuan are the ones who took my uncle. They do not deserve our resp—"

Zulfira slapped her hard across the face, ringing her ear and knocking her off her stool. The cleaver flew from her hand and fell to the floor, where it buried itself into the cheap linoleum like an ax in soft wood.

Zulfira held the skein of oiled noodles in her hand like a club. "And yet," she said, "respecting them is exactly what you are going to do." Flour smudged her chin. Her eyes blazed. "Do you understand me, you spoiled little girl? You go away to your fancy gymnastics school with all the rich children and you begin to believe that you are so much smarter than we poor, unlearned Xinjiang Uyghurs who have not seen so much of the world. Well, let me promise you this, your ignorant aunt will break her broom over your back if you do not show these men respect."

And respect was exactly what Hala showed. It did not matter, even a ten-year-old could see that. The rich odors of Zulfira's *laghman*—stir-fried noodles, spiced lamb onions, and peppers—mingled with the smell of black vinegar by the time the men arrived. Dinner dragged on for over an hour, with the bureaucrat demonstrating from his many helpings of *laghman* why he was so fat.

He tried to make small talk over a sweet pudding of rice, raisins, and shredded carrots, acting as if he had suddenly become head of the household. Hala chewed on her collar, soaking it, chapping the skin around her own neck. She could barely hold her tongue. At length, the bureaucrat excused himself to go to the toilet. Oddly, he carried a small plastic bag with him to the restroom.

As soon as he'd gone, his assistant, Ren, opened his swollen lips to explain why.

"The Xinjiang government has a solemn duty to see to the well-being of all its citizens, especially the poorer, less advanced populations," Ren said. His voice squealed. Annoying, Hala thought, like a mosquito. "As you may be aware, the Central Committee feels it is beneficial for local officials such as Mr. Suo to become especially familiar with the households under his care. He appreciates the delicious meal and very much looks forward to our stay tomorrow night."

Zulfira leaned over the table slightly, hands folded in her lap, rocking as if she had a stomachache. Hala had never seen her aunt look so small and frail. She spoke quietly, barely above a whisper.

"Please assure Mr. Suo that we have everything we need in this household. We are happy to provide him with meals, but it would be unseemly for a man to stay in my home with my husband away."

Ren looked down his nose at Zulfira as if she were a small child and not the woman in charge of her own home. "I can assure you, there is nothing unseemly about it. Mr. Suo has instructed me to spend the night as well, as a chaperone."

"Mr. Ren," Zulfira said, head bowed over her own table to show subservience. "Two men will hardly present a more reputable image than one—"

"Phhft." Ren waved away the notion. "If any of your overly pious neighbors have an issue with the business of the government, they may take the matter up with Mr. Suo's office, at which time they will be reminded that religious extremism is one of the Three Evils." Ren now leaned across the table as well, craning his neck like a chicken to get as close to Zulfira as was physically possible without actually touching her. Hala was sure her aunt could smell the man's horrible breath. "Exactly which of your neighbors do you believe will have a problem with a city official doing his duty? Perhaps this person should attend a few classes."

Hala and Zulfira both knew "taking a few classes" meant being carted off to a reeducation camp.

"All is good," Zulfira said, lifting her chin to give Ren a timid smile. "Please excuse an overreaction from a distraught female. Of course Mr. Suo is welcome in our home. I will prepare a pallet on the floor by the stove and he may have my sleeping shelf."

"Now, Mrs. Azizi," Ren said, shaking his head. "You are a lone woman with no one to take care of you. Who knows if your husband will even wish to come back here. Most women in your shoes are happy to have the guidance of a strong man in the home, someone to teach them, watch over them, to keep them from feeling so alone. Sometimes, mutual feelings blossom—"

Fat Suo's voice came from behind them as he emerged from the narrow hall, drying thick fingers on a white handkerchief from his pocket.

"Do not frighten her, Ren," he chuffed. He smiled broadly, swelling his fat cheeks so they all but eclipsed his eyes. "We are supposed to be helpful to our citizens. The forecast calls for snow. I would not presume to have Mrs. Azizi move from her own bed on a night that is to be so cold." He placed his hand gently on Zulfira's shoulder. "I represent not only the local government, but Beijing—the Party, the Motherland. Mrs. Azizi knows she has no reason to mistrust my intentions."

"Thank you," Zulfira said, trembling, breathing through her mouth. "I was not planning to bring it up, but the pipe under the kitchen faucet has leaked ever since we were told to leave our previous home and moved into this one. Perhaps you could fix that, if you were looking to be helpful."

"Ren will have someone look at it, of course. But in the meantime, you and I will be fine on the same sleeping shelf. You have nothing to fear from me. As I said, it will be cold."

Zulfira's lips parted. "But, sir—"

The bureaucrat clapped his hands together, evidently signifying to his assistant that it was time to go, because Ren was on his feet in an instant.

Zulfira flinched at the noise. Hala thought she might run, but she just sat there, shaking.

"I left a few of my favorite toiletries in your bath," Suo continued. "You have given so freely of your hospitality with this delicious meal, I do not want to take advantage of you by using your soaps when I shower." He turned up his nose, transforming his noxious smile into a pinched sneer. "In truth, I do not particularly care for the odor of the soaps you Uyghurs use. I am not . . . how shall I put this? I am not completely sure that Uyghur products are as effective as they should be at getting the body clean." He clapped his hands again, a judge delivering his ruling. "I will be back tomorrow afternoon. Please feel free to make use of the soap and shampoo I left when next you shower."

Hala wanted to scream, but Zulfira flashed her a hard look, quieting her as surely as another slap to the face.

"You are . . . most generous," Zulfira stammered. "But—"

"Make use of the soap!" He left no room for argument.

The bureaucrat walked out the door without looking back. Ren paused, his slender hand trailing on the wall as he looked directly at Hala.

"I meant to ask you earlier, child. Have you by any chance had any communication with your mother?"

Hala shook her head, collar between her teeth.

Ren's gaze shifted quickly to Zulfira. "And how about you?"

"My sister is dead to me," Zulfira said.

"That is too bad," Ren said, before letting his hungry gaze settle back on Hala. "I would very much like to meet your mother. And, with her gone, that leaves you all alone in the world. Does it not, child?"

Hala pressed against her aunt, who put an arm around her shoulder and drew her close.

"She is not alone," Zulfira said.

Ren stood there in the doorway, black eyes flitting back and forth between Hala and her aunt.

"We will see you both tomorrow evening," he said, and then shut the door behind him.

Neither moved until they heard the vehicle start and gravel crunch as it pulled away on the street.

Hala felt as if a sudden weight had been lifted off her back. Even at ten years old, she knew all too well how vulnerable they were as Uyghur females. There was no one to call to protect them. The police were simply another arm of the XPCC. Zulfira gasped, swaying on her feet. She clutched the table to keep from collapsing.

"You must be careful of that one, Hala." Zulfira's eyes stayed locked on the door, as if she expected the men to burst back in at any moment. "Suo is focused on me, but his stooge, Ren, he is the more dangerous of the two."

"Why did he want to know about my mother?" Hala asked.

Zulfira gave a little shrug, but said nothing.

Hala pressed the issue, pent-up words gushing out all at once like water from a broken pitcher. "I wish we could call her on the telephone and see that she is all right. Do you know where she is? How we might find her? I miss her so much, sometimes I think—"

Zulfira put a finger to her lips and gave a stern shake of her head, unwilling to broach that subject, even now that the men were gone.

"Why did she leave me?" Hala said, sniffing back the tears.

"She did not share her reasons with me," Zulfira said. "She simply went away—and she is never coming back."

"Never?"

"I have told you all I know."

Zulfira breathed deeply, regaining her composure, then began clearing the table.

Hala picked up her own bowl and the serving spoon for the rice pudding, studiously avoiding the utensils the men had used. "They are coming back tomorrow night . . ." She didn't know whether to cry or scream. "What will we do?"

Zulfira stopped halfway between the table and the sink, turning to face Hala, brandishing a fork to drive home her point. "You will become very, very small," she said. "Invisible, like a mouse. And I . . . I will do whatever I must to keep you safe. Now," she said, turning again toward the kitchen counter. She swayed for a moment, then grabbed at the table to steady herself.

Hala went to help her. "Are you all right?"

Zulfira gave a hollow cough, then heaved, like she might vomit. "I am fine," she whispered. "Go to bed."

Hala reached to comfort her, the way her mother had done for her. "I can see to the dish—"

"Go to bed!" Zulfira snapped. "I mean it. And do not speak of your mother again. The stupid woman will get us both killed . . . or worse."

15

M edina Tohti was trained as an engineer, not a killer, but single-minded patience made her exceptional at both.

In China, it was not enough to *want* to be somewhere. One had to show a need to be in a particular place at a particular time. What's more, that need had to agree with the government's assessment. Vacations to National Forest Parks were a necessity, important to demonstrate to the rest of the world—and most especially the West—that China was a worthy tourist destination, and its citizens were happy and content in their heavenly land.

Fortunately for Medina Tohti, the government believed Ma Jianyu, the man behind the wheel, *needed* to be driving the dirty white Ministry of Culture and Tourism van toward Urumqi at this moment.

Dusty headlights worked overtime to cut the inky darkness of the road ahead. Wild double-humped Bactrian camels, or the odd feral goat, sometimes wandered out into the road, causing Ma to swerve violently. A goat would damage the van and raise unwanted questions from the Bingtuan state security forces, but the van would have struck a camel in the legs, sending the big animal through the windshield. Even if Ma Jianyu and the two Uyghur passengers survived, they would have a difficult time explaining the secret compartment and weapons in the back of the van. So Medina and the young Uyghur man named Perhat gazed ahead into the hypnotic blackness as if their life depended on it.

Ma, whom they called Mamut, spoke as he drove, teaching, but more like a religious leader than a college professor. Medina and Perhat listened intently, eyes forward, watching for camels and other signs of danger.

They all saw it at once, the flashing lights of a Bingtuan police checkpoint about the time the faint glow of Urumqi, the capital of the Xinjiang Uyghur Autonomous Area, hove into view on the horizon.

Ma whistled sharply, warning his two passengers. He needn't have. Medina and Perhat were already sliding the boxes in the back of the van to one side, so they could lie down in the hollow area beneath the false floor, what they called "the can."

The government did not recognize Medina's need to be anywhere. She was a fugitive in a part of the world where the Chinese Communist Party surveilled all its citizens. Throughout most of the People's Republic of China, Beijing's Social Credit System used a network of software crawlers, voice exemplars, security cameras, and facial-recognition programs to document the most mundane behaviors of daily life, from social media content, to shopping preferences, to how quickly one paid their bills, all in order to assign a numerical score. Much like a credit score in the West, something in the seven hundreds allowed a Chinese citizen to rent a car, book a hotel, or travel on a train, generally without leaving a deposit. The Social Credit System's avowed goal was to allow honest Chinese citizens to travel freely around the world, but to keep dishonest people "from taking a single step" without being noticed.

In Xinjiang, the frontier province in far-western China, the system was made even simpler—and more onerous. Instead of a numerical score, there were three classifications. Ethnic Han Chinese and a chosen few Uyghur and Hui peoples who had jumped into the government wagon were deemed *Trustworthy*. Uyghurs despised these minority turncoats, and often referred to them as watermelons—Muslim green on the outside but Communist Chinese red on the inside. Uyghur, Hui, Kazakhs, and other minorities were generally classified with a score of *Average*. Anyone in the Average category who had broken one of Beijing's rules, or had a close relative who had broken one of the rules, was given the social classification of *Untrustworthy*, and, more often than not, carted off to be reeducated at one of the internment camps that dotted western China. The offenses were many: worshiping outside a mosque, teaching a child Uyghur history, burying a newborn's umbilical cord, or simply having WhatsApp or Twitter or a long list of other evil applications installed on one's mobile phone.

Medina Tohti tried to stretch out as best she could in the cramped compartment. Pistol in hand, she slowed her breath as the van rolled toward the Bingtuan roadblock. If the XPCC militia soldiers decided to search the van, there was no doubt they would find the hiding spot. All three had agreed they would not be taken alive, vowing to take as many of these militia soldiers with them as they could before they were gunned down. Hopefully it would not come to that. Medina had cried too many tears and cursed too many curses to feel anything close to terror as the van came to a squealing stop. She'd hoped to see her daughter again one day, but had given up on even that. It was a liberating thing being numb to the idea of death—or life, for that matter.

Outside, voices barked orders in Mandarin. The van rolled forward a few feet. Medina heard the metallic whine as Ma rolled his window down. He chatted easily with the policemen, exchanging quick stories about the isolation of government work in Xinjiang, but how he was the kind of guy who liked isolation. He asked the men if they had water and offered to give them some, since he would be in the city soon.

Medina wished he wouldn't wax so friendly at these stops. It took forever, and every second risked discovery.

The smell of cloves from Perhat's mouthwash drifted over with the sounds of his breathing. He was a good man. In his mid-twenties, two or three years Medina's junior, with the pronounced nose of his Turkic ancestors and a heavy brow overhanging dark eyes. Medina knew Perhat had a bit of a crush on her. They'd spent at least two of the last six hours lying alongside each other in the cramped hiding spot with gravel pinging off the thin metal between their backsides and the pavement. The highway was rough, often sending Perhat bouncing into Medina or her bouncing into Perhat. Their proximity made him self-conscious, and he'd asked Mamut to purchase the mouthwash when he'd stopped to buy petrol just before they turned east on the 312 for the final leg of their journey.

They rode in silence for ten minutes after the checkpoint, before another whistle from Mamut let them know it was safe to emerge.

The skyscrapers and glowing minarets of Urumqi materialized from the blackness just before midnight, with a frigid wind from the Heavenly Mountains buffeting the van and chasing away what little warmth the previous spring day might have left behind. There were police checkpoints in Urumqi as well. Bingtuan forces were on constant guard against ESS— events deemed to endanger State Security. The police were so busy keeping an eye on the Uyghur population in their city of three and a half million people that, more often than not, officers manning the checkpoints simply waved Han drivers through with an abrupt nod.

Mamut took a ring road around the downtown, taking side streets to bypass the Uyghur market bazaar.

Mamut nodded to the north, across the street from a tall hospital, as he worked his way between a river of honking scooters and green Volkswagen taxis.

"My mother used to bring me here as a boy," he said, his voice hushed, as if they were passing a holy place. "See those shoddy new concrete apartment buildings, the bright lights of the state-owned convenience stores?"

Medina and Perhat stayed in the back of the van in case they needed to duck out of sight for a surprise checkpoint.

"Less than five years ago," Mamut continued, "this place used to be a wonderful labyrinth of backstreets and alleys containing Uyghur cafés and shops—a place where my mother's people could shop and talk about the old times. Now the only Uyghur shops and cafés are for Han tourists."

"We're getting close," Perhat said, craning his neck so he could look out the windshield and better orient himself with the folded map on his knee. Mamut had a mobile phone, because he would be expected to have one for officers to check if asked. Neither Medina nor Perhat bothered. Mobile phones were far too easy to track, and there was no one for either of them to call anyway.

"Two blocks."

Mamut brought the van to a stop in a small car park behind a large blue trash dumpster. A casual observer would think someone from the Ministry of Culture and Tourism was visiting a friend in the adjacent apartment building. Surveillance cameras lined the crossbeams of every light post like roosting pigeons, downloading massive amounts of data to Bingtuan security servers. Medina and Perhat wore traditional Uyghur costumes in bright colors. Heavy makeup changed the apparent angles of Medina's nose, cheekbones, and chin. Perhat kept a *tebetei* pulled low over his brow. The traditional Kyrgyz fur hat was flashy enough that it said he was not trying to slip under the radar, but covered enough of his face to allow him to do just that. Mamut wore a black ball cap, pulled low, but walked with the confidence of a Han man with nothing to hide, just far enough ahead of the other two that it was impossible to tell they were together.

Half a block from where they'd parked the van, Mamut held up a hand, pausing to allow a knot of intoxicated men to move past them. Medina's fingers closed around the butt of the suppressed pistol in her pocket. It felt cold and incredibly heavy as the men stumbled by. One in three people in western China worked for the Bingtuan security forces in one way or another. Drawing their ire could spell disaster, even when they were drunk and off-duty—perhaps especially then.

Mamut began to preach again as they walked, causing Perhat to glance at Medina and give her an ever-so-slight eye roll under the shadow of his fox-fur hat in the glow of the streetlight.

"At the sixtieth anniversary of the Bingtuan, a Party official spoke of the dangers to Xinjiang and said, 'We must be ready to tightly clench our fists to combat the Three Evils—terrorism, separatism, and religious extremism.' In no place are their fists clenched tighter than here in Urumqi, where this Bingtuan captain who calls himself Kenny Lo would take it upon himself to imprison a young father who did nothing but dare to teach his child to recite Uyghur folktales—and then pester that man's wife while he was in prison until she felt compelled to take her own life. What these Bingtuan monsters do not realize is that a clenched fist is a slow fist. We will move with open hands, slapping and stabbing with lightning speed, causing far more damage than the dull and impotent blows of a tight fist."

Mamut led the way down a dark alley, between two apartment buildings. Barracks for Te Jing—literally special police, the black-uniformed Bingtuan force equivalent to what the West called SWAT—were less than a block away.

A bitter wind kicked up a dusty whirlwind at the end of the alley, rattling the plastic bags overflowing from a long dumpster. Muffled snarls came from the shadows, a dog, guarding some prized piece of trash. The little group moved past quickly, showing they were no threat. As they passed the dumpster, the area behind the apartment buildings opened into a tree-covered courtyard. Spring hadn't had time to green the lawns, but small amber lights on concrete posts formed to resemble ancient stone lanterns lit gravel walkways, bamboo gardens, and a brook that babbled over hauled-in rocks, courtesy of the pump that recirculated the captive water. It was all very bucolic at first glance, but the slightest bit of scrutiny revealed it was fake.

Medina nodded toward the glowing window through a copse of wrist-thick bamboo across a painted footbridge at the center of the courtyard. Clay tile and dragon carvings on the building's wooden beams made Medina feel as if she'd stepped back into a more ancient China, but the colored lights of a television flashing inside against the paper blinds brought her back to the mission at hand. Medina slid a hand in her pocket again, reassured by the weight of the pistol.

A gaudy slurry of blaring music and studio gunfire spilled from under the wood-framed door.

Special Police Captain Lo Han, who had given himself the Westernized name of Kenny—was said to be an avid fan of video games and action movies—Westerns, gangster flicks, space operas, it did not matter. The bloodier the action, the better.

In that respect, Kenny Lo was about to get his wish.

Medina Tohti grieved for her family every minute of the day. Her husband was dead. She would never see her daughter again. Loneliness and despair pressed so hard at the back of her throat that she could hardly breathe. Food ceased to have any taste.

Her only solace came from watching Mamut. He knew the high cost of freedom, and was all too willing to pay it.

A true believer, Ma "Mamut" Jianyu was the son of a Han father and Uyghur mother. He'd been an officer in the People's Liberation Army Second Artillery, learning hand-to-hand combat, field tactics, strategy, and, most important, the tactical methods of the Chinese military and police.

Ma taught doctrine as much as he attacked targets, ensuring his flock of nameless fighters were focused on the same righteous cause. Their fight was not, he said, a religious one. Religion was decided by the heart, not the gun. No, their struggle was for independence from the Chinese boot. Every action they took had to be done under the notion that they were agents of the legitimate free state of East Turkestan. The other "Stans" in Central Asia had gained their independence after the Soviet Union dissolved. It stood to reason that the Uyghur Autonomous Region should be afforded the same treatment by China.

It made no sense to ask the tyrant for independence. One simply had to act independently. Wuming—the Nameless— were soldiers, agents of their legitimate state, fighting a war.

Mamut ran his operations with the righteous indignation of an Israeli hit squad, the brutality of a Russian active mea- sures unit, and the sophisticated finesse of a Hollywood assas- sin. Like drug lords in Mexico and South America, he employed falcons—young people who acted as his spies. Being the most heavily militarized area of the world came with a price. Youth, even nationalistic Chinese youth, were uncomfortable with the oppressive surveillance tactics of the Bingtuan. Everyone had something to hide.

A few questions to the right bureaucrat's disgruntled daugh- ter revealed that officers from the special police detachment down the block often commandeered the apartment complex's community center, chasing off the resident teenagers who liked to smoke weed and play video games in the wee hours of the morning. Captain Lo and two of his friends had just returned from a three-day trip to Karamay with a truckload of Uyghur separatists who would be put to work in the oil fields as part of their reeducation curriculum. It made sense that these road- weary Bingtuan officers would come here to blow off a little steam.

With his pistol in his left hand, Perhat checked the door with his right. It was unlocked, so he pushed it open a crack.

The knob was on the left and Mamut stood on that side of

the frame, ready to slip in the moment his Uyghur friend pushed it open on his signal. Medina stood behind Perhat, her pistol out of her pocket now, clutched in both hands, pointed at the ground between her boots. It was her job to protect their rear until they made entry, at which point she would be third in, behind Perhat.

More shooting punctuated the loud music of a movie soundtrack.

Perhat reached behind him and tapped Medina on the elbow, signifying they were about to make entry. The door yawned open a hair, allowing the small team a quick glance to orient themselves.

Captain Lo and his two companions sat sideways, at a slight angle to the door. All wore their black battle-dress uniform pants. All were shirtless. The one in the center stretched out on a sofa with his feet toward the flat-screen television mounted on the far wall. He nursed a bottle of beer while the man to his left brandished a combat knife at the screen. All three men shouted their support to Wu Jing, the muscular actor in the skintight white T-shirt playing Leng Feng as he battled the heartless American mercenaries. "Blood for blood!" An action hero of the highest order, Wolf Warrior rescued the downtrodden and saved weak African nations from exploitation by a morally corrupt United States.

"Blood for blood!" the policeman shouted again, banging the hilt of a combat knife against the couch. Ironically, the knife was an American design, likely manufactured in China.

Medina did a quick check behind her to make sure they were clear, and then tapped Mamut on the thigh, signaling that she was ready.

Had this been a Hollywood movie, the ominous music

would have begun. There was no announcement, no witty repartee or challenge to the bad guy, before he met his fate.

Only rehearsed, machinelike precision.

Mamut took the lead through the doorway, shooting the farthest soldier in the back of the head. Suppressed pistols spat in quick succession as Perhat followed a meter behind, shooting the nearest man. Captain Lo caught a reflection in the television screen and half turned at the same instant both men put bullets into the back of his head. Medina followed up, twisting at the waist just as Mamut had shown her as she moved down the line, putting another bullet in the back of each head.

In effect, all three were shooting at the same time, overlapping their fields of fire. The shirtless bodies danced at the thudding impact before pitching forward. Subsonic rounds tended to remain inside the cranial vault, but Captain Lo had turned, allowing one bullet to destroy his lower jaw. The other two died with the solemn expressions of hero worship they'd had on their faces from watching *Wolf Warrior 2* a few breaths before.

Medina found her vision locked on the scene, unable to move her feet, until Mamut patted her arm, pushing the muzzle of the pistol gently toward the floor.

She blinked, taking slow, deliberate breaths to clear her mind. Perhat scanned the room, looking for security cameras. Considering the oily odor of marijuana in the air, Medina doubted cameras would be a problem.

Mamut leaned over the couch, one last check of the bodies. "We must pick up the expended brass," he said. "Each one has to be accounted for."

Perhat brandished his pistol toward the flashing screen. "Wait, wait," he said. "They are coming to the crossbow part."

"The what?"

The young Uyghur stood transfixed in front of the television, pistol dangling in his fist, three dead men at his feet. "Watch for yourselves," he said, entranced, breathless. "It is amazing. Leng Feng, the Wolf Warrior, fashions a crossbow out of material he finds lying around and uses it to kill the mercenaries and save the captives."

Medina returned the pistol to her pocket and gave an indignant scoff as she stooped to pick up spent cartridges at her feet.

"What?" Perhat said, wagging his head. "I know the Han Chinese savior stuff is all lies, but I like the action. Okay?"

"Something is seriously wrong with you," Medina said, picking up a fourth piece of brass.

Perhat chuckled, deadpan, still watching Wolf Warrior save the day. "If you are only becoming aware of this, then you are not nearly as observant as you need to be. There is something seriously wrong with all of us." His eyes flicked momentarily to her, then back to the television. "Some may even be beyond help. But after all, God has only damaged people to work with. No? Anyway, I like action movies. As soon as they make one with a Uyghur hero I'll throw away my DVDs of *Die Hard* and *Wolf Warrior.*"

"It is fine," Mamut said, counting the brass on his open palm to see that it was all accounted for. "It is well and good that you are familiar with this trash. Such things are all the rage among youth today. The media even speaks of Beijing's Wolf Warrior diplomacy. It would be foolish to disregard this piece of culture . . . propaganda though it may be."

"Exactly," Perhat said.

"But there is no need to wallow in it," Mamut said. "Now let's go."

They took an indirect route back to the van. It was late enough that the checkpoints on Highway 312 would be manned by different people, but they remained in Urumqi for the rest of the night, so surveillance cameras would not record them leaving the city so quickly after they'd only just arrived.

The killing of Bingtuan special police, especially when one of them was a line commander—was sure to make a splash. In all likelihood, the action would spawn a brutal crackdown by local authorities, making an already difficult life harder for minorities in Urumqi. Mamut had confided this worry to Medina, but felt the long-term goals were worth the sacrifice.

They'd taken great care to leave no calling card on the bodies, nothing that would give them the obvious credit other than the cold precision with which the assassinations were carried out. They left the bodies exactly as they fell. There was no physical evidence other than the slugs buried inside the dead men's brains. The whispers would begin before the bodies were loaded onto a mortuary van. Some would blame the killings on other groups—the East Turkestan Islamic Movement, or some other independence or jihadist group. Captain Lo marked the fifteenth such assassination for Mamut and his group, six of them regional politicians who had made decisions that led directly to Uyghur imprisonment and death. With that many, some in Beijing would surely call it a plot of the American CIA. Local Party leaders, Bingtuan security force commanders, even the soldiers themselves whispered among themselves, jaws tense, teeth gnashing, hiding their fear with bluster and threat to a foe they could not see or even describe. But they knew who was responsible for each of the killings.

The Nameless.

Wuming.

16

D r. Patti Moon rubbed exhausted eyes and lay back on the bunk in her cramped cabin aboard the icebreaking research vessel *Sikuliaq*.

"Are you seriously telling me you don't hear human voices?"

A wide terry-cloth band held black hair, still damp from an evening shower, out of her eyes. The apples of her high cheekbones were flushed pink, warm with the glow that came from working on deck all day in the cold wind. Dressed in gray merino wool long john bottoms and a white T-shirt—she knew better than to sleep in anything less on a vessel that had frequent abandon-ship drills—Moon rolled over toward her open laptop with a groan to study the digital signature of her hydrophone recording for the hundredth time. Her friend and former shipmate Chief Petty Officer Shad Barker's voice crackled on the voice over IP connection. The connection was via satellite, which was slow to begin with, and the lag between each sentence was beginning to make conversation a chore. Sixty miles northwest of Utqiagvik, the Alaska city white people called Barrow, satellite antennas had to be pointed almost at the horizon to get a connection. What few visitors she'd ever taken to her home village of Point Hope were always astounded when they learned that, one, the Native people there had satellite TV, and, two, all the dishes appeared to be aimed at the ground.

Moon and Barker had been at it for nearly an hour. She aboard R/V *Sikuliaq* in the Arctic Ocean, he on the destroyer USS *John Paul Jones,* steaming off the coast of Oahu four thousand miles away. Moon had spent her fair share of months at sea aboard a tin can, some of it with Barker when they were both second-class petty officers, long before he'd become a chief and she'd left the Navy to finish graduate school. They'd made a short go of a romantic fling—while on liberty in Manila. Hooking up on land didn't make her feel as loose as getting under way while under way. Moon didn't want to be "that girl on the ship." It hadn't worked out anyway. They'd both been young and stupid enough to let their hormones take control, but old and wise enough to know that they would be much happier as shipboard friends than sneaking around trying to find some nook or cranny on the destroyer just to get a little privacy—which would have given them both reputations they didn't want.

Turning on her side, she tapped the trackpad on her computer to start the sound bite again.

She pinched the bridge of her nose with her thumb and forefinger, squinting as she focused on the sounds pouring through her headphones.

The recording stopped, leaving her banging her head softly on the industrial-strength bunk mattress. "Now tell me you don't hear that?"

Barker scoffed on the other end of the line. "And you're telling me you hear voices?"

"That's exactly what I'm telling you," Moon said.

"That's a stretch," Barker said. "If that's the case, it has to be a submarine and they're double-hulled. I don't think it's possible."

"I've heard that, too," Moon said. "But I've also heard submariners say they have heard voices on their hydrophones—and anyway, I know I'm hearing something."

"Much more likely to be sea ice, maybe some mating whales or—"

"Why do guys working the sonar always think the whales are mating? Girl whales like to talk at other times, too, you know. And besides, whales don't mate in Arctic waters. They swim south for that."

"Can't blame them there," Barker said. "But I still think what you're hearing could be a whale song. Don't you have narwhals up there?"

Moon clicked some keys on her laptop to slow down the recording. "There," she said. "That's metal banging on metal. I'm sure of it."

"Are you, though?" Barker asked. "I mean, the simplest explanation is the most likely. It's probably the screws of your own ship pinging off an ice chunk. Didn't you say you were in an open lead when you made the recording? That means ice all around you."

"We were," Moon said. "But that's not what this is. I can clearly hear a metal door slamming shut when I slow down the loop. When I filter the lower frequencies I can make out what I think are voices—screaming, panicked voices."

"Okay," Barker said, only a little condescending. "I'll bite. What are these voices saying?"

"I don't know," Moon said. "I think they're speaking Chinese. Shad, if you'd been on the sonar and you heard this, wouldn't you report it?"

"Of course."

"Well, somebody needs to be made aware," Moon said. "And I flat don't have anybody else to tell besides Twitter."

"Wait," Barker said. "You want me to kick this up my chain of command?"

"It's all I can ask."

"I hate to point this out," Barker said, "but nobody is likely to buy this, considering it's coming from you."

"I'm aware of my reputation in the Navy," Moon said. "That's why you should take the credit."

"Not in a million years," Barker said. "This is your baby."

"But you will kick it up?"

"I'll do it as soon as we're done here," Barker said.

Moon rolled onto her back, staring up at the bottom of the vacant bunk above her. She rubbed her face with an open hand, feeling the glow of warmth from a long day in the wind. *"Naamuktuk,"* she said.

Inupiaq for *good enough.*

Barker groaned. "You used to always say that when you were pissed."

"No," she said. "Really. I do appreciate this. I'll send you the coordinates where I picked up the voices—"

"The as-yet-unidentified sound transient—"

She stood her ground. "Voices. I'm certain of it."

"You know I'm in your corner," Barker said. "I'm just reminding you that not everyone thinks the shadows are full of conspiracies and secrets."

"They should," Moon said. "Because they are. Anyway, thanks again for doing this, Shad."

"No worries," he said. "It's good to talk to you."

"You, too." She started to end the call, but was a fraction of a second late getting her finger to the keyboard.

"You ever wish we'd made more of a go of it?" Barker asked. "You know. That time in Manila?"

"That was fun," Moon said. "But nah, I don't think so. To be honest, I like you too much to screw everything up with romance." She returned to the reason for her call. "So, you'll pass this up the chain as soon as we hang up?"

"Roger that."

"Good," she said. "I'm hanging up now. Whoever it is screaming at the bottom of the Arctic Ocean is in your debt."

17

The director of national intelligence was afforded not only an office for herself, but an entire suite of offices that housed her chief of staff and many advisers and assistants. Most were tucked away in other offices or small cubbies off a larger, top-floor lobby. None of these people were more imposing than the woman who greeted Monica Hendricks from behind the immaculately clean desk outside Mary Pat Foley's closed office door. She was tall, even when seated, nearing sixty years old, with broad shoulders, naturally silver hair, and the hint of a perpetual squint, as if she did not quite believe what was going on before her eyes. Hendricks had made a life out of reading people and felt sure this woman had been a police officer of some sort in an earlier life, perhaps in the military. Or maybe she'd just raised a couple of teenage sons.

Secretaries might be called administrative assistants in the modern era, but at a certain level, there was an unwritten rule that they had to act as a sort of guard dog as well—the last line of defense outside the inner sanctum.

The woman glanced at the visitor's badge clipped to the lapel of Monica's navy-blue summer-wool suit. Similar to the ones issued at the J. Edgar Hoover FBI Building, the badge had

a bleed-through strip affixed to the front that would read EX-
PIRED twelve hours after it had been applied and issued.

"Mrs. Hendricks?"

Monica shot her a smile. "That's right."

"The director is just finishing up on a call," the woman said.
"I'll let her know you're—"

The oak door yawned open and Mary Pat Foley stepped out.
"Thank you, Gladys. I'm good now."

Foley took Monica's hand in both hers, patted the back in a
way that might seem condescending from someone else, but
felt genuine coming from Mary Pat.

As usual, Foley was dressed as if she might have to rush off
to the White House at any moment. Black pearl earrings accented the white silk blouse, open at the neck, and a gray gab-
ardine A-line skirt. She was barefoot, but a pair of sensible black
shoes sat akimbo beside a polished mahogany desk that held
little more than a computer screen and a single file folder. She
caught Monica looking and chuckled.

"The sign of an insane mind. Right?"

"It is an awfully clean desk, ma'am."

Foley grabbed the file and then smoothed her skirt behind
her with both hands as she sat down across from Hendricks at
a small meeting table.

"All the clutter is on those desks out front," she said.

"You do have a nice office," Hendricks said.

It was large, though, Hendricks had to admit, certainly
smaller than the seventh-floor sanctum of the D/CIA at Langley. And it was much less imposing than she would have imagined for the person in charge of the sixteen other intelligence
agencies falling under the purview of the National Counterintelligence Center at the Liberty Crossing complex—a large

X-shaped building located across the freeway from Tysons Corner, Virginia. White walls were detailed in mahogany and oak, with crisp blue carpet and a Persian rug. It was de rigueur for those in lofty government positions to display framed autographed 8x10s of them standing on the tarmac beside famous dignitaries during historical moments, presidents, world leaders, Supreme Court justices, even movie stars. Notoriously wary of the camera, Foley had only two photographs of herself that Hendricks could see. One with her family, the other with Jack Ryan, when they were younger, somewhere in Russia. There were, however, plenty of photographs of her boys over the years, playing hockey with a red Soviet flag in the background, graduating from high school, weddings, grandchildren—the vestiges of normal life that people who lived in the shadows clutched tightly in an effort to keep their heads above water.

Foley rested both hands flat on the table, on either side of the closed folder that presumably held Hendricks's polygraph results. "I speak for the President as well," she said, "when I say how grateful we are to you for doing this. Virtually begging you to stay, but then asking you to take a polygraph as a prerequisite."

"It must be important, then," Hendricks said.

Foley patted the folder without opening it. "You passed, by the way."

Hendricks closed her eyes and gave a tired smile. "I know I passed, ma'am—"

Foley kept her hands on the table but raised her brow. "Mary Pat."

"Right," Hendricks said. "Mary Pat. Anyway, I hate polygraphs. They are embarrassing and dehumanizing even if you have nothing to hide. I mean, a pimple-faced kid half my age asking me if I have any deviant sexual tendencies that could embarrass me if they were made known. Can you imagine? For Pete's sake, Mary Pat, I'm Southern Baptist. Talking to that kid about sex at all embarrasses me. I did confess to sometimes peeing a dribble or two when I sneeze. I think that tidbit put the little shit off-kilter."

Foley smiled. "Putting people off-kilter is your superpower, Monica. Anyway, the flutter was a formality to ease the President's mind."

"You talked to President Ryan about me specifically?"

"Of course," Foley said. "Apart from me and the President, only eight people know of the existence of this operation we're calling ELISE. This mole has no idea we're hunting him . . . or her."

"So ELISE is a mole hunt?" Hendricks mused, half to herself.

"Exactly," Foley said. "A traitor within the intelligence community, likely in the CIA. The Chi-Comms refer to him as SURVEYOR. Our computer spit out BITTER ARROW for a code name, but that sounds too much like what it is. The Chinese are wily, and since we're looking for someone inside our intelligence community whom they've turned, we thought it better to choose something a little less on the nose."

"I'm assuming you've snooped through my bank accounts."

Foley gave a tired nod. "Among other things. I can compartmentalize a background check without the checkers knowing why you're being vetted."

"Surely the fact that there are leaks doesn't come as a surprise to you," Hendricks said. "We're taught from the get-go to assume there is always someone leaking information, even without meaning to."

"True enough," Foley said. "But this particular leak is devastating, and intentional."

"And we're sure the Chinese aren't running a disinformation campaign? Sowing mistrust in the ranks and making us chase our own tails?"

Foley gave her a thumbnail sketch of what they knew so far—including the fact that there was a Russian asset in Chinese intelligence.

Hendricks leaned back in her chair, mulling over what little information she had. "I've got to say, you have all kinds of aggressive young counterintelligence weenies who would love to run this kind of investigation. Why pick on a chubby woman about to retire? This kind of operation could make a career."

"Or break them," Foley said. "That's one of the main reasons we tapped you. Think about it, Monica. Untold amounts of information come across your desk every day—information that the Chinese would love to get their hands on. You know as well as I do that if you were indeed one of their assets, Beijing would throw a royal fit if you decided to walk away now. And you'd be stupid for abandoning a seat at the table that assures you a golden parachute when you do leave."

"Or a bullet behind the ear," Hendricks said.

Foley shrugged. "There is that."

"I'll buy your logic," Hendricks said. "But what if I suddenly grew a conscience and couldn't live with myself anymore. Or maybe I'm just afraid the CI weenies are onto me, so I've decided to cut and run. Have you considered that?"

"Cut and run to teach high school?"

"Penance?"

Foley slumped. "No sin is that grievous, my dear."

"I am not this SURVEYOR character."

"I know that," Foley said.

"Only eight people," Hendricks said.

"Plenty more will know as soon as you start to rattle cages."

"Who's my boss?" Hendricks asked. "Who's running the show?"

"Your boss is me," Foley said. "But you are running ELISE. David Wallace from the Bureau will be working with you, but POTUS wants CIA taking the lead in the investigation. FBI will handle prosecution when we get to that point."

"Jack Ryan doesn't know me from Adam," Hendricks said.

"He trusts *me*." Foley slid the folder across the table. "Here's a brief on all we know so far. As you can see from the list on the cover page, of the ten who know about this, almost all are in the President's inner circle or agency heads—the directors of both the FBI and the CIA, the White House chief of staff. There is a field officer who runs the asset who gave us the information."

"Adam Yao?" Hendricks said, without opening the folder.

Foley grinned. "See there. If *you* were SURVEYOR, Yao would have already been compromised."

"Are we sure this isn't disinformation?" Hendricks asked again.

"We've certainly thought about that," Foley said. "The President is clear, and I agree, we don't want another Angleton witch hunt."

Both women were all too familiar with the hunt for the infamous Soviet mole "Sasha" by the enigmatic CIA counterintelligence head James Jesus Angleton. Virtually anyone whose name started with the letter *K* and ended with *-ski* or *-sky* became a suspect—a hard blow to any CIA officers with Polish or Eastern European heritage. Careers were derailed, lives were ruined.

Mary Pat bounced a fist on the table. "That's not happening again. Not on my watch. It would be all too easy to brand every Asian CIA employee a suspect and then bully our way down the list, letting the chips fall where they may—but you know me better than that."

"I wouldn't be sitting here if I thought otherwise, ma'am."

Foley raised her index finger. "That said, this mole is still a problem, our sensibilities toward prejudice notwithstanding. There are too many instances where the Chinese have gotten a leg up on something of ours that they could not have known without inside help. People's lives are at stake. A lot of people."

"Understood," Hendricks said. "But I had to ask. Anyway, Adam Yao's a solid guy. I'm glad to have him on the team."

"He's not exactly on the team," Foley said. "His mission at the moment is tangentially related, but it's out in the field. He does, however, have contact with his asset, VICAR, who has access to the Russian asset."

"Like that kids' game, telephone."

"Not optimum, I know," Foley said. "But Yao's bullshit detector has proven to be solid. He'll work to get you answers for any questions you have as they arise."

"Great," Hendricks said, sounding anything but. She thumbed through the folder. There wasn't much there. Yao's report. Recent cases of two blown CIA operations, one in Australia, the other in Indonesia, where the Chinese did end runs as if they had the local operational playbook. The worst incident was a Chinese Christian asset in Indonesia who'd been compromised by leaked intelligence. He'd last been seen being dragged into a dark van, a white hood over his head. Boots on the ground said he'd been tied to a rubber tree outside of Jakarta and shot—after a lengthy and painful interrogation. The MSS officers who'd done it had left plenty of marks on the body—a warning to anyone else who might decide to cooperate with the West. It was enough to convince Hendricks to stay as long as it took to catch SURVEYOR.

"I'm going to need a much larger team than the President and a bunch of agency heads," Hendricks said, still reading.

"Of course."

"I can pick whomever I want?"

"As long as they pass the vetting process."

"And I run the vetting process?"

Foley seemed to consider this for a moment, then nodded. "It's your show. Why do you ask? Who are you thinking?"

"I understand David Wallace is over from the Bureau, but he will always tend to think in terms of making a criminal case for eventual prosecution. I'd much rather run it like a CIA operation. Prosecution if we can, but discovering the threat so we can stanch the flow of leaked intel has to be our first priority."

"I wouldn't have it any other way," Foley said.

"There's a guy I'd like to be my deputy," Hendricks said. "Retired from the Navy. He helped me get out of Somalia years ago on his destroyer. You and I crossed paths with many good folks over the course of our careers. Most, you simply thank them and move on. But this guy and I clicked. Became good friends." She looked at Foley. "I'm sure there's someone like that in your past."

"Yeah," Foley said. "My guy's the President."

"Then you know what I'm talking about. Honestly, my husband was always a little jealous of my 'Navy friend.'"

"That's not going to be a problem? Nothing that will—"

"Hey, I passed my polygraph," Hendricks said. "Seriously, it wasn't like that. And anyway, look at me. I'm pretty certain the days of my husband thinking some dude's gonna ravish me while I'm out on assignment are long gone."

"Those days never end, my friend," Foley said. "Believe me."

Hendricks laughed and waved away the thought. "Anyway, he's just a really good person. Someone we can trust—and he's of Chinese descent."

"A retired admiral?"

Hendricks nodded.

Foley tapped a finger against her temple and gave Hendricks a conspiratorial wink. "We're probably thinking about the same guy . . ."

B ack in her car in the Liberty Crossing visitor parking lot, Monica Hendricks sent a text via Signal. The messaging app was end-to-end encrypted, but habit made her careful with her words unless she was talking on an STU or some other dedicated secure device.

Her friend was cordial, if a little terse, but that could have been the fact that they were thumb-typing. He gave her a quick rundown on his life like he was giving a bottom-line-up-front briefing to the Joint Chiefs. She did the same. Three sentences to encapsulate the status of her life.

He cut to the chase. What's up?

Something I need to run by you.

Shoot.

Hendricks thought for a moment, then typed. It needs to be in person. She was of the generation that texted in complete sentences and checked her spelling and grammar before hitting send.

Okay. It must be important, then.

Something important enough to keep me from walking out the door. She sent that, then added, I'd come to you, but things are crazy busy. Can you come to D.C.?

Pulsing dots . . . but only for a moment.

I'll break the news to Sophie.

I'm sorry it's last-minute. Today would be best, if at all possible.

Admiral Peter Li's answer came back almost immediately, as she knew it would.

I'll be there.

18

This is exactly the kind of problem you're good at," Cathy Ryan said, slouching across the study in an overstuffed leather chair.

Jack Ryan found himself mesmerized by this gorgeous, rock-solid oasis of sanity in an insane world. Blond hair askew over her forehead, eyes half closed, she balanced an astonishingly bright cobalt-blue Paul Green pump on the toe of her astonishingly beautiful foot.

A world-renowned ophthalmic surgeon, Dr. Cathy Ryan had performed three retinal surgeries that morning. Dealing with vessels and nerves smaller than a human hair, there was zero room for error. Not particularly physical, but heavy lifting nonetheless.

Ryan stretched out on the well-worn cushions of the leather sofa of his private study off the Oval Office, tie loose, shoes off. Hands folded across his chest, his head turned sideways so he could lie down and still look at his wife.

"Not sure if I'm good at it," he said. "But a Chinese mole inside CIA is definitely a problem."

"But that's not the problem you were talking about."

Ryan rubbed his eyes with the heels of his hands. "We have

some incredibly brave and devoted patriots of Asian heritage in our intelligence organizations, and we're about to put the screws to the vast majority of them, basically tell them we've stopped trusting them because of who their grandparents are. But the fact remains, the PRC likes to utilize people who have ties to China, to appeal to their sense of what it means to be Chinese. It's a hard reality."

"Are you sure this mole is of Chinese descent?"

"Not at all," Ryan said. "But we have to consider the possibility. It troubles me that we actively recruit intelligence officers who speak native Mandarin, and then turn on them like this for the same reason we hired them. If we move too far in one direction, I ruin dozens of careers. Don't move far enough, and a mole continues to bleed us dry of critical intelligence, endangering lives. It would be all too easy to have a purge."

"My dear," Cathy said, sounding almost asleep. "The fact that you struggle with this at all puts you a hundred and eighty degrees off a purge."

"Mary Pat and I have hashed this out ad nauseam," Ryan said. "She and her team will do a thoughtful job, but the buck stops with me. Every piece of guidance and advice I give is scrutinized—and heeded."

"I get it," Cathy said. "You can't unlaunch a missile once you say 'fire.'"

"You can," Ryan said, "but the analogy makes the point. The direction I give affects people's lives."

The corner of Cathy's lip perked in a half-smile. "It might be good for the guy on the street to hear Jack Ryan struggle with all sides of an issue once in a great while."

"That's sausage nobody wants to see made," Ryan said.

"Sometimes I worry that my team is banking everything on *me* making the exact right move at exactly the right time."

Cathy's eye flicked open. "You mean like when I alone am utilizing a powerful laser to work around microscopic vessels and blast someone's tissue to reattach the retina to the back of their eye? Yeah, I think I get what you're talking about."

"Sorry for whining." Ryan groaned. "Of course you get it."

"Maybe we should just sneak away," she said. "Because I have to tell you, sometimes, I feel like sneaking away."

Ryan gave a little shrug, chin to chest. The couch in his private study was his second-favorite thinking spot. "I thought this *was* sneaking away."

Cathy looked up at him with a mock pout. "I guess so. At least we're away from that little peephole in the Oval Office door. I trust Betty, but . . . it still weirds me out sometimes to think about you living under a glass bubble."

"Weirds *you* out?" Ryan swung his legs to the floor, patting the cushion beside him.

"I'm too tired to move, Jack."

"Presidential order?"

"Nice try."

She hauled herself out of the chair anyway and plopped down beside Ryan. "Just so you know, I'm moving because I want to, not because you made me."

"Of that, my dear," Ryan said, "I have no doubt."

They leaned back together, staring at the ceiling.

Cathy yawned. "This is a comfortable couch." She closed her eyes. "You have good hands," she said, out of the blue.

Ryan gave her a quizzical look. "I appreciate that . . ."

"Good hands are a gift, Jack."

"Thanks?"

"By the time a would-be surgeon gets to me, they've been through four years of medical school, rotations, practical testing, and an internship . . . at least. Most of the residents who come my way are pretty good at what they do. They'll make good surgeons who can do ninety-five percent of the procedures out there. Every couple of years, though, I get a would-be surgeon who can rattle off the textbook answer to any question I throw out or look at a patient and diagnose the problem with ease. But when it comes to surgery, they are clumsy and inept. We say they have wooden hands."

"Okay . . ."

"I'm telling you, you don't have wooden hands, Jack. You're not one of the other ninety-five percent, either." She rested her palms flat on her knees and heaved a long sigh. "I'm not sure what it's like to be President, but I know what it's like to be a surgeon. It takes a monumental amount of swagger. You have to know you're good enough to step up when everyone is looking over your shoulder with a literal microscope. You are skilled and sure and self-aware enough that you will make the right decision about this. You have good hands . . ." She glanced up at him. "Very. Good. Hands."

"Are we still talking about my dilemma?"

"That depends on—"

Ryan groaned inside when a knock at the door cut her off.

Ryan took a seat behind the Resolute desk, his back to the windows overlooking the Rose Garden. The lingering smell of Cathy's shampoo filled him with suffused giddiness—even after all these decades—and it took every ounce of his energy to give his full attention to Dustin Fullmer, from Defense Mapping.

Arnie van Damm pulled one of the Chippendale side chairs around to the end of the desk.

Fullmer, a twentysomething analyst, stood rooted in place, as if there were yellow footprints painted on the carpet in front of the Resolute. Like virtually everyone who briefed at the White House, he had a fresh haircut and a new suit.

He'd been involved in a handful of briefings, but never as lead. Folio clutched at his waist with both hands, he stood and nodded, meeting Ryan's eye but not saying a word.

"Let's have it, Dustin," Ryan said.

"Have what, Mr. President?"

Van Damm closed his eyes and shook his head. "You told me you needed to brief the President."

"No, sir, Mr. van Damm," Fullmer said. "I said the President needed to be briefed. Commander Forestall is on his way over. Perhaps we should wait for—"

Ryan raised an open hand. "Your bosses trust you."

"Yes, sir."

"It wasn't a question, Dustin," Ryan said. "I know they trust you, or they wouldn't have sent you over to brief me. I've been in your shoes, shoved out in front, so to speak. Believe me, I understand what it's like to stand where you're standing. So take a deep breath and give me what you've got. We can go over it again when Commander Forestall arrives."

"Of course, Mr. President," Fullmer said. "I was . . ." He caught van Damm's gaze and opened the leather folio. "As you're aware, China and Russia recently engaged in a military exercise they called Snow Dragon. Satellite imagery shows three Chinese submarines departed pens in Wuhan and Hainan approximately five months ago. Two Shang Type 093 nuclear fast-attacks, then later a Kilo diesel-electric. The Kilo surfaced to top off batteries every twenty-four hours. They made no attempt to hide. A week later, a *Jin*-class nuclear ballistic missile sub departed Huludao. We picked it up again when it transited the Bering Strait and monitored it during the war game. The Kilo peeled off from the pack near Anadyr, Russia, at which point a fifth Chinese submarine, a *Yuan*, we believe, hull number 771, appeared. Both these subs stayed in the littoral waters around Anadyr, participating with Chinese and Russian surface ships in what we assume was a different round of the same exercise."

Ryan nodded, showing that he was listening. None of this was exactly new information.

Van Damm made an ever so slight get-on-with-it motion with his hand.

Fullmer swallowed, taking the hint. "Satellite imaging, undersea hydrophonic arrays, and P-3cs stationed at Eielson Air Force Base near Fairbanks, Alaska, show the Shang fast-attacks transited the Bering Strait nine days ago, moving southward. The Kilo departed Anadyr at around the same time, but the *Yuan* remained for an extra week before departing to the south."

"Okay . . ." Ryan said.

"Right," Fullmer said. "The point is, the *Yuan*-class sub has turned around and has transited the Bering Strait heading north. We've picked up a coded signal we believe is coming from an area known as the Mendeleev Ridge in the Arctic Ocean."

"A submarine in distress?" Ryan asked.

"A DISSUB would make sense, sir," Fullmer said. "Both

Shang fast-attacks have apparently turned around and passed through the Bering two hours ago. The Chinese Kilo appears to be following."

"Any Russian vessels heading toward the coded signal?"

"There are some standing well off," Fullmer said. "But none approaching. The newest Chinese icebreaker *Xue Long 2* took part in the exercises and remained in Russian waters. It is moving toward the signal from the Laptev Sea." Fullmer swallowed. "Incidentally, *Xue Long* means snow dragon . . . Same as the name of the exercise . . ."

"Interesting," Ryan said, looking at van Damm, amused but for the gravity of the situation. Forestall was on his way. That was a good thing.

Fullmer continued. "It's spring and the Arctic ice is thinning, but it still keeps most surface vessels away."

"So a coded signal," Ryan asked. "And returning submarines . . ."

Fullmer waited a beat. When van Damm didn't offer anything, he said, "The subs that—"

A knock at the door from the secretaries' suite preceded Commander Robbie Forestall's arrival. He apologized for D.C. traffic. Breathing easier now, Fullmer brought the commander quickly up to speed.

Forestall took a stack of 8x10 color photographs from his folder and passed them across the desk to give commentary— and clarity—to Fullmer's earlier brief.

Ryan tapped the humpbacked submarine in the photo. "Tell me what I'm looking at."

"That's the *Yuan*-class," Forestall said. "The *771*."

"And a *Yuan* isn't a nuke," Ryan mused.

"It is not," Forestall said.

"Dustin mentioned the Chinese boomer," Ryan said. "The *Jin*-class. When's the last time we saw her?"

"Our last contact with her was a week ago, north of the Bering Strait."

"So are we thinking this boomer is in distress and calling for help?"

"High probability," Forestall said.

"I can see them sending the Shangs into an overhead environment like an ice floe, but the *Yuan*'s a diesel. Seems like a good way to lose another sub."

"Right," Forestall said. "But the *Yuan*'s not an ordinary diesel-electric. Folks at the Naval Institute describe it as like a Song that resembles the Russian Kilo or a Kilo that has some characteristics of a Song. The *Yuan* has horizontal control surfaces on his sail and a dorsal rudder—like the *Song*-class boats. The Kilos have neither of these features, but they do share the same two-over-four torpedo tube configuration with the *Yuan*. Shipbuilders in Wuhan are turning out this newer class of sub with a rubberized hull coating, seven-blade screw, antivibration rack. State-of-the-art weaponry and sonar come either from Russia and or France. This is a very quiet sub, Mr. President. China has had great success with air-independent power."

"Meaning they don't need to surface and run their diesel to charge their batteries," Ryan said.

"Exactly," Forestall said. "We're not sure how long they can stay under, but at least two weeks. We've inserted a test section with AIP in one of our *Virginia*-class boats for testing, but honestly, sir, we've put most of our eggs in the nuke basket. France sold AIP hardware to Pakistan. Germany is using the technology as well."

"So," Ryan said, "all but one of the Chinese submarines

returning to Arctic waters are capable of staying submerged and maneuvering while doing so for sustained periods."

"That's correct, Mr. President," Forestall said.

"To go under the ice . . ." Ryan said. "Even the Communist Chinese wouldn't want to risk their nascent submarine forces by sailing them into an overhead environment where they could not surface if they had an issue. So a DISSUB sounds on the nose."

"True enough, Mr. President," Forestall said. "We wanted to give you the military picture to give background for what I have next."

19

I would not normally have brought something of this nature to your attention," Commander Forestall said. "But considering the coded signal coming from somewhere around the Mendeleev Ridge . . ."

"I'm all ears, Robby," Ryan said.

"Captain Russ Holland, skipper of the *John Paul Jones*, operating off the coast of Hawaii, kicked something up the chain regarding Arctic waters," Forestall said. "His chief sonar technician is in possession of an audio file purported to contain noises that some believe to be the sound of metal on metal . . . and possibly . . . words . . . Chinese words."

Ryan raised an eyebrow. "A sonar tech in Hawaii?"

"Correct," Forestall said. "These sound transients in question were recorded on a hydrophone during a scientific survey below the ice north of Point Barrow, Alaska. Chief Petty Officer Barker's former shipmate, a Dr. Patti Moon, left the Navy and went on to earn her Ph.D. in physics. She works aboard the research vessel *Sikuliaq*, a light icebreaker operated by the University of Alaska Fairbanks. It seems the R/V *Sikuliaq* was dropping under-ice sensors near an area at the edge of our continental shelf, a place called the Chukchi Borderland, when she recorded the sounds. I should point out that this is less than thirty nautical miles from the point of origin for the coded signal. In any case, Dr. Moon sent the file to her friend Chief Barker on the *John Paul Jones* and he submitted it through his chain of command."

"Does he agree with her assessment?" Ryan asked. "This Barker fellow."

"Enough to kick it up the chain," Forestall said. "Which bears some serious consideration. I pulled Dr. Moon's records. She's originally from Alaska. Received consistently good performance evaluations, but all her commanders noted that she had a penchant for putting far too much credence in conspiracy theories, especially those involving the government. Secret cabals and such. Seems she doesn't trust Uncle Sam to do right by her."

"What words?" Ryan asked.

Commander Forestall cocked his head, not following. "Sir?"

"Dr. Moon's Chinese words," Ryan said. "I'm assuming someone in your office speaks Mandarin."

SecDef Burgess walked through the door, already having read the brief.

"Admiral Talbot is on his way," Burgess said. Talbot was CNO, chief of naval operations. "He was having a root canal."

Ryan nodded and flicked his hand for Forestall to finish answering the question.

"The sound file is extremely garbled, Mr. President," Forestall said. "It could very well be fish or moving ice. But if it is someone screaming, my two Chinese speakers are at odds about what this person is saying. One of them thinks *fire* or *danger.* I've listened to the file myself. Honestly, I find it highly unlikely anyone could pick up human voices outside a submarine. The hulls aren't like in the movies. We make them quiet. Now, you slam a hatch . . . drop a pan of cookies . . . that's a different story. Voices . . . I'm not sure about that. I will say, though, the metallic sounds are extremely convincing, especially with the current situation."

"So," Ryan said. "Let's say these sounds are coming from a DISSUB. The Chinese are homing in on a signal thirty miles away from where Dr. Moon made her recording? Either the damaged sub traveled, or they're looking in the wrong place."

Dustin Fullmer moved his hand like he was going to raise it but changed his mind.

"Let's have it," Ryan said.

"Well, sir," Fullmer said. "I'm not a hundred percent sure of Chinese technology, but what if the DISSUB deployed a submarine rescue buoy? If the cable detached, it could have been carried under the ice and didn't pop to the surface until it was thirty miles away."

Ryan glanced at Forestall.

"I suppose that could be the case," Forestall said.

"Would the buoy have GPS of the original deployment?" Ryan asked.

"I'm not sure about Chinese design," Forestall said. "The buoys are designed to deploy automatically if the timers aren't reset periodically, in case they're unreachable in an accident. The Russians kept having accidental deployments, so they welded many of theirs in place."

"Okay," Ryan said, giving Fullmer an attaboy nod. He scribbled something in his notepad and then looked up at Burgess. "Who do we have up north, Bob?"

"The Navy's biennial ICEX ended a little over a week ago," Burgess said. "Two subs took part. The *Connecticut* was headed home, already abeam the San Juan Islands by the time we turned her around. But SSN 789—the *Indiana*—is still under the ice. We don't have contact with her for the moment, but we're sending ELF signals for her to make contact when she's able to receive. I imagine she's shadowing a Russian submarine. They would have come to lurk around the edges of our ICEX training. If need be, we can send someone up with Deep Siren. Find a lead in the ice and get a message to them that way."

Raytheon's Deep Siren was essentially a low-frequency acoustic tactical paging system to communicate underwater. It had proven itself many times over during several ICEX scenarios. Moving ice was problematic, but as long as there was open water, messages could be sent to the sub. "In addition to the *Indiana*, the USCG icebreaker *Healy* is also present," Burgess added. "We've been in contact and they are moving to investigate the point of this coded signal's origin."

"Very well," Ryan said. "The ice makes it problematic . . ."

Forestall nodded.

"It does indeed, sir," Burgess said. "Surface ships are a no go, other than the *Healy*. And with this many Chinese, U.S., and, surely, Russian submarines playing cat and mouse the chances of someone bumping rises sharply."

Ryan shook his finger. "No bumping."

"Roger that, Mr. President."

"Have your experts keep playing with the sound file and that coded signal," Ryan said, still tapping the desk with his pencil.

"Of course, sir," Forestall said.

"So," Ryan said. "Dr. Moon is from Alaska?"

"Yes, Mr. President," Forestall said. "Her record says she's from a small village on the Arctic. Point Hope."

"Point Hope." Ryan gave a sad shake of his head. "Interesting."

"It's in the top corner of the state," Forestall said. "On the northwest coast."

"I'm familiar with Point Hope," Ryan said. "And some of you likely read about it in college. Shortly after World War Two, some well-meaning but poorly informed folks at the Atomic Energy Commission were trying to come up with peacetime uses for the A-bomb. In their infinite governmental wisdom, somebody decided we should detonate five nuclear bombs a little south of that village where Dr. Moon is from to build a new harbor . . . in an area that stayed covered in ice more than half of the year. The plan was nixed, but it's no wonder she doesn't trust the government. I'm sure she grew up hearing stories about Project Chariot. You work for the government as long as I have, you learn some conspiracies deserve a little extra credence. Given the total of what's going on, there is a strong probability that the PLAN Submarine Force is launching a rescue mission."

"Agreed," Burgess said.

"Very well," Ryan said. "I'll leave the how and how many up to you. But I'd like to be kept informed. Where exactly is the *Healy* right now?"

The Coast Guard vessel *Healy* was one of only two functional icebreakers in the U.S. military inventory. China also had two. Russia had over forty.

Commander Forestall tapped a query into his tablet, waited a moment, then said, "The *Healy* is patrolling north of Kaktovik, Alaska—an old DEW Line station."

DEW Line was a series of Distant Early Warning radar sites, meant to keep tabs on the Soviet Bear during the Cold War. Some three hundred miles east of Point Barrow, the Inupiat village of Kaktovik was on the northern edge of the Arctic

National Wildlife Refuge. It now served as a hub for scientific research on climate change and a thriving tourist destination for watching polar bears that came to eat on the boneyard from the village's yearly harvest of bowhead whales.

Ryan stood. The others were already standing, but van Damm got to his feet as well.

"Who's *Healy*'s skipper?"

Forestall glanced at his tablet again. "Captain Jay Rapoza."

Ryan picked up the pencil again, thinking, then tossed it back to the center of his desk.

"And he's heading for the source of this coded signal?"

"Correct," Burgess said.

"And that will take him near the place were Dr. Moon heard her sounds?"

Burgess glanced at Forestall.

"Right over the top of it, Mr. President."

"Bob, get in touch with Rapoza's chain of command and make sure everyone stays in the loop as things develop."

"Yes, sir," the SecDef said.

"Robbie," Ryan said, causing Forestall to turn. "There's one more thing I'd like you to facilitate for me."

20

John Clark marked the police minders as soon as he boarded the aircraft. Both were Han Chinese men in their forties, seated three rows behind him on either side of the aisle. They read magazines, looking up periodically with feigned disinterest. The one on the right had thinning hair and a long, horselike face. He was dressed like a businessman coming home from a conference, open-collared white shirt, rumpled suit, an overcoat he kept in his lap like a blanket. He talked on his phone a lot—or pretended to. The other was slightly doughy with a blue ball cap and puffy blue ski jacket over a corduroy sport coat that looked too tight to button. Clark noted Horse Face's shoe that stuck half out in the aisle. It was well worn, sturdy, and didn't quite match the business suit. The Uyghurs who'd boarded in front of Clark recognized the minders for what they were as well, and leaned slightly away when they shuffled past, as if the men were contagious.

Clark had the entire row to himself. The China Southern Airlines flight was only around half full, but most of the passengers were Uyghur men. None of them wanted to risk being seen chatting with a foreigner by the two police minders.

The steady hiss of air flowing across the fuselage of the shabby but serviceable Airbus changed to a burbling roar as the pilots deployed flaps and slowed the plane in preparation for landing. Clark's ears popped, alerting him to the aircraft's descent. He hated airports, and didn't particularly enjoy being crammed into a flying metal tube. But he wasn't apprehensive about flying itself. At best, he was ambivalent. For him, slipping the surly bonds of earth was simply a means to an end. Some found the idea of flying a romantic notion. Good for them. Clark understood, a little.

He felt that way about the sea.

The pilots kept the cabin on the chilly side, so most passengers wore their coats or at least a heavy wool sweater during the flight. Most of the Uyghur men wore black fur hats pulled low over their eyes, like the winter hat worn by Brezhnev in all the newsreels. Others wore ball caps, or snap-brims. A couple of the older ones wore large fur Kyrgyz hats, similar to a Russian *ushanka* but wider at the earflaps, perfectly suited to their long white beards and Turkic features. Dark eyes and aquiline noses peered back and forth at the gathering twilight out of the windows on each side of the plane.

Clark watched the ground rise up to meet him out the window to his left. A dusty haze hung over the dull gray of the city and muted brown of the surrounding countryside. Patches of grimy snow clung to the shadows. The canal along the highway leading from the airport northeast of the town flowed full of chocolate-brown water. A convoy of three white-topped military troop carriers rolled down the highway east of the city. Pickups and larger trucks shared the roads with taxis and scooters.

Clark could already feel the grit of dust in his teeth and the chill on his neck just from looking out the window. It was no wonder everyone on the plane wore winter hats.

The plane bounced once, crabbing into a stiff crosswind before straightening up and settling onto Kashgar Airport's only runway.

The police minders followed Clark off the plane and then jumped ahead when he was held up at Immigration and Customs. He was sure he'd see them again. No doubt about that.

The uniformed Han officer grunted as Clark slid his Canadian passport and visa, courtesy of Adam Yao's friend in Beijing, across the counter. The officer perused it with the jaundiced eye of someone accustomed to being lied to on an hourly basis.

He asked Clark a couple perfunctory questions about the purpose of his trip. For his part, Clark tried very hard to hide the predatory edge in his eyes by acting bewildered. The three-thousand-mile trip from Ho Chi Minh City via Guangzhou and Urumqi had sapped him, and he was able to play weary traveler without acting. The officer barked something unintelligible, making the bewildered look easy to sustain.

It sounded as if he'd asked Clark if he had a jeep.

Clark shrugged and tapped his ear. It was better for the officer to think he was simply dealing with an old deaf guy rather than to be offended because Clark couldn't understand his English.

"You have the GPS?" the officer pantomimed, using his index finger like a compass needle. "For navigation."

"On my phone," Clark said, honestly.

"Mobile phone!" The man snapped his fingers. "Give to me."

Clark fished the phone out of his jacket pocket and passed it to the officer without argument.

"Extra battery?"

Clark dug out the spare charging block as well.

"Passcode!

"I . . ."

"Passcode or I do not give back," the man said. He gazed up at Clark without lifting his head.

Clark gave him the code to unlock the screen.

The officer scrolled, perusing the various icons, then said, "Do not use in China."

"The phone?"

The officer gave a disgusted shake of his head, then pointed to the map icon on the screen, raising his voice for the deaf Canadian at his station.

"No JEEPS in China."

"I understand," Clark said. "No GPS."

The officer slid the phone and passport back, but kept the extra battery for himself, giving no explanation. It was a small sacrifice to the Immigration and Customs gods.

One problem down, Clark moved to the next. He traveled with just a carry-on, so he made his way directly through the terminal, past the crowd of passengers. They squatted on tiny plastic stools by their bags, eating instant noodles or shanks of meat, while they waited for flights that rarely departed on schedule.

The two police minders, Horse Face and Doughboy, resumed their tail before Clark made it out the glass doors. Blowing yellow dust muted the glow of the streetlamps, forcing Clark and everyone else to bow their heads against the biting wind. The two minders trotted to keep up as he skirted a group of construction workers in hard hats laying rebar for a new sidewalk between the buses and taxi stand.

He'd let them follow him for now. But sooner or later, he'd have to lose them or lie to them.

Clark was, in fact, extremely good at lying. Sociopathy within proper bounds, the shrinks at Langley called it. Clark had never considered himself a spy in the strictest sense of the term. He was an operator, had been since he was a pup. Operators lied to get where they needed to be—or, more often than not, to get out of the grease after the job was complete. He grabbed intel when he came across it, of course, but in the main, he used other people's intel to go in, do his thing, and then slip away.

A good percentage of the time his thing had to do with getting some spy out—or killing one.

H ala Tohti helped load boxes of oiled noodles onto the back of her aunt's scooter. Her aunt's normally olive skin was chalky pale. She'd been up at all hours of the night, sewing, cooking, reading, anything but sleeping.

"I can take these to the market," Hala said, nodding at the noodles.

"I will be fine," Zulfira said.

A cold wind howled up the dusty street, picking up bits of trash and causing them to dance under the light posts, bristling with security cameras. Zulfira pulled her woolen scarf around her neck and shivered.

"I think you may be ill," Hala said.

"I said I will be fine."

The busy Jiefang Night Market was only a few blocks away,

but Zulfira swayed in the wind as if she might fall over before making the short trip.

Zulfira climbed aboard the scooter with unsteady legs. "I will drop off the noodles to Rami and return at once," she said, head bent against the wind. "Chop the meat while I am gone. We must have dinner ready when Mr. Suo arrives."

Hala's throat convulsed, making her warble like a frightened child—which made her angry with herself. "What if he comes while you are gone?"

"Ren sent word. Mr. Suo is delayed with meetings. He will be here in two hours. Plenty of time."

Hala knew better than to argue. She was a guest in her aunt's home.

Hala watched her aunt's scooter disappear into the dusk before going back into the house. She was no stranger to work—and there was always plenty of it to do. Her mother had taught her to make savory rice plov, and chop mince and vegetables to fill dough for samsa, by the time she was six. She could joint a chicken with her eyes closed, especially with her uncle's razor-sharp cleaver.

She stood on a stool while she worked, chicken carcass on a flat board, cleaver in her right hand. Holding a drumstick— yellow foot and claws attached—away from the breast at an angle, she pressed the cleaver against the joint and popped it away, setting aside the neatly separated leg. What else could she do? She saw the way the fat bureaucrat Suo and his secretary, Ren, looked at both her and her aunt. Oh, Fat Suo liked Zulfira, but Hala was old enough to realize men looked at her as well with glazed eyes and sagging jaws. Fat Suo would be back soon, looking at her like she was a sweet. But Zulfira was strong. Zulfira would protect her.

Hala had seen it before, at the dance and gymnastics academy in Nanjing. Coaches sometimes looked at the older girls that way. They took them on walks or to their offices upstairs. None of the girls ever said what happened when they came back to the dormitory, but they cried a lot. Some of them got so sick that they had to leave the school.

Sometimes, early on when she was still only seven years old and she'd just been identified as a gymnastics prodigy and sent away to train for the glory of the Motherland, Hala wished she would get sick so she could go home like the other girls. Later, when she was old enough to understand some of it, she learned the girls hadn't gone home. They'd left the school in shame, to have babies. Hala had grown up around farm animals and understood the basics, but not the narrow-eyed looks some of the coaches had when they looked at the older girls.

Then she turned ten, and things changed—a lot.

One evening, after practice, Mr. Yun, who trained the boys on the pommel horse and rings, brought her a small piece of cake wrapped in wax paper. Student diets were strictly controlled, but Mr. Yun's gifts became more and more frequent. Each time he gave her anything, he gave her a funny stare. She thought it made him look like his eyes were crossed. Sometimes he even touched her hand, but she was always so hungry, so she'd taken the sweets and wolfed them down without thinking. Then, Mr. Yun had whispered in her ear during supper that she should meet him in the corner, where they stacked the mats—and not to tell anyone. He'd given her a small piece of white cake, filled with cream that was so deliciously sweet and wonderful that it made her head buzz when she ate it. Mr.

Yun rested his hand on her upper arm, squeezing her softly. He promised there were more treats where that came from if he and Hala could become secret friends.

Mr. Yun leaped away when the gym door opened, hands raised, as if Hala was on fire and he did not want to be burned. His wife had just stood there in her white T-shirt and red track pants, blinking at him for what seemed like forever. Mrs. Yun was a strong woman, but she grew smaller and smaller that night. Her entire body began to tremble, her chest heaving enough to rattle the whistle hanging on the lanyard around her neck. She summoned Hala over with a flick of her wrist and walked her to the dormitory without a word.

Hala had always thought Mrs. Yun liked her, or at least respected how hard she trained, but the next day, she called Hala to her office and told her she was worthless as a gymnast. Hala tried to apologize, though she didn't know what for. Mrs. Yun only became angrier and slapped her across the cheek. The blow had knocked out a tooth, which seemed to surprise Mrs. Yun. She'd cried, still shaking, then chided Hala for chewing the collar of her sweatshirt, and called her a stupid, stupid little girl. There was no longer a spot for her at the school. Hala would be put on a train that very afternoon. She would return home to live with her aunt.

Mrs. Yun and the other coaches were surely angry because Hala was doing so much better than their pretty Chinese students. But no, it wasn't that. They'd known she was Uyghur when they sent her to the school. Had it been the sweets? Hala had figured it out while she packed her things and said goodbye to her friends. It wasn't because she'd broken the rules of her diet. Mrs. Yun was angry with her because Mr. Yun had put his hand on her shoulder—and looked at *her* like she was one of his sweets.

That was the past, Hala thought, and resumed dismembering the chicken. There was nothing she could do about it now—

The handle on the front door shook, sending a gush of fear down her back. She jumped, nearly dropping the cleaver, then dipped her head, teeth searching for, then biting, the collar of her shirt.

The door swung open slowly and Zulfira stepped in.

Hala relaxed a notch. "Did you forget some—"

"He is here," Zulfira said, chin quivering.

"Suo?"

Zulfira swallowed hard. She nodded, lips set tight, red in the face, like she was holding her breath.

The fat bureaucrat darkened the door behind her, suitcase in hand. Smiling cruelly, he waved at Hala as if he were a welcome relative, there to visit for the holidays. He had every right to stay—according to the law. Some might even call it duty. Provincial bureaucrats in Xinjiang were ordered by Beijing to see to the needs of backward Uyghur families, stopping in to visit at all hours, and spending the night.

Civilizing them in a decidedly uncivilized manner.

Fat Suo dropped his suitcase to the floor and tossed his head at Hala. "Put that in your aunt's room, child, if you would be so kind. And stop sucking on your shirt!"

Hala let the damp collar fall away. She froze, mouth open, looking at the large case. How long did this fat baboon intend to stay?

Suo's face began to darken.

"Go ahead," Zulfira said, before turning to the fat man. "Please sit and make yourself comfortable in my home. Your assistant said that you would be late, so I was going to deliver my noodles to the market before making dinner."

Suo smiled again. "Do not trouble yourself with a meal," he said. "My meeting ended earlier than expected and I had some rice and pork at the office . . . Does that offend you? That I ate pork?"

"You may eat whatever you wish," Zulfira said. "But I do not."

"I see," the fat man said. He clapped his thick hands and then held them together, fingers interlaced in front of his face as he looked back and forth from Zulfira to Hala. "In any case, I have already eaten. I am tired. Perhaps you could show me the bedroom."

Zulfira nodded to the door off the kitchen. "Through there."

"It is awfully cold, my dear," Suo said. "Perhaps you might come and warm my old bones."

"I . . . I think it would be best if I slept by the stove."

Hala noticed for the first time that her aunt had already moved a stack of quilts out of the bedroom and put them in the corner of the main room.

The fat man touched his lips with clenched hands, peering over his knuckles in thought. "The girl is small, but I suppose she could warm my—"

"No!" Zulfira said. She touched her belly. "It is just that . . . I . . . my husband has only been gone a few months, and I am . . ."

Fat Suo scoffed. "With child?"

Zulfira chewed on her bottom lip but didn't deny it.

Suo put a hand on Zulfira's shoulder, caressing as if trying to calm an animal. Hala clenched her fist, ready to fly at the fat man, but Zulfira flashed her a look.

Suo gave a wry chuckle. "Have you heard of the wild horses of Kalamely Mountain?"

Tears pressed from Zulfira's lashes as she clenched her eyes. She shook her head.

"Przewalski's horses, they're called," Suo said. "Runty little beasts, in the great scheme of things, but they are thought to have been native to Asia many thousands of years ago. A few dozen were reintroduced here in Xinjiang, probably decades before you were born. There are still not very many, less than two hundred, so I am told." Suo cocked his head to one side and then ran a knuckle down Zulfira's cheek. "Every single foal is important to the people who are trying to grow this herd . . . but the stallions do not care about the herd as a whole. They only care about the foals that come from their loins. Did you know, for instance, that when a stronger stallion finds, shall we say, a pregnant mare whose mate he has killed or is no longer around for one reason or another, he simply mounts the mare with such force as to make certain that there is no chance that any progeny but his own survives?" Suo laughed, throwing up his hands. "Of course, we are not horses. There is no need for rough behavior—"

"So long as the mare remains civil," Zulfira said.

"Something like that," the fat man said and chuckled.

Zulfira folded her arms tight across her chest. "Where is your assistant?"

"Ren is busy taking care of another matter."

A tear ran down Zulfira's cheek. "What of Hala?"

Suo took her hand. "She may sleep by the stove." His voice was husky now. "Unless my hand is forced, I have no interest in foals."

21

C lark checked his watch. Two hours. That gave him enough time to catch a cab to his hotel and grab a couple of samsa from a street vendor. He'd let the minders watch him eat dinner while he studied a tourist map of the city he'd picked up in the terminal and waited for Midas to arrive on the next flight.

The two Campus operatives would coordinate but work without direct face-to-face contact with each other. Clark would take the lead, putting eyes on the Uyghur girl, Hala—and hopefully her mother, Medina Tohti, their actual target. Midas would hang back, taking a broader view, acting as backup and overwatch. The point was not so much to provide a safety net for Clark—there was little either one of them could do if the other was somehow compromised and picked up by XPCC authorities. Two sets of eyes, acting in a coordinated fashion, were far more likely to find Medina Tohti if she was anywhere nearby. If something did happen to Clark, Midas could continue the mission.

Though they would not make personal contact, Clark and Midas could communicate via text on a shadowed phone app developed by Gavin Biery, The Campus's IT genius. The app—

Biery called it Walk-to-Me—hid behind a functional pedometer application and wouldn't show up without the correct code.

Clark's phone buzzed as he walked to the line of green-and-
white VW Santana taxis outside the large glass building. The
brrrp and buzz of saws and pneumatic power tools mingled
with the sound of traffic outside. He checked his phone. The
pedometer app said he'd just reached four thousand steps—
meaning he had a message from Midas.

Clark punched in the code with his thumb, then read the
message before it disappeared from the screen ten seconds
later.

It was short and to the point.

Flight delayed. Twelve hours. m

This changed what Clark had planned to do. He was still
hungry, and he still planned to do a quick drive-by of the house
where Medina Tohti's daughter was supposed to live. Now he'd
just do it without any redundancy or backup. If he fumbled
here, screwed up and somehow got himself killed, he'd die alone.

Not exactly a new situation for him. He needed to lose his
two minders . . . Clark chuckled to himself. One thing at a
time.

The message from Midas made him forget about the biting
wind. A bitter gust hit him full in the face as he rounded a line
of waiting city buses, taking away his breath and sandblasting
his squinting eyes. He fished a black wool watch cap from the
pocket of his navy peacoat. Pulled down over his ears, the wool
hat did double duty of keeping him warm and providing natural camouflage on streets where virtually everyone had dark
hair and a hat.

Two Uyghur men stood at the head of a line of green-and-white taxis. Backs to the wind, the men spoke in animated voices with a red-faced Uyghur woman in a scarf. Clark didn't speak Uyghur, but from the frequent exasperated head turning, they were negotiating over the price of a cab ride—and the woman was not having any of it.

The fourth cabbie back in line sat behind the wheel, phone to his ear, nodding gravely to whatever was being said. He wore a ratty black trilby that looked like he might have slept in it. Clark noted that his doughy police minder, also on his phone, ended his call at the same time as the cabbie.

The cabbie pulled forward, out of the queue, stopping to jump out to come around, intent on opening the rear passenger door. Clark ignored him, walking straight for the second cab in line, pretending not to hear.

The driver of this cab was an old Uyghur man who looked to be near Clark's age—certainly past the point of putting up with any bullshit from line-jumping competitors. He wore a white doppa—the embroidered four-cornered skullcap ubiquitous among Uyghur men. A wisp of a whisker curled sideways forming a silver-gray comma off the point of his chin.

"Qinibagh Hotel?" Clark said, opening his door and sliding across the peach-colored seat in the back.

The old man looked over his shoulder, one silver caterpillar brow arching upward.

"Qiniwake?"

The Qinibagh or Chinibagh Hotel was located on the old British consulate grounds near Old Town Kashgar and the Night Market. The site of a good deal of intrigue during the Great Game between Russia and the UK during the early 1900s, it was also known as the Qiniwake.

"That's the one," Clark said, sliding in beside his bag.

The old man shoulder-checked and then pulled away from the curb. "Twenty yuan," he said, once they were rolling. It was twice the normal price for a cab ride into the city—but still about three U.S. dollars. Hardly worth the trouble to haggle over. Clark hadn't exactly been eating caviar off a mother-of-pearl spoon all his life, but his GMC pickup at home in Virginia was likely worth more than this guy would make in his lifetime.

The cabbie turned right out of airport parking onto Yingbin Avenue, following signs above the roadway that read TO KASHGAR/KASHI CITY in English, Chinese characters, and Arabic script. Traffic was moderate, mostly taxis and Chinese-made pickups, small by American standards, but large enough to handle the farm chores of this decidedly rural city. They passed a small field on the right on the far side of a wide irrigation canal. It had long since been picked over, but the telltale white tufts dotted the dry stubble and brown earth.

"Cotton," the cabbie said. He patted his chest and smiled in the mirror. "Very good cotton from here. Your Gucci, Prada, big names, they all use Xinjiang cotton."

"Interesting," Clark said.

"That land," the cabbie said, patting his chest again. "My family once raised cotton there."

"Now?"

"Bingtuan—Han government soldier farmers plant cotton on the land now." He shook his finger back and forth in the mirror. "I no more drive tractor. Now I drive taxi."

"Who owns the land?" Clark asked, knowing the answer, but playing along so the cabbie could tell the story he obviously wanted to tell.

The old man nodded thoughtfully, rubbing his sparse beard. "I think the land is owned by the ones who have the most soldiers . . ."

"I suppose," Clark said.

The light ahead of them turned red and the taxi rolled to a squeaky stop right beside a commuter bus. Clark tipped his head toward a sign beside the entry doors. "What does that say?"

The cabbie eyed him hard in the mirror until they started rolling again. Finally, he said, "Explosives and bearded men are forbidden on public buses."

"You have a beard."

"No beards," the cabbie said. "Unless you are old like me . . ."

"And me," Clark said.

"Ha," the cabbie said, smiling beneath sad eyes. He shook his finger in the mirror again. "No beard for you, young man. You are young and fit, not bent and old like me."

"I wish, my friend," Clark said. He leaned forward in the seat. The streets had suddenly grown crowded with pedestrians. Smoke from myriad wood grills and ovens rose in the cold air and swirled among colorful lights strung back and forth across the side alleys off the main road. "Change of plans, uncle," Clark said. "Drop me off up here at Jiefang Night Market. I'd like to walk a bit. My hotel is not far."

The old cabbie's face filled the rearview mirror as he looked at Clark like he'd gone crazy. "You know the way? It is dark and the wind is cold."

"I'm fine," Clark said. "I have read about your Night Market. It looks interesting."

"And your bag?"

Clark patted the duffel. "It's small."

"Okay," the cabbie said, still unconvinced. "You are the boss.

But there will be checkpoints. You are tourist so perhaps they will not stop you all the time, but your bag will be searched if they do."

"No worries. I have nothing to hide."

The cabbie pulled to the curb a half block away from the lights of the Night Market, before a set of yellow metal barricades in front of a checkpoint. Camouflaged police and black-clad SWAT officers checked Uyghur pedestrians' identity cards. A speaker blared a recording of a woman's voice in Uyghur. Clark leaned across the seat to grab his bag.

"What is she saying?" Clark asked as he handed over a stack of bills.

"'Report terrorism or separatism immediately. Speaking to others on the Internet about separatism is forbidden . . . Speaking on the Internet about terrorism is forbidden . . .'" The old cabbie gave Clark a mischievous wink as he took the money. "'And no beards . . .'"

Clark shouldered his bag and approached the nearest policeman, pointing at the lights of the street market ahead and pantomiming eating. Unwilling to bother with a tourist who probably didn't speak Mandarin, the officer waved him through before turning his attention to the line of docile Uyghur men and women behind the yellow barriers. A group of Han Chinese tourists in fashionable coats and faux-fur mittens and hats were waved through with no more than a cursory we're-on-the-same-team nod from the officers at the checkpoint.

Clark bought a hot samsa at the first stand he came to. The Central Asian meat pie was similar to an Argentine empanada, this one plucked straight out of the tandoori-style oven. Filled with chopped carrot, garlic, onion, and fatty pieces of lamb, it warmed him as he made his way through the market, working east, where he hoped to avoid most of the cameras long enough to check out the house where Hala Tohti was supposed to be staying with her aunt.

A slender man with thick, pink lips like a carp shouldered his way past, cursing at Clark in Mandarin as he went by. He was going in the same direction, obviously in a big hurry to get somewhere.

Hala lay under a quilt in front of the oil stove, fully clothed, chewing on the sodden collar of her shirt. She covered her ears with both hands, trying to block out the noises coming from her aunt's room. Soon it was quiet, but she did not move until the fat baboon Suo yelled for her to get him some tea.

Ren flung open the door before she'd made it to the kitchen. Cold air swirled in around him, and Hala imagined he was a devil, come to curse their house. Then Suo came out with nothing but his sagging undershorts and she did not have to imagine devils any longer.

Zulfira followed him out of the bedroom. Her hair mussed, she clutched the throat of her simple cotton robe with one hand. The other hand she kept in her pocket.

Zulfira stopped cold when Ren shut the door behind him.

"We agreed," she said. "Hala is not to be touched."

"We did agree," Suo said, fat chin to soap-white chest. "That is the truth. But it is also true that I made an agreement with my assistant—and that agreement was made before yours."

Hala glanced at the door, but Ren grabbed her by the arm.

Zulfira set her jaw. "No . . ." she whispered. "You . . . cannot do this . . ."

Fat Suo breathed deeply, as if taking in her smell, and gave her a smug smile. "I have decided that I am hungry after all."

Zulfira's voice rose in pitch and timbre. "This is *my* home. I will not allow—"

Suo struck her hard across the face with the back of his hand. "My dear, you will allow—"

Her hand came out of her pocket with an ornate Uyghur blade that Hala recognized as one of her uncle's. Zulfira struck like a scorpion, hitting hard and fast, pounding over and over at the spot where Suo's neck attached to his shoulder. The knife was more decorative than practical, with an eagle pommel and rosewood grips inlaid with jade and mother-of-pearl—but Zulfira's husband believed that all knives, even those meant for decoration, should be kept sharp enough to shave the hairs on one's arm. The blade was no longer than five inches, but the wicked upturned point did an incredible amount of damage as Zulfira drove it home again and again. A great arc of blood spouted across the room at the first blow, deflecting off her hand and spattering her face and chest each time she struck.

Suo slapped a hand to his neck, eyes wide, collapsing to his knees. Blood poured between fat fingers and ran down his arm in a red curtain to the floor. He opened his mouth to speak, but managed no more than a horrible croak.

Ren relaxed his grip in shock, allowing Hala to pull away and run to her aunt. She floundered midway, slipping and almost falling in the growing pool of blood. Suo's hand that had been holding his neck fell to his side, noodlelike. His eyes fluttered and he pitched forward, smashing his face against the linoleum floor with a horrific thud.

Zulfira brandished the Uyghur knife at Ren. Her attack had

been so furious she'd not noticed that she'd cut her own hand each time she'd plunged the knife into Suo's fat neck. At some point in the process the blade had snapped at the tang, leaving her with nothing but the handle in her blood-drenched hand. She dropped it and grabbed Hala, yanking her out of the way just in time.

Dumbfounded, Ren cried out in rage. His eyes shifted to the cleaver on the table, and he snatched it up. Zulfira blocked his exit, screaming for Hala to go in the bedroom and lock the door.

Ren brandished the gleaming cleaver. His voice was high and pinched. His chest heaved. "I promise you this," he hissed. "I will not be so easy to kill."

And he was right.

22

At once terrified and enraged at the sudden murder of his boss, Ren rushed forward, slashing wildly, intent on slicing Zulfira in half. She picked up a wooden bowl and pushed it out in front with both hands like a shield, but Ren had her on size and reach. One of his swings connected, opening a sickening smile of meat along the length of her forearm. The Uyghur knife she'd used so well to kill Mr. Suo clattered to the floor. Ren cackled maniacally, pressing forward slowly. Zulfira was now unarmed, bleeding profusely.

Without thinking, Hala grabbed one of the wooden chairs near the table and ran as fast as she could, pushing it ahead of her across the slick linoleum floor toward Ren like a battering ram.

Ren wheeled too late, catching the heavy wooden seat directly below his kneecaps.

A ragged scream boiled out of his throat. "You filthy Uyghur bitch! Do you think to win against a full-grown man? I will cut you into litt—"

Hala's trick with the chair afforded Zulfira the opportunity to scoop up a paring knife and throw herself against Ren before he could react with the cleaver. Throwing her head back in a terrifying scream, she leaped onto his back and buried the little knife again and again in his neck and shoulder.

Unlike his boss, Ren expected the attack. He ducked his head to his shoulder, twisting and turning, making it virtually impossible for Zulfira to get the right angle. Though the blade did some damage and drew a copious amount of blood, none of the wounds were arterial or anywhere close to fatal.

The cleaver fell from Ren's grasp at the same moment Hala's feet squirted out from under her in the blood. She landed almost on top of the cleaver, grabbing it up as she rolled and bringing it down on top of Ren's dress shoe, burying the sharp blade across his arch. It would have cut the front of his foot off, had Hala been stronger and her footing more secure.

Ren yowled, flailing for the cleaver, but missing it as his other foot shot sideways, like a goat trying to walk across a frozen pond. He hit the ground with a crack, groaning, rolling in blood. Zulfira fell, too, slashing, opening his cheek with her blade as she sought out his throat. The knife found a home in his shoulder. Ren roared, swatting her away. She landed on her butt, sliding backward, mopping blood on the floor.

Hala rolled away, crouching now, cleaver in hand. Ren wallowed to his feet, looking like he'd been dipped in blood. He drew the paring knife from his shoulder, dragging his injured foot as he hobbled toward a panting Zulfira. Hala slashed at his legs with the cleaver. Ren turned, coglike, catching himself with his good foot to stay upright at every shuffling step. He shook the knife at Hala. Blood and spittle spewed through clenched teeth.

"Whore! Mosquito. I will open your—"

On her feet again, Zulfira smashed a wooden bowl over the man's head.

Stunned but far from out, Ren shoved her sideways, stagger-
ing backward from the blow.

Zulfira barely regained her footing. Blood covered her face
and arms. "Run!" she wailed at Hala. "Go!"

Hala scrambled sideways, wheezing, unable to draw a breath.
She tried to stand, but her muscles were made of stone. Her
aunt's sobbing cries, the wicked man's screams, rattled inside
her head, muffled and disjointed. Her back hit the wall. She
was cornered.

Howling like a madman, Ren lunged for her—but Zulfira
threw herself between them, grabbing the hand that held the
knife and drawing it into her own belly, driving forward to
topple Ren.

"Go!" Zulfira's voice was a shattered scream as she fell on
top of the startled man. "Leave, Hala! Leave now!"

Ren pushed the dying woman away, then lay there on his
back, chest heaving, his shirt gleaming like red satin in the
lamplight. He swallowed, head lolling, to look at Zulfira, who
clutched her stomach, wracked with pain.

Ren started to rise. "B . . . b . . . bitch!" A cruel laugh escaped
his swollen lips. "No one will even know you are gone . . ."

Outside Zulfira Azizi's home, the man's derisive laugh cost
him his life.

Clark had watched from the shadows across the street when
he'd first arrived. He noted the location of security cameras—
on the eaves, light poles, and perched on the top of street signs.
A Han Chinese sentry stood beside a white Toyota Cressida—
the only car on a street filled with scooters. Clark had pulled
guard duty for a big shot before, and knew what it looked like.

This guy wore a long wool coat over civilian clothing, but Clark was reasonably certain he was a policeman, likely a driver of whoever was inside Zulfira Azizi's home. A flame flared behind the sentry's cupped hand, momentarily illuminating his face as he lit a cigarette. He returned the lighter to his pants pocket, opening his coat just enough for Clark to catch the outline of a pistol on his belt. The sentry tapped it before he let the coat fall, and then leaned back against the hood of the car, stretching, taking a long drag on the fresh cigarette. As if struck with a sudden idea, he glanced up at the cameras, then lifted the coat again and tucked it behind his holster. His hand hovered above the weapon and then squared off in the darkness. He pantomimed a quick-draw like a gunfighter in the Old West. He let the coat fall, took three steps, then looked up before repeating the pantomime gunfight.

Clark stifled a chuckle. This asshole knew exactly where the cameras were, and saved his gunfighting theatrics for the moments he was in the black.

Movement in the windows drew Clark's attention away from the buffoon. Lights flickered inside. Shadows shifted oddly, back and forth behind floral curtains near the front door. The sentry's head snapped up at some sound coming from inside. Distance and a moaning wind made it difficult for Clark to pick up the sound at first.

Then a sudden lull in the wind brought the blood-chilling wail of a woman in despair.

Clark came up on his toes at the pitiful sound, preparing to move.

Next to the sedan, the sentry shook his head—and laughed.

John Clark took killing seriously—both tactically and morally. He'd ended the life of many people—some of them in unspeakably brutal ways that he'd never talk about, even to Ding or Sandy . . . especially not to Sandy. He told himself that they'd all been necessary—for the greater good—but that depended on one's point of view. He slept well most nights, but felt reasonably certain that if there was such a thing as judgment day, he could, at the very least, expect a stern talking-to from the Big Man. People who killed others for a living rarely afforded themselves the luxury of fretting over the sin of it. More often, or at least for Clark, it hinged on adherence to a personal moral code.

Sometimes—far less often than one might expect—he'd had the luxury of thinking things through, planning, learning all there was to know about the person whose life he would extinguish. The vast majority of circumstances, though, dictated immediate action, like this sentry, standing between Clark and someone in danger—and laughing derisively at their pain.

Clark closed the distance quickly, crossing the street when the sentry turned to listen to more screams pouring from inside the house—padding up behind him in a spot with no camera coverage.

For as much as he pantomimed the gunfighting action, the sentry was woefully slow on the draw, allowing Clark to give him a quick hammer-fist to the side of the neck and then pluck the small revolver out of the man's holster before he could react. Intent on moving toward the sound of the screams, and unwilling to leave an adversary behind him, Clark pressed the little revolver to the wide-eyed man's belly and pulled the trigger.

He got nothing. Not even a click.

"Shit!" He resorted to using the handgun as a mini–battering ram, driving it barrel-first, again and again, into the man's teeth, before slamming it into the side of his head.

Clark realized the gun was a replica about the time the man collapsed.

"Some gunslinger," Clark spat, anchoring the man to the ground with a boot to the head. He dropped the worthless prop and wheeled toward the door—moving toward the sound of bitter screams.

Hala brought the cleaver down with all her might. Ren flailed, grabbing her hand and shoving the blade away as it came down. It hovered a hair above his heaving throat. Tendons knotted in his neck. Zulfira was there, too, helping Hala press the cleaver down, down, down.

Ren screamed, one hand wrapped around Hala's where she held the cleaver, the other flailing with the little knife, slashing at Zulfira's back as he struck blow after sickening blow. "Why? Won't? You? Die?"

Hala could feel her aunt's strength ebbing. A ghoulish smile crossed Ren's face. He felt it, too.

Hala's stomach lurched and she had to fight the urge to vomit. She was too small to finish this, too weak.

A shadow crossed behind her. Her heart sank. More of Fat Suo's men—

Then a dark boot came down next to her hand, stepping on the spine of the cleaver and driving the blade deep into Ren's neck.

Hala looked up at the tall man who towered above her. He was white—an American, with thinning silver hair and hard eyes that flashed with cruelty. He softened when he met her gaze and put a hand over his heart.

A friend.

Hala rolled away, gasping. There was nothing she could do about it if he decided to kill her. She ignored him and dragged herself across the floor to her aunt, who lay shuddering in a pool of blood on the floor. The man dropped to his knees beside them. He worked furiously to stop Zulfira's bleeding, but her wounds were too many and too deep.

Hala pressed her forehead against her aunt's cheek, whimpering. "Why? Why did you do that?"

The grimace face fell away. Her lashes fluttered. "I told you," she whispered. "We do what we must."

"I'm sorry," the gray-haired man said to Hala after her aunt breathed a final shuddering breath.

Hala looked up at him, wide-eyed, covered in blood and tears. She whispered, "Who are you?"

She'd grown up with a rudimentary grasp of English from working at the Jiefang market, talking to tourists with her father. Few Americans or Europeans even tried to speak Mandarin. Fewer still attempted more than a butchered greeting in Arabic. No tourist at the market had ever tried to talk to her in Uyghur. She was young and smart, with an ear for language. Her father had taught her early on that she could go far by learning English. Classes at the gymnastics school helped refine the basics she'd learned at the market.

"A friend," the man said, hand to heart again. "Are you hurt?"

Hala put the collar of her shirt in her mouth and stared at him, unable to speak. She tasted blood, but did not care. Her head spun. The room grew smaller.

"Are you hurt?" the man asked again, pantomiming a knife against his own arm. "Cut?"

Hala shook her head, then, without another thought, threw herself into the stranger's arms. She wanted to cry, but nothing came out.

23

Gray clouds hung low enough to scrape the ice while Dr. Moon sat in the wardroom and ate a breakfast of steel-cut oats and blueberries. She was dressed for travel: thick socks, heavy boots, insulated Arctic-weight bibs she kept unzipped while inside the boat. A bright red anorak with a wolverine fur ruff lay draped across the packed duffel in the chair beside her. It was custom-made, a gift from her auntie, a famous Inupiat seamstress in her home village of Point Hope.

Moon looked at her watch. It was already ten in the morning. She was ready to go, but skeptical that anything would happen today. Travel this far north meant a lot of waiting.

Utqiagvik did not see the sun from mid-November until late January, but when the light returned, it came back with a vengeance. Now, nearing the end of March, the sun circled overhead from seven in the morning until after nine p.m., giving Patti Moon and the rest of the scientists aboard the research vessel *Sikuliaq* abundant light for their experiments—weather permitting. Sun or not, the Arctic was a fickle place, with weather patterns that changed rapidly and with little notice. Lois Deering, the meteorologist on board *Sikuliaq*, often joked that the high-pressure system was so shallow at these latitudes that good weather could be chased away with a sneeze in the wrong direction.

The morning before had broken bluebird clear. Lois the weather guesser had forecast at least twelve more decent hours—then someone sneezed and blew in a low.

The little icebreaker was in pack ice, young, from the previous winter, but still a good foot thick, so they didn't have to deal with waves. The wind had howled all night. Temperatures fell well below zero—reminding everyone on board that spring in the Arctic was rarely all sunshine and daffodils.

Kelli Symonds came in, wool beanie pulled low, cheeks flushed pink from a stroll on the weather deck.

Moon saluted her with a spoon heaped full of oats. "Looks chilly out there."

"To the bone," Symonds said, sounding, as she always did, like she had salt water instead of blood in her veins. "To the bitter bone." Moon could not help but imagine the pretty young woman wearing a peacoat, smoking a corncob pipe, and calling everyone "matey." In truth, Kelli Symonds was simply a competent sailor who, when she was not at sea on *Sikuliaq*, lived north of Seattle with her retired mother, two Yorkshire terriers, and her husband, whom she'd met while they were both attending the U.S. Merchant Marine Academy in Kings Point.

Symonds threw her wool gloves onto the table and poured herself a cup of coffee from an urn against the bulkhead.

"They're on their way," she said, flopping down across from Moon, holding her coffee mug with both hands, letting the steam curl up and warm her face.

"Seriously?" Moon said. "In this?"

"The skipper got a call on the radio five minutes ago. Chopper's half an hour out." Symonds took a sip of coffee, peering across her mug with narrow eyes. "I've been working in these lofty latitudes for almost ten years, and I've never seen a chopper fly out to pluck someone off the ice who wasn't about to keel over from botulism or some such thing." She took another sip of coffee, then gave Moon a mock toast with the mug. "You must really rate." Her eyes shifted quickly from side to side, and then she leaned over the table and whispered, "Are you a secret agent?"

"More likely that I'm in trouble," Moon said.

"Maybe." Symonds looked into her coffee, then up to meet Moon's gaze. "Do you really think there was someone down there, under the ice? A Russian submarine or something?"

"I know what I heard," Moon said. "And it wasn't farting fish like Thorson says."

The part about the noises sounding like Chinese seemed like something Moon should keep to herself.

"And you don't think it was ice? That stuff screams like a banshee all night long."

"Like you said, it's weird that they're sending a helicopter," Moon said. "Maybe I heard a secret lab under the ice and they're taking me somewhere to keep me quiet."

Symonds laughed at that. "Maybe," she said. "You ever think about how in the movies, when some spy or military dude messes up, really screws the pooch I mean, and the uppity-ups banish him to a science station in Alaska? We must be a couple of first-rate brainiacs, coming, what, five hundred miles off the Arctic Circle of our own free will . . ."

Moon lowered her voice. "Sometimes I think those uppity-ups only say they're banishing the guy to the North Pole for punishment when what they really mean is they're dumping his body down a mine shaft somewhere."

"Like my dad when he told me my dog was in a better place?"

Moon brandished the oatmeal spoon to make her point. "Exactly like that."

Another crewman stuck his head in the wardroom and twirled his finger in the air. "Captain says you should get out on the ice," he said. "Your chariot is fifteen out and they don't want to put down where the ice is chewed up next to the boat."

"They were half an hour out five minutes ago," Symonds said.

Moon got up with a groan, gathering her anorak and duffel. "I get it," she said. "Choppers burn a shitload of fuel every minute. Can't blame them if they would rather have me waiting on the ice for them rather the other way around."

"Maybe," Symonds said. It was her favorite word. She set her mug on the table and stood with Moon. "You'll need a polar-bear guard. I'll get the twelve-gauge and come with. Skipper saw two yesterday morning before the weather got bad, chowing down on an adolescent walrus they'd managed to nab off a haul out."

"I saw the photos," Moon said.

"Brutal to the bone, right?" Symonds said. "The snow was slathered in blood and gore. One look at that shit is enough to make me never venture onto the ice without the shotgun."

"You really think any self-respecting polar bear is going to stick around between us and an approaching helicopter?"

Symonds shrugged and gave Moon a wink.

"Maybe."

The gray twin-engine UH-1Y Venom "Super Huey" helicopter kicked a cloud of white into the air as it settled on thick ice fifty yards from the ship. The pilots kept the rotor spinning while a callow Marine bundled up like the Michelin Man beckoned Moon toward the open side hatch.

She ducked instinctively as she approached, though the rotors were well above her head.

"Dr. Moon?" the Marine shouted above the whumping blades and whining engine. She exaggerated her nod in the big parka ruff. Satisfied that she was the person he'd come for, he waved her aboard. She tried to thank him, but he shook his head, tapping the earmuffs on the side of his helmet and then pointing to another helmet and earphones hanging by one of the vis-à-vis seats inside the otherwise empty cabin.

Moon frowned at the thought of being the only passenger. She'd been only half kidding about the possibility of getting dumped down a mine shaft—or, in this case, into the Arctic Ocean.

In addition to the heavy flight suit, cranial protection, and goggles, the crew chief wore a load-bearing vest that included a sidearm—presumably polar-bear defense if they went down. Moon stifled a smile at the thought. A nine-millimeter pistol was better than your teeth and fingernails against a nine-foot bear who considered you food, but not by much. A cable attached to a line inside the cabin was clipped to the young Marine's safety harness, allowing him to move around the cabin with relative freedom. He helped her put on the four-point harness in one of the forward-facing seats, then had her don the helmet. He pushed the tiny boom mic closer to her mouth.

His voice came over the intercom. "Copy?"

She gave him a thumbs-up. "Five by five."

"Outstanding," the Marine said, sounding much more mature than he looked. "I'm Corporal Goen, the crew chief,

Lieutenant Eggiman is up front on the left, Captain Pelkey is on the right. He's the one in charge of this bird."

"You guys are based in Alaska?"

"Oh, hell, no," Corporal Goen said. "HMLA-269 out of New River. We're doing cold weather out of Utgi . . . Utga . . . Barrow . . . for training with Marines from 2nd Division."

HMLA stood for Helicopter Marine Light Attack.

"I was stationed at Norfolk for a while," Moon said. "Been to New River a couple of times."

She'd dated a Marine from Air Station New River for a while. The three-hour drive had been worth it, but then he'd shipped off with a one-way ticket to Fallujah. She mentioned none of this to Corporal Goen, who, she suspected, was at least fifteen years her junior.

"Navy, huh?" The crew chief gave a wide grin. "That's some different shit, huh, pardon my French. Marines giving you a lift somewhere instead of the other way around."

"No kidding," Moon said. "Hard to believe your commander let you fly all the way out here to get one person."

Captain Pelkey turned to look over his shoulder from the cockpit. He was hooked up to the intercom as well. "That's correct, Doc. Someone further up the chain said make it so, so we're makin' it so. Colonel Cruz wanted to come with us, but frankly we needed the weight for fuel." Pelkey returned his attention to the cockpit instruments again, but kept talking. "Your ship is right at the edge of how far we can go and get back before bingo. Wind's been kind of snarky, and with these cold temps, we're seeing as much as a five percent loss in range."

Moon nodded. "I'll bet. The speed of sound decreases with the temperature, increasing Mach drag on your rotors."

Captain Pelkey turned to look at her again. "You fly choppers in the Navy?"

"Nope," Moon said. "Sonar. Sound. It's sort of my thing."

"Still . . ." Pelkey shook his head. "Anyhoo, weather between here and Utqiagvik is marginal, but we're equipped for it. We should have you back in a little under an hour and a half. I understand there'll be a C-21 Learjet out of Eielson Air Force Base waiting to take you to Washington."

"Unbelievable," Moon said, mostly to herself, but it went across the intercom. "At least I can visit friends on Whidbey Island, I guess . . ."

"The other Washington," Pelkey said. "The one on the Potomac."

Suddenly chilled, Moon looked out the window at the passing ice as the Super Huey banked to the south. If they were going to fire her, they would have waited for *Sikuliaq* to make her next port call. No, Barker had come through and submitted her findings up his chain of command. Someone believed her theory enough to spend a considerable amount of money snatching her off the middle of the ice pack. She could not believe it. They actually wanted her expertise. Unless . . . what if she truly had stumbled on some ultra-secret operation and they were calling her in to silence her?

She'd grown up in the Arctic, a place with no snakes, but she'd seen enough of the world after leaving home to know that in Washington, D.C., there were vipers behind every rock and tree.

24

The American smelled like soap and oiled leather—like the saddle of a horse Hala's father had once set her on at the market. He spoke softly, obviously trying not to frighten her. That would be impossible, she thought. Her aunt had died saving her and now lay on the floor mere paces from the lifeless blood-drenched lumps that had once been horrible men.

He said his name was John, and that he was a friend—but nothing more. He'd saved her from Ren, but that only made him slightly less terrifying. John found some pomegranate juice in the kitchen and made her drink it, telling her the sugar would make her feel a little better. He moved quickly, looking out front a lot, like he thought someone else might be coming.

"We need to go," he said after Hala drank all her juice. "It's not safe here."

She chewed on her collar. "Where?"

"I'm not sure." He looked out the window again, then stepped to the door. "As quick as you can, wash up and change into clean clothes. Sturdy and warm."

"Clothes are clothes," she said. "Why would anyone wear clothes that were not sturdy and warm?"

"Right," the man said. "Quick as you can."

Hala began to panic when he eased open the door. "Are you leaving?"

"I'm not going anywhere without you, kiddo," John said. "But these guys had a friend outside. I need to bring him in so your neighbors don't call the police."

"But you're coming back in?"

"I promise."

"Okay." Hala gave a shuddering sigh, still chewing her collar. "I will go clean off this blood."

The idea had been to watch Hala Tohti. Clark was supposed to ascertain if there was anything about the girl that might lead to her mother's whereabouts. Observe and report. Interview Hala and her aunt if it came to that. Taking either of them had never been on the table. Getting a third party out of any part of China would be difficult enough. Xinjiang, and particularly Kashgar, had so many cameras, checkpoints, and armed patrols that leaving here with anyone would be akin to breaking them out of prison.

Clark dragged the body of the sentry into the house and dropped it in the corner beside a wooden chair. He sighed to himself.

No plan survived first contact with the enemy—which was often a boot to the nose. Things changed. The girl was coming with him, one way or another. She was as good as dead if he left her here.

The room was filled with far too much carnage to fret about the poor kid seeing more of it. He found a cloth vegetable sack in one of the cupboards and filled it with two rounds of naan bread and a shank of roast meat he thought was probably lamb.

The girl had been cooperative so far, apparently accepting the fact that she had no other choice than to come with him, considering the four dead bodies in her living room. Clark knew he could be terrifying, but this girl was incredibly resilient. Judging from her scraped knuckles and the amount of blood covering her body, she'd been smack in the middle of the violence that occurred here. She'd been trying to help her aunt cut a man's throat when he came in—and then watched Clark finish the job. No, she was tough as a boot. And it would take a whole lot more of the same if they were both going to get out of the country alive.

Hala was washed and dressed by the time Clark had dragged in the dead driver and filled the canvas sack with provisions. The wooly fake-fur ruff around the hood of her blue coat looked out of place against the scene behind her.

"I was thinking," she said. "There is an old caravanserai about twelve kilometers away from here. We can take my aunt's scooter."

"Which direction?"

Hala pointed. "Near the livestock market."

Caravanserais were the truck stops of the ancient Silk Road that connected China through Central Asia to the rest of the world. Water and food stops for man and beast. A place for weary travelers to lay their heads and worry slightly less about getting their throats cut at night by robbers wanting to take their animals and cargo.

"No one else stays there?"

"It was empty when I went there before. My father let me explore it when he took me to the livestock market. It is not far away, maybe two kilometers into the desert. The spring there has dried up, so no one goes there anymore."

Clark thought for a moment. The livestock market was RP Bravo, one of six SHTF rally points in and around Kashgar he'd prearranged with Midas, options for places to meet if things hit the proverbial fan—which they had. It was also the location of Adam Yao's in-country contact. The area would be crawling with police and soldiers—especially on a Sunday—but it also was a popular tourist destination, a place where it was said a person could find everything but the milk of a chicken. Clark counted on the crowd to be able to blend in.

"The market is on Sunday," he said. "That's tomorrow."

"It is," Hala said. "But when I saw the caravanserai it was on market day and it was filled with nothing but spiderwebs and dust."

"We can't stay here," Clark said.

"Okay," she said. "I will show you the way."

She tiptoed gingerly around one of the many pools of blood and pushed a chair up to the counter next to the small white refrigerator. Removing the lid of a large clay jar of loose tea leaves, she took out a roll of brown waxed paper and held it out to Clark. "My aunt saved some money for . . . bad times."

Clark nodded. "Emergency."

"Yes," Hala said. "I think this is emergency. No?"

"It is." Clark gently nudged the child's hand away. "But you keep it. Everyone needs to have some money of their own. Now, it's going to be cold. We should bring some blankets." He glanced around the kitchen. "And, if you don't mind, I would like to borrow a knife to take with us."

Hala pulled open the drawer below the cupboard where she'd found the money and retrieved a folding knife with a four-inch blade. A simple folded piece of steel formed a flat handle. The blade was carbon steel, with a wicked-sharp scimitar point.

The knife did not lock open, but had a hefty spring that kept it from closing on the user's hand under normal use. Clark recognized it immediately. It was not a fighting knife, as he'd hoped, but a French utility blade often found in the pockets of Legionnaires during conflicts in Algeria and Indochina. They'd generally fallen out of favor with modern Legionnaires, who now carried the wood-handled Opinel No. 08. The Opinel was more comfortable in the hand, but the older style suited Clark just fine.

It made sense. The wicked little French knife was called a douk-douk, after the Melanesian god of chaos and doom.

Hala took him a back way out of her neighborhood that skirted all but one of the police checkpoints, the last on the outskirts of town, some two kilometers from the livestock market. They had to abandon the scooter and cut through a pasture of fat sheep to get around. Clark took the registration plate off the scooter and then set it on fire before they left, hoping any identifying numbers would be destroyed. It was better that the police respond to a fire than find a bike that belonged to Hala's aunt abandoned so near the Sunday Market.

The walk to the caravanserai was relatively short, but the cumulative effects of jet lag and a near-constant flow of adrenaline left Clark dragging with exhaustion.

As usual, this caravanserai was a fortresslike affair of mud and brick built around a large courtyard where camels and goods could be brought inside while the travelers ate and slept.

An entire side had fallen in—a victim of the siege of time. There was spray-painted graffiti here and there on the remaining walls—tentative, like the artist had been in a rush, terrified of being caught. Clark couldn't read the Arabic, but it was faded and old, much of it naturally sandblasted away by the wind. A bony rat hustled from one pile of stone to another, not nearly as worried about getting caught as the graffiti painter. Peeling paint on a dusty wooden sign out front suggested that someone had once tried to turn the place into a tourist attraction. WONDERS OF THE SILK ROAD, the peeling paint read in Chinese characters and English. For whatever reason, the project had failed—leaving this particular wonder of the Silk Road long abandoned and offering Clark and Hala what appeared to be the perfect place to hide.

Any straw or animal bedding had long since turned to dust, leaving nothing but the dirt ground and the blankets they'd brought with them for beds. Clark found a spot in the back corner of an old room.

There was a vacant hole in the thick clay wall a few feet to the left of his bed—a small window, or perhaps even a gun port. He had no firearm, but he could roll out of his bed quickly and the hole gave him a viable vantage point where he could see anyone who tried to approach from the road before they saw him.

This place would do for now.

He took the secure cell phone out of his pocket. The battery was dangerously low, and there was certainly no way to charge it here. Instead of calling, he entered the code to open the encrypted text capability behind his Walk-to-Me pedometer app and thumb-typed a quick message. It would disappear ten seconds after Midas read it.

Have package. All intact. RP Bravo.

Midas would know to try to meet at 0900, 1400, and 2100 local time. Other than that, there was nothing he could do.

Clark was a planner, a strategizer, and even a gambler if the stakes were high enough, but he didn't waste much time on worry. He'd decide what to do next tomorrow, when a couple hours' rest had cleared his head.

Hala, obviously accustomed to sleeping on the floor, made a nest for herself at Clark's feet. She'd spoken only to give directions since they'd left the house, her collar always in her mouth, her arms trembling as she held on to his waist behind him on the scooter.

"Will you be warm enough?" Clark asked. He was unsure of what to say but felt like he needed to check on the poor kid before passing out himself. He wasn't completely blind to the experience of having a daughter, but was honest enough with himself to know his wife had done the lion's share of the parenting while he was traveling the world kicking ass for flag and freedom. What could he possibly say to any little girl to comfort her? That was Sandy's job.

Hala Tohti was what? Ten years old? When Patsy was that age, she had a comfortable home and a warm bedroom full of Barbie dolls and posters of boy bands. Hala's father was dead, her mother gone. Three hours ago, she'd witnessed her aunt stab one man to death in the neck and then helped her cut another man's throat with a meat cleaver—and she still had the wherewithal to think of this place to hide.

Maybe this kind of kid deserved more bedtime stories, not less.

"I am fine," she said. Her voice quivered as the events of the evening caught up with her. Nights were always the worst— for everyone. "Did you know that I am very good on the balance beam? The government even sent me to a special school."

"You must be good, then," Clark said. For some reason, her small, fragile voice in the darkness brought on him an immeasurable sadness.

"I was going to compete in the Olympics someday," she said, "but I do not think that will happen now."

Clark swallowed, having a little trouble speaking. It was odd the things that got to him lately.

Hala saved him. "May I ask a question?"

Clark rolled up on his side, resting his elbow on the ground as he peered through the dusty darkness at the lump of blankets. He swallowed again, working very hard to smooth the gravel in his voice. Many years of being John Clark had given his personality more jagged edges than he liked to admit.

"Of course," he said.

"Am I . . ." Now she sat up, looking back at him. "Am I your prisoner?"

"Oh, no, no," Clark said. "Not at all. I am going to get you to safety."

"That is what you told me at my aunt's house," the girl said, breathless, like she might get up and run at any moment. "But one can never be sure with men. They give you cake and tell you lies."

"That is true about many men," Clark said. "But not me. I am running, too." He gave a soft chuckle, hoping it would help to calm her. "And I have no cake."

"And no lies?" Stone sober now.

"No lies," Clark said. "We're in this together."

She sighed and lay back down. "The Bingtuan have eyes everywhere. How will we get away?"

"Truthfully," Clark said, "I'm not sure. But we'll meet my friend tomorrow. We can decide what to do then. You should get some rest if you can."

"Okay," she said in the darkness. He could tell she was sucking on her shirt collar again. Poor kid.

Clark pulled the blanket up over his shoulder. He was so exhausted he figured he might even get two or three hours' sleep on the uneven dirt floor before he woke up with his old bones half crippled.

Somewhere in the darkness, the tiny claws of a rat clicked across the dusty floor. The room smelled of a thousand years of camel dung and far more recent rodent urine, leaving Clark to wonder what kind of biblical plagues he might breathe in while he slept. He shrugged away the thought and rested his head on his outstretched arm. It didn't matter. Considering the present situation, a plague wasn't what would kill him.

25

CIA case officer Leigh Murphy ended the call from Adam Yao and leaned back in her chair to work out a plan for her getaway. Dunny blond hair hung just above smallish shoulders. There was some curl to it, but not enough to get her noticed. Now, throw on an LBD—little black dress—instead of her usual faded jeans and loose hooded sweatshirt, dab a little makeup around her green eyes, and she could get herself noticed, all right. She'd learned early in life how to, as her mother put it, "turn her wiggle off and on." A good skill to have as an intelligence officer.

Fredrick Rask, the station chief, slouched in his office. The mini-blinds were up on his window, and he watched the bullpen intently, homing in on her. Rask must have sensed she was up to something. He licked his chops like a male lion waiting for the lioness to go out and hunt because he was too lazy to get off his own fat ass and kill something. That was Fredrick Rask's specialty—benefitting through the efforts of others.

Murphy scribbled the address Adam Yao had given her on a piece of scratch paper and stuffed it into her pocket while she thought through a couple of possible approaches. It was going to be touchy, talking to this particular guy—but that was her strength. Besides, Albania had been on her dream sheet of posts from the beginning, and Adam Yao had helped her get here. She owed him. A lot.

She'd known Adam since Kenya, her first foreign posting after graduating from CIA's Career Training Program and Camp Peary, or The Farm—the facility officially referred to as an Armed Forces Experimental Training Activity. Yao had come up with a lead on a Chinese businessman smuggling a shipment of tramadol from Guangzhou to Mombasa via private charter. Dope smugglers, as deplorable as they were, didn't exactly fall into a CIA case officer's wheelhouse—except this particular load of dope was being smuggled by the son of a Chinese People's Liberation Army general in Guangzhou. The PLA, or at least high-ranking members of it, appeared to be behind the operation—and that information could fill in some big puzzle pieces for the analysts at Langley and Liberty Crossing.

Murphy was fresh to the field then, but she'd been identified by her station chief as a rising star—able to read and recruit assets, from the Chinese ambassador's Kenyan housekeeper to a major in the National Police Service. With the help of Murphy's contacts, Yao tipped the correct dominos to get them all falling in just the right order. In the end, they seized over a hundred pounds of a fentanyl analogue known as China White—worth almost two million dollars—and five peach crates containing seven hundred and fifty thousand tablets of the synthetic opiate tramadol. The fentanyl would have ended up in relatively affluent cities like Nairobi or Johannesburg, where at least some of the population could afford heroin. Slums along the East Africa coast provided outlets for the tramadol. No one involved was under the mistaken impression that they'd suddenly won a drug war—but they'd won this battle, and maybe, just maybe, the tide was held back for a week or two before some other group filled the void in the marketplace. At the very least, they took several million dollars out of the pockets of evil men—while gaining useful intelligence about the PLA's activities in East Africa.

The Guangzhou general's son went to prison, and, thanks to Leigh Murphy's stable of assets in-country, so did a sizable criminal outfit whose operation spanned from Nairobi to Mauritius to Cape Town. Yao added the information he gleaned from the general's son to his intelligence file, but the CIA didn't take credit for busting a narcotics ring, even one that large. The U.S. Drug Enforcement Administration had a robust presence during the operation from the beginning, and they, along with the National Police Service, got the headlines.

Leigh Murphy and Yao had slipped away from the limelight—like good intelligence officers do—and celebrated over a plate of *nyama choma*—in this case, traditional grilled goat—at a quiet bar in the upscale Nairobi neighborhood of Kilimani. The light was low, the afterglow mixed with the slight buzz from her third Tusker lager. Stupidly, like some giddy schoolgirl with a crush, she'd looked into his eyes across the table and tapped the neck of her beer to his.

"*Bia yangu, nchi yangu.*"

He was impressed that she spoke Kiswahili, but she admitted that it was written on the Tusker bottle—*My beer, my country.*

It just sounded cool.

They spent two days together, debriefing . . . and whatnot. The romantic part of the equation never seemed to work out. Both were still working on their careers. Prohibitions against dipping your pen in company ink weren't the problem. Agency relationships made for a tighter circle of trust. Long-distance relationships sucked, though, and could take an operative's mind off the game. Neither of them wanted that. So Adam Yao had slipped back into his secret life of a NOC—no official cover—operative somewhere in Asia—he'd never even told her exactly what his cover was. It was safer that way for both of them. They kept in touch, and Yao had become her behind-the-scenes unofficial mentor and confidant. When it was time for Murphy to have a new posting, he put in a good word with his boss, who talked to her boss, who got her posted to Tirana.

She'd do anything for him, even this. She just needed to figure out how to do it without pissing off her chief—or, worse, doing something to cause an incident and making the papers by pulling back the sugar coating of the Albania she loved.

On the outside, the country was a wonderland, gorgeous mountains, delicious food, friendly people, not to mention the Adriatic, but there was a hidden underbelly—a bad spot on the melon—that required a delicate touch.

Albania—Shqiperia, to the locals—was an incredible place to be a young intelligence officer. *Korrieri*, one of the country's now defunct newspapers, had once run the headline during an American state visit—PLEASE OCCUPY US! Americans might have a difficult time finding Albania on a map, but people from the Land of the Eagles loved all things red, white, and blue—and made no bones about telling the world how they felt. The Albanian ambassador to the United States had once written an opinion piece in *The Washington Times* that said, among other things, "If you believe in freedom, you believe in fighting for it, and if you believe in fighting for freedom, you believe in the United States."

But Langley didn't send her here for the love and good feeling. She was interested in seedier stuff. If she was going to play patty-cake with America-lovers, they had to know something important about people who didn't feel the same way.

Some experts denied the existence of a true Albanian Mafia, but those paying for protection, or being trafficked by one of the Fifteen Families, likely thought otherwise. These families controlled organized and unorganized crime all over the country. Drugs, human trafficking, and, of particular interest to Leigh Murphy, military arms sales simply did not happen in Albania without at least one of the Fifteen having a hand in the pot.

And then there was *gjakmarrja*. Albanians had made the blood feud an art form. The philosophy of a head for a head was part of the social code or canon of twelve books known as the Kanun. Revenge was deeply ingrained in Albanian society, with *gjakmarrja* vendettas passing from generation to generation.

Still, even an asshole station chief, blood feuds, and Fifteen Family hit men who were often more disciplined and brutal than the Russian Mob—the good outweighed the bad. For Leigh Murphy, it was more of a calling than a job post.

Chief Rask made it out of his office on his gouty legs about the time she stood up.

"You know how I feel about lone meetings," he said. "Grab Joey or Vlora to go with you."

Two other case officers looked up from their respective desks in the bullpen, deadpan, clearly not wanting to get involved with more of Rask's BS. Joey was a kiss-ass, but he was almost as lazy as Rask and didn't feel the need to overwork himself tagging along on some meeting that was probably bullshit—like ninety percent of them were.

Murphy remained stone-faced. "Who said I was going on a meeting?"

"We read people," Rask said. "It's literally part of the job description."

"Well, Chief, you misread. Just going to get a haircut."

There was no set of circumstances where she wanted the station chief sticking his nose in this interview before she was done. She told Adam as much and he'd agreed. Besides, Rask would break into a wicked-gross mental fit if he got wind that she'd just been on the phone with a well-respected senior intelligence officer in the Agency—one who cared about the people he worked with and didn't use their backs as rungs on his career ladder. Rask didn't like other lions sniffing around his pride.

He sneered, licking his lips. Maybe he didn't believe her, or maybe he felt deprived of the meat he'd expected when he saw her on the phone. Langley wanted frequent results. How was he supposed to kick intel up the line to make himself look good if his chief hunting lioness worried more about her personal grooming than making a kill?

He screwed up his face like he was about to sneeze. Murphy wasn't sure he even knew he was doing it. The man wore his emotions like a neon sign. The polygraphers surely had a good old time with him.

"You sure you're just getting a haircut?"

The rusty adage of not being able to kid a kidder applied doubly to a liar. But then, lying to a liar was CIA tradecraft 101.

She thought of popping off to him, something like *"You can try and follow me if you want . . . oh, I forgot, you haven't run a surveillance op in ten years . . ."* but a smartass attitude would only give him some juice to write her up on come performance evaluation time. It was her job to work people. Might as well start with her boss.

She gave him her most benign smile. "Yep, just a haircut, Chief." He relished it when subordinates called him that. She looked at her watch, then grabbed a tweed sport jacket from the back of her chair and put it on over the sweatshirt, adjusting the hood so it draped over her collar in back. Her mom back in Boston would have called the outfit a Fall River Tuxedo. "I came in early, and I've got scads of comp time."

Rask waved a hand in the air over his shoulder, already shuffling back to his office. "Better be logged."

Murphy took the Glock 43 and inside-the-pants holster from her lap drawer and shoved it down the waistband of her jeans, over the small of her back. Her dad, a Boston PD detective, had always said that God made that little hollow in a person's back just the right size to carry a .45. He was a big guy, and could get away with carrying a big gun. Just under five-five, she stuck with the baby Glock nine-millimeter. Single-stack, the pistol carried only six in the mag and one in the pipe, but she was a case officer, not some ground branch operator. If she had to resort to her sidearm, things had gone terribly wrong.

She paused, turning to grab a spare magazine from her desk before Rask made it to his desk and turned around again. Wouldn't hurt to go in prepared.

Adam Yao had asked her to interview Urkesh Beg, a Uyghur man who until recently had been held as an enemy combatant at a CIA black site—off the grid and away from the rules of the U.S. justice system. He was released when a military tribunal determined that although he was likely in Afghanistan, training with known terrorists, he was no longer an enemy combatant against the United States. Due to the rules of engagement, Beg's association, and proximity to, known terrorists meant that U.S. forces could have put a warhead on his forehead if they'd hit the terrorist training camp with a couple of Hellfire missiles, but after holding him for four and a half years, decided they were not inclined to keep him in custody indefinitely.

Albania had offered Beg refugee status as a favor to the United States. As far as Yao knew, he'd kept his affiliation with the East Turkestan Islamic Movement, technically still on the terrorism watch list. There was a good chance that if he smelled anything remotely CIA or U.S. government about Murphy, he might not be all that pleased to see her.

Joey Shoop got the summoning whistle from Rask the moment the door swung shut behind Murphy. Shoop stood quickly—that's what you did when the boss called—and tucked the errant tail of his peach oxford button-down into his pants. As much of a slob as the chief was, he liked his troops to look tidy. Vlora cocked her head to one side and looked down her nose at him. She spoke fluent Albanian and lorded it over everyone in the office. She touched her finger to her nose.

"Got a little hanger-on there, Joey."

Shoop knew she was just messing with him, but he wiped his nose just in case on the way to Rask's office.

The chief was staring at his computer screen, working on some memo. "Go after her," he said.

"To her haircut?"

"She's not getting a haircut," Rask said. "Go."

"Right," Shoop said. "I'll have her back."

Now Rask looked up. "I want you to follow her. In your car. Let me know where she goes."

"You got it," Shoop said.

Rask raised both hands, palms up. "Unless you got a tracker on her car, you'd better get on after it."

Shoop grabbed his jacket and left at a trot, hitting the door at the same time Rask called Vlora into his office—probably to keep her from ratting them out.

Murphy turned north out of embassy parking, heading for downtown. It seemed like every other car on the road in Tirana was gray or white, and many of those were Mercedes sedans. Murphy's little Ford Fiesta melted into the background.

She crossed the Lana like she might be going to the city center, but then turned left, paralleling the river. Maybe she was just running a surveillance-detection route, crossing the river before she worked her way back to Blloku, just ahead on her right. It made sense. There were lots of high-end boutiques and shops there. Under Soviet rule, only Party elite were even allowed in "the Block." Now it was the place to go to watch the upper crust of Tirana do their thing. The grim influence of the less-than-halcyon days of Soviet rule had long since been painted over with a riot of reds and yellows and blues. The architecture still resembled large boxes that more attractive buildings must have come in, but now, instead of dull gray cubes, multicolored blocks in the shadow of Mount Dajti lined streets named after U.S. presidents and packed with Mercedes-Benz sedans.

But Murphy didn't turn until she reached the middle ring

road, cutting north now, passing the embassies of Greece and Great Britain as she skirted downtown. She arced to her right, continuing east until she reached the Mother Teresa, at which point she turned right again on Rruga Bardhyl, generally going back toward the office.

Shoop pounded the steering wheel of his Taurus. Did she know he was following her? She was stopping at all the lights, wasn't doubling back on herself, getting on and off a highway, or any of the usual countersurveillance-run maneuvers. She was barely even maintaining the speed limit. Shoop had to ride the brakes to keep from overtaking her. They were doing the same damn route again. When was she going to turn?

He stayed in the shadow of three other cars and a large delivery van with a picture on the side of what looked like the Albanian version of the Three Stooges.

They'd just taken the roundabout past the British consulate, heading east—again—when a silver Mercedes S 500 pulled alongside the Taurus at the same time the delivery van slowed. Boxed in, Shoop tapped his brake. He lost sight of Leigh Murphy for a grand total of six seconds—but when the van pulled forward and gave him enough room to squirt around in front of the Mercedes, the little gray Ford was nowhere to be seen.

Shoop's stomach fell. He smacked the steering wheel again, cursing, craning his head back and forth, searching a sea of gray sedans for *the* gray sedan he was after. He thought he saw it, a gray Ford beneath a scraggly elm tree, pocked with early spring buds—but a fat man got out.

"Think!" Shoop chided himself.

A concrete median divided the boulevard, so she must have taken one of the two streets to the right. No way she had enough time to make it to the next cross street. Had she?

Shoop would have seen her if she'd taken the first right, so he turned down the second right, trying to put himself in Murphy's shoes.

He didn't know where she was going, but it sure as hell wasn't to get a haircut.

26

Leigh Murphy took the first left after the roundabout, working her way through the narrow streets and double-parked cars in front of a mix of boxy apartment buildings and back-street shops that sold everything from pastries to truck tires. Zoning appeared to be an afterthought here. Sides of beef or mutton might hang in a butcher's window next to an engine repair shop. Mehmet Akif High School for Boys was just over a block from Prison 313, a windowless fortress of brick, chipped concrete, and concertina wire.

Urkesh Beg lived between the school and the prison, in a tired-looking concrete six-story apartment building surrounded by a mote of gravelly alleys and a spooky overgrown lot that had once been paved but was probably rubble when the Russkies ruled Albania. An overpowering smell of garbage hung in the chilly air. The little ditch next to where Murphy parked gurgled merrily along with what she felt reasonably sure was sewage. A tumbledown brick wall—the kind where gobs of mortar look mashed from between each brick like the layer cake of an overzealous baker—ran along the street. In the shadow of the wall, an eight-by-eight block shed with a rusted tin roof sat tucked into the scrub brush. Murphy found herself wishing she'd parked farther away—or even on the other side of the apartment building. This place looked like a private stockade, or the cottage belonging to a resident witch. Either way, it creeped her out and she sped up, ready to deal with a disgruntled Uyghur.

He was smaller than she'd expected him to be. She'd looked up his photo while on the phone with Adam, and seen his descriptors. This guy might have been five nine, a hundred and seventy pounds at some point, but not anymore. Life had pounded him down good and hard, bending him where people were not meant to bend and shaving pounds and surely years off his life.

Murphy didn't speak Uyghur or Chinese, so she greeted him in Arabic.

"As-salamu alaikum."

He eyed her warily, bent as if he might topple forward at the slightest breath or misstep.

"Wa alaikumu as-salam," he said.

He spoke English, haltingly, but assured her that he understood it very well from his time in U.S. custody.

Murphy introduced herself as a member of an NGO that was working to reunite Uyghur refugees with their children. To her surprise, he invited her in immediately.

"Come, come," he said, raking the air with a cupped hand. "Please. I make you tea."

He lived alone, with no family and few hobbies, from the looks of the sparse interior of the shabby but clean apartment. His nails were long, his hair unkempt. His only friends appeared to be the neat stacks of books and magazines in Arabic script and English stacked in various spots around the living area. Murphy noted just a few of the English titles—*A Raisin in the Sun, 1984, The Invisible Man,* assorted Kafka . . . A well-worn copy of *To Kill a Mockingbird* sat open and facedown next to a mug of tea on a small table beside a sagging easy chair, as if he'd been up to the business of reading it when she'd knocked on his door. Not exactly books she'd expected to see in a Uyghur refugee's home in the suburbs of Albania, but there was definitely a theme. You could get only so much by reading a person's file.

He brought her tea and then retrieved his own, using a strip of white paper to mark his spot before reverently closing *To Kill a Mockingbird* and setting it gently on the table. Sitting across from Murphy, he told her that he was sorry but he could not help because he had no children to be reunited with. Where an American or European man might bawdily joke that he had no children "that he knew of," Urkesh Beg looked at her soberly and left it at the apologetic denial.

Murphy learned early—likely well before The Farm—that a lie was easier to swallow when buttered with some truth. She set her teacup on her knees and bent forward, trying to make herself seem as small and unthreatening as possible. "Mr. Beg," she said. "I am here on a very delicate matter. There are members of certain . . . shall we say . . . groups that China has deemed . . . outside the law—"

Beg's countenance fell dark at the mention of China.

Murphy held up her free hand. "Please understand, I am in no way connected to the Chinese government. On the contrary, I do not even represent the American government."

"That is good," Beg said. "Because I hate the U.S. only a little less than I hate the Chinese government."

Murphy had read the man's file. She felt the urge to explain that although there was no question that the Uyghur people had been severely mistreated, it was no small thing to align oneself with Taliban forces, even for training, and then fire toward U.S. troops. Urkesh Beg was, in point of fact, fortunate to be upright and still breathing. Still, criminals in the United States did less time than he had for a hell of a lot worse. It wasn't Leigh Murphy's job to prove to him how right the United States was or was not in detaining him for so long. She needed to find out what he knew.

She took a contemplative sip of tea, letting the silence sink in before beginning. "The people I work with represent separated children, not nations. Unfortunately, members of the groups I'm talking to you about do not contact authorities regarding the location and fate of their little ones because they are afraid the Chinese government—"

Beg scoffed. "Or the U.S."

"Or whomever," Murphy continued. "Parents aligned with groups operating on the edges of the law fear making contact, leaving my organization with no way to find extended family for the children in our care—many of whom are too young to communicate with us."

"Maybe you give me names of the people you are looking for," Beg said. "I am not part of all this you speak of, but I know people who know."

"I have a list at my office," she said. "Perhaps we can meet tomorrow or the next day and speak in more detail. I do remember several of the smaller children had family members in the ETIM . . ." Murphy listed two other known Uyghur groups before bringing it home. Yao had been vague about why he was looking for Medina Tohti, but did mention she had a daughter. Murphy flipped the script on the details but kept the issue of parent and child the same. ". . . at least one, a three-year-old boy, if I am correct, has a father who is part of . . . I'm not sure I'm saying it correctly, the Wuming group."

Beg shook his head emphatically, lips pursed, a child refusing to eat his oatmeal. He took two slow, deep breaths before saying, "Wuming?" His hand trembled as he took a sip of tea. "*Wuming* means nameless. Nobody."

"Anonymous?" Murphy offered. If this man was reading *A Raisin in the Sun* and George Orwell, he had a decent vocabulary.

"Yes," Beg said. "Anonymous. Maybe other groups do things and Wuming gets the blame."

"Or the credit," Murphy said. "The Chinese believe they are behind several killings." She put her hand to her chest now, over her heart. "This boy I spoke of, he believes his father is Wuming. I hope they are real. Someone needs to fight the Chinese oppression."

Beg leaned back in his chair, eyeing her carefully. "Do you know of *Baihua Qifang?*"

Murphy thought for a moment, then shook her head. "I don't recognize it."

"The Hundred Flowers Campaign," Beg said. "Decades ago, Mao allowed open criticism of the Communist government. 'Let a hundred flowers bloom and a hundred differing thoughts contend.' A Chinese poem." Beg turned up his nose. "Far inferior to Uyghur verse."

He was certainly finding his vocabulary now.

"I have heard of the Hundred Flowers Campaign," Murphy said. "It did not go well."

"It did not," Beg said. "Some say it started with good intentions, but I think Mao told everyone to speak the truth of how they disagreed with him so he could kill them or put them in prison later."

"Fair assessment," Murphy said. "But what does that have to do with us?"

"You come to my house, telling me you are happy with crimes committed against Han Chinese military and police. You think this will make me agree with you and get me in trouble."

"I told you," Murphy said. "I represent no specific country, but I am obviously not Chinese."

Beg gave a derisive laugh. "You Americans believe only people who look Chinese help Beijing. China has lots of money. Americans who look like you help China, Africans help China, even some greedy Uyghur work for China against other Uyghur. I told you, I am not a part of any organization you are asking about and I have no children." He stood. "There are Uyghur families in many free countries who I imagine would happily raise these children. I think you should go and use your time to contact them."

"I will," Murphy said, getting to her feet. The fire in Urkesh Beg's eyes made her grateful for the weight of the little Glock in her waistband. "But I would still like to try and place the children with family if possible. You said you know people who might know. This little boy who says his father is Wuming is so—"

"Wuming is no one. Little children's stories, yes, but that is all. Wuming is just story."

Murphy bit her bottom lip, making her chin quiver. She could not only turn her wiggle off and on, but the waterworks as well. "Honestly," she said, sniffing for effect. "Hundred

Flowers Campaign be damned. Think whatever you want. Whoever is doing these things, Wuming or whatever they are called . . . Who could blame them? There are evil people out there, taking children from parents, husbands from wives . . . I worry about the children, but you're probably right. It would be better to place them with unrelated Uyghur families. Chinese authorities are relentless. They will eventually find and imprison everyone who even thinks a separatist thought, even the Wuming."

"I will tell you this much," Beg said, growing animated. "If Wuming was real, no stupid Han Chinese soldier would be able to find them. Wuming is shapeless. No . . . how do you say it? Formless. Wuming can never be caught. They would never preach. Never say a bad word against China. Never talk aloud of a free East Turkestan. He shook his head again, snorting, almost a chuckle. "Wuming is no one, but could be anyone. So many borders, they will never be found. They don't speak of what they must do, they do what they must. If anyone looks, they will only disappear into wilderness like fox or melt back into the fabric of regular folk."

"I understand," Murphy said. "Do you have a mobile?"

Beg looked around his modest apartment and gave a wan smile. "A phone is expensive," he said. "And I have no one to call."

"I'll check back tomorrow or the next day," she said.

"As you wish," Beg said. "But I doubt I can help."

She said her good-byes and left a card with a hello-phone callback number—the voicemail gave an extension, not a business name. Pondering what a colossal dead end this had proven to be, she rounded the brick wall on the way back to her car and nearly jumped out of her skin when Joey Shoop stepped from behind the creepy witch's cottage.

"Nice haircut," he said.

"Hey," she said, trying to remain nonchalant.

"Hey, my ass," Shoop said and sneered. "I about smacked into a meat truck trying to find you. What's with trying to lose me back there?"

"I wasn't trying to lose you, nimrod." She wagged her head. "I was running this little thing we do in intelligence work called a surveillance-detection route. Maybe you've heard of them."

Shoop just stood there, glaring at her. "Rask was right to wonder about you. You got something going on, don't you?"

"You're an idiot, Joey. You want to hear him yell at me, I'm going back to the office to type up a report now." She gave him a disdainful shrug. "I guess you're welcome to follow me if you think you can keep up."

27

Adam Yao was running out of options. Two days of interviews and meetings hadn't got him any closer to finding Medina Tohti. Leigh Murphy had come up dry as well. The Usenovs were his last shot.

Adam Yao arrived unannounced, but that did not matter. Kambar Usenov answered the door, heard Yao say he was a journalist from Taiwan who had a few questions, and waved him inside out of the chill. Russian was the lingua franca of Kazakhstan, but the Usenovs were Oralman—literally "returnees" who had come back to their ethnic roots after living for generations in another country. Kambar and Aisulu Usenov had fled Xinjiang, so their first language was Mandarin— making Yao's job much easier. His Russian was halting at best, but he spoke Chinese like a native—which at first appeared to put Usenov on edge, until Yao showed him the Taiwanese journalist credentials. Usenov, a bear of a man with a slight limp, gripped Yao's hand firmly with both of his. He peered into Yao's eyes for just long enough to make Yao think he might have to pull away.

At length, Usenov gave a satisfied grunt and let go, welcoming Yao into his home as if he was a long-lost relative. Mrs.

Usenov set a third plate at the low table situated on the colorful Asian rug in the middle of the Usenovs' main room. She was a quiet Kazakh woman with flour on her dress and a light blue scarf tied above a handsome oval face. She wore little makeup, but a thin black pencil line connected her dark eyebrows. Yao had seen it many times before on women in Central Asia.

Mrs. Usenov shuffled back and forth from the kitchen, bringing tray after tray of noodles, boiled meat, and fried bread, as if they'd been expecting company.

Kambar put Yao where he normally sat, at the head of the table—a place of honor for the guest. He waved a wind-chapped hand over the top of the feast his wife was busy bringing in.

"We went to a cousin's wedding," he said in Mandarin. "My cousin's wife, she makes the best *beshbarmak* I have ever tasted." He smiled, high cheekbones squinting his eyes. "Except for my wife, Aisulu, of course. She is a most excellent cook."

CIA case officers received language and culture training before heading off to any long-term posting, but most colloquialism and nuance could be learned only firsthand. After ten minutes at the Usenovs' table, stuffing himself with *beshbarmak*—literally "five fingers," because that's the way the mixture of noodles, boiled horse, and onion was eaten—Yao realized no instructor had ever covered the dangers of too much hospitality.

He took a drink of *kumis*—fermented mare's milk—and got down to business.

"Forgive me for being forward," he said. "But I understand you and your wife were in a Chinese detention center in Baijiantan."

Aisulu leaned forward, grease dripping off her fingers from the *beshbarmak*. "Someone reported that Kambar was studying

Russian. The authorities said that meant we were thinking about leaving China, so they put us in a camp to remind us that the grass is not greener in Kazakhstan."

Kambar shrugged. "If I am being honest, we were studying Russian so we could leave. Kazakhstan is the best country in the world. No offense meant to Taiwan."

"What business is that of theirs if we leave China?" his wife snapped. "We are Kazakh. We should be able to come home if we wish."

"I agree with you," Yao said. "If I may ask, were you treated harshly in Baijiantan?"

"We were fed," Kambar said. "Our heads were shaved and I was separated from my wife. We attended many classes, sang songs about the Motherland, told we should love and respect President Zhao, things of that nature. I was not beaten, if that is what you mean, but I saw it happen many times."

Mrs. Usenov covered her mouth with an open hand as she chewed a large bite of fried dough. She swallowed. "Same for me. But you do not have to be beaten to be mistreated . . ."

"I am sure," Yao said. "I would like to return to the conditions inside at another time, perhaps when we are not in the middle of such a delicious meal."

Kambar looked heavenward while he chewed, remembering. "Though they never beat me, it was the worst time of my life. One day, after two months, they let us go. It took two days, but I was eventually reunited with Aisulu. She was so frail and gaunt, and both of us had terrible coughs—everyone in the camps did."

"But they came back," Yao prompted. "The Chinese authorities, and arrested you again?"

Usenov nodded, heaving a great sigh. "I have no idea why.

Maybe they needed more numbers for their quota. Maybe they felt they were in error letting us go the first time."

"But you escaped?"

Mrs. Usenov rocked back and forth on her cushion, excited at the memory. "Kambar and I were in the back of the same van. The van stopped so quickly it threw us all forward. We heard shouting, then gunfire—and then the van began to move again. We drove for a long time, hours maybe. I fell asleep so I do not know."

"I, too, slept," Mr. Usenov said, nodding for his wife to continue the story.

"I felt my ears begin to pop, so I knew we were going up into the mountains. I thought maybe they were taking us far away to kill us, but one of the other men said that the Chinese were in charge. If they wanted to kill us, they would not have to drive out of their way to do it. Finally, the van stopped and the doors opened. A man in dark clothing motioned us out, unlocked our shackles, and pointed us toward the Kazakh border."

"Who rescued you?"

"They wore hoods," Usenov said. "They did not say it, but I believe they were Wuming."

"Wuming." Yao took another drink of fermented mare's milk.

"You have heard of them?" Mrs. Usenov asked. "They are angels, I think. Allah's helpers here on earth. Most in the van had thought to grab a blanket or put on a coat. Kambar made sure I had a jacket, but the policeman dragged him out before he could retrieve his own. It was bitter cold, snowing, and Kambar was in his shirtsleeves. One of the Wuming saw this and gave my husband his coat."

"I would love to interview a member of the Wuming," Yao said.

Mrs. Usenov exhaled softly. "I do not know how that would happen. Surely that would be much too dangerous for them. The Chinese government would kill them all if they could."

"That's true." Yao shrugged. "They sound like incredibly good people, giving you their own coat."

"I still have it," Usenov said proudly. "It is the best coat I have ever owned." He scrambled to his feet, belying his age. "I will show you."

Yao wiped his hands with a towel Mrs. Usenov gave him and stood, stepping back from the low table to look at the puffy down ski jacket Kambar Usenov brought out from the bedroom.

"Very nice." Yao opened it to read the tag, knowing he wouldn't find a name, but checking nonetheless.

Usenov reached into the pocket and showed him something almost as good.

Yao called Leigh Murphy on his secure mobile.

Excited at the prospect of a lead, he began to speak as soon as she picked up. "Tell me again what Beg said about the woods."

"Hello to you, too," Murphy said. "You must have something."

"Maybe," Yao said. "So go over Beg's statement again. The part about the Wuming disappearing."

"He said they would disappear into the forest, that they could slip over many borders to escape—if they exist at all. Why, what do you have?"

"Not sure," Yao said. "Maybe nothing. There were some ticket stubs in the pocket of a coat that may have come from a member of the Wuming. They're only partial stubs, but they're for a boat tour. It's something about a monster fish."

"Lake Kanas?" Murphy said.

"It's not on the ticket, but I assume the boat tour could be on a lake."

"The tickets are Chinese, right?" Murphy asked.

"Correct."

"Then Kanas Lake makes sense," Murphy said. "They have their own version of the Loch Ness Monster." She paused.

"You still there?" Yao asked.

"Yup. Just checking a map. This looks promising, Adam. Lake Kanas is north of Urumqi, tucked into a little thumb of land that is surrounded by Kazakhstan, Russia, and Mongolia . . . It's extremely rural, with many borders over which to escape— and lots of forest—just like Urkesh Beg said."

"That's thin," Yao said. "But it's a hell of a lot more than I had an hour ago. I appreciate this."

"No prob," Murphy said. "When are you coming to Albania so I can show you around? We need somebody with a brain to be our station chief. Rask chewed my ass for interviewing Beg without his blessing. I told him I wasn't allowed to tell him who asked me, which really pissed him off."

"Sorry about that," Yao said. "I'll make a couple of calls and get you top cover. In the meantime, don't mention the Lake Kanas connection to anyone. Okay?"

"You got it, Chief."

"Don't," Adam said and chuckled. "I'm not chief material."

"Don't be a stranger," Murphy said. "It's hard to find good friends."

"In this outfit?"

Murphy sighed. "Anywhere, Adam."

———

C IA Station Chief Fredrick Rask hunched over his keyboard, fuming, fingers blazing as he typed a cable. No, this could not be allowed to stand. Leigh Murphy was forgetting her place in the food chain.

A mentor had once told him to get up and go to the restroom before sending a cable or e-mail when you were angry. Good advice, to be sure, if you wanted to be civil, but Rask wanted a piece of somebody's ass. He was either the station chief or he wasn't. No one had the right to run an op on his turf without at least letting him know. And he'd be damned if he was going to let some secret-squirrel shithead from Langley sneak into his bailiwick and task one of his case officers without asking his permission. Not to mention the task in question was to chat up the former U.S. detainee about his continued association with Uyghur separatists. The guy had already been interrogated for four and a half years. This kind of shit had the propensity to blow up in your face. The media, Congress, his bosses in D.C.—they'd be all over him if they found out one of his people was harassing a guy they'd let go.

Someone at HQ needed to know about this—if only so Rask could cover his own ass from the blowback. He fired off the cable, making his boss aware of the situation, and then leaned back and sent a copy to his buddy on the Central Asia desk. If someone was poking around looking for Uyghur separatists, he'd want to know.

28

An hour into the seven-hour flight on the C-21A, the U.S. military's version of the Bombardier Learjet 35, Dr. Patti Moon decided this kind of luxury was something she could become used to. They made a short stop to refuel at an FBO in Calgary, Alberta, and then continued direct from there to Washington Reagan. She had the plane to herself—just her and a couple of hotshot pilots who liked to practice near-vertical takeoffs and then explain how the Lear was really a fighter jet in a suit and tie. And anyway, somebody up the chain wanted her in D.C. ASAP, the pilots said, so they were told by their bosses not to spare the horses.

The closer they got to D.C., the more fretful she became. The whole suit-and-tie thing didn't help. Moon's mother, an extremely devout and weekly attendee of the Tikigaq Bible Baptist Church in Point Hope, had drummed into her from an early age that the devil would not be dressed in rags when he came to tempt her. He would, in fact, be dressed in fine furs . . . or even a suit and tie.

She'd worked herself into a lather by the time the little jet lined up left of the Potomac River and settled into a grease-smooth landing at Washington Reagan.

To make matters worse, the tall man in Navy khakis who met her in the lobby of Signature Flight Support at the south end of the airport introduced himself as Commander Robbie Forestall, a national security adviser to the President of the United States.

Navy habits abided long, and she very nearly introduced herself as Petty Officer First Class Moon. She caught herself, shook the commander's hand, and then stepped back and let him lead the way. A meeting with the national security adviser . . . That was going to be weird. Still, Moon supposed she'd asked for it by asking Barker to push the recording up the chain.

The Marine helicopter had picked her up at breakfast, and the entire trip had been relatively short, but the time difference between Alaska and the East Coast meant it was already well into the evening by the time Commander Forestall showed Moon to a black Lincoln Town Car. He gave her a bottle of water and offered to help her with her bag, but she refused and held it on her lap instead.

Traffic on George Washington Memorial was a steady flow of red lights and headlights—a shock to Moon's system after the high lonesome solitude of the far north where she spent much of her life. The ice floe was dispassionate and could crack loud as a gunshot, but there was silence there, too, and, when the sky was clear, the bowl of stars and aurora brought peace to Moon's ever-wary soul.

D.C. had the opposite effect. On steroids. Being plunked down here in the middle of a rat race made her chest tight to the point she thought she might be having a heart attack. By the time Forestall took the 14th Street Bridge across the Potomac into D.C. proper, Moon resolved that she would attend her little meetings, answer some bureaucrat's questions, and then haul her ass out of here as fast as she could.

Then Independence Avenue and the National Mall appeared in the windshield and she began to wonder where they were going. Her theory had gone up through Navy channels, so she'd figured they'd put her up somewhere in Crystal City. There were some damned fine hotels there that gave the government rate and were always crawling with service members from all branches that had business at the Pentagon. *Must all be full*, she thought.

"What hotel am I at?"

"I'm not a hundred percent sure," the commander said, easy and honest, like they were old friends. "I'm thinking they have you at the Willard. It's just a block away, but I'll drive you over. It's no problem at all."

Moon had read somewhere about the Willard, but couldn't place it.

"A block away from what?"

"The White House," Forestall said. "That's where your meeting's at."

Moon leaned forward, craning her neck over the front seat. "Wait, wait, wait. Commander, are you telling me that the national security adviser wants to meet with me at the White House about the noises I recorded under the ice?"

Forestall gave her a wry smile. "Not exactly."

"Whew," Moon said. "Because that would have given me a stroke."

The commander laughed out loud. "I am so sorry," he said. "Your meeting isn't with the national security adviser. I thought you already knew . . ."

———

J ack Ryan had just walked into the Oval from the colonnade, still wearing his black Orioles baseball jacket against the evening chill, when Commander Forestall entered from the secretaries' suite. Arnie van Damm, Mary Pat Foley, SecDef Bob Burgess, and Admiral Talbot, chief of naval operations, were already present.

Dr. Moon was not.

Ryan raised his hands, palms up, shooting a glance at Forestall. "Did she escape?"

"I apologize, Mr. President," the commander said. "I have her signed in and set up with a visitor's badge, but she insisted on calling her father before coming in. She's standing outside the entrance by the press briefing room to make the call. Millie from Secret Service Uniform Division has an eye on her, but giving her space."

Ryan sat down beside his desk.

He'd already been to the Residence and grabbed a quick dinner with Cathy—crab salad with quinoa that was tasty enough but left him craving crab cakes from Chick & Ruth's in Annapolis. He'd changed out of his suit, thinking that since Dr. Moon was coming straight off a plane, she'd be more relaxed if he were dressed in jeans and an open-collared shirt.

"I'm really sorry, sir," Forestall said. "She was very insistent."

"It's not your fault, Robbie." Ryan waved off the apology, resting his elbows on the desk, looking glum as a schoolboy benched during a ballgame. "At our level, you get used to people waiting on you instead of the other way around."

Forestall chuckled. "Our level, Mr. President?"

"You know what I mean," Ryan said. "In charge of things."

Van Damm crossed to the door. "I'll go get her."

"Give her a second," Ryan said. "Everyone processes these meetings differently. What we have here before us, as my dad used to say, is the opportunity not to be assholes. He held leaders to a high standard, my old man. You were either a good leader or a bad one. Good leaders could make mistakes, but the higher up the chain they were, the better my dad expected them to treat their subordinates." Ryan's eyes glistened. "Remember that anecdote about the Army private who was late for formation and he ran around the corner and knocked General Eisenhower to the ground. There they were, the bottom rung of the enlisted ladder, and the five-star supreme commander of Allied Forces. Remember what General Eisenhower said to the kid?"

No one answered.

"'You better be glad I'm not a lieutenant,'" Ryan said. "I don't even know if it's true, but it's a damned good story."

Dr. Moon arrived two minutes later, giving a decidedly jaundiced eye to everyone in the room. Ryan took her hand and smiled. "I'm not going to beat around the bush," he said, "except to say that we're reading you in to some extremely sensitive subjects that shouldn't be discussed with anyone outside this room unless you clear it with Commander Forestall."

"Understood, Mr. President," Moon said, her face a granite wall, impossible to read.

"All right, then." Ryan took a seat in his customary chair by the fireplace and offered Moon the chair beside him while everyone else took the couches. "A lot of big, giant brains seem to be divided about whether your recordings depict something made by man or fish noises. Certain events have transpired that give weight to the 'man-made' argument, but you're the closest person we have to the source. I'd like you to make your case."

It took less than two minutes for Moon to recount what she'd heard and where she'd heard it, after which she glanced at Commander Forestall's tablet. "Are the audio files I sent you on that?"

The room listened to a series of whistles and grunts and buzzing sounds, illustrated by a dancing bar graph on the computer screen that rose and fell with the pitch and volume of the sounds.

"That's a recording of an Atlantic cod, *Gadus morhua*," she said, before opening a second file on the heels of the first. It was hollow, eerie, and haunting. "This one is *uguruq* bearded seals, recorded from my father's boat." She tapped the tablet and a green graph appeared, superimposed over the red lines that depicted the seal song. "Now we add the ice." The whistles, screams, and chattering groans sounded incredibly human.

She tapped the screen again. "We'll mute the ice and the biologics, but leave up the visual graphs while we add the recording in question."

The room sat enthralled by the distinct splash as the hydrophone slipped beneath the surface and the burble as it descended into the deep. A wailing whistle, somewhere in the distance, overlaid significantly with a red graph—the bearded seal. The screech of the ship's hull against floating ice closely matched the green. Ryan had listened to the file before, but heard it differently now.

The new yellow graph suddenly jumped as new sounds came over the tablet's tiny speakers. The room sat in rapt silence as the sounds blanked out and then reappeared a few moments later when the hydrophone cable was retrieved.

Ryan took it all in, impressed with the young woman's forthright demeanor—folksy, from a life lived close to the land, yet bolstered by science.

Moon folded the cover over the tablet screen and gave a somber nod. "This is not fish flatulence, Mr. President, as some of my fellow scientists have suggested. And I do not believe it is ice. I've spent my life listening to ice talk and sing. I know what it sounds like."

Ryan gave a contemplative nod. "I agree."

Moon's eyebrows inched up, just a hair, but enough that Ryan noticed. That might be the most emotional outburst he was going to get from this stoic woman.

"It is interesting," Ryan continued, "that the voices you recorded appeared and then disappeared as the hydrophone went deeper. I'm assuming that you're working with some sophisticated equipment. I've listened to your recording and it sounds almost like the flip of a switch, as if someone turns off the voices and turns them back on again. Why would they not fade away as the hydrophone grew more distant?"

"I've thought about that," Moon said. "There's still a lot we don't know about the Arctic Ocean and surrounding seas. For years—decades, really—phantom shoals have appeared on some charts, but not others. One Navy sonar picks up a submerged reef that looks as though it should rip the keel off the ship, while another steams by with nothing between them and the bottom but three hundred fathoms of cold water. Some say these are caused by rising biologics—schools of fish, plankton clouds, even giant squid. Others believe there is a magnetic anomaly and the charts are simply wrong. The point is, Mr.

President, the Arctic is a mysterious place. That's why I'm there, doing what I do. There's a good chance we're more familiar with the surface of the moon than we are with what's down under the ice. Subs are gathering more and more data every day, but it's a big place, with lots of secrets. What we do know is that the area around the Chukchi Borderland is toothy. There are all sorts of ridges and ledges jutting up from the seabed. A couple of them reach within a few fathoms of the surface. I suspect that whatever . . . whoever . . . made the sounds I recorded was located on the opposite side of one of those ridges. Sound waves travel long distances through water, but they are easily attenuated by solid rock, at least as far as my hydrophones are concerned."

Ryan nodded slowly, picturing the scene.

"So," he said. "For the sake of illustration, whatever is making voices is on one side of a ridge, say, a hundred meters below the peak, and you lowered your hydrophone on the opposite side. The sounds would be picked up as the hydrophone descended, and then blocked by the underwater mountain when the equipment went below the top, in the rock shadow, so to speak."

"Exactly, sir," Moon said.

Forestall put up his hand. "If I may, sir."

"Go ahead, Robbie."

"Given this scenario," Forestall said, "knowing that the sounds came from the direction of the ridge in relation to the hydrophone, we may be able to triangulate on the signal strength as the instrument descended and the known depth. In theory, that could get us a general location from which the sounds emitted."

"He's right," Dr. Moon said, turning Forestall's tablet around so Ryan had a good view. The others leaned in. The screen depicted a cross-sectional view of the seabed with the research vessel *Sikuliaq* on the surface. A series of knifelike ridges rose from the bottom, one almost directly beneath the ship. She tapped the screen and a small box representing the hydrophone appeared beneath the surface. "I began picking up the sounds here," she said, "as soon as the instrument made it below all the surface clutter—ice, ship noise, et cetera. Then lost it here."

Foley leaned closer, adjusting her reading glasses. "The hydrophone is still above the ridgetop," she said. "Not in the shadow yet."

"Ah," Dr. Moon said. "But it would be in the shadow if the sounds emanated from this point." She tapped the screen again, bringing up the red triangle, five hundred feet down, resting on a ledge on the opposite side of the ridge as the hydrophone. "Any sounds coming from here would travel upward, spreading out just enough to allow me to pick them up for a few meters. But if the sounds are coming from here, close to the wall, the shadow starts much higher, before the instrument passes the ridgetop."

Ryan looked around the room. "Anyone else have questions for Dr. Moon?"

No one did. The matters they had to discuss would take place out of her presence.

"Very well." Ryan got to his feet. "Thank you for dropping everything for this trip."

Moon worked her way around the room, shaking hands.

"I wonder," Ryan said. "Would you mind staying around D.C. for a couple of days?"

"Of course," she said. "But I've already told you everything I know. My field of study is relatively narrow. I'm not sure what help I could offer."

"You're smart," Ryan said, "and you stick up for what you know when peers and superiors try to wave you off. It's only a request, mind you. If you have something pressing, I understand, but I would appreciate it if you could stay. Commander Forestall will get you set up at the Willard and see that you get a few bucks in per diem." Ryan walked with her to the door, struck with a sudden idea. "The First Lady is accompanying me to Fairbanks day after tomorrow, where I'm hosting some meetings with the polar nations. You could fly up on Air Force One as my guest, and then I'll get someone from Wainwright or Eielson to get you back to your ship. If this is what I think it is, things are likely to develop fast, and I'd like to have you around."

Moon's brow inched up again. "And what do you think it is, Mr. President?"

Ryan opened the door for her. "The same thing you do. A Chinese submarine that has gotten itself into trouble."

29

It seemed a simple assignment. Pick three names, one of which would be randomly selected for a suicide mission.

Wan Xiuying sat alone in his quarters, curtain drawn, listening to the terrified sobs of the young crew, smelling the stench of melted metal and the cloyingly sweet odor of cooked flesh. Hunched over his small, fold-out writing desk, the thirty-one-year-old executive officer of the PLAN nuclear ballistic submarine *Long March #880* clutched at his forelock with one hand while he tapped his pencil on the blank sheet of paper.

The captain's only criteria were that the candidates be brave, calm under pressure, and physically fit enough for the mission.

Wan pushed the pencil so hard with his thumb that it snapped in half. How could he pick the next men to die? Most of them were mere boys. Fifteen were already dead, burned to death or killed by smoke inhalation when PLAN nuclear ballistic missile submarine *Long March #880* suffered an engine room fire. A dozen more were sick or injured. All of them were terrified. One seaman's apprentice who had witnessed the fire had gone out of his mind, screaming "Sixty-one, sixty one," over and over as he ran back and forth in the narrow passageways. In 2003, all seventy crewmen aboard the *Great Wall #61*, an older, *Ming*-class sub, had suffocated at their stations when the diesel generator failed to turn off and used up all the oxygen on board. Any submariner in the fleet who denied having dreams about the disaster was lying.

This should not have happened to Wan Xiuying. He was an up-and-coming star of PLA-Navy's relatively nascent blue-water submarine force. He'd wanted to be a submariner since he was a small boy, reading every book and watching every movie about submarines that he could get his hands on. Most of the movies were in English, which had afforded him a perfect opportunity to study American idioms. Though they were meant to make the Americans look heroic, they almost always showed the captain and the first officer at odds over command of the vessel. Commander Wan hoped that was the truth. It would make beating the Americans easier in a pitched sea battle if the two men who were supposed to be in charge of the ship were constantly at each other's throats like they were in *Crimson Tide*—or in the book *Run Silent, Run Deep* . . . In *U-571* the captain did not trust the XO to make difficult decisions—decisions like Commander Wan now found himself facing. The list of conflicts was almost endless.

Wan revered and respected Captain Tian. He felt certain the feeling was mutual. Were it not so, Captain Tian would have, no doubt, personally stuffed his XO in a torpedo tube and gotten him off the boat.

Tian was a senior captain, would have certainly been promoted to admiral after this tour. He had quite literally grown up with the Chinese Navy and understood the pressing need not only to build excellent submarines, but to build excellent submariners. He worked very hard to pass on his knowledge to those next in line. From the time Wan had come aboard, it was clear to him that Captain Tian demanded strict discipline, a hard-as-ironwood boss who was focused not only on the command of his submarine, but on making certain his new XO was equal to the task when he got his own boat.

But none of that would happen now.

The experimental Mirage silent propulsion system was a twisted heap of charred metal. Fifteen men had died horrible deaths, including the ship's medic. Twelve more were too severely burned to work. Worst of all, the chief engineer and three of the five engineering mates were dead. The remaining two, still in their teens, were from poor counties that still used oxen in the field. They'd only recently graduated from submariner school in Qingdao, but their training specific to the engine operation and maintenance was to have taken place aboard the boat. Even then, with a new, experimental propulsion unit, they could do little more than stare at the mess while holding a wrench, clucking to themselves like a husband who did not want to admit to his wife he had no idea how to fix a stalled car.

When it had become apparent that the fire involved the submarine's propulsion unit, Captain Tian had considered an emergency blow—that is, sending compressed air into the ballast tanks and blasting them to the surface. Both the United States and Russia provided periodic analysis of ice and possible open water. The United States called theirs a FLAP analysis— Fractures, Leads, and Polynyas (the Russian word for open water surrounded by ice). But the ice here was moving, a flowing solid, with jagged keels that hung down like ax blades, capable of chopping the 880 in half during an uncontrolled ascent.

Fortunately, the nuclear reactor was in the compartment forward of the Mirage drive. The reactor itself and all but two of the pumps were still operational.

If the charts and calculations were correct, the *880* lay belly-down on a rocky ledge, one hundred and seventy meters below the surface, with an undersea mountain rising to starboard. Collision with the rock face on the way down had ripped a four-meter gash in the outermost hull of the double-hulled vessel. The inner hull was still intact, keeping the crew alive— for the moment—but with the ballast tank damaged, an emergency blow was now problematic.

To port, off the edge of the ledge, the seabed lay some eleven hundred meters below—well beyond crush depth, even for a powerful double-hulled submarine like *880*. If the baby-faced engineering mates were able to somehow get the boat moving in any direction other than up, she might simply shuffle off the ledge and plummet straight to the bottom.

Of course, that would solve Commander Wan's problem.

At first it seemed like they had one ace in the hole. Professor Liu Wangshu should have been able to fix the drive. It was his design. That's why he was on the boat, to make sure it worked. And work it did. When the pumps—one of the loudest parts of a nuclear submarine—were rigged for ultra-quiet, the gearless Mirage drive proved to render the *880* all but invisible. The fire appeared to have started in one of the pumps, some sort of lubricant ignited by a spark, one of the youngsters surmised. Wan wondered if they would ever know. Over and over, history had shown that it was often a string of simple, relatively minor mistakes and seemingly insignificant design flaws that led to catastrophe.

Liu Wangshu could have seen the problem at once, had he not been sick. *Sick* was not nearly a strong enough word to describe what was wrong with him. Only a handful of the crew knew Professor Liu's background. He dressed in regular engineering officer's coveralls, and he spoke with the authority of a professor, which was not uncommon among officers in any branch. He had the shoulder boards, so the crew obeyed him, even though he was new and unknown to them. Oddly, the fire itself had not hurt him. His lungs appeared undamaged by the toxic smoke. No, this was something else. The XO guessed it was a stroke, judging from the man's sagging face and the gibberish he spoke. Probably brought on by the sudden stress of seeing his life's work destroyed by fire.

They'd given him aspirin and confined him to bed with two junior submariners watching him. Either he would get better or he would not. If he did not get better, then everyone on the sub would eventually die. Some sooner, when they went insane and began to kill one another. One of the sonar techs had already gotten into a fight with the cook. Some later, when their food ran out.

As long as the reactor continued to function—decades, if no pumps broke—they had power for heaters, the amine CO_2 scrubbers for clean air to breathe, the water maker, and the pumps to take waste off the submarine. Commander Wan anticipated they had almost three months of food—now that there were fewer mouths left alive to eat it. Marooned in their bubble island, they would simply starve to death.

There was an alternative—that only Commander Wan and the captain knew about.

Rigged against bulkheads in the 880's nose and tail were two explosive disks, each over two meters in diameter. The experimental Mirage drive was the only one of its kind. Ordinarily, Professor Liu, the only person who could re-create the mechanism, would never have been allowed on the submarine. But he'd somehow pulled strings. He wanted to see his creation work in the real world.

Command wanted the drive and the professor protected if at all possible, but their orders were clear. In the event of an emergency, *Long March #880* was not to end up in American—or even Russian—hands. The Mirage drive was Chinese technology, not stolen through tradecraft or purchased from a disgruntled U.S. Navy scientist. It had been developed by China and tested by China, and would eventually be utilized by China. It was a point of national pride—and Beijing wanted it to stay that way.

The self-destruct disks were alarmingly simple to operate. Unlike the nuclear missiles on board, which required the simultaneous use of keys carried by both the captain and the XO to activate the command-and-control system, the self-destruct system could be initiated by the captain alone, or, in his absence, the executive officer.

The captain had met with Wan in private, discussing their options. Tian was no coward. He would detonate the disks if ordered to do so. But he was a patriot and did not want to deprive China of technology that put them ahead in a race that they'd lagged in for so long.

He felt certain command would want to salvage what was left of the drive, and, if possible, nurse Professor Liu back to health. If he destroyed the vessel, the United States would not get it—but, without the professor, China might not be able to re-create it, either.

For years.

Hydrophones had remained operational. The sonar tech listened to the screws of the surface vessel almost directly overhead. Oblivious to what was occurring five hundred feet below, it departed the area shortly after the accident.

Tian waited four hours, and then, when it became apparent the drive was inoperable, he released the rescue buoy affixed to the exterior of the ship. It was programmed to release after six hours anyway if the timers were not continually reset by each oncoming watch. That way, if all on board were killed in an explosion—or, as in the case of the *61*, died at their stations, China could come and retrieve her submarine.

The distress buoy was attached to the submarine by a long cable that reeled out when it deployed.

Had the buoy made it to the surface, the fleet would have received coded satellite transmissions and then sent someone to rescue the *880* or destroy them. Either way, the captain would have his answer.

But heavy ice had moved in above. The hydrophones picked up the burble of the buoy's departure, and the unmistakable thud as it impacted the ice. Moving ice tugged at the cable, finally separating it completely and carrying the buoy away without it ever having seen the sky to make its call. A remote underwater autonomous vehicle met the same fate in the unforgiving ice. The Americans had ALSEAMAR SLOT 281s, buoys the size of baseball bats that carried a recorded message to the surface and then scuttled themselves. The *880* was too secret to be equipped with such devices.

The captain decided to try one last option before detonating the self-destruct disks. It was low-tech, and the odds of success were practically nil, but the odds of everyone dying if he did not try were one hundred percent.

He would send a man to the surface.

A torpedo would blast a hole through the ice, hopefully

pulverizing a good portion of it. This would almost certainly bring nosy Americans, but he always had the explosive disks as a fallback if that occurred. A volunteer would use the escape trunk to leave the submarine immediately following the fish, rising to the surface in a neoprene escape suit—with a satellite phone in a waterproof bag.

Commander Wan had thought the idea insane, but one did not confide such feelings to a submarine captain. It was either this, the captain had explained, or they all died immediately when the captain initiated the self-destruct mechanism, taking the priceless Mirage drive with them. In time, Wan saw that this was the only way forward—the last way.

And so Wan Xiuying found himself hunched over his desk, clutching his forelock, trying to decide which of his men he would volunteer to climb into the escape trunk, wait for it to fill with water equalizing pressure with the sea, all the while waiting for the horrific banging of the hammer that signaled it was time to open the outer hatch and swim into the cold, dark water . . . one hundred and seventy meters—five hundred and sixty feet—below the surface.

He used the edge of the desk to carefully tear the paper into three equal pieces—and then wrote his own name on each one.

30

"Y our request must be denied out of hand!" Captain Tian snapped, pulling the second, and then the third folded paper out of the cup in Commander Wan's hand. "I need you here, by my side. These are incredibly important decisions that must be made. If, by some chance, any of us survive this, it should be you. You are the future of our Red Star, Blue Water Navy."

Wan kept his voice low and even, knowing full well that he would never win an argument with the captain. The man simply did not argue. He would discuss, he would listen to reason, but if for one moment he believed that someone was arguing with him, he would, as the Americans said, pull rank, or, more often than not, simply walk away.

"I understand," he said. "But if I may, you have said many times that you depend on my counsel. I humbly give you that counsel now. You know how important the Mirage drive is. I am in full agreement with you that if there is any way to save it and Professor Liu, then we should attempt it. Honestly, the chief engineer would have been the best candidate. He was extremely fit, and knew more about the drive than anyone besides the professor. But, sadly, he did not survive the fire. Considering our options dispassionately, I am the next logical choice. I am older than almost any of the submariners, so I am less likely to panic, and in much better physical condition than any of the more mature division chiefs. I swam competitively in secondary school and am a trained scuba diver, accustomed to the water."

Tian took a long breath, puckering, as if smelling his top lip—it was what he did when he thought and was often copied by the men, though never in his presence.

"This is a suicide mission," he said. "A one-way trip. No return. One way or another, you will die when you leave this boat. No question about it. In all likelihood, your lungs will rupture during ascent, or you will drown, hopelessly trapped beneath the ice. If you reach the surface alive, there is a better-than-average chance that you will be ground to flotsam by jagged pieces of floating ice. If, by some miracle, you are able to drag your broken body onto the ice and make the call, rescuers may save the ship, but the chances of anyone arriving in time to save you are almost nonexistent."

"So," Wan smiled, "there is hope?"

"You will eventually freeze to death."

"If we do nothing, we all die. It would be my great honor to give my life for the crew and for China." He shrugged, hoping it looked humble rather than haughty. "And I have heard that dying from cold is not at all unpleasant," Commander Wan said. "They say one falls asleep."

"A pleasant way to die indeed, unless your slumber is interrupted by a passing polar bear." The captain pursed his lips again. "Soviet cosmonauts were issued shotguns to take into space for the eventuality that their capsule landed in Siberia when it returned to earth." He shivered, trying to shake a memory. "I once saw the body of a man who had been partially eaten by a bear, in Siberia. The beast had broken the poor man's neck and then eaten his kidneys. I believe he was alive during—"

"With all due respect," Wan said, smiling, "I would just as soon die as imagine such horrible things."

The captain took him by both shoulders, tears of pride welling in his eyes, calling him by his given name. "Xiuying, it has been my great honor to serve as your captain . . ."

"Thank you, sir!"

Tian stepped away. "But if we are to do this, then we should do it without delay. I am sorry that there is no more time for you to prepare."

"I assure you, Captain," Commander Wan said, "I would rather not linger. I was prepared from the moment I wrote my name on the papers."

The PLAN Submariner Academy in Qingdao ran every student through egress exercises. Wan still remembered his experience putting on the full-face mask and "horse-collar" flotation aid before crawling into the modified torpedo tube and waiting for it to flood. When the hammer clanged three times on the hatch, he opened the flooded tube and kick-floated his way through a few feet of slightly cool water to the surface, into the arms of waiting instructors who wore scuba equipment to save him if he got into trouble.

This was not going to be like that.

The ungainly orange suit was a Chinese copy of the Submarine Escape Immersion Equipment, or SEIE, suit, designed and manufactured by RFD Beaufort Limited and utilized by, among others, the U.S. Navy. The operation was relatively straightforward. He would enter the lockout trunk wearing his suit, and attach the tube from his suit to an air connection that, when the time came, would fill the enclosed hood and provide him with flotation and breathing air on the way to the surface. The function of the trunk was exactly the same as that of the training tube in Qingdao, with the exception that this one was much larger, to accommodate several Special Forces divers, should the need arise. There were no Special Forces divers on this trip, or one of them would have had this honor.

Because of the unpredictability of the ice after it was broken—if it broke at all—it was decided that Commander Wan would enter the lockout trunk and flooding would begin as the Yu-6 torpedo was fired. Coordinates were plotted and the 880's fire control guided the fish via its trailing wire umbilical, sending it as close to straight above their heads as possible.

Sweating profusely in the waterproof suit, Wan opened the escape trunk's inner hatch. He saluted the crew, who had crowded into the forward torpedo room, and then hung the rubber pack containing the satellite phone around his neck, clipping it to a belt around his waist to keep it from becoming an entanglement hazard.

Captain Tian stepped forward, gave him another pack with a short shotgun inside.

"The chief sawed off the barrel, to make it easier for you to carry." The captain pursed his lips again, patting Wan on the shoulder. "I would hate for you to see a polar bear."

At that, the captain nodded to the assistant medic, who'd had little training but for what he got on the job. He carried a long steel needle. "The medical manual suggests submariners egressing from depths perforate their eardrums prior to leaving, to avoid a more violent tear during rapid ascent."

"Very well," Wan said. He did not know if puncturing an eardrum would hurt, but he thought having one ripped apart by pressure might render him incapable of making the decisions he would need to make at the surface. He pushed the SEIE suit's hood back to expose his ears. "Please go ahead."

"Me?" the seaman stammered. "I had thought . . ." He held up the needle with an unsteady hand.

Wan smiled, rescuing the young man by taking the needle from him and deftly popping both his own eardrums, quickly, one after the other, before he had time to think. It smarted, but, to his surprise, it was not excruciating, and he could still hear.

He returned the needle and entered the escape trunk. The heavy door closed behind him with a resounding metallic *thunk*, muffling the sound of the cheers coming from the crew.

Almost immediately, seawater began to flow in around his feet, filling the metal box, the rising pressure causing the holes in his eardrums to hum.

He did not hurt—yet.

31

C aptain Cole Condiff, skipper of the *Virginia*-class fast attack submarine USS *Indiana* (SSN 789), stood in the control room, behind the officer of the deck. They were
three hundred feet under the Arctic ice, eight hundred miles
south of the North Pole, approaching the point where the Beaufort Sea became the Chukchi.

A second U.S. sub, the *Seawolf*-class USS *Connecticut*, had
departed the latest ICEX the week before, but Condiff had
held his boat back, running drills, waiting. Russian subs were
well aware of the U.S. Navy's biennial Arctic combat and tactical readiness exercise. There had been nearly fifty personnel at
the camp above the ice for almost three weeks. The Russians
did the same kind of training, maybe even more, if you considered the proximity of their sub bases to large sheets of ice. The
Chinese were throwing up ice camps, too, attempting to show
some polar connection. Their subs were also here, or so he'd
heard, charting, learning.

With new shipping lanes and trade routes coming into play
as the ice opened up more and more each year, every nation
with a toehold in the Arctic worked to make sure they had the

right tools to navigate and protect their interests. If the Russians knew about ICEX, then they would be lurking, waiting on the fringes for the U.S. subs to go home.

Captain Condiff's predatory drive kicked in at the thought, and he'd decided to let the *Connecticut* draw away any lurkers, and then he would fall in behind, hunting his way home.

Indiana had been under the ice for six days—since they'd said good-bye to their friends at the ice camp. Thick floe and huge daggerlike ice keels prevented deployment of the ELF antenna, making communication with the outside world impossible. Condiff expected open water by the end of watch, where the ELF could pick up any traffic from command. Until then, his sonar technicians watched the wavering green waterfall on their screens for the sound signatures of a Russian submarine.

Condiff took a deep breath. He was long past smelling it, but knew there was an odor there that those on land found disquieting if not disgusting. His wife made him wash his uniforms three times as soon as he walked in the door after a deployment. Even then, she relegated them to designated plastic totes that stayed on a shelf in the garage until the next time he went to sea.

Reusable water bottle in one hand, the skipper chatted with one of the newest members of his crew, a twentysomething woman named Ramirez. A freckled farm-boy lieutenant from Nebraska named Lowdermilk was officer of the deck at the moment, leaving Condiff to conduct his training. Unlike older submarines, *Virginia*-class subs like *Indiana* had consolidated the watch positions of dive, helm, outboard, and chief of the watch into pilot and copilot who both sat at a console in front of the officer of the deck, who gave them maneuvering orders. Combat control consoles ran along the starboard side. Sonar technicians sat at consoles to port, opposite combat control.

Along with approximately ten percent of her crewmates, this was Ramirez's first tour. Participation in ICEX was a surprise bonus for these newbies, since Blue Noses, submariners who'd crossed the Arctic Circle, were relatively rare. It was one of the few missions a young submariner could brag about while ashore without getting into trouble.

Ramirez was taciturn, a quality Condiff liked if he did not share. Even better, she was a quick study. Her formal training was to be a sonar tech, or STS. Captain Condiff had no doubt that she would eventually become an outstanding one, but before that, he liked to have his newbies take a tour through the specialties, sonar, combat control, engineering, communications, among others, even the galley. Everyone on the sub drilled in emergency procedures, so she got plenty of that as well. Not only had these few weeks of round-the-boat training taught her a little about most of the systems, she'd been able to see firsthand how components of the crew acted and interacted. The rest of the crew also got to know Ramirez and her fellow newbies.

Each new submariner also spent half a day shadowing him. Mentally exhausting to be sure, but it had borne fruit in the form of a crew of cohesive submariners and junior officers who were ingrained with the concept of servant leadership.

Today was Ramirez's day. She stood off his left shoulder, Rite in the Rain notebook and pen in hand, eager to learn.

"Tell me about our enemy, Seaman Ramirez," Condiff said.

"Our enemy, sir? Here, at this moment?"

"Yes," Condiff said. "Here on this sub."

". . . Russia, sir?"

"Not at the moment," Condiff said. He turned to Lowder-milk. "Lieutenant?"

"The sea, Skipper," Lowdermilk said. "The sea is our enemy."

"You are correct, Mr. Lowdermilk," Condiff said. "You may continue driving my boat."

Lowdermilk grinned. "Aye, aye, sir."

Condiff took a swig from the water bottle and winked at Ramirez. "I'm not kidding, you know. Even now, Mother Ocean would love to crush our hull with her bare hands. And if she's unable to do that, she would sink and flood and freeze us with-out a second thought. Don't believe me? Punch a tiny hole in the sub and then try to make friends with her. No, ma'am, the sea is an invasive species." He took another drink and then raised the bottle as if in a toast. "And I love it more than just about any other place on the planet."

He gestured at the nearest sonar technician. "So Petty Of-ficer Markette, there, is keeping an eye on a surface ship mak-ing its way through the ice . . . Right, Petty Officer Markette?"

"Aye, Captain," the STS said. "Bearing two-five-five. Heavy, slow screws. Turn count suggests it's the *Healy*. Getting a lot of interference from the ice floe, but we're estimating her at eight miles."

The U.S. Coast Guard icebreaker *Healy* had been in the area before they dove. They'd picked up her groaning screws off and on throughout the week as she maneuvered through the ice, along with the periodic groans of a smaller boat they assumed to be an Arctic research vessel.

"Thank you kindly, Petty Officer Markette." Condiff glanced at Ramirez again. "Ice . . . just frozen water . . . so still the enemy . . ."

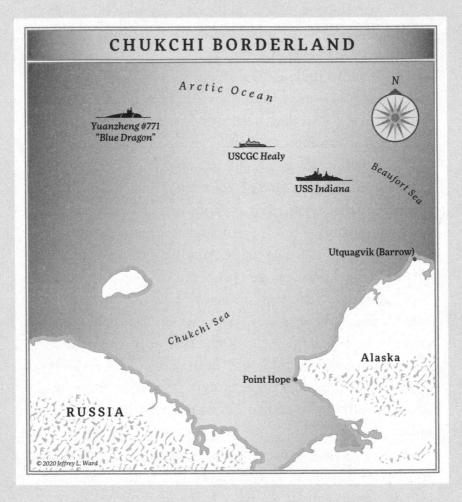

CHUKCHI BORDERLAND

Arctic Ocean

Yuanzheng #771
"Blue Dragon"

USCGC Healy

USS Indiana

Beaufort Sea

N

Utquagvik (Barrow)

Chukchi Sea

Alaska

Point Hope

RUSSIA

© 2020 Jeffrey L. Ward

Markette sat up straighter in his chair.

"Con. Sonar. Contact," he said, all business. "Sound transient, far, bearing two-four-zero . . . Explosion. I think it was a torpedo."

"I have the con," Condiff said, moving forward.

"Captain has the con." Lowdermilk stepped out of the way, deftly nudging Seaman Ramirez with him.

"Station a tracking party," Condiff said before turning toward sonar.

Lieutenant Lowdermilk relayed the order on the 1 MC, or main communications circuit, alerting the entire ship that a contact needed tracking, but the captain was not quite ready for battle stations. Designated crew, along with the XO, were needed in control.

"Report," Condiff said.

"Nothing, sir," Petty Officer Markette said. "The sound of the launch blended with ice noise at first. The fish launched and then detonated . . . six seconds later."

"The *Healy*?" Condiff said, feeling bile rise in his gut.

"Heavy screws are still present, sir," Markette said. "Turn count is accelerating. She's speeding up."

"Assessment?"

Markette listened to a playback of the noise. "There it is," he said. "Hiss, crack, boom. I think the transient was a sub firing a torpedo through the ice."

"No other contacts?"

"No other contacts," Markette said.

Lowdermilk said, "Shall we find open water and send up an X-SUB?"

The X-SUB was a communication buoy developed by AL-SEAMAR, that, when deployed by tether, allowed two-way communication between the submarine and ships or land while staying at depth.

"Not yet," Condiff said. "I'm not ready to show our hand on the surface quite yet—even with a little buoy. No telling what kind of air assets are up there." He addressed the petty officers in the pilot and copilot seats, giving them the coordinates and speed he wanted.

". . . Take us toward the sound of gunfire . . ."

32

The other members of ELISE filtered into the secret space by ones and twos, bringing small boxes of supplies for their desks—a favorite type of pencil that couldn't be nabbed at the supply closet, a coffee mug that had served them through many overseas assignments, or maybe a framed photo or two to help anchor them to normal life . . . whatever that was. Smartwatches, Fitbits, iPads, or outside electronics of any kind were not allowed.

Hendricks, Wallace, and Li had worked through a pool of thirty prospective personnel files and sent nine names to DNI Foley for approval. Once Foley signed off, Hendricks and Wallace had met with each of them personally and invited them to apply to participate in a special project that would require in-depth background checks, including a polygraph and a financial review that one of the men later described as more intrusive than a lingering prostate exam. Hendricks, Wallace, Li, and even Director Foley worked around the clock to complete the vetting process.

No one on ELISE knew how long the assignment would be, but once they found out it was a mole hunt, they were in it for the long haul.

Monica Hendricks sat at the head of a long oak conference table, flanked by David Wallace of the FBI and retired rear admiral Peter Li, her longtime friend and unofficial deputy on project ELISE.

With the last two team members less than five minutes out, Hendricks asked the others to stow their belongings quickly and join her at the conference table. She'd already laid out twelve yellow legal pads and twelve black Skilcraft government pens.

It was often said that it took a spy to catch a spy. Monica preferred to think that it took a spy to catch a rat. Turncoat, sellout, traitor, quisling—many pejoratives fit the bill, but *rat* was a much better descriptor than *mole*.

Moles lived underground, out of sight. They were hard to find, but they were blind and witless, digging away toward the smell of food or a mate. Beady-eyed and conniving, rats, on the other hand, slinked through the darkness, eating grain stores, shitting on what they didn't eat, and spreading plagues.

Rats who sold out to Israel or Taiwan or France, while they couldn't be forgiven, might at least be understood. Rats who gave up their knowledge to Communist countries were beyond redemption.

Of the twelve people assigned to ELISE, there were seven women and five men. Two were black, three were of Chinese heritage, and two were Hispanic. The rest were white. There was one Southern Baptist, one Lutheran, and one Jew. Agnostics, Mormons, and Catholics tied at three apiece. Everyone in the room spoke at least two languages. More than half, including all the Mormons, spoke fluent Mandarin. Most had graduate degrees, one from Harvard Law School, two were former cops, and two had taught high school. Nine were parents. Three had grandchildren and would gladly show you dozens of photos, though they did not post them on any sort of social media.

An extremely diverse group, but for all their differences, every single member of ELISE hated Communism with the intensity of a thousand suns. Socialism was no better, just Communism by another name. All of them had been around the world and witnessed firsthand the damage Communist regimes rained down on the people. Voicing the notion aloud made one sound like a crazed zealot, but experience had taught everyone in the room that Communism was a fairy tale on paper, the cold reality of which brought riches to the rulers and sorrow, starvation, and death to the ruled. The record of the United States was far from perfect, but those who worked for Monica Hendricks made no apologies for the fervent belief that theirs was not a fight against merely an alternate dogma to democracy, but against evil.

The brush did not paint as broadly when it came to people. Communism was evil, but not all Communists were evil. Some were idealists, caught up in the dream. Others were simply trapped in the cogs and wheels of a great and terrible machine, unable to slip away without being crushed. There were tens of millions of good Chinese people who identified as Communists but would have happily gone another way if not for fear of being run over by a tank.

Whatever Hendricks's moral views on the Communist regime of the People's Republic of China, they were a formidable enemy, capable enough to penetrate the CIA with an as-yet-unknown agent in place. She did not intend to underestimate their resolve or their abilities at espionage.

For the protection of all involved, ELISE would be run out

of a nondescript office off the mazelike underground mall in Crystal City, Virginia, rented under the name of a fictitious advertising corporation set up by and paid for with funds from the good folks at FBI Counterintelligence Division, where David Wallace served as section chief of counterespionage.

The space, an open bullpen, was large enough for a long conference table Admiral Li was already calling the Big Deck. Fifteen desks, including Hendricks's, surrounded the table. Two computer servers occupied one of the two closets at the far end of the room, next to a small supply closet. The room had been transformed in a matter of hours by technical surveillance and countermeasures experts, also from FBI, into one big SCIF. This Secure Compartmented Information Facility guarded against what the NSA called TEMPEST—the leakage of electronic signals and sound that could be picked up by an adversary. A typical suburban home spilled enough TEMPEST information from its routers, mobile phones, smart devices, vehicles, and even pacemakers to piece together a large intelligence file.

The room had no windows. False walls and a second ceiling, six inches lower than the existing one, formed a room within the room, impregnated with metal foil to act as a Faraday cage. Everyone who entered, including the IT specialist, was deeply vetted and read all the way in to ELISE. In the unlikely event that they received a visit from, say, an FBI or CIA assistant director or White House staffer, a rotating red beacon would begin to flash annoyingly in the center of the ceiling, reminding everyone that there was an outsider in their midst. They should cover their work product and keep any details of the mole hunt to themselves.

All computer and most telephone lines going in and out of

ELISE space were encrypted and firewalled. The handset of each regular landline phone was affixed with a large red sticker that warned it was not a secure communication device. Cell phones—even Hendricks's and Wallace's—stayed in cubbies in the outer lobby with a plainclothes officer from CIA police whose job it was to run force protection. Even the cell-phone cubbies were enclosed with Faraday film to keep anyone with a scanner and a Yagi antenna from grabbing a list of the phones parked in front of the location. It didn't seem like much, but that information formed another piece of the puzzle that Monica Hendricks did not want to give up.

The George Bush Center for Intelligence, AKA Langley, was less than ten miles up the George Washington Parkway. The White House was three miles to the north across any number of bridges. FBI HQ was just six blocks east of that. Crystal City was only two metro stops away from the Pentagon. Arlington National Cemetery was one more on the Blue Line. Joint Base Anacostia–Bolling, the now-not-so-secret second home of the HMX-1 (Marine One) presidential helicopters, as well as the headquarters of the Defense Intelligence Agency, was directly across the Potomac. You couldn't hear them in the SCIF, but every few minutes, the walls of the ELISE office space gave a tremulous shake signifying the takeoff of a commercial aircraft from Reagan National Airport on Runways 1 or 33 to the north, a scant two blocks away.

Restaurants and shops in and around Crystal City were accustomed to military and civilian government types staying at one of the many hotels while on TDY to Washington. Some experts reckoned, correctly, in Hendricks's estimation, that with all the government knowledge floating around, Crystal City was one of the most heavily trolled places in the United

States by foreign adversaries. Amazon was buying up office space in several high-rises connected to the Crystal City underground, and now it was even odds whether the people in line at Starbucks or Ted's Montana Grill worked for Jeff Bezos or Uncle Sam.

"First off," Hendricks said, once everyone had arrived and the door was secured, "thank you all for participating. I don't have to tell you what a sensitive matter this is." She introduced herself, and then went around the table and had each person give a two-minute thumbnail of their background. When it got back around to her, she said, "You see that only six of you presently serve as counterintelligence officers. That is by design. If you do, we want your expertise. If you don't, we want your different point of view. You've each been briefed individually on what we know about SURVEYOR—which is precious little, so there's no need to go over that again at this point."

She glanced at Wallace.

"Thanks, Monica," he said. "I would only say that I'm from the FBI and I'm here to help—"

The two agencies' rivalry went back to J. Edgar Hoover's days and this brought a round of good-natured chuckles from the CIA officers in the room. Wallace took it in stride.

"Generally speaking, the Bureau would take the lead in a case of this sort, but the powers that be have decided that's not the case this go-around. And I honestly understand why. SURVEYOR will undoubtedly be someone many of you know personally. Maybe you've had coffee with him, sat across from her at lunch or dinner. Your children may play together. Your spouses could be close friends. This will feel personal, because it is. SURVEYOR works among you. That is why you are the people to catch him or her. I know very few people at Langley.

I am here to provide you someone with arrest authority on U.S. soil, extra bodies when we need them, and an extra point of view from someone in a gun culture. How many of you have fired a sidearm in the past year?"

Half of the hands went up.

"As I thought, and that's normal. Guns might not be a big part of your job when gathering intelligence, so you may not necessarily think about arrest procedures and tactics when you're not overseas. Our hunt for SURVEYOR has been a secret up to now, but in a few minutes, we will take it on the road. We will conduct interviews, sit surveillance, and dig through copious files. I have the U.S. attorney for Northern Virginia on speed dial, so subpoenas shouldn't be a problem. Secrecy might. The vast majority of all interviews and polygraphs will be conducted at hotel rooms off-site, away from Langley or ELISE offices. In the next few hours, SURVEYOR will know we are looking for him or her. I won't get too far into the weeds with site and personal security, but I would remind each of you from the outset that, as Chief Hendricks has pointed out, we are dealing with a dangerous foe, who would have no trouble killing anyone here to protect themselves or their asset. SURVEYOR is a tremendous coup for them and they will likely protect him or her at all cost . . ." Wallace glanced down at his notepad, tapped it a couple times with the tips of his fingers, and then smiled. "You know us FBI guys, we can't bring ourselves to shut up when we're given the floor, but that's all for now."

"Okay." Hendricks stood and clapped her hands lightly together. "As my oldest boy would say, 'That was the drumroll, Mom, what you really got?' Ladies and gentlemen, the clock is ticking. It is not an overstatement to say that lives are at stake.

To that end, we must think outside the box. I'd like each of you to take ten minutes and come up with a list of the people at the Agency who bug you. Don't think too hard. Just go with your gut. Maybe you think this person is disgusting enough to betray their country, or they just strike you as odd. You don't even have to have any evidence."

A couple of the younger case officers began to squirm at the notion. Hendricks raised a hand and gave a motherly tip of her head. "I know it sounds judgmental and unscientific, but many studies have shown our instinct, our gut, if you will, is correct much of the time. Jeanne Vertefeuille and Sandy Grimes used this very technique at the outset of the hunt for the mole who turned out to be Rick Ames."

Aldrich "Rick" Ames, a CIA case officer for thirty-one years, was convicted of espionage in 1994. His betrayal of Russian CIA assets cost at least ten lives and brought recruitment of new Russian intelligence assets to a screeching halt for fear that they, too, would inevitably be betrayed and killed.

"Remember," Hendricks continued. "At this point, we're not talking about building a case for court. This is simply a move to get us started. I would point out that Ames was high on many people's list."

David Wallace's chair creaked as he rocked backward, subconsciously showing his doubts at the idea.

Admiral Li raised a hand. Hendricks gave him the floor. They'd already rehearsed this.

"In the 1960s," Li said, "a gifted outside-the-box thinker with Naval Projects named John Craven was assigned to locate a hydrogen bomb that had been lost in the Mediterranean. Amid a crowd of naysayers and cynics, Craven put together a team of mathematicians and engineers, who used something called

Bayes's theorem of subjective probability, an algebraic formula that, to put in simple terms, assigns a numerical value to a gut feeling. Craven's team took what data they had, and then used Las Vegas–style betting—wagering bottles of whiskey—on where they thought the missing item would be on a grid. Their hunches were basically weaponized with mathematical formulas—the bomb was found, right where the odds said they would be. A short time later, using the same weaponized hunches, he found the USS *Scorpion*, which had gone missing in the deep Atlantic. The Coast Guard still utilizes this formula in its search-and-recovery missions."

Li dropped his pen onto the table and glanced at Hendricks before taking his seat.

"Okay," Hendricks said, resuming her role as both cheerleader and whip. "So listen to your guts. Work independently." She started to sit down but then added, "After you're done, please pass your papers to Special Agent Wallace or Admiral Li . . . You know, in case I'm on your list."

What Hendricks did not mention was that there were two more members of ELISE, unknown to everyone but her, Wallace, and Foley. Vetted just as thoroughly as the people in the room. Unknown even to each other, these two would continue to work their assigned desks at Langley, reporting back to Hendricks with reactions in the ranks once the cages began to rattle.

Introductions and instructions over, Hendricks picked up her pen and began to compile her own list.

33

CIA case officer Tim Meyer had not started out to commit treason. His goal was to show the Agency where its holes were. To demonstrate how some people with the CIMC were letting things fall through the cracks. At least, that's what he told himself. What he really wanted was to tank Odette Miller's career.

In the end, treason had just happened. The money wasn't bad, though the Chinese didn't pay nearly as well as he'd heard the Russians did. Fred Rask didn't know it, but he'd come through with some juicy stuff that might up Meyer's payday. If he played his cards right, this might be enough to get out, go to some beach somewhere in the South Pacific and just hang.

He'd heard about the mole hunt, of course. Rumors were flying all around Langley. Trusted employees were being dragged in and given polygraphs. The poly didn't scare Meyer. He'd passed every one he'd taken, and he had plenty of things he didn't want to disclose. At one point, the examiner had noted a possible deception, but that was just because Meyer was laughing inside. They gave him a retry and he breezed through.

Still, they'd catch him someday. They always figured it out. The trick was knowing when to get out of town. Sooner or later, Meyer knew, someone would snap to the fact that he was selling secrets to Beijing. He'd told his handler just that. Made it clear to her that he wanted to maximize his work so he could minimize his time under the gun. She handled him like a boss, though, and sent him back for more.

Now they were asking questions. Too many questions. Everything was about to change, one way or another.

The function of the CIA's Counterintelligence Mission Center was to look for attempted penetrations of U.S. intelligence. The CIMC had had a complete makeover in recent years, transforming a duty that was once seen as a career-stopper into a professional and well-run organization. As spy hunters, they were extremely good at their job—but as good as they were, they had yet to catch Tim Meyer.

In their defense, Meyer had been spying for the Chinese for only four months—and he worked counterintelligence.

Meyer was forty-six, with seventeen years under his belt at the Agency. He had a reputation for doing adequate work and not being overzealous about much of anything. Performance appraisals generally showed him average and acceptable, and they couldn't fire you for being acceptable. Right?

As in any organization, dysfunction had sought out its own, and Meyer had been able to find bosses who were all too happy not to have anyone in their shop make waves. Intelligence operations often took years, and it was no big trick to slack if the planets aligned and two or three people in the chain between boots and management wanted to coast a bit and recharge their batteries after all the life-risking they had to do in the field.

Meyer developed the reputation as a guy who got things done—just in the nick of time. But, hey, he got it done, and that was the important part, right? He got along with most of the guys. He got in trouble once for telling an off-color joke in the breakroom—but that was back when things were just turning to be all woke and politically correct.

You couldn't even ask a girl from work out anymore. Well, you could, but you had to be extremely careful because your life was pretty much in her hands if you accidentally crossed the line. Meyer had seen it happen. Fortunately for him, he was a quick study, as well as a high-functioning sociopath, and he figured out how to make his intentions appear much more benign than they were. People had a hard time "getting a read" on him. He liked that.

He'd dated an analyst from counterproliferation for a while and she'd tried to describe it. "You're just so . . ."

"Enigmatic?" he'd offered.

"No," she'd said. "That's not the word . . ."

But it probably was. And anyway, being unreadable was a good quality at CIA.

Assigned to the Central Asia desk, Meyer's job was to assist the referent. Referents, the CI officers sent over by the Counterintelligence Mission Center to the various geographical divisions, were sometimes looked at as outsiders, not part of the same team. Meyer's boss, the baron running Central Asia, wanted to make sure that did not happen on his watch. A mandate came down to cooperate fully with CI, which meant virtually opening the book on every sensitive op so the referent could do his or her job.

In this case, the referent was an officer named Odette Miller. At thirty-two, she'd started with the Agency right out of college and moved up fast—a real blue-flamer. She wasn't really Meyer's supervisor, and, when he was honest with himself, she didn't try to be, but it chapped him that she could waltz in and have the run of the place. He got over it, though, and asked her out for a drink. She'd pretty much told him that he was too old for her. Oh, she was nice about it, on the surface. But he could tell she was laughing at him on the inside. They were what, fourteen years apart? That was nothing. But she laughed like he couldn't possibly be serious and said he reminded her of her uncle.

He'd just said okay and walked away smiling, to figure out how to sink her. It wouldn't be hard. Blue-flamers were easy to shoot down.

The best way was probably to find something good himself that she'd missed.

When he'd been approached by the Chinese woman, it had been a no-brainer. China butted up to most of the countries in his division, so there was always crossover. The woman, she said her name was Dot, short for Dorothy, was pretty, she smiled a lot and touched his arm when she talked, like they were old friends, and she was happy to be around an American man instead of the Chinese guys she worked with who didn't treat her so good. He'd answered a few questions at first, always telling himself that he would reel her in just a little further and then turn her with his enigmatic personality.

There had been no big reveal, no traumatic moment when she'd said, "Sorry, Tim, you've gone too far with us. We have you now." He'd just known it. In truth, he'd enjoyed the work, the feeling of superiority he got from sitting at his desk and knowing when everyone else did not. Clandestine CIA officers felt that a little bit when they just went to the store, or to a family reunion, but pulling the wool over everyone at Langley— and getting paid for it—that had to be the most satisfying feeling in the world. And if he got to topple the imperious Odette

Miller off her lofty career ladder when he popped smoke and left right under her nose, that was just gravy.

Rask had unwittingly passed on intel the Chinese had been salivating to get for years. Oh, the stuff about the Albanian op was interesting, and Meyer's handler had paid him a bonus for it. Meyer had done a little digging, tangentially, so he didn't get his hands dirty, and it turned out that the same officer who Leigh Murphy mentioned in her report was planning something big. Meyer could only glean bits and pieces. Requests for some unspecified activity in Novosibirsk, Russia, and a safe house in Almaty, Kazakhstan.

All of it was good stuff—get-imprisoned-for-espionage stuff—but Dot pressed him hard for one thing above all else. She wanted to know the identity of the case officer who had called Leigh Murphy in the first place, the person who had asked her to interview the Uyghur. According to Rask, she must have known him well. They'd probably worked together on a past op. Murphy had been stationed in Africa before, Meyer had that much. Maybe they'd been stationed there together. He'd do some checking, ginning up some connection to a CI case he was helping with. Hell, maybe he'd just call Murphy, tell her he was running something down and needed her help. Rask said she seemed like a ladder-climber. She'd probably be happy to help out someone from HQ. He'd play her a little and get some leads. The thought occurred to him that the Chinese might talk to her first, but he put that out of his mind.

With the mole hunters poking under every stone, Meyer needed to work quickly so he could get out of here before they started casting wider nets. So far, nobody expected he would know anything about the China desk. In fact, no one expected him to know much about anything at all.

He'd find out what Dot wanted. Rask had told him about Murphy's after-action report, how she was vague to the point of insubordination. She'd identified her friend only by a crypt-onym, an NOC, or officer with no official diplomatic cover. This guy wouldn't get booted out of the country and declared persona non grata if he was caught. He'd be imprisoned or killed. If the Chinese were smart, they would watch him for a while, learn who his assets were, and then scoop everyone up at the same time.

Meyer had heard the cryptonym before, and it gave him a place to start.

CROSSTIE.

34

F u Bohai woke to the hum of his mobile phone on the nightstand next to his hotel bed. He peeled back the Egyptian cotton sheet, sodden with sweat, and rolled away from the naked Russian woman who lay draped across his chest and thigh.

She stirred, smacking her lips in sleep. "Tell them to crawl away and die," she said, her Russian thick with the aftereffects of too much blini and Ossetra caviar, and precisely the right amount of vodka and sex.

Her name was Talia Nvotova. They'd met that evening at a Chinese embassy function in Moscow where Fu had been tasked to look into a Chinese diplomat suspected of selling secrets to the Russians. They were "strategic partners," Russia and China, tenuous allies. But, as the adage went, there were friendly countries, but not friendly intelligence services.

Fu Bohai was known by his superiors to be particularly un-friendly, and it was this quality for which he was sent to Moscow. His direct supervisor, Admiral Zheng, who commanded PLAN intelligence, operated by what he called the fifty-fifty rule. If Fu was fifty percent convinced that the diplomat had turned traitor, he was to take care of the matter then and there, sparing the Motherland the bother of a trial. Beijing had suspected for over a year that someone within the Ministry of State Security or PRC military intelligence was leaking classified information to both the Russians and the Americans. They hadn't narrowed the field very far as of yet, and could not very well approach the SVR and say, "One of your spies who has betrayed China is also betraying you to the Americans," though Fu Bohai suspected it would come to that eventually if the traitor could not be found, in order to plug the leak. He smiled at the idea of the mushroom cloud that would cause in both countries.

Officially, Talia was a Russian/Mandarin translator for Moscow state television. Her surname was Czech, but she was a Russian citizen. Fu made certain of that. Well-known in diplomatic circles, Talia had been invited to the function because of her beauty and ability to keep the conversation going. Fu Bohai felt she was probably a case officer with SVR, the Russian foreign intelligence service akin to MSS and the American CIA. He was a newcomer to the embassy, so the alluring Miss Nvotova had naturally done her job and cozied up to him at the party. It did not hurt that he was over two meters tall, had a boyish face but the experience of forty-two years, and could bench-press over a hundred and fifty kilos. He happily went along with the getting-to-know-you charade, inviting her to stroll with him around the park across Druzhby Street from the embassy. Moscow springs are notoriously chilly and Talia looked ravishingly Russian in her silver fox coat and sable *ushanka*. She'd complimented his fedora; he'd complimented her cold pink cheeks. They'd ended up together at his hotel, where she looked ravishingly Russian with nothing on at all.

She tried to roll back to him, but he pushed her away again, harder this time, giving himself distance.

She snorted, collapsing onto her back in a huff, not bothering with the sheet while he lifted his fedora to retrieve the phone under it.

Fu spoke in Chinese, knowing Talia understood every word. He shifted in bed so his thigh ran alongside hers as he talked, skin to skin. He kept the volume of the phone low, so she could hear only his side of the conversation.

It was Admiral Zheng.

SURVEYOR had information that someone from the CIA office in Albania had spoken with a Uyghur refugee who had links to separatist groups in China, possibly the Wuming. It was weak, as far as intelligence product went, but it had caused some movement from the Americans. The admiral wanted Fu to speak to the Uyghur and the woman from CIA—find out what they knew that might help lead him to Medina Tohti, and then do with them what he did best. Fu did not know the entirety of the situation with Tohti. He did not need to. What he did know was that it was a sensitive matter that the admiral did not trust the Ministry of State Security to handle. What's more, the admiral cared little about finding anyone associated with the terrorist organization known as Wuming. Locating them would provide a method to capture Medina Tohti. She had to be brought in alive and able to think and communicate. The last was an important detail. A prisoner could be very much alive, but unable to do much beyond a blink or grunt. Anyone else should be terminated if possible, but Fu was not to go out of his way for that. Wuming was a problem for law enforcement. The admiral wanted Medina Tohti in custody sooner rather than later—and the fewer people who knew about it, the better.

Fu picked up his watch, a Tissot, also on the nightstand by his hat. "I will check the flights," he said. "But it will take all day to get there via commercial airline."

Talia's beautiful thigh tensed—possibly because he spoke about leaving . . .

"Stand by," Fu said, muting the phone and holding it away from his ear to check the distance between Moscow and Tirana, Albania, on the Internet. He turned the phone away so Talia could not observe his search.

The movement brought a whiff of Talia's shampoo and he had to rub a hand across his face to stay focused.

"If I take a company plane I can be there in under four hours," he said.

Her leg tensed again. Relaxed. A delicate foot tick-tocked back and forth at the end of the mattress, red toenails bright and stark against the white sheet. Her brain was working through some problem. Was it how to get Fu to stay with her, or was she instead envisioning a large map, as he would have done had he heard her having this same conversation? Was she trying to work out what important destinations a corporate jet might reach in less than four hours?

The admiral easily agreed to Fu's use of the company plane, a Cessna Citation CJ3 registered to an Internet gaming company in Beijing. The company did not mind the use of their name on the international paperwork, and members of Admiral Zheng's intelligence service enjoyed some degree of anonymity when they traveled. Four of Fu's men were already in the air from Beijing. They would meet him in Tirana.

Fu ended the call and set the phone back on the nightstand beside his hat. He waited for Talia to speak.

She rolled toward him, draping her leg across his thighs again, nuzzling his neck with her button nose, kneading gently at his shoulder with her chin. "Do you really have to leave me, *dorogoy?*" My darling.

"I am afraid so," Fu said, attuned to the reaction of the muscles in her belly as she lay flush against his hip.

She groaned, pouting, pulling herself closer to him, as if getting any closer were even possible. *"Ya nye magu byes teebya zheet."* Fu didn't understand her, but he'd observed many times since he'd taken her to his bed that though her Mandarin was near perfect, she stuck to her native Russian in matters of the heart. She stuck out her bottom lip and translated. "I cannot live without you."

She did not ask where he was going, which made him doubt his earlier assessment. Instead, she asked when he was coming back.

"I am not certain," Fu said, being honest. He did not know if he would ever return to Moscow.

She nuzzled him harder, breathing against his neck. "You have at least one more hour, no?"

He shook his head. "I must leave now."

She pulled away, far enough to lift herself up on one elbow and stare down at his face, head tilted, auburn hair draped to one side, exposing the small diamond stud in her beautiful ear. She kept her leg where it was, hooking him gently with her heel.

"What could be so important that you have to rush away?"

"Work," he said, leaving it at that. Now her questions would come. The angled interrogation of a spy hiding under the guise of a wistful lover.

Instead, she collapsed beside him, dejected and glum, and pressed him no further. "Very well," she said. "I am not accustomed to this. It is usually I who leaves."

Fu kissed her on the shoulder and got out of bed.

Talia pulled the white sheet to her chin and rolled on her side to watch him get dressed. She slipped back and forth between Chinese and Russian as she talked about all the things they might do together when he came back to Moscow.

She was still in bed, naked but for the sheet, when he shrugged on his long wool coat and pulled his gray hat snug. The odds were sixty-forty against her working for the Russian SVR—and that saved her life.

For the moment.

35

Commander Wan's exposure suit gripped him like a fist as water flooded the trunk and pressure equalized with the sea outside. He climbed the short ladder and unlocked the hatch. He took a deep breath before he gave it a kick. It opened easily, and he pulled himself through, clinging to a small exterior handle long enough to shut the door behind him, throwing him into complete and utter darkness.

And then he let go.

The sonar technician aboard *Long March #880* had been off watch during the accident and sustained burns to the side of his face as part of the fire-suppression crew. At his station now, he turned his bandaged head toward the captain.

"Con, Sonar. Heavy screws. Close. Zero-five-zero."

Captain Tian pursed his lips. Perhaps the distress buoy had gotten through the ice. "Another submarine?"

"Negative, Captain. A surface ship. Icebreaker."

In training, Commander Wan had been taught to yell "ho, ho, ho," like Santa Claus all the way to the surface to keep venting air so his lungs would not burst as the pressure increased as he shot to the surface. In truth, he simply screamed. The huge hood shot him upward at two meters per second, as if pulled by a hoist, arms outstretched over his head like Superman. Even moving so quickly, it took almost a minute and a half for him to reach the surface. Ears squealing, his lungs on fire, his face felt as though he'd been beaten with a hammer as pockets in his sinuses struggled to deal with the rapid ascent. And the cold. It was very cold, even in the suit. He imagined for a moment that he was falling, not rising, plummeting from a fifty-story building. If he hit overhead ice, the results would be close.

He'd been terrified through the entire journey, from the moment he'd dogged the hatch on the lockout trunk, but a minute in he began to fight true panic. The kind of panic that makes a submariner hold his breath or rip away some important piece of gear. The kind of panic that would kill him. He kept breathing out. Why was it still so dark? He had to be near the surface. Had they gotten the time wrong? Was it night? Did polar bears hunt at night? He should be nearing the surface by now. Ah . . . He'd been closing his eyes. Light. Gray at first. Then blue. Something pale passed in front of his eyes, scraping the hood, spinning him as he bounced away.

Ice.

His hands struck the base of the ice sheet first, his arms folding in on themselves as the speed of his body carried him up. The air in the bubble hood protected his skull from the worst of the impact—rattling him, but not breaking his neck as he'd feared. He followed the light, rebreathing what little air he had left in the hood as he crawled along the bottom of the ice, pulling himself toward what he hoped was the edge.

At some point, he'd have nothing but carbon dioxide.

Blue-white chunks of ice as big as cars bobbed and rolled in a slurry of smaller slush, basketballs, soccer balls, baseballs, all jagged and sharp, tearing at his suit. A sudden shock hit the small of his back as freezing water began to seep in. Floundering, he kicked toward what looked like the edge. One of the crew had made him a set of spikes out of two pieces of a mop handle and sharpened bolts. Fighting the swaying current, terrified of being sucked under, he popped the protective corks off the sharpened ends and used them to pull himself upward. Kicking was difficult within the cumbersome suit, but he powered himself up—only to be rolled off the other side as what he thought was a shelf turned out to be a small, tippy berg. Water began to seep into his suit again. If it filled, he would, at the very least, freeze to death. If he lost the flotation, he would return to the sub, very slowly and very dead.

He found the edge, a two-foot-thick shelf. It was much too high for him to get a correct angle with the ice spikes without taking the suit off. That was not going to happen.

He swam along the edge, searching, pushing away every time a swell threatened to drag him under. His nose bled profusely, spattering the clear face of the hood with every breath. Overwhelmed with cold and fatigue, he found himself wondering what would come first, complete exhaustion or the inability to see what he was doing. A bergy bit the size of his father's car nudged him from behind, at first startling him, then giving him an idea.

The first one had held him for a time, before tipping him off. If he could clamber up on this one, he might be able to use it as a stepping stone . . .

"We did not talk about this," Wan muttered inside his bubble hood as he worked. "Drowning. Yes. Kidneys torn out by bears. Yes. But there was no mention of the insurmountable wall . . ."

Using all his reserves, he finally dragged and kicked himself out of the water to collapse on the ice shelf. He rolled onto his side and unzipped the hood with trembling fingers. The sudden slap of cold air took what was left of his breath away. A white moonscape of ice dazzled by the sun stretched forever around him in all directions.

The thought of it made him laugh out loud. He'd struggled so hard, only to drag himself to a different place to die.

Commander Wan's suit had begun to freeze to the ice by the time he remembered he had something else to do.

The satellite phone. *Yes. That was it. Call in the report . . .* and then, whatever happened happened . . .

He fumbled with the bag containing the phone, teeth chattering, shivering badly, his hands like unworkable claws. The simple squeeze buckles seemed impossible, and he had to put his hands under his armpits for several minutes just to warm them. He finally opened the bag—only to dump a steady stream of seawater onto the ice. He could not see any rip, but it had flooded nonetheless. The phone was useless. A plastic brick.

The bag with the shotgun was still around his neck. He could use that if he needed to. If freezing to death wasn't as painless as they said. Or if a bear came for him. He looked at the plastic buckles, then at his blue unworkable fingers and shook his head. The neoprene bag might as well have been a bank vault. However he died, the shotgun would not be a part of it.

Wan rolled onto his back. An unbearable sadness washed over him as he stared up at the incredible blue. The men on the stricken *880*, his men, five hundred feet below, would all perish without another look at the sky.

Two hours after Wan Xiuying collapsed, a strange rumble carried across the ice. He felt it before he heard it. The shivering had passed now and he was warm. In fact, the suit worked much too well, and he thought of taking it off to cool himself. He'd watched movies in his mind as he drifted in and out. *Crimson Tide, Run Silent, Run Deep*—the book was better. He'd found a copy in Mandarin, but he learned more from the one in English. *U-571 . . . What was the Russian movie? China needed something . . . Wolf Warrior should make a good submarine movie . . .*

The rumbling grew louder, shaking the ice under his head. A surge of adrenaline coursed through Wan's body. A bear! Head lolling. He pushed himself onto his side with great effort.

"Come here!" he shouted. "Come and get me, you—"

But when he lifted his head, it was no bear he saw, but a large red ship in the distance, eating its way through the ice—and an orange bird hovering directly above him.

36

Captain Jay Rapoza, commanding officer of the USCGC icebreaker *Healy*, met the medical officer outside sick bay. Rapoza was a big man, burly, fit, barrel-chested, with a slight squint in his left eye that made him look as though he should be clenching a pipe in his teeth. He was a sailor's sailor, fibbing just a little to his wife when he told her how heartbroken he was every time he went to sea.

"How's he doing?" Rapoza asked.

Fortunately for the guy they'd scooped off the ice, the *Healy* was the only cutter in the Coast Guard to have a licensed physician's assistant and an HS—health services technician (called a corpsman in the Navy). Lieutenant Shirley Anderson peeled off a set of blue nitrile gloves and shook her head.

"Pupils are still dilated and his heartbeat is irregular. Core temperature is eighty-seven—about a degree from gonersville in most people. We're warming him up slowly. Have to be careful the cold blood from his extremities doesn't rush back to his core and give him a heart attack."

"Hope that guy plays the lottery," Rapoza said, "because he is one lucky young man."

"Roger that, sir," Lieutenant Anderson said. "If I may ask, sir. No sign of a boat or snow machine?"

"None," Rapoza said. "The 65 made two more passes after they dropped him off. Just a big hole in the ice. The SEIE suit suggests he escaped a submarine."

Anderson shivered.

"I don't like thinking about subs underneath us, sir. Creeps me out. But it does make sense. This guy is extremely talkative—mostly about submarine movies."

"Odd," Rapoza said. "Sonar shows the seabed at over a thousand meters. There are some underwater mountains, maybe . . ." He glanced at the door, then at the lieutenant. "What exactly is he saying?"

"He was talking about Lipizzaner stallions when I left."

Rapoza saw a junior officer from engineering at the end of the passageway and called him by name. "Find Chief Cho and have him come see me."

"Aye, aye, sir," the ensign said. "Right away. I just passed him."

Rex Cho came through the hatch a half minute later, cover in hand.

"Captain," he said, presenting himself.

The whole ship knew they were heading toward an unknown radio signal, possibly a Chinese submarine. And, of course, they knew about the lone Asian man in the exposure suit they'd picked up off the ice, but they'd not all been told the details.

"I'm sorry, Captain," Cho said. "I haven't spoken Chinese since grade school, since my *nainai* passed away."

"Understood," Rapoza said. "But I'd like you in the interview with me, just in case you pick something up. He's kind of out of his head. He might see you as a friendly face and be a little more forthcoming."

"Aye, sir," Cho said.

It took all of ten seconds for the man to tell Chief Petty Officer Cho that he was "Commander Wan Xiuying, executive officer of *880*." He drifted off twice, rambling about enigma machines and Nazi U-boats when he awoke. Some of it was in English, and Rapoza recognized them as lines from Hollywood movies. He first answered Chief Petty Officer Cho in Chinese, but when Cho repeated the question in English, Commander Wan threw his head against the pillow and rolled his eyes as if to say, *Oh, you want to play that game? Okay . . .* and then answering in English. Most of it seemed like nonsense, but many recent events over the past few days fell squarely in the unbelievable column.

Coded signals, strange noises from the bottom of the Chukchi, and now a Chinese submariner coughed up on the ice like some Jonah—Captain Rapoza grabbed a piece of paper from Lieutenant Anderson's desk and took notes.

Though the Chinese submariner seemed fluent in English, his physical and mental state slurred his rambling words, rendering them difficult to understand. There had been a fire on a submarine . . . a professor Liu was dead or near death. Rapoza got that much.

Commander Wan lifted his head, tugging against his IV line, attempting to get out of the bed.

"Must call," he said. "Crew . . . destroy . . ."

Anderson and Cho each took a shoulder and guided him gently back to the pillow.

"Burned," he said, thrashing his head back and forth. "Save crew! *Hai shi shen lou* . . . no good. Destroyed . . . Fire. *Hai shi shen lou* . . . Gone! *Hai shi shen lou* . . ."

Chief Cho gave an excited nod. "Wait, wait . . . I think I

know this one . . . I always thought it was funny . . . *Hai shi shen lou*—towers and cities built by clams—it means *mirage*."

Commander Wan's heart rate rose and he began to thrash harder.

"Captain . . ." Anderson said.

"Right." Rapoza took his notes and walked toward the door. "I need to make a call. This is a little above my pay grade."

"Sir," Lieutenant Anderson whispered before he made it into the passageway. "Are we still heading toward the distress signal?"

Rapoza thought for a moment, and then shook his head.

"I think this guy *is* our distress signal. We'll see what Higher says, but unless otherwise directed, we'll stand by at this location for a bit."

"Do you think there are people alive down there?" Anderson shivered again. "On a submarine?"

"Down there, yes," Rapoza said. "Alive . . . I don't know. But I think we're going to find out."

37

CIA case officers Leigh Murphy and Vlora Cafaro habitually kept an eye open for surveillance. Being aware of one's surroundings was part and parcel of PERSEC—personal security—for spies, and for anyone else, for that matter.

They'd done no full-blown surveillance-detection run on the way to the bar. They had no need to arrive in the black—that is, without a tail. Everyone at the embassy, and likely everyone on Elbasanit Street, knew they went to the Illyrian Saloon at least three nights a week after dinner. Sure, it was predictable, but there were only so many good bars within walking distance of the embassy. The Illyrian was only four blocks away, on the other side of the Air Albania stadium. They were just two women going to unwind after work, not spies doing spooky spy shit.

And they were young and invincible.

Murphy saw the tall man in the gray fedora when she left the Serendipity restaurant on her way to meet Vlora at the bar, around the corner at the southern edge of the upscale Blloku district. Eating alone was a natural depressant, and there was nothing about the man to make him stand out on a dark street where most everyone wore some kind of hat against the cold spring evening.

He'd been out front, loitering by a newsstand on the corner. Vlora had seen him, too. Both women were trained observers, and both had noted he was tall, good-looking, and probably Chinese. Neither woman mentioned him to the other, and both promptly forgot about him when they entered the warm bosom of the bar.

Vlora hadn't eaten, and ordered kebabs. She sat across the small wooden table in a dark corner of the bar and bobbed her head to the live band while she ate, her long black hair piled high on her head with a yellow pencil. Murphy drank her Korca Bjonde and listened to the music.

Wood-planked walls and parquet flooring dampened the chatter and clink of voices and bottles, but conversation was difficult to hear over the music, so both women were content to sit and take in the vibe of the place for the first hour, unwinding from a long, and in Murphy's case, excruciating, day. It took a couple of drinks for them to become lubricated enough that they didn't mind that they'd be stricken with bar-voice the next day from shouting over the din at each other all night just to carry on a conversation.

The band tonight was playing a damn good cover of "Welcome Home (Sanitarium)" by Metallica, and the guy on lead guitar looked the part of an ancient warrior with his massive, coal-black beard that reached the middle of his chest and a crested bronze helmet that should have been guarding the hot gates of Thermopylae. The waitress, who was always giving patrons some little tidbit of Albanian history, had pointed out when she brought Leigh Murphy's fourth bottle of Korca that the Illyrian tribe of Albani had been mentioned in the works of Ptolemy. Albanians took great pride in their Illyrian warrior heritage, as did many Balkan peoples—and the walls of the saloon showed it. Murphy had been here so many times she knew all the trivia by heart. She liked the bellicose motif— bronze helmets, short swords, broad-chested men with spears. When she was growing up in Boston, her middle school PE teacher had called her pugnacious. She'd gone home and looked the word up on Encarta on her dad's new home computer, and decided that, yes, she was indeed pugnacious, and happy to be so. Maybe that was why she liked Albania so much—and why she put up with an asshole chief of station like Fredrick Rask.

Vlora finished her kebabs and twirled her glass of plum rakia while she stared transfixed at the band.

"He's cute," Leigh said, toasting the swarthy drummer with her bottle of Korca.

Vlora bobbed to the music. "You know what they call a drummer in a suit?"

Murphy shook her head.

"The defendant," Vlora said, buzzed, chuckling at her own joke. She turned to face Murphy. "Anyway, I'm not looking to start a romance—too much paperwork. I'd have to file an Out-side Activity report with Rask, and I don't want that son of a bitch knowing any more about me than he has to—especially when it comes to my love life."

Murphy tipped her beer and toasted in Albanian. "*Gezuar* to that." She looked at the bottle and groaned, feeling ex-hausted and more than a little buzzed.

"Speaking of Freddie Rask," Vlora said. "You okay? It looked like he was ripping you a new one today."

"Yeah, well," Murphy said. "I probably deserved it. I should have told him what my friend wanted me to do. I was just afraid he'd say no."

"That's exactly what he would have done," Vlora said. "*No* is the default answer for a boss like Rask. Makes life easier on them." She took a drink of her rakia and then leaned across the table, licking her lips. "So, tell me about this mystery guy. He's one of us. Would I know him?"

"How'd you know my friend was a guy?" Murphy said.

"Leigh . . ." Vlora said. "What is it again that you think I do for a living?"

"Whatever," Murphy said. "Anyway, we're just friends. Life's too complicated to have it any other way. For now." She drank the last of her Korca, thought about another, but then decided against it. Her apartment was only five blocks away, but she wanted to go running in the morning. She looked at her watch. "Shit! It's almost two a.m."

Vlora shrugged. "Let me get this straight, this mystery guy, whatever his name is, sends you on a secret mission to interview a Uyghur guerilla fighter and gets your ass on the chopping block. Sounds like a real peach sending you out on something that radioactive without telling your boss."

"Most of the shit we do is radioactive," Leigh said. "Besides, he needed help."

"All men need help, sweetie." Vlora polished off her drink and waved at the waitress, asking for another. The waitress shook her head, which in Albania meant "yes."

"I've gotta call it a night," Murphy said. "You're staying?"

"For a minute." Vlora gave a long sigh, staring at the drummer again. "I'm rethinking my aversion to writing that Outside Activity report." She looked up suddenly, bending to her philosophical side now that she had a few glasses of rakia in her. "Don't get too mad at Rask. I mean, yeah, he's a dick, but don't you carry that burden of him being what he is. No matter where you go or what you do, there will always be a Freddie Rask—they just have different faces and names."

"I know," Murphy said. "I just didn't appreciate him keeping the blinds to his office open so everyone could witness my beheading. I mean, I'm not some junior case officer straight out of training. He knows that."

"*Dans ce pays-ci, il est bon de tuer de temps en temps un amiral pour encourager les autres.* In this country, it is good to kill an admiral from time to time"—Vlora tapped her empty glass on the table, making sure the waitress didn't forget her—"for the encouragement of others."

The street was dark and cold and quiet when Murphy stepped out of the Illyrian Saloon. A young couple came out of the bar behind her, giggling and cooing at each other and making her feel more alone than she already did. Vlora was a good drinking bud, but not someone Murphy would have hung out with had they not been in the same office and shared a mutual hatred of Rask.

A scooter putted by, heading east toward the stadium. A dog barked somewhere down the street. She was thinking about how you didn't hear many dogs in the city during the day, when the unmistakable sound of a boot scraped the pavement behind her. Continuing down the sidewalk, she shot a nonchalant glance over her shoulder. An Asian man in a skintight leather jacket, going the same direction she was. He was short, maybe not even as tall as Murphy, but looked broad in the shoulders, a weightlifter, maybe. His short stature and sudden appearance made her think of a Pukwudgie—the creepy little swamp goblins her dad used to tell her about to keep her from venturing away too far in the dark.

She'd been too tipsy to notice him. *Amateur.* Not that the guy was a threat, but Murphy shouldn't have let anyone get that close without noticing him. Then she remembered the Asian man in the hat who had been loitering on the corner. A coincidence? Not likely. Adam had just sent her to have a heart-to-heart with a Uyghur separatist who might have information on the whereabouts of the Wuming.

Murphy quickened her pace, suddenly grateful for the weight of the little Glock 43 resting under her jacket in the small of her back. Normally, she would have continued west, to the T, before turning left on Sami Frasheri. Her apartment was two long blocks down, with a view of the Tirana Grand Park. If Pukwudgie was a state actor, the last thing she wanted to do was let him know where she lived. Protocol said she should have gone straight back to the bar where Vlora was, but this was probably nothing.

Murphy looked behind her again. He was still there, smoking a cigarette now, making no effort to hide, but was slowly closing the distance between them. She cut left down Janos Hunyadi, behind University of Tirana. It was a wider street and didn't lead directly to where she lived.

She fished her phone out of her pocket and voice-dialed Vlora. It rang three times and then went to voicemail.

Shit!

Behind her, she heard footfalls on the pavement as Pukwudgie made the turn as well.

She thought of dialing 112—Albania's 911 equivalent—but if something was about to go down, it would all be over before the police could get here. She stuffed the phone back into her jacket, wanting to keep her hands free.

Twenty, maybe just fifteen, steps back, Pukwudgie coughed. Loud, fake, the way you cough when you want someone to know the toilet stall is occupied. She didn't even have time to check before a second man, also Asian, stepped around the corner at the intersection ahead and started walking toward her. This one was taller, with glasses and a puffy gray ski jacket. There was a street to her left, an alley, really, flanked by a scabby vacant lot and a run-down four-story apartment building. There were no streetlights, but she figured she could use that to her advantage. Tirana was her turf. Pukwudgie and his friend were trying to pinch her on *her* streets, the very route where she ran virtually every morning. She could cut down the alley, and then squirt out the end by the market, and then hang a left and run straight back north to the Illyrian, where Vlora was probably still making time with the drummer.

She made the turn, skirting a parked sedan, picking up her pace, running through the darkness.

She felt the man in the hat before she saw him, her gut registering some clue nanoseconds before the conscious part of her brain picked up on it. He stepped out of a little alcove to her right, midway down the block, less than ten yards away. She slowed, trying to make sense of the situation. Her hand flew to the gun at the same instant the man lit a cigarette. His motions were slow, methodical. The match lit his face under the low brim of the fedora. Then he held the flame sideways, so it illuminated the alcove beside him—and the lifeless body of Joey Shoop.

Murphy's breath caught like a stone in her throat. She

stutter-stepped, slowing her draw of the pistol when she should have sped up. These men had known she would take an alternate route if pressed when she left the bar. They had driven her to this exact spot.

Something heavy impacted her right knee at the same moment her hand touched the Glock. White lights of pain exploded through her body. Instinctively, her left leg propelled her away from the impact. She hopped sideways, trying to regain her balance as she brought the weapon up toward the man who'd hit her. He hit her again, with a metal bar—probably a collapsible baton, but it was too dark to see for sure. The second blow caught her across the top of the arm, impacting her radial nerves. The gun flew from her hand. At the same moment, a powerful hand struck her hard between the shoulder blades. Her right knee destroyed, her arm still aching from the blow, she threw her left hand out front to arrest her fall. Her wrist snapped on impact.

She choked out a scream, her senses flooded with nausea from the pain. Scrambling onto her back, she chambered her good leg, ready to kick any son of a bitch who came near her again. She screamed again, ragged, torn, her voice already hoarse from the bar.

The tall man in the hat stood there looking down at her, almost bored, while the other two approached from her head and her feet. It was impossible to fight them both at once, injured like she was. She felt someone move and turned in time to see the syringe the moment before Pukwudgie jabbed her in the neck.

She felt herself detaching, floating away. This was bad.

The pain in her knee and wrist faded away . . . No, that wasn't right. It was still there. She just didn't care. The men stood back, waiting for the drug to take effect. The syringe was huge. Whatever they'd given her, it had been a big dose.

Then she saw the spiders. Hairy. Black eyes. Obsidian fangs, dripping with venom. Dozens of them pouring out cracks in the ground. She tried to run, but floundered, falling again—into the path of the spiders.

A light came on in one of the apartments above. Someone shouted in Albanian—muffled, distorted. In her stupor, Murphy couldn't make it out.

"It's okay!" the man in the hat yelled in English. "My friend has had too much rakia!"

A dark panel van screeched down the alley and they shoved her inside facedown on the metal floor, leaving poor Joey where he lay.

Her face pressed against the cold floor, she tasted blood, smelled puke and urine. So dizzy . . . Her lungs were heavy.

This was where they'd killed Joey . . .

She came to slowly at first, willing her eyes to open, then jerking, jolted by the cold chill of the van's metal floor against her bare skin. She was naked, hog-tied, hands and ankles zip-tied behind and then tied together. Arched backward by the bonds, it put excruciating pressure on her injured knee and shattered wrist.

Whatever they'd given her, Murphy metabolized it quickly. Probably a ketamine dart—straight into her muscle. That would explain why she hadn't dropped immediately. Her memory of the attack was fraught with gaping holes. She remembered the spiders, though. She'd never forget those. Yeah, it was ketamine, all right.

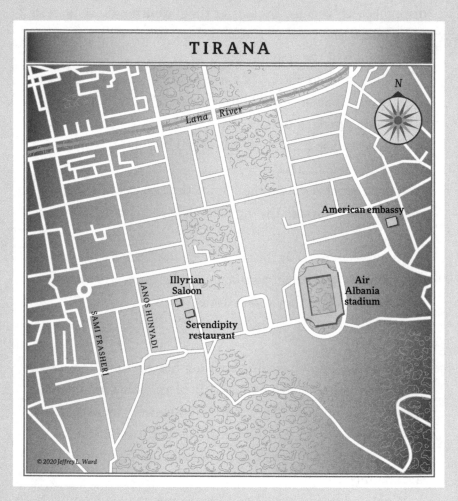

The van was moving, bouncing over a rough road. That told her nothing. Many of the streets around Tirana were in a constant state of repair. The men spoke among themselves in hushed Mandarin, ignoring her for the time being.

Murphy shut her eyes, struggling not to let her breathing get away from her. She needed to calm her thoughts, no easy task naked and bound in the back of a van with three dudes.

Pain and the drugs had turned her brain to mush. Her thoughts were fuzzy, unhinged and without defined edges. Nothing made sense. Everything hurt.

Was this random? Did they plan to take her somewhere and rape her? Panic bore down, crushing her chest. *No.* Rapists didn't tie your feet together. *Did they?*

Come on, Leigh. Think. They trained you for this at The Farm.

No, they didn't. Not really. There was no way to train for something this horrific, this futile.

They wanted her awake. That meant they wanted to question her. She blinked, trying to remember. *Adam. They would want to know about Adam.*

The man in the gray hat sat on an overturned bucket behind the driver. He reached down to pat her cheek, gently at first. Hard enough to rattle her teeth when she clenched her eyes.

He'd cocked his felt hat back, revealing a high forehead and passive eyes, accustomed to hiding their cruelty. "We are going for a drive in the countryside." He smiled benignly. "How long we drive is up to you."

She licked her lips, then craned her neck to get a better look at him, trying to speak. He raised a hand to shush her. "I do not want to kill you," he said. "But it is important that you know I will."

"Just get to—"

The man in the hat nodded to his companions. The short one, Pukwudgie, flipped her on her side, and then pressed his boot to her injured knee, bearing down hard, slowly, like grinding out a cigarette.

She screamed and kept screaming until the one in the hat kicked her in the face.

He took a folding knife from his pocket. It was small, with a turned-down Wharncliffe blade. The needle-sharp point and scalpel edge allowed him to perform extremely intricate work. "Listen to me carefully. I will now ask you a few questions about your conversation with Urkesh Beg, the Uyghur man you spoke with today. If you lie, I will make a small cut, somewhere on your body. I have not decided where yet. If you refuse to talk, I will do the same." He gave a long, sad sigh and then leaned back on the bucket, crossing his knees, bouncing the butt of the knife against his thigh, almost as an afterthought. "In my experience, the process works better if it is done slowly, so you have more time to consider your answers between each incision. Unfortunately, I do not have much time. How did you learn of Urkesh Beg?"

Murphy began to sob. "I . . . I don't know what you're talking about."

The man's hand flashed, like a viper, his blade neatly bisecting the brow over her left eye. It stung, but the pain wasn't as horrible as she'd anticipated. Blood poured from the wound, burning her eye, a constant reminder that she'd been cut.

He prodded her with the toe of his boot. "I have many questions and little time." He waved the blade over the top of her body. "It is a shame to ruin such beautiful skin."

Head lolling, cheek against the cold steel of the floor, Leigh

Murphy clenched her eyes shut. Tears pressed from her lashes, mingling with the blood.

Pukwudgie readied another syringe.

Leigh Murphy began to tremble, her entire body wracked with sobs. *Oh, Adam. You told me too much.*

I may have a location," Fu Bohai said when he telephoned Admiral Zheng four hours later.

The American CIA officer had been incredibly resilient. She'd borne much of the pain in silence, passing out much later than others to whom he'd given the same treatment. In the end, no one could hold up to drugs and pain. The mind simply let go.

The admiral grew animated on the other end of the line as Fu repeated the details of what she'd given up.

"You must go at once," the admiral said, breathless. "Take as many men as you need. Kill the Wuming filth, kill the Americans, or do not. I do not care. But you must bring me Medina Tohti alive and intact. I cannot stress that enough. I need her coherent and talking. Now go, take the company plane. I want you at this mysterious lake as soon as humanly possible. Before that would be even better."

"I understand," Fu said. "But . . ."

"What is it?"

"Forgive me," Fu said. "But please trust my expertise in this area. Even the most determined person will eventually talk, but the more determined one is, they are often far from coherent when they do finally break."

Admiral Zheng scoffed. "Do not concern yourself with that.

Just bring Medina Tohti to me. Your expertise is not required beyond finding her and getting her to my office. Harsh
methods will not be necessary. Her daughter and sister are
in Kashgar. Their safety will be all the incentive she needs to
assist us."

38

Clark's eye flicked open at the sound of shuffling footsteps—too big and heavy to be a rat. The room was hazy with the muted gray light of an overcast dawn outside the tiny window. He moved slowly, feeling the familiar pops and cracks that greeted each morning even when he slept in a soft bed. A cloud of white vapor blossomed around his face when he breathed.

The sound bounced off the clay walls, making it difficult to pinpoint where it was coming from. He caught movement in the shadows, tensed, then relaxed a hair, falling back into his blanket when Hala's silhouette came into focus, her small face framed by the white fake fur ruff of her coat.

"You okay?"

"John . . ."

The urgency in her voice brought him fully awake. He sat upright, throwing off his blanket.

"What is it?" he whispered, still raspy from his sleep.

Hala went to the window. She had to tiptoe to peek out. She ducked her head away as soon as she'd looked. "He's coming!"

Clark rolled to his feet and drew the girl near so she could explain quietly. "Who's coming?"

"I'm sorry," she said again. "I had to pee. There was a man

driving by on the road. I think he had stopped to pee as well. I did not think he saw me at first, but then he called out. I'm very sorry. It was an accident—"

"It's okay," Clark said. "Is he a policeman?"

She shook her head. "No. I do not think so."

"Is he alone?"

She nodded. "I saw his car. There was no one else. Maybe he is—"

A wary voice called from outside the walls of the caravanserai. She was right. The man was Uyghur—and he was close.

Clark held up his hand to shush her while the man spoke, then leaned in so she could whisper in his ear to translate.

"He . . . He wants to know what I am doing out here all by myself."

The man outside spoke again, louder this time, bolder, more demanding.

Hala gasped and began to shake at what she heard.

"What is it?" Clark asked.

"He knows the Bingtuan are looking for a runaway child," she said. "He said he will not call them if I do not fight him." She looked up at Clark. "He is a very bad man."

"Yes, he is," Clark said. He stood, stepping sideways inch by inch, "cutting the pie" until he brought the shadowed figure outside into view.

He was dressed like a workingman—dark trousers, white shirt, dark sport jacket under a heavier wool coat. He wore a black fur hat with the earflaps down against the morning cold. Clark estimated him to be in his early thirties, but it was difficult to tell in this part of the world. Life in western China tended to age people beyond their years. He could just as easily have been twenty-five.

Clark assessed the man quickly as an opponent. He didn't appear to have a weapon. His hands were empty. No cell phone at the ready. He could have already called and reported his find, but Clark doubted that. Not if he wanted to be alone with his newly found young treasure. No, he'd wait until he was done—or, more likely, he'd forgo calling the police at all. He'd just do what he wanted and leave. Fugitives didn't call the police, if he even let her live.

The man called out again, whistling as if summoning a pet.

Hala's hand shot to her lips, covering a gasp. "He said he's coming in. He warned me not to run . . ."

Clark scanned the room. There'd been nothing to use as a weapon when they'd come in, but maybe he'd missed something.

Nope.

Clark dropped to his knees in front of Hala, taking her by both shoulders. "I need you to trust me."

She nodded. "What do you want me to do?"

Clark stood and took the little douk-douk out of his pocket, opening the scimitar blade. He placed it on the ground, and then stepped on the handle, pinching the two metal sides together, effectively turning it into a fixed-blade knife. The cutting edge was just four inches long, not optimal for stabbing, but there were other ways to cause chaos and doom with a knife.

Clark nodded toward the entrance. The place where the wall had collapsed formed a natural funnel that would send the man to them.

"He's going to come from there," Clark whispered. "I will stand by the door. When I raise my hand, you make a noise. Don't call to him, but let him hear you. Do you understand?"

315

She looked up with brown doe eyes, nodded around a mouthful of shirt collar.

"When you see him at the door, I want you to run." Clark pointed to the far corner of the room.

"Run where?" Hala whispered, terrified. "There is nowhere to go."

Clark gave her a reassuring pat on the shoulder. "True," he said. "But he does not know that. He will not be able to resist chasing you."

"What if he catches—"

"He won't," Clark said, already moving to the door. None of this would work if the man saw or heard him.

Clark had the newcomer in height and weight, but that whole vitality-of-youth thing would be a problem. Fortunately, Clark had what Ding called "old-man strength," which was really not strength at all, but cunning and pure meanness in the face of battle. He didn't intend to let this evolve into a contest of strength or determination. In fact, if Clark did this right, there would be no fight at all. It would be an assassination.

Clark stood to the right of the door, opposite where the man's sight line would be when he heard Hala. He held the douk-douk in his right hand, firmly but relaxed. A clenched fist moved much too slowly for what he needed to do.

He raised his left hand, listening for the tentative footsteps. The man called out again, just a few feet down the dark hall. Clark couldn't understand a word, but the cruel intent came through clearly enough.

Clark let his left hand drop.

At the signal, Hala gave a gasp, shuffling her feet on the ground as if scrambling to get away.

The man laughed, whistling again, calling out. Clark imagined him saying, "I have you now . . ."

Clark caught movement to his left, checked his breathing, lowered his center, ready to move.

Hala sprang from her spot, digging in as though she intended to run straight through the far wall of the earthen chamber. Clark hadn't told her to scream, but she did, and it only added to the effect.

The man's predatory drive kicked in immediately at the sight of his fleeing quarry. He shouted at her to stop and bolted after her, thinking there must be a door in the shadows, and unwilling to let her slip away.

Clark stepped sideways, snaking his left hand behind the man's neck and around his face, forearm to forehead, yanking him backward as his legs tried to run out from under him. At the same moment, Clark buried the blade into the side of the man's exposed neck, impacting the brachial nerve so hard that his body jolted as if hit with an electric shock. The little doukdouk's scimitar point slid in as if the flesh were butter, just behind the windpipe. Clark felt a sudden pulse of blood slap his arm, moist and hot. This wasn't his first rodeo, and he'd rolled his sleeve above the elbow in anticipation of this to keep it clean.

With the edge of the blade facing forward, Clark pushed at the same time he gave a sharp backward tug on the man's forehead, severing the trachea with a sickening pop.

The man struggled, but only for a moment, before becoming heavy. Clark let go, allowing him to pitch forward, faceplanting on the floor.

Hala ran to him, ignoring the dying man's agonal gasps, to

grab Clark's arm with both tiny hands. She was frantic with worry at the blood dripping from his elbow.

"John, you are hurt!"

He took a deep breath. "No," he said, turning so she faced away from the gore. "I'm fine. It's his. Not mine."

"Okay," she said, panting, lifting his arm to check it thoroughly, unconvinced.

He switched the open douk-douk to his left hand to keep from accidentally cutting her.

"Really," he said, "I'm okay."

Clark rubbed as much of the blood off his arm as he could with a blanket, and then went to look out the window. He'd thought to move the man's car before anyone noticed it, but there was too much traffic for that. A steady line of open trucks and trailers filled with camels, cattle, goats, donkeys, and the odd, fat-bottomed sheep of the region formed an early-morning parade line toward the market grounds. None of them paid any heed to the thirty-year-old Dongfeng sedan that had apparently broken down on the side of the road.

Clark turned to see the girl standing over the dead man.

"Gather your things," he said. "We should find another place to wait. It's only six thirty. Still over two hours until we can meet my friend. This will be difficult to explain if anyone else happens along."

Hala didn't move until he took her gently by the shoulder and herded her into the corridor.

"I'm sorry you had to see such awful things," he said.

She leaned against his leg and sighed. Still trembling, she spoke matter-of-factly, like a woman twice her age. "It *was* awful, that is true, but if you had not been here, it would have been much worse."

318

39

Midas Jankowski was pretty damned certain that no one in the history of history had ever calmed down because someone else told them to "calm down." Fortunately, no matter what Gerry Hendley was reading into his tone, Midas wasn't spun up, he was just surrounded by camels and goats and weird-looking big-assed sheep.

A Uyghur with four goats stacked like cordwood on the back of a three-wheeled motorcycle truck barked *"bosh-bosh, bosh-bosh"* as he nosed Midas aside with the front tire and rode past. Hendley must have heard the change in Midas's voice and was doing his level best to try and talk him off some ledge.

A woman's voice playing an incessant loop over a loud-speaker forced him to cup his hand over the phone in order to be heard.

"Seriously, Boss," Midas said. "I'm fine. Just got *bosh-bosh*ed out of the way."

"What the hell does that even mean?"

Midas thought of telling Hendley to think about calming down, but decided being a wiseass to the boss's boss was not the smartest thing to do.

"Not sure," Midas said. "Probably 'get out of my way.' Anyway, something's come up with our mutual friend." The line was presumed secure, but he still refrained from using names.

"All right," Hendley said. "Let's have it."

"Everyone's intact," Midas said. "Our problem is egress. Our friend's message said he has the package."

"*Has* the package? With him?"

"Sounds like it," Midas said. "From the sound of things, something really bad went down in the neighborhood he was looking at. I'm not sure about the details, but I'm hearing three dead."

"Our friend?" Hendley asked.

"Well enough to send the message," Midas said. "He must have rescued the package."

Midas's plane had arrived in the middle of the night, really in the wee hours of the morning, when he would have been getting up to do PT during his days as a lieutenant colonel in the Unit, commonly known as Delta Force. Halfway around the world, Gerry Hendley was hungry to know what was going on.

They spoke over an encrypted Internet connection, the virtual IP address bouncing around the globe to discourage local authorities in Kashgar from monitoring the call or tracking his signal. This had been the first opportunity Midas had been in the clear enough to call in with a report.

He'd done his usual TSCM—Technical Surveillance Countermeasures—sweeps covertly as soon as he arrived in the hotel room, always assuming the walls were bugged and equipped with at least one camera. Chinese security services surveilled everyone on the street, and it stood to reason that they wouldn't pass up the opportunity to bug the rooms where foreigners spent the night. He'd found two listening devices, one in the lamp by the house phone—too obvious—and another at the corner of the bathroom mirror. Those wily MSS guys, assuming people might conduct their nefarious conversations while sitting on the john. Midas had used enough laser listening devices himself that he left the draperies closed to keep anyone from picking up the subtle vibrations of his voice against the window glass.

In case anyone happened to be watching, he'd used his phone to take the obligatory YouTube video of his Chinese vacation, getting a 360 of his room. Pinhole cameras in the walls would show up as shiny dots. Lenses in other objects—smoke alarms, wall hangings—might or might not give themselves away.

Even so, covert phone conversations from a hotel room in Communist China were too big a risk, so Midas waited until he got to the market—Rally Point Bravo, where Clark's message had said to meet.

He'd just begun to bring Hendley up to speed on the new turn of events when the goatherd *bosh-bosh*ed his way past.

"We've got an emergency bugout plan," Midas said. "But it didn't take the package into account. We should be meeting up soon."

"Very well," Hendley said, obviously not wanting to end the connection and be left in the dark. "Three dead, you say?"

"As far as I know," Midas said. "We passed a bunch of XPCC armored personnel carriers and troop trucks rolling into the neighborhoods behind Jiafang market this morning on the way in from the airport. My driver said he heard through the cabbie network that three officials were murdered with knives. XPCC and cops are saying it was Uyghur terrorists. I guess they're already rounding up the usual suspects, at least the ones who aren't already in detention camps."

"Any word that a foreigner might be involved?"

"None so far," Midas said, sidestepping a fresh pile of what he believed to be camel shit. "You need to cut back on the fruit, Mister," he said under his breath.

"Pardon?"

"Sorry. Nothing," Midas said. "The most important point is, our friend says he's intact. Knowing him, I'm sure he has some kind of plan worked . . ."

Midas's voice trailed off as he watched a half-dozen SWAT officers in black BDUs and helmets swagger through the crowd. Each had a small rifle Midas recognized as a QCW-05, a Chinese-made SMG, slung diagonally across his chest. Long wooden riot clubs hung from rings on their Sam Browne belts. The mass of marketgoers parted in front of them. Midas glanced to his left, and saw another group of officers, this one moving down the next aisle where food vendors sold grilled versions of the same animals that were still on the hoof just a few feet away.

It was clear from the way they scrutinized the crowds that these officers weren't just out on patrol. They were looking for someone in particular.

At the other end of the line, Hendley grew agitated at the long silence. "What is it?"

"Have to go, Boss," Midas said. "I got officers in hats and bats strolling around hunting for somebody. I need to make sure it's not our mutual friend."

Midas promised to check in soon and ended the connection, stuffing the phone into his coat pocket. Strolling slowly, he checked out the different livestock and food vendors, keeping tabs on the nearest group of XPCC troops out of the corner of his eye. A grizzled little man in a dark suit coat and four-cornered doppa hat stroked a wispy beard with one hand and held up a straight razor with the other, offering to give Midas a shave. Midas smiled and shook his head. Yeah, sitting down in these crowds and letting a stranger put a blade to his throat didn't seem very tactical at the moment. A woman selling hot soup called him over with a flick of her wrist and held out a steaming cardboard cup. He figured soup from a boiling cauldron was about the best chance he had not to catch street-meat two-step. It was good, salty, with a few more globules of fat floating on the surface than he was used to, but it warmed his hands, and carrying it made him look like a tourist. Just yards from the soup lady, a man in a ratty military-surplus coat butchered a black goat. A pool of fresh blood in the dust said he'd just killed the thing. When Midas drew closer, he realized the hatchet that the man used to cut the animal was connected to a concrete block with a length of chain—one of the Bingtuan's prohibitions about Uyghurs possessing weapons.

He checked his watch. Almost 0900.

While the bulk of the livestock market visitors were Uyghurs, there were plenty of tourists, Han Chinese and European alike, *ooh*ing and *aah*ing and snapping photos at every camel and sheep. The guy with the chained hatchet got a lot of attention. Midas took a photo there, too, more to get a pic of the officers behind the man than the bloody carnage.

At first Midas thought the troops were singling out European tourists specifically, but further study made him realize they weren't zeroed in on any particular ethnicity at all. Their focus appeared to be on taller men who happened to be with children. It made sense. Clark would have worn a hat that

323

covered his face, but they must have security camera footage that showed a big guy in the company of Hala Tohti.

One of the policemen caught Midas looking in his direction and glared, a challenge to come closer. Midas smiled, ducked his head subserviently like a nervous tourist would—all the while thinking he could surely take this skinny dude, body armor and all. The real problem was Rally Point Bravo, where he was supposed to meet Clark, was on the other side of this officer and his heavily armed friends. With any luck, Clark had seen the patrols and was staying away.

Midas made a right, nearly running into a different patrol. He smiled again, stifling the urge to speed up. That would look like he was trying to avoid them. Instead, he worked his way in the opposite direction from the rally point, taking the long way around. Clark would wait fifteen minutes before he left the area. Midas would stand off and watch, approaching only if they were in the clear—which wasn't looking very likely, since the place was crawling with XPCC cops.

Midas stopped to look at a rack of colorful pashmina scarves as two more officers sauntered by, chatting with each other like they were at the beach instead of an occupying force. Their wooden batons rattled against black riot armor.

The Uyghur woman behind the scarves smiled at him, covering her sales bases. "Three for five euro. Two for five dollar."

Midas bought three. "A lot of police," he said, giving the lady a smiling grimace as he gave her a U.S. five-dollar bill. "Did something happen?"

She folded the scarves neatly and put them in a flimsy plastic bag. "Nothing happen," she said. "Always police. They here every day."

Midas thanked the woman and walked on, swinging the

sack full of scarves in one hand while he sipped the fatty soup with the other—the perfect tourist cover.

"Mr. C.," Midas said, blowing a blossom of vapor into the cold, musty-smelling air. "What have you gotten yourself into?"

Clark tapped Hala on the shoulder so she'd follow when he left the rally point. Midas was twenty minutes late, which meant they'd have to try again at 1400. There was too much law enforcement roaming the livestock market to tarry in one spot for long. They needed to get somewhere out of sight—away from the dead man at the dilapidated caravanserai.

With his phone battery near zero, he had no way of knowing if Midas was free to move around the city or if he'd picked up a tail. There was always a chance he'd been compromised. Clark would cross that bridge when he came to it, but in the meantime, he decided to pay a visit to Adam Yao's contact, a woman named Cai, who sold handwoven carpets. Her presence at the market was the reason Clark had picked it as one of the meeting points in the first place.

The authorities appeared to be looking for someone with a child, so Clark whispered where they were going and then had Hala walk a few paces ahead, mingling with the other marketgoers. She blended in well with the crowd, always alert, stepping behind a string of camels or sheep when she spied approaching officers.

The clatter of hooves and *baas* of sheep drew Clark's attention over his shoulder.

"*Bosh-bosh!*" the boy driving the sheep said.

Hala stepped close enough to tug at Clark's sleeve, translating before putting distance between them again. "Make way."

Clark knew the general area where Yao's contact would be set up, but he supposed assigned spots could shuffle from week to week with so many people being taken away to camps.

To his left, a young man wearing an embroidered green doppa hat and a white apron over his coat arranged small glasses of pomegranate juice on a table to tempt passersby. A girl about Hala's age—his daughter, perhaps—stood behind him, leaning on the handle of a juice press twice her size to fill a large metal bowl with the vibrant red liquid. Beside her, a man fanned smoke away from a line of fatty mutton kebabs that had likely come from a friend of one of the flocks the next row over.

Across from the juice stand, a cobbler tapped at his bench beside a mountain of refurbished shoes as high as his waist. Beside him, blue tarps covered a stall with shelves of assorted Uyghur pottery.

Yao's contact, Mrs. Cai, came into view as he walked, on the other side of the blue tarp. A stout woman with high cheekbones and a sun-pinked face, she wore an ankle-length brown coat of heavy wool over broad, workingwoman shoulders. A few strands of black hair escaped her white headscarf. A Hui Muslim, one of China's fifty-six recognized ethnicities, Cai's ancestors had likely been Central Asian travelers from Kyrgyzstan or Kazakhstan on the ancient Silk Road.

Clark kept his distance, watching the young cobbler tap tiny nails into the new heel of a gnarled pair of leather shoes, while he waited for a German couple to haggle over a Central Asian rug the size of a bathmat.

They finally got the price they wanted, and walked away with their tiny rug. Mrs. Cai glanced up at Clark but didn't acknowledge him as she stuffed the Germans' cash into a metal box underneath her table. Clark noted the tarp over the potter stall next door blocked a good portion of the security camera on the nearby electric pole.

"Nice carpets," he said in English, keeping his back to the camera and the pottery seller.

She smiled but said nothing.

Clark smiled back and waved a hand over the hand-knotted display rug of rich maroon and deep blue wool. "Like Aladdin's magic carpet," he said.

She looked at him for a long moment and then nodded. "I've heard it said that Aladdin's rug was Persian."

Clark gave her Yao's passphrase response. "I've heard that as well," he said. "I have also heard that all Persian rugs are Oriental, but not all Oriental rugs are Persian."

"You are John?" Cai whispered. Her expression never changed, and anyone who looked on would have thought they were still discussing carpets.

Clark watched her closely. Initial meets were always touchy, but at some point, you had to commit. To paraphrase Hemingway, sometimes the only way to know if you could trust someone was to trust them. There were so many soldiers and police around that all she had to do was raise her voice and he would be toast.

"Yes," he said. "I am John."

Like usual, the travel alias retained his real first name, so John was the given name on his Canadian passport. Cai would not know or care if it was his real name or not.

Her head dipped in an almost imperceptible nod toward Hala, who stood watching the shoemaker a few feet away.

"The girl is safe, then?"

Clark picked up a small rolled carpet, perusing the golden fringe. "She is," he said. "But getting her out is a problem."

"I will help," the woman said.

"I would appreciate anything you could do," Clark said. "The person we were supposed to meet hasn't arrived."

Cai pretended to explain the details of the carpet. Her wrists peeked from the sleeves of her long coat, exposing a cluster of scars when she reached to unroll the edge—cigarette burns that didn't look accidental. It was no wonder she was helping Yao. Sadly, the fact that this woman had likely been tortured by the same people who were after him allowed Clark to relax a notch. She had her personal reasons for fighting the Han government.

"I am to give you some special items." She took the carpet they were looking at and reached below her table to retrieve a small one, deep red and coal black, about the same size as the one she'd sold the German couple. Stepping closer to the blue tarp wall of the pottery stall to block the security camera's view, she unrolled it enough to reveal two handguns. One a semiauto Norinco known as a Black Star, a Chinese copy of the venerable Russian TT-33. Two magazines of 7.62x25 Tokarev ammo lay nestled in the carpet beside the pistol. Clark wasn't a big fan of Norincos, but you took what you could get at times like this.

Mrs. Cai unfurled the carpet a few more inches to reveal a puggish stainless-steel derringer with the words SNAKE SLAYER and BOND ARMS engraved on the side of its three-inch over and under barrels. Elegantly simple, the little gun was chambered to fire either two .45 Colt or two .410-gauge shotgun shells.

Cai had no .45, but provided six .410 shells loaded with number-six birdshot—a snake slayer indeed. Always a gun guy, Clark resisted the urge to pick up the derringer and handle it.

Cai rolled the carpet and tied it with a piece of strong cord.

"Some Bingtuan police carry 7.65," she said. "Others nine-millimeter. The derringer was given to me by a friend. I would like the girl to have it."

"Of course," Clark said. He marveled that the little Texas-made gun had somehow found its way to the frontier city of Kashgar, about as close to the rough and tumble of the real Wild West as anywhere left on earth. "It will be perfect for her, should we need it."

"I fear you may have many opportunities before you are out of this country," Cai said. "These guns are small but powerful. Perhaps you can use them to obtain other weapons."

"Getting out of the country," Clark said. "I understand you have the contact for the route."

"You must leave the city as soon as possible," she said. "Too many cameras here. They are looking for the girl, saying she has been kidnapped. If they have her photo, facial-recognition software will eventually identify her." She scribbled an address and a new passphrase on a piece of paper, holding it out of view of the surveillance camera while she showed it to Clark. "Memorize this."

He nodded, reading it to himself and committing it to memory before she rubbed the pencil marks away with her thumb.

"This person will help you get out of the country. You can trust him."

She handed him the carpet and held out an open hand.

Clark looked at her.

"You have to pay me," she said. "People will think I am giving things—"

A commotion on the other side of the cobbler's stall drew both their attention up the aisle. Four XPCC soldiers moved among the crowds, stopping every few steps to look at people's phones and question them. They were led by a tall officer with dark glasses and a gray hat of curly Karakul lambskin. This kind of hat, known as a *papakha*, was traditionally reserved for Russian officers of higher rank. The way this man moved led Clark to believe that the hat might have the same significance for the Bingtuan of western China.

Behind Clark, Hala gave a startled gasp. He turned to find her crouching behind the stack of carpets at the far end of Mrs. Cai's stall. Deathly pale, she chewed away furiously at her collar, rocking forward and back as if she might bolt at any moment.

Clark stepped closer.

"Do not run," he said, keeping his face passive, his voice low and even. "They will notice us more if we look afraid."

"It is him," Hala whispered.

"Ren Shuren," Cai said, running a hand across one of the carpets for the benefit of the security camera that viewed that end of the table. "A major with the local Bingtuan police service. His younger brother, Ren Zhelan, works for the Kashgar building council."

"It is him," Hala whispered again.

"Ren," Clark said under his breath. Of course. He'd heard Hala use that name before. The major bore an uncanny resemblance to the man Hala and her aunt had been fighting with when Clark first stepped into their home—the same man he'd finished off with the cleaver.

Major Ren Shuren waved his men along, scanning the crowds like a machine as he stalked forward. He hadn't made eye contact with Clark yet, but he was close, less than thirty feet away, and closing fast.

40

There'd been no way for Midas to reach the rally point on time. He was nearly run over by police patrols twice. Black uniforms were around each corner, beside every flock of sheep, their boots visible beneath the bellies of standing camels. They were everywhere. Midas resorted to combat breathing—four seconds in, four seconds out—willing himself to remain calm. It made no sense to rush into danger when he could stroll his way out and approach the situation from a more strategic angle. So he walked slowly, taking in the sights, doing his best to play tourist.

At half past nine, he decided to go check out the carpet lady. There didn't seem to be quite as much law enforcement in this area of the market, and it made sense that Clark might try and link up with Yao's contact when Midas missed the meet.

A shepherd with a half-dozen sheep *bosh bosh*ed him again just as he reached the corner, grabbing his attention for an instant. A cloud of greasy meat smoke hit him in the face as he made the turn. When he stepped out of the smoke, he forgot about his combat breathing entirely.

Forty feet away, John Clark stood by a pile of colorful carpets, chatting with a round lady in a white scarf and heavy coat. A group of very grumpy-looking soldier cops stalked directly toward him.

A man to Midas's left held up a glass of red juice, grinning broadly. His daughter, a girl of ten or twelve, sat behind a table full of glasses, pressing more juice. Without a second thought, Midas turned toward the man, nodding, reaching for the juice. Up until now, he'd worked hard to make himself insignificant, small, a tourist not worth noticing. Now he straightened up to his full height, making no attempt to hide the hint of belligerence that was usually present in his bearing. Two feet from the man, he dragged his lead foot, stumbling forward in the gravel. He knocked the glass from the man's hand, spilling the juice and crashing headlong into the table. The array of full glasses flew everywhere, shattering into the ground. The table was a flimsy affair, nothing more than a few wood planks set atop two sawhorses. It gave way quickly, allowing Midas to stumble past the cursing man and into the juice press where the young woman sat, knocking her to the ground.

Midas caught the girl by her hand, mid-fall. She cried out in surprise, covered in bright red pomegranate juice and seeds from the juicer. She hit the ground on her butt, startled but uninjured.

The XPCC authorities were looking for a tall man with a Uyghur girl, and when the man approaching Clark turned at the sound of breaking glass to look at Midas, that is exactly what they saw.

Midas scrambled to his feet, helping the girl. She tried to pull her hand away, but Midas held her for a moment, long enough, he hoped, to give the impression that she was with him.

Her hand locked in his, Midas looked toward the officers. They were all running in his direction. He released his grip, allowing the girl to scramble to the safety of her father. On the far side of the oncoming policemen, John Clark caught Midas's eye for a fleeting second and gave him a nod of thanks for the distraction.

"I'm sorry," Midas said to the juice seller, taking out his wallet as he watched Clark hustle Hala Tohti away. He shoved a wad of cash toward the other man. "I can pay. I'm sorry. I'm sor—"

A blur of black body armor bowled him over, cutting his apology short and knocking the wind out of him.

You're on your own now, Mr. C., he thought, as a knee speared him in the small of his back and a forearm smeared his cheek into the dust.

The commotion with Midas drew every available soldier and policeman at the market, leaving Clark and Hala unimpeded as they left the scene. Clark found a likely vehicle at the far edge of the parking area—an old Toyota flatbed truck with the key still in the ignition. Even the farmers were interested in Midas's commotion, so the area was all but deserted.

Cai's contact was a sheep farmer ten kilometers farther out of the city. He knew they were coming, which meant it could be a trap. Clark reasoned that if Cai had wanted to turn him in, she could have done it at the market—unless, of course, she wanted to blame it on someone else so she could keep the arrangement with Adam Yao. Unless . . . It was all too easy to work yourself into a lather on what might happen. That was one of the greatest stresses of intelligence work. Everyone involved was lying. Some lied to safeguard their own skin, some to protect secrets—or a ten-year-old Uyghur girl. Some lied for money or to settle ancient feuds. Hui and Uyghurs hadn't always gotten along, each contending the other group were the outsiders. But then, the Uyghur man at the caravanserai had proven that people were people, and he could not trust someone with Hala's safety simply because they shared a common ethnicity. Conversely, he could not write off Mrs. Cai simply because she did not.

Circumstances often forced an intelligence officer to approach strangers in strange lands. Time and again, these people were no more than the proverbial friend of a friend—or, worse, the enemy of a common enemy. No matter how tenuous the connection, there had to be some trust to move forward in any mission.

And then there was the problem of the mole hiding out somewhere in the ranks of the U.S. intelligence community. Yao's contacts in and around Kashgar didn't have to be bad themselves. They could simply be compromised—and that would drop everyone in the grease.

The driver's-side door of the old pickup creaked and groaned when Clark pulled it open. Too late to quit now, he didn't even look around to see if anyone had heard. Instead, he waved Hala in ahead of him. She scuttled quickly across the bench seat and ducked down while he shut the door. The inside of the truck smelled like tobacco and lanolin—sheepherder smells. Exploring, Hala opened the glove box and found a loaf of bread and a can of apple juice.

"Lunch," she said, holding them. A half-moon of saliva dampened the collar of her shirt, but she was smiling now instead of chewing it—breathless and elated at having gotten away.

Clark was relieved, too, but had enough experience to know

all of that could change in a heartbeat. Midas would be fine, so long as his cover held.

Clark turned the ignition. The truck started up without a fuss, and he pulled out onto the road, rattling east, out of town, away from the dusty livestock market, and the dead man in the slumping caravanserai—outlaws on the Silk Road.

41

Illegal entry into a hostile nation was beyond tricky.

Adam Yao weighed the pros and cons carefully of which point of entry would be best to take the Campus operators across. Holograms and embedded biometrics had rendered forged passports all but anachronistic. Fortunately, stolen passports still worked, so long as the offended country didn't report the missing numbers. The Finnish documents Yao provided were genuine, with matching biometrics and authentic barcodes. To add a touch of even more veracity, VICAR, Yao's agent in place in Russian SVR, had arranged for a Russian entry and exit stamp, with which Yao was able to mark each visa. Travelers with some history drew less scrutiny—at least that was the theory. Thanks to Yao's contact in Beijing, the last-minute Chinese tourist visas were all in order. Probably. Trust was always a risk. CIA did have the mole, but Yao told himself he'd mitigated that by keeping his asset off the radar, paying him off the books with discretionary funds. Assets were supposed to have control numbers, files. Langley, and, more important, Congress, liked to know where their money was going. Thank God he'd broken the rules on that one.

They'd seriously considered crossing by bus at Maikapcha-gai, Kazakhstan, into Jeminay, a sparsely populated county in western Xinjiang. Locals used the crossing, so tourists, even benign Finnish ones, would raise a fuss. Still, the border guards were poorly paid, and Yao felt certain he'd be able to sort it out with a few hundred well-placed American dollars. Scrutiny sometimes wasn't quite as tight at land crossings as it was at airports.

The problem was one of logistics. Entry with a stolen pass-port was one thing. But regulations at the Maikapchagai/Jemi-nay crossing required them to take a bus rather than a private or rented vehicle. It was much closer to their destination on a map, but the realities of vehicle procurement and border delays could add hours or even days to the journey. A commercial flight into Urumqi had put them seven hours away, but at least they had the independence of their own transportation. Secu-rity had been tense, but they'd been admitted with Yao, a Hong Kong resident, acting as their guide and minder. Yao slapped magnetic signs on both sides of the rented van, pro-claiming them a "Sun Country" guided tour to ease the minds of jumpy security patrols. Chavez had wanted two vehicles, but the XPCC officials were suspicious of outsiders as it was. An extra vehicle without someone Chinese driving it would be an extra chance for random search—particularly in the off sea-son, when tourists were rare and personnel at the checkpoints had little to occupy their time. So far, they'd passed three, and Yao had gushed about the beauty and glory of mainland China at every turn.

A Web search revealed Lake Kanas, a day's drive north of Urumqi, was situated in a mountainous forest on a small protru-sion that was bordered by Kazakhstan, Russia, and Mongolia. It was remote, and difficult to police. It was also famous for a large fish that was said to drag unsuspecting horses into the water while they were drinking. Beginning in May, tourists would flock to the lake for the numerous tour boat excursions, hoping to catch a glimpse of China's version of the Loch Ness Monster.

Ding Chavez rode shotgun, with Adara and Lisanne behind him. Ryan took the rearmost seat with some of the luggage. They didn't have much, just a duffel apiece, but needed enough to pass for tourists. Most had grabbed catnaps along the way, wanting to be as fresh as possible when they arrived so they could hit the ground running.

An hour south of Burqin village—the entrance to Kanas Lake Park—Chavez got everyone's attention. Yao was guide, but as an NOC, he operated by himself so much that he was more than happy to yield the role of team leader.

"Let's do a quick gear check," Chavez said. "Everyone up on commo?"

The group answered in turn.

Gavin Biery had modified their cell phones so they could function as radio and intercoms, allowing them a common net even when there was no cell service. Gone were the copper near-field neck loops and belt-pack radios. Linked to the Sonitus Molar Mics attached to each operative's rear tooth, the entire communications system had been reduced to what looked and outwardly functioned exactly like a normal cell phone, and a piece of plastic that resembled a small retainer. It would be discovered only during an extremely invasive search.

Chavez looked across the front seat at Yao. "I know you didn't want to dig out weapons prior to the checkpoints."

"Now is probably okay," Yao said. "Ryan, grab that camera bag in the back."

Ryan did, passing it over the seat to Lisanne, who gave it to Chavez.

Yao nodded at the hard plastic case. "They're in there. Two wide body cameras, a couple of lenses, and ten rolls of film."

Chavez scoffed. "You're still using film?"

Yao chuckled. "I'm not taking pictures, dude. Those little black film canisters are about the same size as the suppressors. Helps them blend in. The pistols are wedged in the camera bodies. Should be four total. One for each of you."

Adara and Lisanne leaned forward to get a look. All the way in the rear, Ryan looked on glumly, chin resting in his hands over the backseat, waiting his turn.

"How'd you get this through security at the airport?" he asked.

"I didn't," Yao said. "The case was waiting for me at the rental car place in Urumqi."

"You've got some serious contacts, my friend," Lisanne said.

"A lot of people in this part of the country are good and pissed at their Chinese overlords," Yao said. "I can usually find someone willing to do something for me as long as they figure I'm sticking it to Beijing. I use a couple of assets as cutouts, to keep my face off the transaction." He shrugged. "Plus, you can accomplish more with a good cause and a duffel bag of cash than you can with a good cause alone."

Chavez flipped open one of the cameras. "What the hell?" He held up a small black Beretta semiautomatic Bobcat.

"You got us toy guns?"

Ryan groaned from the rear seat. "You know what Colonel Jeff Cooper said about the .25 auto? You better not carry one because you might have to shoot someone with it, and if you shoot someone with it, they just might realize they were shot and it might piss them off . . . or something like that."

"Shows how much you know," Yao said. "These Bobcats are .22-caliber."

"A .22 . . ." Ryan fell back against his seat. "Well, that is just fabulous news."

Chavez passed one of the diminutive black pistols over the seat for Adara and Lisanne to look at.

Lisanne activated the lever on the side, flipping up the barrel, obviously familiar with the weapon. "My mother had one of these. The tip-up barrel made it easier for her to chamber a round without having to work the slide. Pretty nifty, if you ask me."

"I agree with Ryan," Chavez said. "I'd take nine-millimeter over nifty. Beggars can't be choosers, though."

"They cannot," Yao said, tapping the steering wheel with an open hand as he drove. "We're in the Wild West, my friends. Adapt and overcome." He nodded sideways to the case again, eyes on the road. There were wild horses there, and the occasional camel. "Unscrew the lenses. There should be five blades in there. Some of them are better than others. Give Ryan the Halo. Maybe a good Microtech will appease him."

Ding unscrewed the plastic cap on the end of a telephoto lens and dumped the knives out in his hand. All of them were Microtech automatics with OTF, or out-the-front, blades. The Halo was the largest, with a blade just over four inches long.

"Excellent," Chavez said. "Just in case I need a sexy knife to cut open an MRE."

"You will find the icing on the cake next to those film canisters we talked about," Yao said. "It took some doing to get those babies. Everybody on my pipeline kept wanting to steal them."

Chavez held up a black metal cylinder, an inch in diameter and just under three inches long.

"Small for a suppressor," he mused.

"You know as well as I that these things aren't mouse-fart quiet," Yao said. "But with subsonic ammo this thing is amazing. Solid, too. Instructions don't call for you to shoot it wet, but I've put a little lithium grease on the baffles and . . . I've gotta tell you, it is sweet. Jack could pop a round in the backseat and we'd think we ran over a rock."

"Custom job?" Adara asked.

"No," Yao said. "Made by Bowers Group. They call it the Bitty. These are the same, they just don't have any manufacturer's markings, in case we have to ditch them."

Adara screwed it onto the threaded barrel of the Beretta Bobcat and hefted the little setup. "Bowers Bitty 'Black,'" she said. "Makes the .22-caliber much more interesting."

She passed the gun over her shoulder to Ryan, who gave it a nod of approval. "I guess the little cuss grows on you after a while," he said.

Chavez laughed and looked back at him. "Like somebody else I know." He turned to Yao. "There are only four. What are you going to carry?"

"I'll make do." Yao chuckled. "Frankly, if things turn to shit, I plan to run screaming into the woods . . ."

Yao knew something was wrong when the Han woman at the front desk at the Hongfu Lake Kanas Resort fanned the collected passports in her hands like a poker hand, pushing his upward to separate it from the pack. She set that one aside and then gathered the rest into a neat stack before placing them on the counter. Probably in her mid-forties, her black hair had the slightly auburn tint of a person who spent a great deal of time outdoors. The tag on her navy-blue cardigan said her name was Ming.

Absent the frown lines of someone who looked as grim as she did at the moment, she was probably a very nice woman, or she would have been had not the two hawkeyed police officers been watching from the lobby—one a bulldog, the other a whippet.

"*You* may check in," Ming said, loud enough that the two policemen could hear. "But I am sorry to inform you that we are too full to accommodate the foreign guests."

"I see," Yao said. He knew full well they had plenty of rooms, but it would have done no good to call her on her lie. Instead, he gathered the Finnish passports and passed them back to their respective owners. This would have certainly been the problem if he'd tried to get them rooms at one of the hotels right next to the lake. They were notorious for telling foreigners at the last minute that they could not be accommodated. He'd hoped to mitigate it by staying in Jiadengyu fifteen minutes away. "My secretary made the reservations," he said. "I will speak to her about the error."

"Perhaps," the desk clerk said. "Or perhaps it was a problem with the computer system. It happens."

Yao started to leave, but then turned, as if struck by a sudden idea. "What if we were to upgrade the rooms for my foreign guests? Their budgets are large. I'm sure they would happily pay for any larger suites you might have available, and, of course, any surcharges such upgrades might include."

The clerk glanced at the bulldog, who gave an almost imperceptible nod.

"Would your friends pay in cash?" she asked.

"Of course," Yao said.

This brought nods from the bulldog and the whippet. The desk clerk took the passports again and made copies for her records. She'd saved face and Yao was able to secure the exact same rooms he'd originally reserved for a mere doubling of the cost. It was a small price to pay.

Yao moved to retrieve the passports again, but the whippet policeman walked over and put his hand on top of the stack. He looked them over one by one, examining each photo, comparing it to its owner.

"Finland?" he said to Adara in Mandarin. "I have seen photographs on the Internet. Forests and lakes like here, no?"

Of all the Campus operatives, Adara spoke the best Chinese. There was no need for them to know that, so Yao translated.

Adara smiled and unleashed her baby blues. Nodding enthusiastically, she said, "Yes, yes."

"Okay," Whippet said, and stuffed the passports into his pocket.

Yao protested. "They need those."

"I have to make a report at my office," Whippet said, pointing at the double doors with a slender chin. "One of you may retrieve them in . . ." He whispered to Bulldog, who thought for a moment and then grumbled something back.

"After dinner," Whippet said. "And you must get them tonight. You will be unable to eat at a restaurant, take a boat or horse tour, or any of the other park concessions without your passports."

"But—"

"Retrieve them after dinner," he said again, nodding his skinny face once to show that the matter was closed.

42

Seated to Ryan's right beside Chief of Naval Operations Admiral Talbot, near the head of the polished Situation Room table, Secretary of Defense Bob Burgess got straight to the point, as he always did. He was brash, outspoken, sometimes downright combative, but, as Lincoln had said describing General Grant: "Where he is, things move." Ryan didn't often yield to Burgess's hawkish nature, but it was good to have a plan. As Ryan's dad had told him: Decide what you're going to fight for, and how you plan to do it, then, when the time comes, you don't have to waste any time making those decisions.

Bob Burgess provided Ryan with the military options, so he didn't have to search for them himself.

The Situation Room, not exceptionally large to begin with, was packed to the gunnels. Arnie van Damm was there, along with Foley, Forestall, Commander Carter with the Coast Guard, and a dozen other military men and women—and their aides.

Commander Carter had completed his brief regarding the *Healy*'s recently acquired new passenger—and the fact that the Chinese icebreaker *Xue Long*'s Z-9 helicopter was already buzzing dangerously close to the *Healy*, while she closed the distance at a steady six knots.

Carter stood to leave, but Ryan asked him to stay, stating his desire to have all the smart nautical brains the room could hold.

"Mr. President," Burgess said. "We believe the *880* is the *Long March 880*, the Chinese Type 094 *Jin*-class nuclear ballistic missile submarine that took part in the Snow Dragon war games. Last year, President Zhao gave an address to the Central Committee where he noted a 'revolutionary' propulsion system for their submarines that would render them as quiet as any in the United States' arsenal. It was, Zhao said, a new dawn for the PLA-Navy that would take them out of littoral waters and into the blue—an 'underwater Great Wall' of weapons that could protect Chinese interests from anywhere, and remain undetected."

Burgess nodded to an aide against the wall on the other side of the room. A moment later, the two images appeared side by side on the screen at the end of the table and Admiral Talbot took over.

"These are both satellite images of a submarine believed to be *Long March 880*."

"The sub on the left is shorter," Ryan noted. "By at least . . ."

"Twelve feet," Talbot said. "We believe this indicates the addition of their new propulsion system, similar to our gearless pump jets. To the consternation of his admirals, President Zhao even called the new device by name—*Hai shi shen lou*—Mirage."

Ryan nodded to Commander Carter. "The man the *Healy* plucked from the ice used this same term."

"He did, Mr. President."

"Any chance the Chinese know we have Commander Wan?" Ryan asked.

Carter shook his head. "Very slim. Captain Rapoza was closer. His Dolphin picked up the commander a good twenty minutes before the *Xue Long*'s chopper overflew the scene. Rapoza sent the bird back out again to recon, so for all the Chinese know, we are trying to figure out what happened as much as they are."

"This guy, Wan, mentioned a professor as well," van Damm said. "The missing Professor Liu?"

"Just so," Burgess said. "He's one of their top propulsion engineers. It's not a great leap forward to think that Liu is on the DISSUB. Whoever it was sounds like he had a heart attack or some other debilitating injury. Commander Wan is much more taciturn now that he's warmed up."

"Nice work by Captain Rapoza, by the way," Ryan said. "Engaging him while he was still hypothermic." He leaned back in his chair. "In any case, if Liu is on board and badly injured, there may not be any way to make repairs to the *880*."

"Heck of a lucky stroke," Arnie said. "The rest of the submariners are fortunate that the *Healy* picked up their guy since their rescue party is looking in the wrong place."

Burgess, Talbot, and Ryan looked at one another, and then at van Damm.

"What?" the chief of staff said, in the crosshairs.

"Arnie," Ryan said. "Those subs are coming to make sure we don't get our hands on it, even if they have to destroy it—"

Van Damm cut him off. "I guess this rules out your Fairbanks trip. A ballistic missile sub off the coast of Alaska . . . that's the last place you need to be."

"The icebreaker *Xue Long* will be on station with the *Healy* in . . ." Ryan looked up at Carter.

"Six hours, sir," Carter said.

"There you go," Ryan said. "And their *Yuan* submarine three times faster than that. A few hours and this is all going to be over, one way or another." Ryan turned to the SecDef. "Bob, I don't want to escalate this any more than we need to, but with the *Xue Long*'s chopper harassing *Healy*, let's get a couple of F-35s from Eielson to let Captain Rapoza know he's not alone on the ice."

43

T hat, my friend," Ding Chavez said, "is one of the worst
plans in the known history of plans."

White vapor blossomed around his face as he spoke,
the sight of which made this kid from East L.A. tug the wool
hat down over his ears.

He closed his eyes, inhaling the pungent odor of fir trees and
a hint of woodsmoke. Gone was the cloying odor of cigarette
smoke, gasoline, and garbage that went hand in glove with ur-
ban China. The breeze blowing off the pristine lake nestled
between tree-covered mountains was clear and clean and cold
enough to hurt his face. He could have been someplace in Col-
orado or Montana.

The sun was low, about to dip behind the frosted mountains
to the west, giving the area a pink evening alpenglow to accent
the cobalt-blue water. All of them had zipped up their coats
and put on hats as soon as they'd gotten out of the van.

Behind a pair of binoculars, Yao tried again with his pitch.
"I'm just saying it's the only—"

"Bad idea," Chavez said. "We'll think of something else."

Adara Sherman lowered her own binoculars a hair and narrowed an eye at Yao. A tear, brought on by the chilly wind, ran down a rosy cheek. "For what it's worth, I agree with Ding."

"Okay . . ."

More than a dozen tour boats bobbed against their moorings on a long wooden float that ran parallel to the shore. Three piers, continuations of the boardwalks that ran from the hotel parking lot, led to the boats. Three of the boats, including the one that issued tickets identical to the stubs Yao had gotten from the Kazakh, were just returning from a day on the water. Tourist season was still weeks away, but each had a handful of tourists and their local crews.

They were focused on a boat called the *Xiantao*, which Yao translated as *Eternal Peach*. Chavez estimated it to be a fifty-five-footer. It had an enclosed cabin with large windows for when the weather was bad, and a long aft viewing deck for when it was clear.

"Interesting name." Ryan tipped his binoculars at the tour boat.

"Typical for China," Yao said. "The Jade Emperor's wife, Queen Mother of the West, looks after the Xiantao—the Peaches of Immortality. Eating them is said to give the gods their long lives."

"I could use a peach," Adara mumbled to herself.

"I could use a coffee," Ryan said.

Chavez stamped his feet to get the circulation going and snugged down the wool watch cap. Not that there was much call for it in Southern Cali, but his aunt had always told him, "Feet cold—put on a hat." Right now he needed a bigger hat.

There was still snow at the higher elevations. Ice had gone off the lake only in the past couple weeks and tourists were just beginning to migrate from skiing—Xinjiang-style, with a single guide pole—to boat tours in search of the famed Kanas Lake Monster—thought by most to be a giant, landlocked Siberian salmon called a *hucho taimen*. The Chinese government designated Kanas a Five A park, top of the line. A considerable amount of advertising dollars went toward making people aware of this hidden gem that had much more in common with the Russian taiga than it did with China.

Binoculars and cameras were expected here, making at least the logistics of surveillance straightforward. The problem was, they had no idea what any member of the Wuming might look like. The only photo of Medina Tohti was so old and grainy they could have easily been looking at surveillance footage of Zoe Saldana in a headscarf.

Adara spoke into her fists as she played the binoculars slowly back and forth across the lake. "Let's talk this through, then," she said. "We think these people work on *Eternal Peach*, but they could be on any of the other boats as well . . . We don't know what they look like, or how many there are . . ."

Yao chuckled, blowing out more vapor. "Hence my aforementioned plan."

Adara ignored him. "I say we watch *Eternal Peach* and see who looks like a terrorist."

"Freedom fighter," Yao said.

"Right," Ryan said. "So, the Wuming whack some XPCC troops and spring the Uyghurs and Kazakhs to keep them out of the camps. One of them who works on *Eternal Peach* is a kindhearted fellow and gives one of the poor refugees his coat—forgetting to take the stubs out of the pocket . . ."

They'd been over this before, but it never hurt to hash out the details a few times.

"It really does make sense," Ryan continued. "The concessions would make a great cover. From what I've seen, there are as many Uyghur working here as there are Han Chinese. It's like the surveillance state hasn't quite made it out here yet."

Adara kept the binos to her eyes, but gave a slight sideways nod toward the light pole on her right and the nearest pier. "Oh, Big Brother still has his eye on everyone," she said. "Make no mistake about that."

Lisanne turned a slow 360, taking in the scenery. "Maybe a kind of a Potemkin village when you consider the atrocities going on in other parts of Xinjiang, but it's still beautiful. It's like terrorism hasn't made it here."

Yao half turned, binoculars still up and trained on the second boat over. "Freedom fighters," he said again. "Not terrorists."

"Tomato, tomahto," Chavez said. "The mujahideen were freedom fighters when we were helping them fight the Russians in Afghanistan. Then they were terrorists when they linked up with al-Qaeda and the Taliban to fight us. Same guys, doing the same thing, just to different people."

"Preach on, brother," Yao said. "And right now, we're dealing with freedom fighters. So far, the Wuming haven't hit a single civilian target, only military and government targets we would dub as enemy combatants, were we at war with China."

"But we're not," Chavez said.

"Depends on how well we behave ourselves," Yao said. "Anyway, the fact that there's no freedom-fighting going on around here is another indicator that our guys could be using this as a home base. Bigwigs from the Central Committee, the XPCC, and even the military love to come here and play. Judging from the people who've been on the Wuming hit list, this would be an extremely target-rich environment. Not a single hit has occurred within three hundred miles. That tells me they're not shitting in their own backyard."

"It was enough to get us here," Chavez said. "But it's still too thin to get my hopes up. We can separate and go for a couple of tours tomorrow. Compare the ticket stubs to the ones you got from your Kazakh friend. That will narrow down the boat. Looks like five or six crew members on each vessel. That gives us a lot of people to follow in a small resort with just a few of us. We'll get burned in a matter of minutes."

"Right," Yao said. "That's what I'm saying. You guys start to spread the word that my family is big in Beijing politics. Make me out to be a nationalist, anti-Uyghur prick, too big a target for them to pass up—"

"We're not using you as bait, Adam," Chavez said. "That. Is. All."

"It could take weeks," Yao said. "And I don't feel like getting to be buds with those two cops from the hotel."

Lisanne Robertson cleared her throat. She was humble, polite, and generally soft-spoken, but as a former Marine and police officer, she had no problem with speaking up.

"Can the newbie make a suggestion?"

"Go for it," Chavez said.

"Okay," she said. "There are cameras at the end of the docks and at various points in the parking lot and lakeshore. I've counted and, like you said, Jack, surveillance is spotty here. There are quite a few blind spots."

Chavez made a nonchalant pass along the shoreline with his binoculars. "And that benefits us how?"

"I'm willing to bet," Lisanne said, "that members of any organization as secretive as the Wuming will have each and every camera mapped and tagged. They will want to avoid as much notoriety as possible."

She nodded to the last gaggle of tourists that were, at that moment, stepping off the wooden piers and returning to hotels and tour buses. "See how they walk in straight lines? They couldn't care less about security cameras. The boat crews will get off work in the next few minutes. All we have to do is figure out where the lapses in security coverage are, and then wait and see who takes a more varied route in order to avoid cameras." She shrugged, looking at Adara. "I mean, I do the same thing at work. Don't you?"

Ryan dabbed away a mock tear. "Look at how she's all grown up."

"That might actually work," Chavez said. He checked his watch. It had taken them just under twenty minutes to get there from the hotel in Jiadengyu. They'd grabbed a bite and scouted the area, burning another two hours. "Let's spread out a little and focus on the people getting off *Eternal Peach* for the time being. We should start seeing movement off the boats anytime."

Lisanne tucked her chin deeper into her jacket, shivering. She nodded to a line of taxis, waiting to pick up the last few tourists. "Somebody has to go get our passports from the Keystone Kops. Gonna be harder to get a cab all the way out here by the lake after all the boats are empty. Should be easy to find one in town, though. I can be back in less than an hour."

"We can all go back in the van," Chavez said. "When it's time."

"He's right," Jack said. "Not a good idea for any of us to go off on our own."

Lisanne laughed out loud. "That is the most hilarious thing

I've heard all day, coming from you, Mr. Lone Wolf. Seriously, have you guys forgotten what my primary title is? Director of transportation. This is literally what I do." She looked accusingly at Chavez. "Tell me you wouldn't assign me exactly this task if John hadn't been brought into ops."

"The kid's right," Adara said. "Somebody has to do the grunt work. We can't all have the exhilarating task of shivering our asses off in the cold and staring at the end of a pier for two hours."

"I still don't like it," Ryan said. He treated Lisanne like she was his kid sister most of the time. It had been clear to everyone on the team for some time that he harbored some unresolved feelings.

Chavez hooked a thumb toward the taxis. "Go," he said. "But be back in an hour. And keep your phone on."

"I should go with her," Ryan said.

Adara put an arm around his shoulders. "You're with me, Jackie boy. Let's go check out the other end of the pier before you embarrass yourself."

Lisanne mouthed *Thanks* to Adara after Ryan's back was turned, and then started for the cabs. "Just a quick trip to town," she said over her shoulder. "I'll be fine."

44

Fu Bohai took five men on Admiral Zheng's "company" Cessna Citation CJ3 from Tirana, Albania, to Burqin/ Kanas Airport. With a maximum cruise speed of over seven hundred kilometers per hour, the pilots made the trip in just over eight hours, including a lightning-fast fuel stop in Baku, Azerbaijan, that would have put a Le Mans pit crew to shame. It did not hurt that everyone on board had seen Fu Bohai at work and endeavored to do everything in their power to be certain they never had cause to see him take out his knife with them in mind.

Pretty Leigh Murphy, the CIA officer with the fierce eyes, had proven more difficult to break than he'd imagined. Oh, he knew from the outset that she would be tough. Women customarily held out much longer than their male counterparts. One of his men once suggested that their resilience under torture was because of their threshold for pain. Fu suspected it had more to do with the sheer stubbornness it took to push a child from one's body. Pain had little to do with the process, in any case. Anticipation of pain was what turned the tide, caused people to give him the information he needed to know.

Fu had not even opened his blade, let alone cut the other

CIA officer, before he started blubbering. Joey was his name. He didn't know much anyway, which had proven fortunate for him. A quick death was in his cards, not torture and questioning. According to the information Fu had received through the admiral from SURVEYOR, the girl was the one with the answers. Joey had simply presented himself as an opportunity. He'd been following Murphy, which put him in the right spot for Fu to take advantage of his presence. As the proverb said, sometimes it was necessary to kill a chicken to scare the monkey and make him dance.

The sight of her dead coworker had added an air of gravity to the situation that no threat could have. From that moment, Leigh Murphy had no doubt that Fu was serious. Even so, she'd held her secrets for almost four hours. Finally, the well-tested combination of drugs and anticipation of pain had broken her, as Fu had known it would.

Urkesh Beg, the Uyghur Murphy had spoken with, was wise enough to disappear into the shadows soon after her visit. Fu and his men could have located him, given time, but it no longer mattered. They had enough. Murphy admitted that she'd talked to another intelligence officer who was also after Medina Tohti. This other officer had some sort of ticket for a boat tour that mentioned a monster fish. The CIA officers believed the ticket to be for a tour operation on Kanas Lake, so Fu believed that as well. He'd never been to that part of China— almost to Russia, but the proximity to Urumqi, the prevalence of friendly Uyghurs, and the many places to melt away made it a likely spot for vermin like the Wuming—and Medina Tohti— to hide.

Interestingly, Murphy had never given up the other intelligence officer's name. Perhaps he was her boyfriend, or even her husband, working in a different office. Fu had heard the Americans were foolish enough that spies sometimes married spies. Whatever her relationship, it did not matter where Fu cut or which drugs he shot into her veins, Murphy steadfastly refused to utter the man's name.

Fu was certain of one thing. Whatever his name, he was either at Kanas Lake or on his way—and he was likely not alone.

45

Major Ren Shuren tick-tocked back and forth in his chair behind a gray metal desk in his shabby little office at Xinjiang Production and Construction Corps' regional military headquarters on the outskirts of Kashgar while he poked through each page of Midas Jankowski's Canadian passport with the eraser of a yellow pencil. His hair was neatly parted and just long enough to comb up in front with a bit of pomade. A pair of black glasses perched on the end of a smallish nose. He wore civilian clothes—white shirt, loose polyester tie. He'd hung his suit jacket over the peg behind him to reveal a holstered pistol on his hip.

Midas had been handcuffed at the scene, and then frog-marched to a waiting van while everyone seemed to try and decide what to do with him. For a short time, he thought they might let him go at the market, then the major got a call on his cell and they'd all ended up here. Instead of putting him in a holding cell, they'd brought Midas straight into Ren's office and stood him at attention in front of the desk.

The three other soldiers wedged in beside Midas wore black SWAT uniforms, complete with helmets and exterior body armor. They'd kept their submachine guns—Chinese-made

QCW-05s, from the looks of them, as well as their SIG Sauer pistols. The gas heater on the wall turned the cramped space into a sauna, but none of them had made any move to take off their gear when they'd come in, leading Midas to conclude that they didn't intend to be there long.

He turned out to be very wrong.

Ren went over every page of the passport, even the blank ones, using the eraser to push the paper. He turned the passport upside down, smacked it against his desk, and even tried to erase some of the printing with his page-turning pencil.

After at least ten excruciating minutes, he pitched the passport to the side and then leaned back in his chair, bouncing a fist on his thigh, swiveling his chair back and forth as if unable to sit still.

"My brother was murdered last night," he said, staring at Midas's eyes. His English was perfect, with the hint of a British accent, like the devil in an old movie.

Midas frowned. "I'm sorry to hear that," he said.

Ren continued to stare at him, swiveling, saying nothing.

"Wait," Midas said. "You . . . you're not suggesting I had anything to do with it?"

"Did you?" Ren said, unwavering.

Midas gasped. It was an honest reaction. "Of course not! I'm here on vacation."

Ren reached for the passport again. "Ah, yes," he said. "Vacation. You travel the world alone?"

"Look," Midas said. "Sir . . . I don't want any trouble. I'll pay for whatever damage I did when I fell. It was an accident."

"Perhaps you were looking for a Chinese prostitute," Ren said, peering over his glasses. "American minds are always in the gutter."

"I'm Canadian," Midas said. "But you have it all wrong, sir. My girlfriend was supposed to come with me on this trip. China was her idea."

"But she conveniently did not," Ren said. "Leaving you free to roam the streets in search of prostitutes—"

This guy had a one-track mind. "No, no, no," Midas said. "That's not it at all. She got called in to do an emergency surgery. Since we had the tickets bought, I thought I might as well not waste the chance to see your beautiful country."

Ren snorted, swiveling his chair so he could peck away at his computer and open Facebook. Apparently, the network used by the XPCC did not have to worry about the Great Firewall of China and the preemptions against most Western forms of social media. His fingers hovered, twitching above the keyboard.

"Your girlfriend's name."

Midas paused.

The soldier nearest him cuffed him in the back of the head. Hard. Midas envisioned snatching the asshole's pistol away and killing everyone in the room, but gave up his fake girlfriend's name instead.

"Angela," he said. "Dr. Angela Garner."

Ren opened the page and scrolled through the posts. Gavin Biery had done a yeoman's job backstopping the legend, providing a dozen or so recent posts with a blond woman and Midas at restaurants, on a beach, in a boat. He'd never even met the woman, but the editing software Gavin used would hold up to all but the most sophisticated forensic examination.

"She has an account, but like I said, she's a doctor. Not a lot of time for social media."

"What do you do, Mr. . . ." Ren looked at the passport, but waited for Midas to answer.

"Stevens," he said. "Bart Stevens. I was in the Canadian Forces, but I'm between jobs now."

"The military?" Ren mused.

"I was," Midas said. "PPCLI, 1st Battalion out of Edmonton, Alberta." It was hopeless to try and hide his military bearing, so he thought it better not to try. Better to make it part of his legend.

"What is PPCLI?"

"Princess Patricia's Canadian Light Infantry," Midas said. He'd worked with a couple troops from PPCLI in Afghanistan, back in the day, before he moved to the Unit. Solid guys.

Major Ren turned up his nose. "How intimidating," he said, dripping with sarcasm. "Sounds very . . . tough."

"As a boot, sir," Midas said. "The Vicious Patricias, they call us."

"And you say your wealthy girlfriend paid for your trip to China?" Ren looked over the top of his glasses and shook his head. "You have a word for that. What is it . . . ? A sugar mama?"

"I guess so," Midas said. "I just didn't see any reason to waste the ticket."

"And you would take a polygraph to that effect?"

Midas shrugged, hoping it was a bluff. He hated polygraphs. The best ones made you feel like shit, and he imagined this one came with its own set of thumbscrews.

"Sure."

Major Ren drummed his fingers on his desk for a time, thinking, and then picked up his phone. He spoke rapid Mandarin and then hung up the receiver, herky-jerky, like everything else he did. A moment later, a young man in a suit came and entered the office, turning sideways to work his way around the uniformed soldiers and take a place beside Ren.

The major gave a curt nod, and the same soldier who'd smacked him stepped behind him to unlock the handcuffs.

Midas rubbed his wrists to get the circulation back while Ren took one last look at the passport and then slid it across the desk.

"China is a very large country," Ren said. "I suggest you go and see some other part of it. Xinjiang is not safe for you."

"But why am I—"

Ren held out an open hand and frowned. "In this country, there are no *whys*. Now go, Mr. Bart Stevens. I want you on the next flight out of Kashi."

"Yeah, um, okay," Midas said. "I'm really sorry to hear about your brother." He started to leave, but turned. "There aren't any flights out until later tonight. Can I at least look around a little bit? I'd really like to see your Sunday Market."

Ren considered it for a moment, then waved him away. "See that you are on the next plane out. Other than that, I do not care."

Ren Shuren closed his eyes, wracking his brain for what to do next. Kashi—what the Chinese called Kashgar—was a long way from his ultimate bosses in Beijing. His immediate superior was busy juggling his wife and two mistresses, so he had little time to supervise, and *his* boss was in Urumqi, fifteen hundred kilometers away. Ren was accustomed to handling things his way on his own terms in his own time. There had been balance in his life. Harmony. They'd been watching Hala

Tohti for some time with no problem, something to do with her missing mother that was above Ren's need to know. Then, out of nowhere, Admiral Zheng of PLA-Navy intelligence had called and ordered him to pick up the girl, on the day after his idiot brother had overstepped his bounds and scared her away—not to mention getting himself killed. Ren saw no need to trouble the admiral with trivial details. The girl would be found soon. There was nowhere for her to go. Security cameras had captured several images of her and the man who had taken her. His face had been covered, but he was tall, and carried himself with the swagger of an American—

His aide drew him out of his thoughts. "Pardon me for saying so, Major," the young man said. "But you would let the Canadian wander about, with all that is happening at the moment?"

"He is a kept man, dependent on the good graces of a woman like some child, still dragging on the teat. He's too much of a buffoon to be involved in our matter," Ren said. "He tripped over his own feet. Not exactly foreign operative material."

"He admitted to being in the military," the soldier said.

"He did," Ren said. "And he is obviously in good physical condition, but I doubt his fitness is because of his job. Note the CrossFit logo on his shirt. Americans and Canadians alike treat their gymnasiums like churches. He may have been in the military, but I guarantee you that all his action was behind a desk, not a rifle."

Ren dismissed the aide and turned to his computer.

"Wait," he said, before the aide reached the door. "Follow the Canadian soldier and see that he boards the plane as instructed."

The young aide braced. "Of course, sir. May I take Corporal

Len? Two men would be better if we are to follow him discreetly."

"Nonsense," Ren said, swiveling back to his keyboard. "Did I tell you to follow him discreetly? I need all available personnel to find the Tohti child and the man who murdered my brother. If this Vicious Patricia attempts to evade you, shoot him."

46

Timur Samedi was an hour early—and Clark didn't like it.
Showing up unexpectedly allowed one to get the lay
of the land, take the high ground, spot bad actors who
weren't supposed to be there. But arriving early and making
contact early were two different things. You stood off and
watched until the appointed time, not an hour early. There
were too many unknowns. Early meant either this guy didn't
know what he was doing or something had happened to rush
the timetable.

Neither was good.

A constant wind rattled and shook the metal warehouse,
muffling the sound of the truck until it was almost on top of
them. Clark heard the rumbling engine, the pop of gravel as
tires rolled to a stop out front, to the left of the yawning double
doors—where trucks came to load their cargo. The old warehouse was empty but for a stack of bolted cotton cloth as high
as Clark's shoulders. Covered with canvas tarps, the bolts were
presumably waiting for Samedi to pick up when he came for
his passengers—Clark and Hala.

Clark waited in the shadows. The girl squatted a few feet
away, weight on her heels, elbows on her knees, the way chil-

dren all over Asia learn to squat when they are still toddlers and carry it with them to adulthood. She smiled quietly at a speckled hen and five peeping chicks that scratched at the dirt in front of her, inside the barn and out of the wind. After all they'd seen together, it was easy to forget she was only a ten-year-old child.

Clark gave a low whistle, waving Hala over at the sound of a slamming vehicle door. She heard it, too, and scampered over to stand behind his leg.

A Uyghur man appeared at the door, backlit by the dazzling yellow landscape.

Hala tensed and stuffed a hand in the pocket of her blue coat, no doubt touching the Snake Slayer. *Good instincts*, Clark thought. He patted her on the shoulder to let her know everything was fine—though he was far from sure himself.

"It's okay," he whispered. "We are expecting him."

She began to chew on her collar again, leaning against Clark's knee.

They'd already discussed how to use the Bond Arms derringer. Unloaded, she'd demonstrated she could cock the hammer with the meat of her thumb and rearrange her grip and press the trigger. She wasn't going to be doing any quick-drawing, but that was fine. In her case, the little derringer was more of a get-off-me gun. The whole thing exhausted Clark to his core. He believed in starting children early, but if he'd given a ten-year-old kid a pocket pistol in Virginia, society would have sentenced him to five days in the electric chair.

He wanted to calm Hala, but he kept his own hands in his coat pockets, his right curled around the butt of the Norinco pistol.

The Uyghur remained in the doorway unaware, or at least

unsure, that they were there. He scanned the interior of the warehouse—apparently unconcerned that he'd made himself a target in the fatal funnel. This didn't make him harmless, just ignorant. Clark knew from experience that there were plenty of idiot bad guys out there.

The Uyghur craned his neck but made no move to come inside.

"Helloooo?"

Clark motioned for Hala to stay back, and then took a deep breath, stepping out of the shadows. His hand remained in his pocket and on the pistol while he gave the initial passphrase. His words echoed in the hollow confines of the empty warehouse.

"It is dangerous to travel the roof of the world."

The Uyghur's head snapped toward the sound, seeing Clark for the first time. He shuffled from side to side, clenching and unclenching his fists, nodding excitedly. "Yes," he said. "Yes. There are many devils there."

The word *many* wasn't in the passphrase, but the man was obviously nervous, so Clark cut him some slack.

"And angels," Clark said.

"And angels, too," the man said, confirming.

Clark made his way across the warehouse. "Samedi?" He shook the man's hand, wanting to get a read on him.

"Yes," the man said. His grip was firm, but he withdrew his hand quickly. "Yes, yes. I am Samedi. I get you out . . ."

It was almost a question.

Samedi was about Clark's height, thin, with gaunt cheeks and dark BB eyes that darted constantly from point to point. He wore fingerless rag-wool gloves and a ratty *karakul* hat of curly black wool that looked as though it had been dragged behind a truck. Oddly, he had no overcoat against the bracing wind. His dark sport coat hung open. Beads of sweat dotted sunburned skin over bushy caterpillar brows.

The Uyghur grinned, showing several gaps where there should have been teeth. "You are ready?" The BB eyes bounced around the shadows. The muscles in his face, unencumbered by fat, tensed and twitched beneath patchy black stubble. "Where is the girl? She is ready to go?"

Clark ignored the questions, but asked one of his own.

"Tell me our route."

Clark watched carefully as Samedi explained how he planned to stack the bolts of cloth so that a hollow space remained inside, and then drive them to "the border"—though he did not explain which one. It would be "easy," "no problems," "for sure."

Samedi's nonchalance about crossing the border—the most dangerous portion of the trip—while he continued to sweat his ass off just talking in the cold barn set Clark's teeth on edge.

Customarily, Clark held to the rule of threes—one hiccup could be an anomaly, even two, but three hiccups, no matter how small, and he'd shut down most ops for a fresh start. Samedi's arrival ahead of schedule, the almost-correct passphrase, the sweating—all of it could be explained away, but . . .

Hala walked out of the shadows, chewing her shirt.

"Come, come, child," Samedi said, brightening. "Time to go." He turned to Clark, less twitchy now, but still sweating. "Will you help me load?"

"Of course," Clark said, releasing a pent-up sigh. He relaxed a hair—but still followed Samedi out to make sure he didn't call anyone while he backed his truck into the warehouse.

The loading went quickly, with the Uyghur directing more

than doing. It would be a relatively short ride, so the vacant cavern they'd left in the middle of the stack was just large enough for both Clark and Hala to sit down. Samedi used sharp wood dowels to pin the interior bolts of cloth in place. He'd done this before.

Finished, Clark used the rear bumper to climb out of the truck and turned to find the muzzle of a black Makarov pistol pointed directly at his chest.

Samedi grabbed Hala's coat by the shoulder, but she yanked away and ran to Clark.

Clark raised both hands. "It's okay," he said, trying to calm the girl. He cocked his head at Samedi. "Is there a problem I don't know about?"

"There is no problem." Samedi shrugged, keeping his Makarov level, his bony finger curled around the trigger.

With ballistics falling between a .380 ACP and a nine-millimeter Luger, the little 9x18 Makarov was plenty capable of ruining Clark's day. They were five feet apart, not quite close enough to make a move without risking Hala.

Samedi thrust the muzzle forward, driving home his point. "You pay one hundred thousand American dollars and I drive you out. Simple. No problem."

Clark kept his right hand up but pulled Hala closer to him with his left. His hand remained there, resting behind her hood.

"We can discuss this like businessmen."

"There will be no discussing," Samedi said. "One hundred thousand dollars."

"Then we do have a problem," Clark said. "Because I can't get you that kind of money until we are out of China."

"That is your problem," Samedi said. "Not mine."

Hala's shoulders began to shake. White-hot fury swelled in Clark's gut. He took a deep breath, tamping down the anger.

It would come in handy later.

"You frighten the girl," he said, flicking his raised hand, getting Samedi accustomed to movement. "Look, I'm not lying to you. I do not have that kind of money with me."

The pistol dipped an inch, but steadied quickly. "How much you have?"

Clark groaned. He had yet to decide if it was better or worse that this guy was such a moron. "About five hundred dollars." He lowered his right hand as if to reach into his coat.

Samedi barked. "Do not move! I know you have gun in pocket. I will shoot the girl. I swear it!"

Clark's hand went back up. "Okay," he said. "It's okay. Do you want the five hundred or not?"

Samedi's bushy brow was no longer able to keep the sweat out of his eyes. He squinted, attempting to wipe it away with his free hand. The pistol never wavered off Clark.

The Uyghur chewed on the idea for a long moment, and then gestured at Hala with his chin. His top lip curled into a derisive sneer. "The girl should bring a good price elsewhere. I will take your money and turn you in to the Bingtuan." He snapped bony fingers, ordering Hala to him, keeping Clark at bay with the Makarov. "Come, child. I won't hurt you."

Clark held the back of Hala's coat, keeping her beside him. "Yeah," he said. "We're not going to do that."

Hala spit out her shirt collar and spoke up. "I have money," she offered. Breathless. Hopeful. She dug into her coat pocket.

Samedi laughed. "I can have your money no matter what. Now come."

"You may as well shoot me now," Clark said, drawing Samedi's attention off Hala as she withdrew the Snake Slayer pistol from the coat pocket. Her hand swung behind her back with the derringer. She tried to cock it, but Clark gave her neck a gentle pat.

Completely unaware, Samedi brandished his Makarov, feeling in control enough that he shuffled a half-step forward. "You would bring more money alive," he said. "But I will shoot you. I promise."

Hala began to sob. "I am scared, John." The tears were real, and her shoulders shook so violently that Clark feared she might drop the derringer.

Samedi took another half-step, beckoning impatiently with snapping fingers.

Right hand still raised, Clark crouched as if to comfort the girl. His left slid down her back to take the little derringer. He studied Samedi, gauging the distance—a scant four feet.

"It will be all right," Clark said, calm, but loud enough that Samedi heard it. "You must do exactly as I say. I won't let him hurt you. I promise."

Hala nodded.

Samedi snapped his fingers.

Clark cocked the pistol.

"Run!" Clark said.

Samedi's head snapped up, shocked. His eyes shifted to Hala, only for a moment, but it was long enough for Clark to spring forward, past the other man's gun, while he brought up the Snake Slayer. Clark fired instantly.

The blast took Samedi in the teeth, the force of the point-blank explosion and over a hundred tiny lead pellets tearing away his lower jaw. The Makarov slipped from his hand and he teetered there, blinking, before crumpling to the dust.

Clark scooped up the Makarov, quickly press-checking the chamber and making certain it was not cocked before dropping it into his coat pocket opposite the Norinco. He was certain the Snake Slayer worked, so he kept it in hand as he herded Hala away from Samedi's body.

Clark squatted in front of her with a low groan. "Are you all right?"

She nodded, her little chest wracked with sobs. "What now?"

Clark released a long breath. "Honestly," he said. "I have no idea. But you did good there. You saved our lives."

She buried her small face against his chest and began to cry in earnest. Clark patted the back of her head, his mind going a hundred miles an hour. "We'll figure something out," he said, trying to convince himself as much as her. "How about you sit in the truck while I take care of something really quick?"

She leaned away, looking up at him with doe eyes. "You have to hide him?"

He nodded.

"Can I play with the baby chickens?"

Clark dragged Samedi's body to the corner, dumping it in the shadows behind a metal desk. It was the best he could do in an otherwise empty warehouse. He knelt beside the body, checking for an extra magazine for the Makarov. Finding none, he opened the man's wallet. The ID card was in Chinese, with the Uyghur name spelled out in phonetic characters with Arabic beneath. Clark's Arabic was rusty, but if he read the script correctly, this man's name was Yunus Samedi, not Timur Samedi, whom Clark was supposed to meet.

Clark left the wallet on top of the body, open, to lead authorities to think Samedi had been killed in a robbery. He could hear Hala jabbering at the chickens, and stooped so he could look under the belly of the truck.

Halfway down, he froze.

Hala was kneeling in the dirt on the other side of the truck, at ease, smiling, completely unaware that less than ten feet behind her, a man stood, watching.

47

Derringer in hand, Clark used the truck as cover and padded quickly to the doorway, where he risked a quick peek outside, suspecting the man with Hala might have friends.

He appeared to be alone.

The stolen Toyota was around back, out of view from the road, and the only other vehicle in the lot was a hulking Czech ten-wheeler called a Praga that looked like an old M35 Deuce and a Half with a botched nose job. It couldn't have been there long, but the windshield was covered with a fine layer of yellow dust—as everything was eventually in this part of the world.

Clark had only gotten a view of the newcomer's legs, and he was surprised when he stepped around Samedi's box van to find not a soldier or policeman, but a bent old man, leaning on a polished stick. Probably no more than five and a half feet tall in his youth, age had now stolen a good chunk of that. He stood passively, hands folded on top of the stick, a half-smile on his weathered face. His features were Han Chinese rather than Turkic. A sun-bleached ball cap that had once matched his red down coat took the place of a fur hat or more traditional Uyghur doppa. Clean blue jeans suggested he had enough money to get out of the dust when he wished. Clark couldn't help but picture him in with a group of other old men, John Deere and Caterpillar hats tipped back on graying heads, reminiscing about the good old days over eggs and coffee.

Clark moved the derringer to his coat pocket, out of sight, and stepped around the corner.

The old man looked up, still leaning on his cane, not at all surprised.

"Ni chi le ma?" the man asked. A polite greeting, it literally meant, "Have you eaten?" Age and his uneven teeth added a slurpy rasp to his Chinese.

Hala spun in the dirt, scrambling to her feet, and ran to Clark at the truck. Clark gathered her to him with his free hand and returned the greeting.

The old man dipped his head, bowing slightly, both hands still resting on the cane, and began to speak. Clark's Chinese was passable, but he tapped Hala's shoulder, asking her to translate so he got it all.

"He knows I am the Tohti girl," she said. "The police are looking for me . . . They say I was kidnapped by a European or American man . . . They offer a reward . . . Seven thousand yuan."

A little over a thousand bucks. Not exactly America's Most Wanted, Clark thought, but it was more than half the yearly income of some of the farmers in Xinjiang.

"Okay," Clark said, his hand gripping the pistol in his coat pocket. "Ask him what he plans to do."

The old man hunched over his cane and listened. When Hala finished, he launched into a lengthy dissertation, one hand remaining on the stick, the other waving around the warehouse to illustrate his story.

Hala whispered the translation as he spoke.

"He says we are none of his business . . . He does not need the Bingtuan reward money. His name is Wang Niu, but everyone calls him *Xiao Niu—*"

The man smiled broadly, looking directly at Clark.

"He says to tell you *Xiao Niu* means little ox."

Clark dipped his head, introducing himself as John.

Little Ox waved a hand at the hen and then peered into the darkness at the back of the warehouse.

Hala listened for a moment, then answered back before translating. "He says there is a dry well behind this building. We should hide the dead man in there so his cousin does not see him."

"His cousin?"

Little Ox nodded as if he understood. Hala translated his answer.

"Timur Samedi and Yunus Samedi both drive this truck," she said. "Timur is a pretty good man. Yunus is not so good man . . . Yunus always thinks there is more to . . . I do not know the word . . . get more money for a business deal."

"Negotiation," Clark said.

Hala nodded enthusiastically.

"I see there is another truck out front," Clark said. "Is he a driver, too?"

Little Ox squinted, listening intently to the question, and then turned to Clark and said something that made Hala laugh. "He says he came here to visit his chickens."

The old man kept talking.

"He says we should not worry," Hala said. "He was once Bingtuan, when he was young and foolish, but not now. He . . .

He has many Uyghur friends. He believes Timur Samedi will help us, but not if he finds out we killed his cousin."

Hala spoke directly to the old man for a moment, and then turned to Clark. "I asked him how we can know Timur is good when Yunus was also Uyghur, also Muslim, and he tried to rob us."

Little Ox leaned against his stick and gave a sad chuckle before he began to speak in accented English. "Yunus Samedi was watermelon—green on outside—good Muslim, but red on inside—like Communist Chinese. Muslim, Christian, it does not matter. Religion only teach people what is right, child. Maybe they do it, maybe not . . ."

The old man looked at Clark with narrowed eyes. "We must hurry and hide the body. Timur Samedi will take you to cross at Wakhjir Pass. Long drive down Karakoram Highway, then you walk in Afghanistan. Very high. Very hard. Many checkpoints on highway, but not so much after you start to walk—"

Clark drew Hala closer, surprised the old man knew their route. "Who told you this?"

The old man smiled, showing his teeth, or what was left of them. He took a cell phone out of his coat and waved it around the interior of the warehouse. "These my chickens. Samedi work for me. I truck carpet and cloth for woman you speak to at the market. She call and let me know you need help. My trucks go across borders all the time, Pakistan, Tajikistan, Kyrgyzstan . . . all over. Bingtuan and border guards know all my drivers, even Uyghurs hardly ever searched."

Clark rubbed his face, frowning. "'Hardly ever' doesn't sound good," he said. "And it seems like the entire world knows we're trying to get out of Kashgar."

Hala translated and the old man shrugged.

"Only peoples who can help you know," he said in English. "Like I say, police know my trucks. We pay them good baksheesh to . . . how do you say, oil the gears, wave us through checkpoint. Probably nobody suspect you get out that way."

Hardly ever. Probably. Not odds on which Clark would have normally based a plan. He considered his options—which were damned few—then asked, "You say your trucks get waved through checkpoints? That gets us down the Karakoram Highway, through Tashkurgan, but the Wakhjir isn't a border crossing, it's a rural pass, likely guarded by foot patrols."

"Truth." Little Ox nodded, pursing his lips in thought. "Much opium come over that pass. Smugglers, they pay big baksheesh to keep border guards away." The old man gave an emphatic shake of his head. "Probably not many patrols."

There was that word again. *Probably.*

Clark pressed the issue. "What are our chances of getting across the Wakhjir? Be honest."

Hala translated again.

The old man leaned on his cane and thought about it. "Fifty-fifty," he finally said. "Would be better if you had help on other side. Timur be here soon. We should hide the body." He stuffed the cell into his vest pocket. It was an iPhone, resembling Clark's.

"I may be able to improve our odds," he said. "If you have a cell-phone charger in your truck."

The old man leaned against his cane and gave a single nod. "I do."

48

G ot him," Adara said, binoculars to her face. She was angled away from the tour boat, as if looking at the wooded valley beyond the parking lot.

Instead of binoculars, Yao used an SLR camera with a zoom lens. So as not to draw attention with them all looking at the same spot, he and Ryan concentrated on the lake and the handful of crewmen who remained aboard *Eternal Peach*. He panned sideways, bringing the parking lot into view.

Gray clouds had rolled over the mountains surrounding the lake, and a light snow began to fall with the dusk.

"I see him," Chavez said. "Tall guy in the blue parka."

"Yep," Adara said. "That's the one. No idea if he's who we're looking for, but he's definitely zigzagging to stay in the black with the cameras."

"Adam," Chavez said. "Tell me you don't think that guy is Han Chinese."

"He's not Uyghur," Yao said after a moment. "You're right. He *is* Han. Maybe mixed blood."

Chavez took a deep breath, let his binoculars hang against his chest, thinking. "The Wuming are separatists," he said. "I'd assumed anyone associated with them would be Uyghur."

"That's two of us," Yao said. "But this makes a hell of a lot of sense. The authorities rarely even stop Han citizens at checkpoints. When they do, the scrutiny is light. This could explain how they've stayed hidden."

"He's stopped to talk to another guy at the hotel," Adara said. "Taking a smoke break . . ."

"Keep an eye on him," Chavez said.

Yao swung the camera back toward *Eternal Peach*, pausing now and then to snap photos. The falling snow, tree-covered mountains rising straight up from the shores of the crystal blue lake and into the clouds—he had no shortage of subjects.

Adara gave a peaceful sigh. "Best surveillance ever . . ."

Yao's phone buzzed in his pocket.

It was Foley. A call from the director of national intelligence would have been an anomaly a week ago, but she'd taken the idea of a mole personally. Where everyone else with a corner office in D.C. delegated to the nth degree, Mary Pat Foley rolled up her sleeves and went to work. It was easy to see why the President relied so heavily on her counsel.

"Can you talk?" she asked as soon as he picked up.

"Yes, ma'am," Yao said, mouthing Foley's name to Chavez so he'd know the call was important enough to take in the middle of a surveillance op. "Just taking in the sights. May have a line on one of those guys we wanted to talk to."

The line was secure, but Yao spoke cryptically out of habit. Foley did not.

"You're in the black?" she asked. "No one is looking at your face right now?"

"No, ma'am . . ."

Deep breath on the line. "Adam, Leigh Murphy has been

killed." She waited a beat for him to digest the news, then said, "I read the ops report you sent in yesterday. We have to consider the strong possibility . . . no, probability, that Leigh's death is related to what you're doing."

Yao rubbed a hand across his face, felt his pulse throb in his neck.

"A robbery?" he asked, already knowing it was not.

"I'm sorry, Adam," Foley said. "Another case officer was murdered as well, Joey Shoop. Police found his body in the city, we think in the location where Leigh was abducted. A couple of teenagers stumbled on her in one of those abandoned Soviet artillery bunkers."

Yao gazed out across the water, dizzy, like he might throw up. "Shit!" He shook his head. "I'm the one who asked her to interview Beg. This is my fault."

"No," Foley said, her voice weighed down with the exhaustion that came from knowing heavy things. "It is not. I hate to tell you this on the phone, but you need to know. Leigh was tortured before she died, methodically and extensively. Toxicology screen is still preliminary, but the coroner contracted by the embassy found traces of ketamine, midazolam, and scopolamine in her system."

"Dissociatives," Yao whispered. "Interrogation drugs. This is absolutely my fault. They wanted to know what she learned from Urkesh Beg . . . Someone should check on him—"

"He's disappeared," Foley said. "Could he have had something to do with this?"

"Not from the way Leigh talked when I spoke with her," Yao said, thinking how that had been just the day before.

"Listen to me carefully," Foley said. "Whoever killed her

wanted information, and we have to assume that they got what they were after."

Yao chewed on his bottom lip, trying to steel himself against the sudden flood of emotion. Everyone eventually broke under interrogation. Resistance training was about holding out long enough that your handlers could change codes or get assets to safety. No one was expected to hold out forever, not when drugs were involved.

"The mole got her killed," Yao said, clenching his teeth. "SURVEYOR must be someone who has access to my field reports."

"You're partially right," Foley said. "We're doing our best to wall you and what you're doing off from the rest of the intelligence community—for obvious reasons, including the team you happen to be working with."

"But?"

"But there's another way SURVEYOR could have found out."

"How?"

"We're working on that now," Foley said. "I'll be able to let you know next time we talk."

"Don't shut me out," Yao said, knowing he was overstepping his bounds, making demands of a member of President Ryan's cabinet, not to mention his closest adviser. "Please."

"You'll be in the loop the whole way," she said. "Now we don't have much to go on. According to my contact at RENEA"—Albania's counterterrorism squad—"a woman in an apartment overlooking the alley where police found Joey Shoop's body saw a tall Chinese man in a long coat wearing what she called a 'gangster hat.'"

"That's the same general description we got from the Russian woman who escaped the bakery massacre in Huludao," Yao said.

"Looks that way." Foley paused again to let him process. She was good that way. A beat later, she said, "We have to assume this guy with the hat is extremely dangerous, and that he's looking for Medina Tohti. If he knows you went there looking, he may already be there as well."

Yao agreed to call Foley back with a situation report as soon as was practical, and she agreed to let him know if any new information popped up about Leigh Murphy's murder.

"Listen up," he said over the net as soon as he ended the call. "We have a situation."

I don't like this," Jack Ryan, Jr., said after Yao gave them the news. "Lisanne's out there on her own."

"Keep trying her phone," Chavez said. "She's probably just in a spot with no service."

"I really want to meet this tall guy with a hat," Adara mused, still on her binoculars. "He's—"

She stopped short, watching the hotel. "Smoke break's over. Our guy is taking a trail off the back lot, heading for the tree line."

Chavez let the binoculars hang around his neck, thinking, rubbing his hands. The temperature was falling fast as darkness settled in. The Uyghur in question wasn't that far away, maybe two hundred yards, but the shadows along the edge of the forest rendered him almost invisible to the naked eye.

Yao was clearly preoccupied with the information about his friend's death. Chavez understood. It was natural to want retribution. Justice. That would come later. Yao was professional enough to know that. He just needed time to process, time they didn't have.

"What's back there?" Chavez asked, giving him something to focus on.

Yao snapped out of his stupor for the moment. "Hemu Village. Beyond the hotel to the east. Cattle farms, log houses, very rural, smack in the middle of a nature preserve. The village itself is ten miles away or so, but the map shows several cabins scattered throughout the forest."

"Lots of chimney smoke hanging out above the treetops," Adara said. "Good place to hunker down and hide if you were an anonymous freedom fighter."

Ryan looked up from his binoculars long enough to catch Ding's eye. "Still four people on the *Eternal Peach*. How do you want to play this? It'll be too dark to see soon. Those guys could be spending the night on there, as far as we know."

"Let's keep an eye on the boat as long as we can," Chavez said. "Just in case this Han guy doesn't pan out as Wuming." He looked around the parking lot, the plank viewing platform, and surrounding shoreline. Snow fell harder now, huge popcorn flakes, giving the entire valley the feeling of a snow globe. As tourists, the group had made no attempt to hide their curiosity at the sights. As soon as it got dark, people would start to wonder why they were still hanging around with binoculars and cameras. "You and Adara keep trying to reach Lisanne."

"We could try the sat phone," Adara said.

"No good," Jack said. "I'm getting her voicemail, so I have a signal. Either she doesn't have a signal or she's not able to pick up."

"Okay," Chavez said, thinking over his options. "Maybe they're giving her the runaround at the police station." He pitched the extra set of van keys to Ryan. "Give her an hour. If you don't hear something by then, go get her. Adam and I will head toward the hotel like we're going to get a tea or something, and then cut into the woods, see where this Han character leads us."

"Roger that," Ryan said. "We—"

Adara cut him off. "Hey, guys," she said, all business, a tense edge to her voice. "Uyghur female at the edge of the tree line. My two o'clock. White ski jacket. Fur ruff around her hood." Adara paused, took her eyes off the binoculars, blinked to refocus, and then looked through them again, speaking into her hands. "I'm thinking this could be Medina."

Chavez took a quick look. "Same nose. Dark brow . . . Only one way to find out." He tucked the binoculars inside his jacket so they wouldn't swing and started walking. "Adam," he said. "You're with me." He shot a quick glance at Ryan and Adara as he passed them. "Belay that order about picking up Lisanne. Medina Tohti is the mission. Give us five minutes for spacing, then follow at a distance." He tapped his cheek over the Molar Mic. "Keep trying Lisanne, though. Tell her to get her ass back here ASAP."

49

Fu Bohai was seated in the back office of the Jiadengyu police station when his man Qiu told him about the woman.

The local police sergeant, a cadaverous fellow with eyes that sank deep in his skull, clicked a few buttons on his keyboard and brought up the lobby camera.

"Ah," he said. "Yes. One of four Finnish tourists. She came to retrieve the passports for her group. I spoke to them earlier at their hotel. I believe their Chinese guide has taken the others to view the lake."

"You say they are Finnish?" Fu watched the monitor as the woman exited the front door. He flicked his fingers at the sergeant, getting him to switch to an exterior camera. "Do you get many European visitors?"

"Oh, yes!" the sergeant said, brimming with pride. "Tourists from all over the world to view our magnificent park. Russians, Japanese, even Americans. Our scenery is quite pop—"

Fu held up his hand to shush the babbling fool and then leaned forward to get a better look at the woman. The sergeant switched from camera to camera, staying with her as she walked down the street, moving in and out of other tour groups, who were out for evening strolls. The footage was re-markably clear considering how dark it was, allowing Fu to see the flashing shift of the woman's eyes as she studied her sur-roundings. Periodically, a flake of snow loomed large, almost obscuring the view as it fell inches from the lens.

Fu ignored the local sergeant and spoke directly to his man. "Notice how she stops periodically," he said. "Turning to face a shop or café window as if to look inside, but . . . there, she casu-ally steps into a shop, and then almost immediately back out again to see if she is being followed. What sort of tourist runs countersurveillance in a scenic park?"

Fu stood, retrieving his hat from the sergeant's desk. "Follow her," he said. "The rest of us will go check the tour boats."

"Yes, Boss!" Qiu pulled down sharply on the hem of his skintight leather coat, making it pop—as he always did after he received an order. Fu had begun to think of it as a sort of salute—and liked it.

50

Hollywood depictions of military vs. CIA bad blood notwithstanding, Captain Alan Brock, team leader ODA-0312, actually got along well with Roy Grant, his counterpart from that Other Governmental Agency.

Stationed at Camp Vance, a stone's throw from Bagram Air Base in eastern Afghanistan, Brock and his men made up a U.S. Special Forces Operational Detachment Alpha, commonly called an A-team. The four-numeral ODA designator, 0312, signified Brock's team was 0–10th Special Forces Group, 3–3rd Battalion, 1—first company in 3rd Battalion (A Company), 2—second team in the company, in this case, mountaineers and horse soldiers.

ODA-0312.

It was Grant who'd spun up this mission—less than an hour earlier, bursting into Brock's team room with a contagious air of secret urgency. The guy knew how to get a team excited—without telling them a damn thing. All he'd said to this point was that they were going to "recon up the Wakhan" riffing on the rhyme as he said the words.

Since the Global War on Terror began, cable programs had made much of the notion that Afghanistan was this unconquerable graveyard where every army that set boots on its plains came to grief. Pundits observed that the Soviets became hopelessly embroiled. The British Empire had failed to conquer. Even Alexander the Great had failed.

Brock knew it wasn't all that simple. Alexander's Greeks had ruled the area for something like two hundred years—not too shabby, as empires go. The Russkies pulled up stakes and left for a number of reasons, chief among them because of the kickass work that CIA had done arming and advising the mujahideen (though U.S. forces would eventually fight these men's sons and grandsons). The British Empire of the nineteenth century had suffered some horrific defeats in Afghanistan, but in the end they'd gotten exactly what they wanted, a thin strip of land to separate British India from the Russian Empire in Turkmenistan—the Wakhan Corridor, roughly two hundred and twenty miles long and forty miles wide, wedged between the high Pamirs to the north and the Karakoram Mountains to the south, and terminating at the border with China. The area was so far removed from the rest of Afghanistan that many of the tribes who lived there didn't even know there was a war on. A portion of the ancient Silk Road, the far-flung paths and trails through the high Pamirs, was still used by the occasional opium smuggler—though there were much easier routes into and out of China than trudging over impossibly high mountain passes in a place locals called the Roof of the World. The battalion S2 had intel on some recent Chinese patrols in the corridor with the Afghan Border Police. The ABP brass denied it, but border guys were hanging way out there by themselves—and the Chi-Comms could be awfully persuasive if they showed up in force and wanted to "help hunt terrorists."

Brock had inserted into the Wakhan half a dozen times, for

recon and training with Afghan forces. It was a wild place—beautiful, and, like much of Afghanistan, something out of an Edgar Rice Burroughs novel.

Now Roy Grant wanted to go on recon for some yet-to-be-explained reason. He was worried about leaks, he said. Moles. He'd brief them on the chopper, he'd said, but pack for a three-day mission.

If it had been anyone else, Captain Brock might have nailed him to the wall until he gave up more than that, but Roy Grant was different. Instead of BDUs or the khaki tacticool pants and polo shirt many of the SAC/SOG guys wore under their rifle plates on missions, Grant had on tan shalwar kameez, the traditional baggy trousers and thigh-length shirt of Afghanistan. Brock and his men sometimes dressed the part as well, when the mission called for it, but generally preferred good old American load-bearing gear. Besides, it was difficult to truly fit in unless you skipped a shower or two and carried around a shitstick like the locals. Brock preferred toilet paper, but Grant went native, the whole shebang, stick and all. You couldn't blame him. The dude was by himself enough that he needed to blend in to the fabric of Afghanistan. At first, Brock thought it would be unpleasant to ride next to a dude like that on a chopper, but the whole country smelled like woodsmoke and a sewer fire, so he didn't really notice. Grant spoke fluent Pashto and worked outside the wire enough that the dark beard and local dress had become part of his persona. From a distance, the only way to tell him apart from a local was his propensity to carry around a cup of coffee from the Green Beans on Bagram.

The two men could have been brothers. Both were tall, runner-fit, with workman's hands and dark, grizzly-bear beards like many of the guys at Camp Vance. As OGA spooks went, Grant was a good shit. Brock wasn't even sure if that was the guy's name. He looked like a Roy Grant, but then, this *was* headquarters for Combined Joint Special Operations Task Force, or CJSOTF—home for both white operations and the more secretive black ops—hence the highest percentage of beards per acre than on any other U.S. military base on the planet.

Brock's five-year-old son had recently told him via Skype that he looked like a caveman. Brock had agreed and said he wouldn't have been surprised if a bunch of velociraptors came stampeding over the desolate mountains beyond the base. The brainy little shit had set his dad straight about "humans and dinosaurs not living during same period."

Brock missed that kid—but if he had to be away from home, this was the place.

When op tempo was high, Camp Vance was crawling with U.S. Special Forces A-teams like Brock's, along with Marine Recon, Air Force combat controllers, Navy Special Warfare DEVGRU, Delta Force, Task Force Orange surveillance operators, air ops guys from 160th SOAR, operators with British Special Boat Service and, of course, the spooks from CIA Special Activities Center/Special Operations Group. The atmosphere was often like a reunion when the SAC/SOG came in from training. More often than not, the Agency recruited its fresh meat from among the active duty ranks operating at Camp Vance.

Half the guys there could have been named Roy Grant.

At the moment, Captain Brock and his six-person split-A, or half his Alpha team, were dressed in full battle rattle, gunned up and ready to go in the back of a Sikorsky UH-60

Black Hawk, piloted by two of the Task Force Brown guys from the 160th. Brock had flown with these two before and trusted them to put them where they needed to be, and, more important, to come back and get them when the work was done. The other half of the split, led by Brock's second-in-command, Warrant Officer Morales, was aboard an identical chopper. Morales had the team sergeant with him. Peplow, the 18F—intelligence sergeant—acted as Brock's second in Morales's absence. Once they were on the ground, the team could merge back into one, or remain split—depending on what Grant had in store. Sergeant Peplow had noted when they boarded that both choppers were wearing stub-wing tanks, indicating a mission likely greater than the Black Hawk's combat range of around three hundred and seventy miles.

Four of Brock's five men carried M4 rifles with EOTech sights, six thirty-round magazines, SIG Sauer M17 nine-millimeters, four pistol magazines, thermite grenades, radios, PVS-14 night-vision goggles, ear pros, assorted knives, chemical light signaling spinners, food and water, blood chits, medical pouches, and, among other gear, next-generation poncho liners that helped hide their heat signature. Morales called it the "woobie of invisibility." Townsend, the weapons sergeant, carried the same basic loadout, but instead of an M4, he carried an FN SCAR-H in 7.62 NATO.

Captain Brock waited for Grant to get buckled in, then tapped his headset. "Okay. Let's have it."

Grant gave him a thumbs-up.

"We're heading toward the Wakhjir Pass."

"To China?"

"In that general direction," Grant said. "Two MQ-9s started

that way . . ." He checked his G-Shock. "Twenty-one minutes ago."

Peplow, the 18F, cocked his head. "The Chinese have troops stationed at a Tajik base less than twelve clicks south of the border. They'll spot the Reapers *and* us, even if we fly nap of the earth, scraping our gear on the valley floor . . ."

"Maybe," Grant said. "Maybe not. We'll be in Afghan airspace, and the Afghans are on board with our trip, being a rescue mission and all."

Brock gave the CIA officer a wary side-eye. "A rescue mission?" He shook his head and settled back in his seat. "You should have led with that."

The pilot in command, an Army warrant officer named Avery, half turned from the right seat. The engines were already whining, and he spoke over the intercom, doing one last safety check with his crew chief.

All good in back and gauges in the green up front, he lifted off.

"As rescue missions go," Grant said, "this one is . . . unique."

51

Chavez groaned, staring into the trees behind the hotel. "Are you seeing this?"

The young woman they believed to be Medina Tohti led her Han Chinese friend to two saddled horses she'd apparently left tied to the top of a corral. A half-dozen trail horses from the hotel concession munched hay off the muddy ground inside the fence, ignoring the two saddled animals outside. All of them were Mongolian ponies, short and stocky, still woolly from a long winter.

Medina climbed aboard a small bay, the man on a slightly larger sorrel the color of a new penny. He spoke nonstop as he brought his horse up to walk beside the woman's, illustrating various points by waving his hands or shaking his index finger.

Medina listened dutifully, fur parka ruff tilted to one side, taking in every word as they clomped down the muddy trail to disappear into the dusky forest.

Chavez breathed out hard, blowing a cloud of vapor, sounding like one of the horses. "I was never a cavalry soldier."

Yao started for the corral the moment the two riders were out of sight. "Didn't you ever go to summer camp?"

"I grew up in East L.A., *mano*," Chavez said. "Our summer

camp was trying not to get jumped walking to the corner stop-and-rob."

"These are trail-ride horses," Yao said. "We'll probably have trouble getting them to go."

All the animals looked to have been fed and watered and turned out. The wranglers, too, had gone home for the night. The saddles were all locked up in a wooden shed, but that didn't matter. They didn't have time for that anyway.

"Mounted operations . . ." Chavez muttered, picking what he hoped was the gentlest of the beasts—a cow-hocked gray with winter fuzz around the muzzle that made it look like a bearded old man.

Yao found a lead rope and attached it to the halter of a stout little mouse-colored horse, forming makeshift reins. Facing the animal's ribs, he put both hands on its back and then pressed himself up, throwing a leg over.

"Damn it!" Chavez said, trying to follow suit, but resorting to using the rails to climb aboard, even with the short horse.

"There's a technique to it," Yao said, leading the way out of the gate.

"No kidding," Chavez said, wishing for some mode of transportation that had wheels instead of hooves. He spun the little gray in two complete circles before finally getting it pointed in the same direction as Yao.

Five jostling minutes later, Yao raised his arm to a square and made a fist, cavalrylike. He listened for a moment, shoulders hunched against the cold.

Chavez brought his gray up next to the other horse, pulling back on the lead rope. He needn't have. The gray didn't intend to leave its buddy for one minute.

"What is it?" Chavez said. Snow drifted down through the

evergreens, melting as soon as it hit the mud and moss—a spring snow. The tracks were easy to follow, and fresh enough that water was only now seeping back into them. "You think they're running a surveillance-detection run on horseback?"

Yao slouched easily on his horse, legs dangling, scanning, patting the animal periodically on the side of its broad neck to keep it calm. "Nah, they're just riding home. We need to give them a minute, though. Our horses want to catch them, so we're getting too close." He gestured forward with the tail of his makeshift reins, causing the horse to flick an ear. "Smell that?"

Chavez sniffed the cold air, catching a hint of woodsmoke and the slightly sweet barnyard stench of more animals.

"A cabin," he said. "Gotta admit, you're shattering my cowboy stereotypes."

Yao kept his focus through the trees. "Don't know a thing about cattle," he whispered, sounding an awful lot like an Asian Gary Cooper. "We should move in a little closer with the horses and then go the rest of the way on foot."

"Sounds good," Chavez said. "Nothing yet from Lisanne. I'd like to make contact with Medina as soon as we hear what's going on in town."

"Yep," Yao said, still sniffing the air. "I'll make a call to my contact and confirm our boat." He gave his horse another pat on the neck. "I'd hoped to hear back from Clark by now about the daughter. We're gonna need something to keep Medina Tohti from shooting us in the face when we go to the door."

John Clark felt the truck slow beneath him, brakes squealing. He and Hala swayed forward, bracing themselves as it came

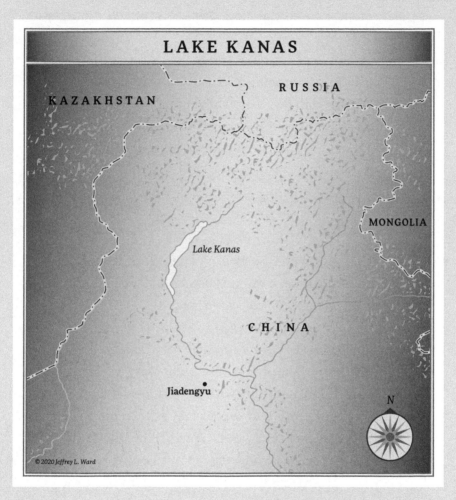

LAKE KANAS

KAZAKHSTAN

RUSSIA

MONGOLIA

Lake Kanas

CHINA

Jiadengyu

N

to a stop. Another checkpoint, the second in less than an hour. Anywhere else and Clark would have thought the authorities were conducting a full-blown manhunt, but here in Xinjiang, security stops were so common, one was often within sight of the next.

It was completely dark in the hollow cavern they'd built beneath the piled carpets and stacked bolts of cotton cloth. Clark had given Hala a small flashlight that she used while they were underway, but he had her turn it off each time they stopped. He could hear her tentative breathing now that the truck was stopped again, and wondered what it must be like for her, a small child, trusting her life to the hands of a stranger— an old man, no less, someone she'd met only twenty-four hours earlier.

The truck's rear doors squeaked open. Muffled voices outside. Clark put his arm around Hala's shoulders, and they both held their breath. More voices—a long discussion—then the doors slammed shut. Hala began to shake as the truck moved on. She flicked on the light, blinking at the sudden brightness. A child again now that they were underway, she moved the beam back and forth, playing with the shadows it made on the uneven stacks of cloth and carpet tassels in their cozy little cave. Clark leaned on the carpets along the outer wall, careful not to dislodge the stack, and watched her smile.

They still had a long way to go—and Hala wasn't the only one putting trust in strangers.

Omar Alim's wife called the People's Armed Police office in Kashgar to report her husband missing after a fellow taxi driver had seen his cab abandoned by the old caravanserai a few kilometers south of the livestock market. A missing Uyghur near a Uyghur bazaar—certainly a Uyghur problem. The officers had taken almost six hours to go to the scene. Ren doubted the fools would have responded at all, but for the fact that he'd sent word to every station reminding them that two prominent members of the government had been murdered and the fugitives remained at large. Even the most insignificant events should be closely examined.

At least the responding officers had enough sense to follow footprints from the abandoned vehicle into the caravanserai. The blood and carnage inside were difficult to miss. Major Ren arrived a short time later, calling in a dog from an XPCC detachment on the other side of Kashgar. The dog, a German shepherd they'd recently gotten from Beijing, was more of an intimidation asset than it was a tracker, but it led them straight to Omar Alim's body.

Ren and his lieutenant climbed into the shallow coulee behind the building where the body had been dumped.

"His throat has been slashed," Ren's man observed.

The major stared at the wound, and thought of his dead brother, murdered in much the same horrific manner. With little access to firearms, crimes of violence in and around Kashgar most often involved a knife or an ax. Still, three deaths, two with their throats cut, in the same twenty-four-hour period. A coincidence? This was clean, as much as such gruesome work could be.

As an officer with the Production and Construction Corps, Ren's primary responsibilities lay with enforcement—keeping the resident Uyghur population in check, not solving their murders. Ordinarily, he would have had little interest in finding out who had killed Alim. That was a job for the local People's Armed Police—who in all likelihood would have filed it away as a case involving no civilized individuals—a Uyghur-on-Uyghur incident.

Ren took a handkerchief from his pocket and held it to his nose while he stooped for a closer look at the torn flesh and glistening gore on Alim's neck. Green flies were already congregating on the wound, even with the chill, smelling the scent of death and decay. This was the work of someone desperate, someone on the run—someone who had killed before.

"The Canadian," Ren said suddenly, giving his man a start. "You saw him board the aircraft?"

"Yes, Major," the lieutenant said.

"To Beijing?"

"To Urumqi," the lieutenant said. "Connecting to Beijing."

"Of course," Ren said. "And there were no other Canadians or Europeans on the flight?"

"Not that I observed."

"The perpetrators will try to leave," Ren said. "To flee across the border. Alert all border crossings to be extremely cautious, to double-check all vehicles, especially any with small girls. Send them a photograph of Hala Tohti. Alert check—"

"Major," the lieutenant said, holding up his phone. "Border guards in Tashkurgan report an incursion by American military aircraft."

Ren gasped. "Into China? That would be an act of war."

The lieutenant read further. "No," he said. "Not across the border, but approaching it at a high rate of speed, as if they intend to do so. Two remotely piloted aircraft believed to be

MQ-9 Reapers passed near our joint Tajik base near the Afghan border eight minutes ago. Radar is also picking up two ghost readings moving west to east in the Wakhan Corridor. They show up only periodically, but estimating their speed and altitude, they are believed to be helicopters."

"Remotely piloted aircraft . . ." Ren mused. "Moving toward the Wakhjir Pass?"

"It looks that way, Major."

"I have read that the Americans have devised a rescue pod that can be attached to the hard points on these drones, the same place where missiles are usually affixed. Let us suppose that the person who killed my brother, Mr. Suo . . . and this man, is attempting to take Hala Tohti to America. The elevation of Wakhjir Pass is extremely high. It would not be easy to get across with a child. But if one was simply able to climb into one of these escape pods and then back to a U.S. military base in Afghanistan . . ."

"Forgive me, Major," the lieutenant said. "But do you not believe this is a bit far-fetched?"

"The Americans love such plans," Ren said. "They believe life is a movie and they are the stars. Contact the checkpoint in Tashkurgan at once. Have them stop everything that moves—trucks, taxis . . ." He jabbed the air with his finger. "I do not want so much as a donkey cart to get past without a thoroughly invasive search. And alert the border guards to increase patrols leading up toward the pass."

"Of course, Major," the lieutenant said. "It seems foolish for the Americans to place these pods where their weapons customarily go. Their aircraft will be completely defenseless."

"Ah," Ren said. "Do not forget the 'ghost readings'—helicopters flying in and out of radar contact. They are surely there for defensive purposes. But we will be prepared for that as well . . . Speaking of helicopters, find me one immediately. I wish to be there when this killer is apprehended and Hala Tohti is retrieved."

52

Secretive and compartmentalized as the Central Intelligence Agency was, it took a grand total of two hours from the time Monica Hendricks and her team began their first interviews for the buzz of the mole hunt to reach virtually everyone at Langley—and a good portion of the CIA stations around the world. Savvy officers already knew something was up. Overnight, silos had dropped down over certain information, making it next to impossible for some to do their jobs. In the Great Game of spy vs. spy, it was often enough to make one's opponent believe they had a traitor in their midst, forcing them to waste precious time and resources chasing shadows. Viable intelligence operations against the Soviet Union had very nearly ground to a halt during Angleton's tenure in CIA.

Director Foley's mandate for ELISE had been clear: Catch the rat, but don't set the entire ship on fire to do it.

Hendricks knew word would get out as soon as she began. She kept a weather eye for rats looking for a way off the boat. People, being what they were, almost all had something they wanted to hide. A spate of surprise dates on the flutter—the polygraph—put everyone on edge.

Monica asked the same questions at each pre-polygraph interview, first and foremost: "If you were going to spy for China, how would you go about it?" The answers displayed two antipodal schools of thought. *"This is a horrible, terrible, awful, no-good thing for our agency. Let me help however I can."* Or *"I am deeply offended that you would think I, of all people, could possibly be a spy! After all I've done for the Agency, for my country!"*

Her last interview for the day was with a redheaded grandmother Hendricks had worked with on and off for almost two decades and who was now the chief over Near East. She'd smiled politely, batted her ginger lashes, and said, "I'd shove this question up your ass, Monica."

Oddly, there were few moderates. One analyst, a guy named J.T., had his spy game all plotted, pointing out myriad security weaknesses and how he'd get the Chinese to use cryptocurrency to pay him instead of dead drops or brush-pass handoffs. Hendricks and Li both concluded that this guy was either such a brilliant criminal mastermind that he was able to line out his entire conspiracy without batting an eyelash or he had no guile at all and simply answered the question as directly as they had posed it to him.

Hendricks put J.T. in the "maybe" box, with a few of the other supercompliant "helpers."

She found it difficult to trust either camp merely on the face of their indignation or volunteerism. It was not lost on her that Soviet spy Rick Ames had approached the counterintelligence team conducting the mole hunt (for him) and demurely asked if there was anything he could do to assist.

In law enforcement, a strong denial after confrontation was expected from a truly innocent party—but CIA officers were taught to lie, to circumnavigate the truth. They drummed it into you at The Farm: You must learn to deceive everyone you meet—outside of the Agency. In other words, *lie to everyone but us.*

Polygraphs were passed. Egos were bruised, but they were no closer to identifying the mole.

And then Joey Shoop and Leigh Murphy were murdered. Hendricks was aware of Murphy's recent connection to Adam Yao, so ELISE turned its focus to anyone who had knowledge of operations in Albania.

Fred Rask's recent cable bitching about the violation of his turf was already making the rounds with the brass on the seventh floor. Most laughed it off as another *Rask writ, writ by Rask,* an homage to the old John Wayne movie. Some, however, were not amused at Murphy's behavior. There were only a few, but these bosses had bailiwicks of their own to consider, and didn't warm to the idea of case officers locking them out of activities.

Hendricks called Foley for nitty-gritty, and found Yao had called Murphy to interview the Uyghur. Foley gave no details about the contents of the interview, other than to say it yielded enormous fruit, while at the same time pissing off Rask enough that he fired off the missive.

Hendricks had worked with Rask a half-dozen times, the last in Tokyo, where her counterpart with Japan's national intelligence service had privately observed that Rask had "sanpaku eyes" where the sclera was visible on both sides of the iris and beneath—*three whites.* Crazy eyes. Hendricks had noticed it, too, along with his truculent nature and tendency to color himself as the most vital component of every operation in the after-action reports.

Freddie Rask was, in fact, third on Hendricks's list of people in the Agency who rubbed her the wrong way.

Rather than beginning with him, she'd called Vlora Cafaro, the case officer who'd been with Murphy earlier the night she was killed.

She conducted the interview via SVTC, a secure video tele-conference. Admiral Peter Li was present, listening, observing, but off-screen.

Still reeling from the death of two coworkers, Cafaro looked as if she'd slept in her clothes. Her eyes sagged. She rocked slightly in her chair, obviously trying to stay alert. Hendricks suspected she had a bit of a hangover in addition to the ex-haustion. Above it all, the young case officer was open and cooperative, firm in the knowledge that she had nothing to hide. She also made it clear that she planned to exact swift vengeance when she figured out who had murdered Leigh Murphy. Hendricks couldn't blame her there. She'd served as one of Leigh Murphy's class mentors during a short rotation at The Farm. They'd never worked together, but she seemed like a great kid.

It was clear that Cafaro was fiercely devoted. Hendricks had friends like that. Hell, Li was one, and he wasn't even CIA.

Cafaro went on for two full minutes about what she would do to the killer/s, and that her chief of station probably wasn't even going to do anything about it, he was such a fat worthless son of a bitch. Fatigue was an excellent truth serum, and this woman was so tired, notions from her heart came straight out of her mouth.

Hendricks glanced at Li, who shook his head, having noth-ing to add.

Hendricks put both palms on the table, pushing back in her chair slightly. "Thank you, Vlora," she said. "I have one favor to ask of you before you get some much-deserved rest."

———

Hendricks scribbled a couple notes on her legal pad while she waited for the SVTC call to connect.

The chief of station Albania glared at the camera as if he wanted to climb through it to Hendricks. He rubbed a hand across his face and frowned, scrunching his nose as if he smelled something rotten.

"Monica, I have a lot on my plate right now. We need to make this short."

Hendricks gave a cursory nod but didn't speak, scribbling on her notepad. *I'll be with you in a minute* . . . She let him stew, forcing him into the next move.

He stood to leave. "Seriously—"

"Sit down, Rask," Hendricks said, without looking up.

He did, probably out of curiosity—or fear that she knew something.

"You're not going to pin those kids' deaths on me," he said. "I'm not a hundred percent sure the two events are even related. Shoop could have just been in the wrong place at the wrong time and Murphy, don't even get me started on her. Murphy was so far off the reservation, it's—"

"Yeah," Hendricks said, struggling to keep her voice calm, dispassionate. "Tell me about how she'd gone off the reservation."

Rask began to air all his woes. Murphy thought she was smarter than everyone. She worked her own little operations without clearing it first. She didn't keep her files current.

Hendricks had yet to look at her camera, and it was killing him. She tapped her pen on the paper, pondering. "Did Murphy ever speak to you in an insubordinate manner?"

"Her *actions* were insubordinate," he snapped.

"And you had her followed?" Cafaro had volunteered that, illustrating the leadership tone in the office. "By Shoop."

"I did," Rask said. "And I'm not apologizing for it. Look, I didn't have shit to do with those murders and you know it. I've already told everything that needs telling to my boss. I'm not going to sit here and—"

"Let me ask you this, Fred," Hendricks said. "If you were going to spy for the Chinese, how would you go about it?"

Rask fell back in his chair like he'd been slapped. "What are you talking about?"

"Answer the question."

"I heard you were accusing half the China desk of being spies," he said.

Hendricks kept writing. "I'd like to know who told you that."

He shot to his feet again.

Now she looked at him.

"I said sit down!"

Off-screen, Li spoke into a desk phone. Almost immediately, the door to Rask's left swung open and a very large security officer stepped inside. Vlora Cafaro entered behind him. They said nothing, but it was apparent that they were there to keep Rask compliant.

Li gave another order over the phone, which was connected to the earpieces Cafaro and the security man wore. They both nodded and then exited the room, leaving Rask at once blustering and dumbfounded.

"I am not spying for China," he said. "And if anyone says I am, they're spewing bullshit."

"But if you were," Hendricks said, goading him, watching his reaction. "Hypothetically, how would you do it?"

"I said I'm not."

"Okay," Hendricks said. "Tell me who is."

"Monica," Rask said through clenched teeth. "So help me . . . I have friends. Your career is—"

"I'm on my way out the door, Freddie," Hendricks said. "Retiring. No career left for you to screw with. Now answer my questions. And you may consider this a pre-interview for your polygraph."

"So this is all about your mole hunt, not Murphy and Shoop?"

Hendricks bit her lip, fighting the urge to take the discussion in an unfruitful direction. She couldn't put her finger on it, but something this piece of trash did had gotten the girl killed.

Peter Li stepped in, giving her time to get her bearings.

"These are just questions we're asking everyone with access."

Rask leaned forward, squinting at the screen. "Who are you?"

Hendricks spoke again. "He's the good cop."

"Get to the point, Monica."

"You sent the complaint regarding Leigh Murphy up the chain, trying to find out who she was working with, get that person's ass in the wringer."

Rask wagged his head. "There's these things called protocols. Murphy and her friend broke them, I made a note of it."

"Did you talk to her?"

"Of course."

"Dole out some punishment?"

"Befitting the offense," Rask said. "Look, I don't see how it's any of your business how I run my office."

Hendricks made a show of pitching her pen on the table,

like she was fed up. She didn't have to act. "Who else did you talk to about it?"

For the first time, Rask squirmed in his seat. He knew full well that talking about operations outside a clearly defined circle of those who needed to know clearly violated his beloved protocols.

"No one . . ."

Hendricks scoffed. "Come on, Fred. You were pissed at this girl because she didn't kiss your ring and seek your permission. Even you had to have some inkling that your expectations were chickenshit. Surely you confided in some buddy, a chickenshit soulmate who is equally as chickenshit, so you could, you know, feel better about yourself. It's a lonely thing being the only turd in the punchbowl."

Rask crossed his arms. "We're done here."

"Oh, Fred," Hendricks said. "We are far from done."

Peter Li spoke into his handset. Vlora Cafaro and the security officer returned to take up positions behind Rask.

Hendricks leaned forward, moving the mouse up to the *invite* button. A moment later, Mary Pat Foley's face popped up on the split screen. She wore a silk blouse with the top button undone. Her makeup was perfect and a string of pearls hung just below her collarbones, as if she'd been called away from an evening out with her husband, or an important dinner with the President.

"Madam Director," Rask said, trying to stand.

The security officer put a hand on his shoulder, stopping him. Ten minutes ago, the chief of station would have called him *"my* security officer."

"We've not met, Mr. Rask," Foley said. "But I see you are a

slow learner. It would be better if you keep your seat. I need to know who you spoke with concerning your troubles with Ms. Murphy."

"Ma'am, I . . ."

"I can get POTUS on the line if you need me to," Foley said. "But I've gotta tell ya, that would sink what little vestige of a career you have left."

Fredrick Rask broke, as they say, like a cheap clay pot, giving up his confidant, a case officer on the Central Asia desk named Tim Meyer.

It made sense. What happened in China or Russia cast a shadow over much of Central Asia. The entire Silk Road had been home to traders and spies for centuries, and nothing had really changed.

Hendricks instructed him to board the next flight to Dulles. Vlora Cafaro would accompany him to be certain he didn't try to contact anyone en route. The security officer took his cell phone and dropped it in a Faraday bag to block any emitted signals. Rask looked as though he might cry. Cafaro beamed. Exhausted or not, she was more than happy to bird-dog the man who would soon be her former boss all the way back to Dulles.

Rask's portion of the video link went dark, leaving Hendricks and the DNI on the screen.

Foley glanced down at the legal pad where she'd jotted notes while Rask spilled his guts.

"You think this is SURVEYOR?"

Hendricks rubbed her forehead with a thumb and forefinger, trying in vain to tamp back her headache.

Peter Li rolled his chair around so he was shoulder to shoulder with Hendricks. "There's a good chance we have him, ma'am. Monica is much too humble to admit it, but he's been at the top of her creep list since we stood up ELISE. We were simply not aware that he had access."

Foley patted the table on either side of her legal pad. "Okay, then. We need to catch him in the act."

"I have an idea," Li said. "There's a risk, but if it works, we'll have him."

Foley reached to end the SVTC connection, but paused. "Call in David Wallace. Work out the wheres and wherefores and then get back with me so I can brief the President. In the meantime, I need to call and warn a friend that his cover could be burned to the ground."

Foley ended the call.

Hendricks got a bottle of ibuprofen from the lap drawer of her desk and took four—grunt candy, the Marines called it.

She washed them down with a swig of stale coffee and leaned back in her chair, staring up at the ceiling tiles.

"Could it really be this easy?"

"I'm not sure I'd call what we've been doing easy," Li said.

"I expected it to take months."

Li nodded. "We still have to catch him in the act of espionage. That could take months. Rask suddenly going incommunicado might spook him."

"Yeah," Hendricks said. In truth, she'd regretted going down that line of questioning as soon as she'd uttered the words. "I should have subpoenaed his phone records, checked his e-mails, found out who he spoke to around that time. We're going to have to come up with some kind of plausible story. Even so, SURVEYOR is already paranoid. He'll smell a—"

Hendricks's phone rang. It was Mateo, the analyst assigned

to ELISE. His voice quavered with excitement, like a kid who just made the varsity team.

"Where are you right now?"

"ELISE HQ."

"Stay there," Mateo said. "I'm ten minutes out and there is something you have to see." Hendricks expected him to end the call, but he couldn't contain himself. "It's bank records, a shitload of bank records for an account opened under the name of a dead aunt. Twenty-seven deposits over the last two years, each for just under the ten-thousand-dollar reporting thresh-old. Only a quarter million, but it's more than a GS-9 makes. The money hasn't been touched, so we're not going to see any lifestyle change."

"Wait," Hendricks said. "A GS-9?" FBI special agents and CIA case officers hit journeyman around GS-13.

"Yeah," Mateo said, crestfallen. "That's what she is, a GS-9. I thought you'd be more excited. We found her. Gretchen Pack has to be SURVEYOR."

G retchen Pack? Isn't she an analyst and briefer for the direc-tor's office?"

Mateo, at the ELISE bullpen now, gave a you-bet-your-ass nod.

"Didn't she just have a baby?"

"She did," Mateo said. "And get this. I did a cross-check of the deposits with the time she was off on maternity leave. Nada. They stopped. Then, two weeks ago, after she came back to work, the payments started up again, like clockwork."

Peter Li, who was working on the other lead, looked up

from his desk. "What else? Just being devil's advocate here. What do we have besides bank deposits?"

"Glad you asked," Mateo said. "As you know, the PRC likes to use people with ties to the Motherland."

"My grandparents were from China," Li said. "I've been pitched a couple of times."

"Right," Mateo said. "Gretchen Pack's husband is from China. His father came over from Fuzhou with a snakehead when he was a child. His name was Pak then. He changed his name to Pack because he thought it looked more American."

Hendricks pulled up Pack's personnel file on her computer. "I can't believe we didn't catch that."

"The Agency?" Mateo said. "Oh, she disclosed it during the hiring process. It's all on the SF-86 she filled out. We, meaning those of us working ELISE, didn't snap to it. She was on Coleen Ragsdale's creep list, though."

Peter Li leaned back in his chair. "You know," he said. "This is tragic if it pans out, but it also provides us with a sudden opportunity to make Tim Meyer feel like the pressure is off. If we identify Gretchen Pack as the mole, maybe he'll relax."

Mateo's head snapped up. "Wait. What do you mean Tim Meyer?"

Hendricks ran down their theory.

"Holy shit," Mateo said. "That means SURVEYOR isn't a spy . . ."

Hendricks groaned, doing the math on when she could take more ibuprofen. "I know," she said. "It's a spy *ring*."

53

Timur Samedi took his eyes off the road just long enough to watch the military helicopter thunder and thump overhead—and almost ran his truck into a herd of double-humped camels. He cursed, swerving wildly to miss the lumbering beasts, certainly dislodging his load in the back of the truck. The camels did not move—all large eyes and jutting teeth, they also stared skyward at the helicopter that followed the path of the highway, almost low enough to touch.

Helicopters were not uncommon up and down the Karakoram Highway where China touched not only Kyrgyzstan but Afghanistan, Tajikistan, and Pakistan in the space of a few hundred kilometers. There were many borders to patrol. Samedi knew nothing about helicopters. He'd never flown in any kind of aircraft, preferring to keep his feet on the ground. This one was dark green and large enough to carry perhaps a dozen troops.

Samedi heaved a sigh of relief when it flew down the highway toward Khunjerab Pass and Pakistan.

He relaxed his grip on the steering wheel, flexing his hands to rid the joints of stress. The next checkpoint would not be until Tashkurgan, ninety kilometers ahead. He could relax until then.

The cold waters of Karakul Lake were on his right. Usually deep green or sparkling azure, the frigid waters had taken on the slate gray of the evening sky. Already at an elevation of over thirty-five hundred meters, the lake was dominated by three great mountain ranges, and several seven-thousand-meter peaks. Kongur Tagh and Muztagh Ata loomed across the water, their peaks vanishing into the clouds.

Some of the Kyrgyz women who lived in the nearby yurts sold hot tea and kebabs of grilled goat. Samedi often stopped. Not tonight. He had to reach Tashkurgan.

A colorful jingle truck—so called that because of all the bells and decorations Pakistani drivers liked to hang on them—rattled past going north while Samedi was still catching his breath from the near-miss with the camels.

A kilometer ahead, the helicopter banked sharply to the right, arcing over the lake to turn back to the north. It came in low, throwing spray off the water's surface and scattering a flock of sheep that were grazing up from the shoreline between two white canvas yurts. Samedi slowed, stomach in his throat as the aircraft hovered directly in front of him, blocking the entire highway before settling onto pavement.

Samedi was not certain, but he believed the pods on the sides of the helicopter contained rockets—all pointed directly at his windshield.

Six men in black SWAT uniforms and helmets poured out of the side doors the instant the skids touched the ground. Each carried a rifle, ducking as they ran up the highway directly toward Samedi's truck. Behind them, the rotor blades came to a halt and another man climbed out. Instead of a uniform, this one wore a business suit. A politician. The one in charge.

Samedi slowed his truck, unsure of what to do. Were they here for him? He groaned. Of course they were here for him. He was the only truck on the road—and they had not come for the camels.

Five of the men aimed their rifles at Samedi's windshield while the fifth directed him to halt at the side of the road. He raised his hands above the steering wheel.

"Reach out the window!" the SWAT leader barked. "Open your door from the outside! Keep your hands visible at all times or we will open fire!"

Two of the riflemen kept their guns pointed at him, while the three others ran to the rear of the truck, boots thumping on the pavement. Samedi watched them in the mirrors as they took aim at the doors.

The SWAT leader barked again. "Get out now! Slowly!"

Samedi complied, hands raised.

The man in the suit stepped forward. The riflemen fanned out so they still had clear shots.

"I am Major Ren of the Corps," he said, looking down his nose over dark-rimmed glasses. "And you are?"

Samedi's throat convulsed when he tried to speak. It seemed to take forever to get the words out.

"You are very nervous about something, Mr. Samedi," the major said. "What do you have in the truck?"

Clark tapped Hala's arm when the truck slowed, reminding her to turn off the flashlight. He cupped a hand to the side of his head, straining to hear, but got nothing but the sound of

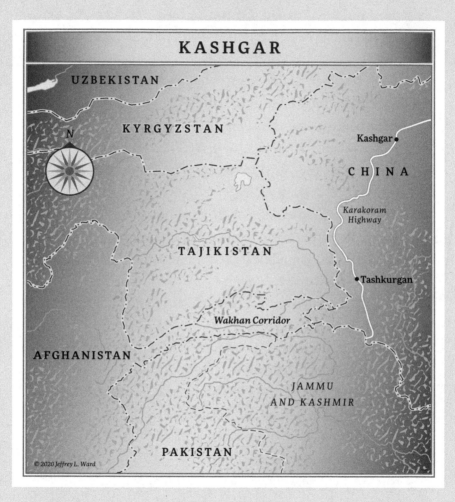

KASHGAR

UZBEKISTAN

KYRGYZSTAN

N

Kashgar

CHINA

Karakoram
Highway

TAJIKISTAN

Tashkurgan

Wakhan Corridor

AFGHANISTAN

JAMMU
AND KASHMIR

PAKISTAN

© 2020 Jeffrey L. Ward

Hala chewing on her collar. The stop seemed to last forever this time. He checked the glowing hands on his watch. Three minutes.

Voices now. Someone shouting.

Then they were moving again, slowly, barely rolling—then another stop.

This one was shorter, less than a minute before they were on their way.

Hala flicked the light on. "What was that?"

Clark took a deep breath, patting her arm again.

"I'm not certain," he said, as the truck slowed again and made a right-hand turn before coming to a stop. The back doors creaked open. Boots thudded on the metal floor as someone climbed into the back. A sharp tap accompanied shuffling foot-steps. A cane. Clark reached for Hala and the light, turning it on, as Little Ox pulled away a roll of carpet and peered down into the hollow compartment.

"Welcome to Kyrgyzstan," he said in slurpy English.

Hala looked up, wide-eyed, and then collapsed against Clark's leg, exhausted from the stress.

She spat out her collar. Her eyes welled with tears. "We are no longer in Xinjiang?"

"We are no longer in China," Clark said. He stood and shook Little Ox's hand. "No trouble at the border?"

"I told you," the old man said. "I pay big baksheesh. They love me here. No trouble at all. If the Bingtuan stop Samedi's truck, they will find nothing but carpets. Come. I take you to a place you can sleep until your friends arrive."

Clark took out his phone, grateful that service had reached even small border towns like Irkeshtam.

Hala was breathing deeply now, as if trying to steady herself. "We are safe?"

Clark punched in the number and looked down at Hala while he waited for it to connect. "We are safe," he said.

Thirty miles from the Chinese border, Warrant Officer Avery looked over his shoulder toward the back of his Black Hawk. "Mr. Grant," he said. "I am to let you know you're supposed to call 'that number,' whatever the hell that means."

"Copy," Grant said. He plugged a satellite phone into his headset and attached a cable that led to an external antenna affixed outside the Black Hawk's window—effectively blocking Captain Brock and the other members of ODA-0312. He spoke for only a few seconds, gave a curt nod, and ended the call, a broad smile almost invisible under his bushy beard.

He reconnected his headset to the intercom.

"Back to the barn, boys," he said.

Captain Brock leaned forward against his harness and shook his head. "I thought this was a rescue mission?"

"It was," Grant said.

Brock glared at the spook. "What were we, decoys?"

"That," Grant said. "And a backup plan."

"Who'd we help rescue?" Sergeant Peplow asked.

"Honestly," Grant said, "I'm not a hundred percent sure. An operative and a very high-value asset. That's all I know. The counterintel folks at Langley crawled so far up my ass they could see my tonsils. You would not believe the grilling I got before they deemed me trustworthy enough to be tasked with this. This mole has us all seeing shadows. Hard to trust anyone."

"Roger that," Brock said. Spooks not trusting spooks . . . imagine that.

Grant leaned his head back against his seat, closing his eyes. "We did God's work tonight. Sometimes that means the blade cuts. Sometimes it just gets waved around. Either way, it needs to be sharp."

Ren Shuren thought seriously about shooting Samedi on principle. Carpets. Nothing but carpets. Ren had been certain this was the escape route. They had stopped the only five vehicles between Kashgar and Tashkurgan capable of smuggling people. Samedi's truck was the last.

He walked toward the lake, then wheeled, barking at his lieutenant. "A hidden compartment, perhaps? Under the belly of the truck."

The lieutenant shook his head. "I am sorry, Major. We have already inspected there."

"I do not understand . . . They must have gotten past us. Perhaps they are further down the road, already past Tashkurgan. Contact the border guard at once and warn them."

The lieutenant made the call on his satellite phone. A pained look crossed his face when he ended the call.

"The American aircraft are now moving west. They appear to be returning to their base."

"What?" Ren punched his open palm with his fist. "How could they have picked the fugitives up so quickly? They must have crossed into China. We should make Beijing aware of this—"

"Major," the lieutenant said. "It appears the aircraft never touched down. They flew to within approximately forty kilometers from the border, and then simply turned and went back the way they had come."

Ren's mouth fell open. "It makes no sense . . . Unless . . . You are certain that Canadian . . . what was his name? Bart Stevens . . . you are certain he boarded the plane to Urumqi?"

"Yes, Major," the lieutenant said. "I watched him myself. Urumqi, where he was to have caught a connecting flight to Beijing."

"Call the airline and make sure."

The lieutenant did, the pained look returning to his face. "Mr. Stevens changed his ticket when he arrived in Urumqi and caught a flight to Bishkek that same hour."

"Kyrgyzstan . . . I . . ." He gazed across the lake, suddenly cold to his core.

The lieutenant leaned closer so as not to be heard by anyone but Ren. "Sir," he said. "What do you wish to do with the driver?"

"Release him." Ren flicked his wrist to the south, feeling sick to his stomach.

He had no idea how, but the Canadian must have been involved in helping his brother's killer escape. He doubted the man was even Canadian. Worst of all, Ren now had to explain to Admiral Zheng how he'd let a ten-year-old Uyghur girl slip through his grasp.

54

Chavez tied his gray pony to the base of a scrubby fir tree. The snow had picked up and he stood for a moment, patting the animal on the shoulder, sharing its warmth. There was no wind, and every thump of a hoof seemed to reverberate through the forest.

Yao expertly looped his horse's lead rope around a branch of a nearby tree and tied it into what he called a bank robber's knot—one yank and it would pull free.

The growing darkness helped to hide their approach, but it also made it difficult for them to see as they crouched low, moving quickly through the underbrush. Now that they were away from the prying eyes of security cameras, Chavez took a PVS-14 night-vision monocular from his pocket. Lightweight, the roughly four-inch tube could be mounted to a helmet, on a long gun, or, as in Chavez's case, handheld. It would certainly raise suspicion if Chinese authorities found it on his person, but they'd be too busy with the little semiauto pistol and suppressor to worry about it. The night-vision device made the low light of evening come alive, but, as it stood, it did not magnify the target.

Fifty meters away, through stands of tall green pines and ragged fir trees, the Han man disappeared inside a cabin of rough-hewn logs. Chavez guessed it to be about twenty by twenty feet, with a small porch out front and a stone chimney on the side. A path off the rutted mud driveway led to a plank-board outhouse, hidden in the trees.

The woman turned the two horses out in a split-rail paddock next to the house, checked their water, and then fed them each a large flake of hay from a stack outside the fence. She stood beside a little bay while it ate, petting it on the shoulder as if she were talking to it. Chavez watched for a moment, cold from the wet ground seeping through the belly of his coat. At length, he shook his head and rolled half onto his side, passing the PVS-14 to Yao.

"Your eyes are younger than mine," he said. "How sure are you that this is Medina Tohti?"

Elbows braced against the mossy forest duff, Yao looked through the monocular. "Nose looks right. Age, height, build all match. Pretty sure."

"Sure enough to knock on the door?"

Yao lowered the monocular and looked sideways at Chavez. "It's either that or snatch her later when she goes to use the outhouse."

Yao gave a sudden start, as if he'd been stung or bitten. It hadn't been that long ago that Chavez met the business end of some particularly brutal murder hornets in Indonesia.

He froze. "You good?"

Yao nodded and took out his phone.

Ding's brow shot up. "Lisanne?"

"Foley," Yao whispered.

"Take it," Chavez said. "I'll keep an eye on Medina."

Yao crawfished backward into the brush, giving him some distance to talk without his voice carrying to the cabin.

Chavez traded the night vision for his binoculars and worked his way to a clump of scrubby buckbrush that offered a little better view. The trickle of smoke from the chimney grew thicker, leading him to believe the cabin had been empty before Medina and the Chinese man arrived and stoked the fire. Headlights played through the trees. Chavez lowered his binoculars to avoid reflection, ducking reflexively. He eased up behind the bush again when the lights went out.

A four-door Great Wall pickup had pulled up alongside the cabin and stopped. Chavez could see at least two heads through the window. They sat there for two minutes, engaged in animated conversation, before the driver got out. He looked Uyghur, or at least more so than the man inside with Medina. Another Uyghur male exited on the passenger side. Chavez froze as this one scanned the tree line. A young woman in a black tam and down parka poked her head out the back door, surveying the area before she got out.

They were all sure as hell acting paranoid enough to be Wuming.

Brush rustled as Yao returned. He was grinning. "Clark made it out," he whispered. "He has the girl."

"Outstanding." Chavez lowered his forehead to the ground, relief washing over him. He still had the rest of his team to worry about, and Medina, and getting his team out of China . . . but he was going to have to eat this elephant one bite at a time. "No word from Lisanne?"

"Negative." Yao gestured toward the cabin with his chin. "I saw lights. What did I miss?"

"Three new arrivals." Chavez passed him the night vision.

"Two males, one female. All Uyghur . . . or maybe Kazakh. I can't be sure. Not Han, though."

"Okay," Yao said. "I spoke with my contact at the lake and confirmed the boat for exfil. He'll be waiting—as soon as we talk Medina into coming with us."

"And the contacts to actually get us across?" Chavez asked.

"Good to go," Yao said.

Chavez groaned. "We now have five people in the cabin. Until Ryan and Adara get back with Lisanne, it's just you and me, a couple of knives, and this little get-off-me .22 pistol."

"You're forgetting our most valuable asset," Yao said. "We have John Clark, and he has Medina Tohti's daughter."

55

Lisanne Robertson felt the presence of someone behind her when she was two blocks from the police station. Her original intention had been to return to the hotel and then catch a taxi back to Kanas Lake from there. Per her training with Clark, she'd decided instead to do a surveillance-detection run on the way. The bad guys she'd hunted as a cop would have called it a "heat check." No matter how gorgeous the green mountains and pristine lakes, she didn't forget that she was operating in hostile territory—uncharted waters. Like the ancient mariners' maps said, there were dragons here.

Jiadengyu was little more than a large concession for the park—hotels, tour companies, shops, and parking lots in the middle of the woods. The gateway to the park, it provided a jumping-off point for tourists who wanted to access the wilderness around Kanas Lake. Bus tours would pick up in a month, but for now, most of the park visitors on the street with Lisanne appeared to be of the hard-core adventurer type. Hikers, ski buffs, and mountain climbers, most of them young, fit, and wearing lived-in clothing, huddled in small knots in front of hotel restaurants and specialty shops that sold souvenirs and outdoor equipment.

Low clouds and a gentle snow brought warmer temperatures than earlier in the day—but warm was relative in the mountains, and the air still bit her cheeks and made her fingers numb. Adrenaline from being followed warmed her some—or at least made her forget about the chill. The weight of the Beretta in her jacket offered some comfort, but with it being a semiauto, she risked a malfunction if she attempted get more than one shot off from inside the pocket. A revolver would have been better, but you took what you could get. She told herself she was much more likely to go mano a mano than use a firearm, and warmed her hands as she had on uniform patrol, two fingers at a time, refraining from stuffing her entire fist down inside her pocket. She'd have access to the Beretta, while allowing her to bring both hands quickly into play—if she needed to, as her dad used to say, "go to town on somebody."

She took a deep breath as she hustled down the sidewalk, letting the chilly air invigorate and settle her. She could do this. Her dad would be proud—and so would John Clark.

The stout little guy in the leather jacket ducked in and out of the crowd, turning when she turned, stopping when she stopped. At one point, she turned suddenly, backtracking a few feet to go back into a pastry shop—as if she'd changed her mind. She bought a cookie to nibble on while she walked, and resumed the circuitous route to the hotel. Leather Jacket was still there, thirty yards back, leaning against a wall, conspicuously ignoring her.

She knew he wouldn't be alone, and began to scan the people across the street who were moving in the same direction. She saw the second man at the next intersection, approaching on her left from halfway down the block. Wool watch cap, dark glasses, and a gray ski jacket. She waited a beat before crossing the street. He slowed his pace, almost imperceptibly, so he didn't catch up to her.

As Lisanne suspected, Gray Coat fell in behind her, taking the eye from Leather Jacket, who turned to the right, surely trotting to make the block and parallel his teammate to catch up a few blocks ahead. If there was a third, he was better than these two, because she couldn't spot him.

It was time to call in reinforcements.

Ryan picked up on the first ring. "Hey! We've—"

"Flash, flash!" Lisanne said, indicating she didn't have time for formalities. She gave her location first, using hotels, landmarks, and then street names. Chavez and the others had the ability to run a common operating picture on their phones, displaying icons that depicted team members' positions on a moving map. Reception could be spotty in the mountains and buildings. "I've picked up a tail," she said, giving a thumbnail description of the men she'd identified. "Team of two so far. Nothing hostile yet, but I don't want to lead them back to your position."

"No trouble at the police station?" Ryan asked.

"None. If they'd wanted to hold me, they could have done it then. Pretty sure they're hoping they can follow me back to you."

"Copy that," Ryan said. "Things heating up here. Can you—"

Lisanne cut him off, bonking the radio for a split second by talking over him. ". . . The one behind me is picking up his pace," she said. "They're definitely crowding me. I expect they'll make contact soon. Wouldn't mind a little help here . . ."

Fu Bohai was less than two kilometers from the lake when Qiu called. Headlights through falling snow looked like a video-game spaceship jumping to light speed. Fu's driver, a young fellow named Gao, hunched over the wheel, concentrating to negotiate sweeping mountain roads.

"She knows we are following," Qiu said.

Fu, seated in front, stared out the passenger window at the darkness. "Then detain her," he said. "She will only lead you in circles."

"Yes, Boss," Qiu said. Fu could envision him bracing at the other end of the call.

"Find out what she is doing here—"

"Boss," Qiu said, his voice as sharp as the snap of his leather jacket. "I don't speak Finnish."

Fu groaned, rubbing his eyes with a thumb and forefinger. "I doubt very much that will be a problem. Find out if she is involved with the search for Medina Tohti. See how much she knows. Get the location of her friends . . . and then sink her body in the lake."

"And if she is not involved?"

"Her fate remains the same," Fu said, shrugging, though the man on the other end of the line could not see it. "The questions you ask will, by necessity, reveal the nature of our mission. If she is a professional, as I suspect she is, since she was alert for surveillance, then your interrogation may be messy. There will not be much left of her for you to release. As I said, sink her."

Ryan and Adara briefed Chavez over the net as they drove.

"Got it," Chavez said. "We'll hold it down here. Watch your speed on the road. The weather's turned to shit where we are.

You won't do her any good if you get yourself smeared over the Chinese countryside."

"Roger that," Ryan said, chattering the van's tires against the pavement as he took a sweeping curve.

Adara grabbed a handful of seatbelt as he made the turn.

"Sorry about that," Ryan said.

"I'm not," Adara said. "Let's see some of that fancy Jack Ryan, Jr., driving your Secret Service detail taught you. We won't do Lisanne any good if we're late, either."

Approaching headlights glowed through the darts of driving snow. Ryan let off the gas momentarily in case it happened to be a police car. A white Toyota sedan passed them, going toward the docks. Adara turned in her seat and looked out the rear window, watching the taillights fade away in the distance.

"Time to haul ass," she said. "You know what they say, faint heart never won fair maiden."

Hands at nine and three o'clock, Ryan took his eyes off the road long enough to shoot a quizzical glance at Adara.

"Fair maiden?"

"I'm not one to judge," Adara said. "Just saying, it's obvious."

"Whatever," Ryan said, slowing just enough to keep control as he approached a turn and then accelerating through the sweep, using up the entire road, cutting corners when he could, shaving every second possible from the drive.

Service was spotty at best, and nonexistent in most places. They were still unable to reach Lisanne.

"Get me a location on the COP as soon as you get a signal," Ryan said. The COP, or Common Operating Picture, gave the team the ability to see one another's location—as long as they had cell or, with the right equipment, satellite service.

"Working on it," Adara said. The dash lights bathed her face in a green glow. "She knows what she's doing, Jack. Clark never would have brought her on board if she didn't."

"I know," Ryan said. "But we shouldn't have let her go alone. She's too new."

"She's a decorated Marine," Adara said. "And an experienced cop."

"You're right," Ryan said. "It's just . . ."

"I know," Adara said. "Me, too." She gave a little fist pump and then held up her phone to display a pulsing blue dot. "Got her. We're eight minutes out."

Ryan attempted to raise Lisanne on the net. No answer. "Try calling her through cell service instead of the radio," he said.

Adara tapped her cheek over the Molar Mic and then held up the phone again. "Trying now . . ." At length, she turned to Ryan. "No joy. She's not picking up."

Ryan raised Chavez on the net, quickly bringing him up to speed. "I don't know how you plan to convince Medina to come with us, but you'd better do it now. I've got a feeling we're going to be coming your way at a run."

56

Domingo Chavez was a smart man—and he knew it. Sure, he started off a little slow, barely getting out of East L.A. to enlist in the Army. He'd gone on to become the first male in his immediate family to attend college, and then later, under the mentorship of John Clark and the man's brainiac daughter, he'd finished graduate school. Fluent in three languages, he was conversant in two more. He could hold his own in forensic accounting, had enough flight time to land a small plane if he had to, or rig a communications radio with little more than a few household items and a foil wrapper from a stick of Juicy Fruit.

He was *good* at a lot of things, but he was *best* at brute force. That was probably why he got along so well with his father-in-law.

Unfortunately, force was off the table for the moment. He had to appeal to his kinder, gentler angels, to sweet-talk a woman who had aligned herself with a bunch of terrorists . . . freedom fighters . . . convince her to come with him of her own free will. Now there was another team out there, poaching the leads Adam Yao had come up with. They were surely the ones following Lisanne—and they also wanted to talk to Medina

Tohti. Judging from the body count they'd left behind in Hu-ludao and Albania, their kinder, gentler angels had gone on terminal leave.

Chavez had to get to her first. Doing that without getting shot was going to be tricky.

The area in front of the cabin had been cleared of brush and trees, making a stealthy approach impossible. Chavez ruled out working their way around to the rear of the cabin. It had likely been cleared as well, and the time it took to check would be wasted.

"We'll ride in on the horses," Yao said. "They'll think we're tourists who got lost on the trail."

"That could work," Chavez said, though he didn't relish climbing aboard the fuzzy little gray again. "If we try to creep up, they'd just shoot us for sure—"

The harsh voice from brush behind them caused both men to roll onto their backs. Chavez let the binoculars fall against their strap and reached for his Beretta.

He froze when he saw Medina Tohti and her Han friend, both with pistols aimed directly at them. Medina looked at Chavez's gun hand and gave a tut-tut shake of her head. Her pistol remained rock-steady, finger on the trigger.

"You are correct," the Han man said in perfect English. "Had you tried to creep up to the cabin, we certainly would have shot you. But that raises a question. What is to keep us from shooting you now?"

The Han man, whom Medina called Ma, obviously had some military or police experience. It took him only a few sec-onds to zip-tie both Chavez's and Yao's hands behind their backs, then pat them down for weapons. He was particularly interested in the Beretta, but said nothing. Satisfied for the moment, he dragged the men to their feet and gave a shrill whistle as he walked them none too gently out of the clearing.

The two men who'd arrived earlier in the Great Wall pickup came out of the cabin, each assuming control of one of the prisoners, shoving them through the door.

A woman sat at the back window, her eye to what looked like a Russian-made infrared scope.

"No movement," she said when the men came in.

Though they were Uyghur, everyone spoke Mandarin, apparently in deference to Ma, who was clearly their leader.

The young man beside Chavez held up the Beretta, which he had already cleared, along with the Bowers Group Bitty.

"An assassin's weapon, to be sure," he said.

The one next to Yao played with one of the Microtech knives, actuating the button so the dagger blade sprang out the opening in front. A few years older than Chavez's guard, this one had several days of dark scruff on his face. "Assassins indeed," he said.

Ma took the Beretta and inserted the magazine, then tipped up the barrel to replace the round in the chamber before reattaching the Bitty suppressor. He aimed the pistol at the floor, giving a satisfied nod at its heft—before turning to point it directly at Adam Yao's face, three feet away.

The Uyghur guard stepped clear, obviously having seen Ma shoot someone in the head before.

"Wait, wait, wait," Chavez said in English. "We're friends."

The Han man stayed aimed in, but took an almost conciliatory tone.

"Friends . . ." he said. "Well, my friends, if you have found

437

me, then others surely will as well. Now, I need one of you to talk to me, but I do not need you both." He took a deep breath, head canted in thought. "I will give one of you five seconds to tell me how you found me. I do not care which one."

Yao spoke, also in English.

"Hala Tohti."

Medina gasped, springing forward.

"What did you say?"

"Please understand," Yao said, looking at Ma. "We have no issue with you. We need to speak with Medina about her daughter."

Ma's face darkened. The nail bed on his trigger finger whitened. "So you bring an assassin's weapon."

Medina's face went pale. "What do you know of Hala?"

"There are men looking for you," Chavez said. "Men who would use Hala to get to you—"

"Is she—"

"She is safe," Chavez said. "My friend is protecting her."

Ma moved the pistol to Chavez, disgusted. "Your friend is holding the child prisoner?"

"No," Chavez said. "My friend got her away from danger. Away from the men who are after her." He looked at Medina. "To get to you."

Medina blinked, shaking her head as if she were in pain. "I . . . She . . . Where is my daughter now?"

"Safe," Chavez said.

Tendons knotted in Medina's neck. Her jaw clenched. "Safe where?"

"At this moment, she's in Kyrgyzstan," Chavez said. "On her way out—"

"I want to speak to her," Medina said.

"We can try," Chavez said. "But right now, they're driving toward Bishkek. I'm not sure if they can get a signal."

Medina choked back a sob. "I must speak to her . . ."

"Listen to me," Yao said. "We have to hurry. There are very bad men here, in the park, the same men who would have used your daughter to get to you. We are on your side. I swear it. But the others have killed many people trying to locate you. Even now they are following one of my friends."

Ma seethed, the Beretta lower now, at his belt, but still pointed at Yao. "This friend, he will come to you for help, and lead these men straight to us."

"No," Chavez said. "*She* is leading them away from you."

"How?" Ma asked. "How did you find us?"

Yao told him about the ticket stubs from the tour boat, speaking quickly. "I will explain when we are on the road. But we must leave."

The female at the window shot a scornful look at the youngest Uyghur man. "Perhat," she said. "You did not think to check your pockets before giving away your coat?"

Perhat hung his head. "I—"

"My friend is right," Chavez said. "You are all in grave danger. We need to go. Now."

"Enough!" Medina sprang forward, shouldering Ma out of the way and pressing her pistol to Adam Yao's chin. She turned to scowl at Chavez. "We are not going anywhere. You will let me speak to my daughter, or I kill your friend."

57

Lisanne picked up her pace, attempting to put distance between herself and the two men. They'd fallen in beside each other now, not even trying to hide the fact that they were following her. Her first thought was to run inside a café, but when she turned to look through the window, she saw families inside with small children. She considered turning around and running back to the police station, but realized these men had likely come from there. That would be a dead end in the purest sense of the word.

So she hustled forward at a fast walk, a hand wrapped around the little Beretta Bobcat in her pocket. She heard . . . felt static vibrate on her Molar Mic. Jack and Adara were en route. The lake was fifteen miles away. With any luck, they'd be here before Leather Jacket and Gray Coat attempted to make contact. Jack and Adara were likely trying to contact her now, just out of radio range—hence the static.

She made a left toward a large hotel, looking left as she crossed the street. The men were less than fifty feet away and closing. Rounding the corner, out of sight of her pursuers for a few seconds, Lisanne broke into a run. She cut down a side street, behind the hotel, skirting two large trash bins, before settling among a small group of elderly Chinese tourists, stroll-ing back to their hotel from dinner.

Adara's voice came across the net, vibrating her jaw via the Sonitus Molar Mic.

". . . read me?"

"Five by five," Lisanne said, breathless now. She made a quick right, thinking it would lead her to the front of the hotel. She'd misread the signs. The main hotel entry was at the far end. What she thought was the back had been the side. The Chinese tourists had gone in the back doors, and now Lisanne found herself on the other side, on a vacant street, with nothing but a line of dark woods beyond.

Footfalls on the pavement behind her grew louder. She turned to see Gray Coat trotting toward her, open hands out to his sides, as if to say, "What's going on?" She turned to run, but saw Leather Jacket ahead of her. He'd continued straight when she made the turn, sprinting around the building to meet her head-on.

"They have me trapped," she said, searching frantically for a way out. "I could really use some help here."

Adara's voice buzzed again, "inside" Lisanne's head, on her jaw. "How many?"

"Still two," Lisanne said. "I'm between a hotel and the woods, can't read the name. Southeast corner of town."

"We've got you on the COP," Adara said. "Hang on. We're two minutes out."

Two minutes . . . This would be over long before that.

Lisanne sidestepped inside a concrete alcove as the men closed in. Recessed into the wall of the hotel, the alcove put her in a box, but it also put her back to the wall. A large rolling metal door told her it was a service entrance. She tried the smaller door to the right of the roll-up, but found it locked. Thought about pounding on it, then decided she might be better off handling this without witnesses.

Gray Coat still had his hands open. "Miss!" he said. "Hey, Miss! We do not hurt you. Want to talk."

"You guys better hurry," she said over the net, not caring if the men heard her or not.

"Ninety seconds," Adara said.

Leather Jacket rushed her before she had time to respond.

He slowed as he got closer, stepping from side to side, herding her backward, into the corner—which was where she'd planned to go as soon as she saw it. She would use the angles to her advantage, forcing both men to come at her head-on rather than flanking her. No man wants to be beaten by a woman, and these two seemed confused that she did not simply submit and let them take her into custody.

"We are police," Leather Jacket said, rolling his shoulders and puffing out his chest like a little bantam rooster. "You come with us, Miss."

Neither Adara nor Jack could hear what the men were saying, but they would be listening to her side of the conversation. "I'm not going anywhere with you," she said. "You're not police."

"You are correct." Gray Coat laughed. "We are not police. And you are not from Finland." He nodded to Leather Jacket, who moved in. Out of the corner of her eye, Lisanne saw Gray Coat take a syringe from his coat pocket—big, metal, like something you'd use on a horse.

Leather Jacket came in low and fast, attempting to take her in a flying tackle. She shuffle-stepped out of the way at the last minute, grabbing a handful of leather collar as he went past and using his momentum to help him headfirst into the concrete wall. Stunned, he staggered sideways in time for Gray Coat to rush in, attempting to stab her with the horse syringe.

Lisanne parried with both arms, attempting but missing a grab for the man's wrist for an arm bar that would have knocked him on his ass—and, with any luck, destroyed his shoulder. Surprised at her sudden aggression, he twisted away, presenting the perfect opportunity for her to deliver a lateral kick to his knee.

Gray Coat yowled in pain. The syringe slipped from his hand, but he flailed out, catching Lisanne directly in the temple with his knuckles. Accidental or not, the blow rattled her. She staggered backward, seeing stars, vaguely aware of the short one coming at her. He drove a fist into her ribs, knocking the wind out of her and driving her sideways, bouncing her off his partner, who was still cursing and clutching his knee. Lisanne used Gray Coat as cover, darting around, wheezing, trying in vain to draw a full breath. Leather Jacket grabbed his own partner by the shoulder and yanked him out of the way, eyes ablaze.

Lisanne fished the little Beretta out of her pocket and brought it up a hair too late. Leather Jacket swatted it out of the way, jarring her radial nerve so her hand opened reflexively. The pistol clattered to the concrete. She sidestepped again to avoid another bum rush, catching a glancing scrape as his shoulder impacted her chest.

The blow spun her, but bought her some distance. She clawed the sides of his face with both hands, raking, screaming, fully intending to rip both the ears off his head. Pain caused him to come up on his toes, allowing her to drive a knee into his unprotected groin.

Leather Jacket doubled over, gagging like he might vomit. He yelled something at his partner. Lisanne gave him a slap across one ear for good measure, then wheeled to face a new assault. Jack and Adara would be here any second.

Gray Coat didn't rush her, or try to attack her at all. Instead, he stepped to the side, moving closer to his partner. Lisanne spun to put her back to the wall again, keeping them both in view.

Tires squealed around the corner, on the other side of the hotel. The glow of approaching headlights cut through the falling snow, playing across the woods. Lisanne wanted to call for them, but didn't have the breath to waste.

Leather Jacket pushed himself off his knees with both hands. He spat on the ground and reached behind his back, drawing a black pistol.

"No!" Lisanne screamed, turning to run. Jack and Adara were almost here—

The first bullet took her in the left arm, high, under her deltoid, shattering bone. It felt like she'd been hit with a hammer. She was vaguely aware of the report of a second and then a third shot. Had he missed? She hadn't felt another impact . . . Arm dangling, she dug in, trying to run. Something was wrong. She coughed. Her feet . . . Would. Not. Move. Rooted in place, she tasted salt . . . Blood.

Headlights lit up the night, blinding her. Doors opened. Disjointed voices shouted behind the light.

Lisanne sank to her knees, gasping for air. A thousand-pound weight bore down against her chest. The headlights began to dim. Were they leaving? *No, no, no.* She needed help. They wouldn't leave her. Jack wouldn't leave her . . .

Fu Bohai stood in the snow on the aft deck of a thirty-foot cabin cruiser tied at the end of a pier behind the Lake Kanas Resort and listened to Qiu's voicemail. This was his third unsuccessful attempt. Fu cursed to himself and snugged his hat down tighter against the chill. For a brief moment, he considered what his life would be like if he simply threw the mobile phone over the side and into the cold, black water. Mountains and lakes were beautiful, to be sure, but they were also an incredible nuisance.

He slipped the phone in his pocket and returned his attention to the boat's skipper, a Uyghur man named Qassim. Qassim had proven to be more than talkative from the time they'd found him waiting alone on the boat. In fact, Fu thought, he might have to shoot the man to get him to shut up. Qassim was forty-six years old, had two children—both sons, thanks be to God, because his brother had two daughters and daughters were a curse. His wife nagged him, as he suspected all wives did, mostly about money and the creature comforts of life that she believed a wife like her deserved to have. She hardly cooked for him anymore now that his boys were grown, and the house was always a mess. She was, he pointed out, his father-in-law's daughter, and, like all daughters, a curse . . .

Fu finally put a boot to the man's shin to get him to focus. He freely admitted to being hired over the phone by a Chinese man to take a group of foreigners on a night excursion. He did not know the details, only that he was to be paid in cash when they arrived. The appointment had been made less than an hour earlier and he'd come down to the boat to get it ready. His wife had nagged him about going out again after dark and accused him of having a mistress. The old ewe would eat her words when he brought home all that money—

Fu kicked him again. "Are night excursions commonplace?"

Qassim shook his head. "Not common, but not unheard of. Crazy foreigners think they can get a better glimpse of the Kanas Lake Monster at night. We took a television crew out last fall." He raised his brow up and down, winking at Fu. "The producer was quite attractive. My wife was certain I was . . ." He trailed off, at least smart enough to stop before he earned another kick.

"Where are you to take these foreigners?" Fu asked.

"I do not know," Qassim said. "It is that way sometimes. Monster hunters bring a chart of the lake and tell me they have heard of sightings here or there or some other place. I charge by the hour, so it does not matter to me where we go." He smiled, unable to help himself. "Plus, it lets me get away from my bothersome wife."

"But they are coming tonight?"

"That is what the man on the phone said."

"What time?" Fu asked.

Qassim shrugged. "I do not know. I brought tea and noodles, so I am prepared to wait. He said he would pay me for ten hours even if we were only out for two."

Fu nodded to one of his men. "Restrain and gag him so he can't raise an alarm. Put him up front in the V-berth, out of sight."

"Please, sir," Qassim said. "You do not have to tie me. I do not know these people. I have no allegiance to them. If they have done something wrong, I am happy to help you capture them."

Fu ignored him, nodding again to his man to get on with it.

"Could I at least call my wife?" Qassim asked. "She worries."

Fu sat on one of the bench seats and took out his knife. It had seen much use lately and needed some time on the stone. Blessedly, Qassim fell quiet at the sight of it.

"Better," Fu said, closing his eyes for a moment to enjoy the sound of the Uyghur's silence. He set his hat on a small chart table beside him, and took a whetstone from his coat pocket, drawing the blade across it as he spoke. "At times, I want my bait to make noise, to draw my prey in closer with their screaming."

The Uyghur licked his lips, swallowing hard. His eyes wide as teacups. "I . . . I . . . can scream. You do not have to cut me."

Fu smiled. "Tonight," he said, "I want my bait to be silent. You will be gagged, so the rats will come to you. Remain quiet and you may survive to return to the arms of your bothersome wife."

Fu set the knife on the chart table next to his hat and tried calling Qiu again. Still nothing. Odd that he would not answer. The man knew Fu expected a report. What could possibly be taking them so long? A lone woman should pose no problem for them at all.

58

Ryan bailed out of the van before it skidded to a complete stop. The transmission chattered, protesting being thrown into Park while the wheels were still rolling.

Ryan had slid in sideways, putting himself directly on top of the action but forcing Adara to run around the vehicle to engage.

"Shit, Jack!" she snapped, flinging the passenger door open.

Surprised by the oncoming van, the two Chinese men had bunched together, shoulder to shoulder, throwing up their arms against the headlights, firing blindly. Bullets thwacked off the hood. Glass shattered as at least one round hit the windshield. Another took the side mirror off the door, missing Ryan by inches.

He didn't care.

Microtech Halo in his left hand, Beretta pistol in his right, Ryan ignored the oncoming gunfire and charged straight at the men as soon as his boots hit the pavement. Instead of moving off-line, the pug in the leather jacket attempted to backpedal, firing as he went. Ryan brought the Microtech around in a tight arc, burying the blade in the side of the man's neck, yanking him sideways by the collarbone in a combination brachial stun

and hooking maneuver. Momentum threw him sideways before he realized his throat had been cut.

Pivoting a hair, Ryan brought the muzzle of the Beretta in
line with the other shooter's face. He fired four shots in rapid
succession. The Bowers Group Bitty muffled but did not completely silence the report. It didn't matter. The guy was well
beyond hearing anything after the first round. Mouse-gun .22
though it was, the little thirty-five-grain slugs had done their
job, and done it well.

Ryan turned back to where the pug lay clutching his neck,
blood pouring from between his fingers. Ryan anchored him
with two quick shots behind the ear. He had been the one to
shoot Lisanne.

Four seconds after he left the van, Ryan stood and scanned
the sidewalk. A thin curl of gray smoke rose from the muzzle
of the Bowers Bitty.

Adara was on her knees, one hand pressed to Lisanne's upper arm, the other under her shirt, searching for other wounds.
"Help me get her to the van! Stay with me, Leese."

Training overcame panic, and Ryan lowered the hammer
on the Beretta before stuffing it into his pocket. He grabbed
Lisanne's legs as gently as he could. Her head lolled to the side,
a swath of arterial blood bathing her cheek. Adara carried her
under each arm.

Hi-Lo sirens wailed in the distance.

"Get her in the van, Jack," Adara said. "I'll work on her
while you drive."

Ryan climbed backward through the side door, lifting
Lisanne so she rested on the backseat, her head and shoulders
in Adara's lap.

Lisanne's mouth opened and closed, making croaking

sounds like a fish out of water. She arched her back at a sudden pain, and then collapsed from the effort. Her eyes fluttered and she looked up at Adara.

Her words were a forced whisper. "You . . . guys . . . came . . ."

"Of course we came," Adara said, sounding much calmer than Ryan felt. "You can't have all the fun." Adara searched frantically through torn flesh and shards of shattered bone for the bleeder under Lisanne's biceps.

Ryan grabbed her medical kit from the back and touched Lisanne's cheek. "She's gonna fix you up."

The sirens were getting louder, closer—just blocks away now.

Adara glanced up at Ryan, her hands, her face, the front of her coat, covered in Lisanne's blood. "Jack." She shook her head, gritting her teeth, squinting away tears. She unwound a rubber tourniquet and wrapped it high and tight under Lisanne's armpit as she spoke. "Turning her over to the authorities might be the only chance she has."

Ryan nodded toward the dead men on the ground—the men he'd just killed. "I think those were the authorities. They didn't have any intention of taking her to a hospital. If we take her with us, at least she has a chance. Leave her behind and . . ."

Adara shook her head, eyes welling with frustration and the unbearable pain of losing another friend. "Jack . . ."

Ryan knew exactly what she meant. In all likelihood, Lisanne Robertson would die no matter what they did. Ryan put the van in gear and made a U-turn, avoiding the street with oncoming police cars as he headed north toward Kanas Lake.

At least this way she would die among friends.

59

Yao's heart fell when Chavez lowered the phone and shook his head. Medina was at the end of her rope, unstrung, a mother helpless to aid a child in danger.

Chavez had turned off his Bluetooth in order to attempt the call, and Ryan's frantic voice crackled over the net for all to hear. Chavez started to answer, but Ma held a finger to his lips.

"Ding! Adam!" Ryan hailed again. "I'm not reading you. Transmitting in the blind. Lisanne's been shot. It's bad, Ding." His voice caught, as he found it difficult to speak. "Really bad. We're headed for exfil. In the black now, but not sure for how long. Hope you're getting this." His voice dropped lower. "Hurry . . . Like I said, it's really bad."

Yao pressed his jaw against the muzzle of Medina's gun. "Go ahead and shoot if you're going to," he said. "The men after you have already tortured and murdered one of my dearest friends, and now they've severely wounded another."

Yao had made a career of reading people, but Medina's face was stone. There was nothing else to do but lay all his cards on the table. He spoke quickly. Ryan would beat them to the boat if they didn't leave in the next five minutes. "Hala is with one of the most capable men I know."

"My sister?"

"Listen to me!" Yao snapped. "We don't have time if you stop and ask questions. Your sister was killed trying to save Hala. My friend killed the man that killed her. He got Hala out of China and she is safe. The men after you are with the Chinese intelligence. They believe you have information that could help them find a missing scientist, Liu Wangshu."

Medina's mouth fell open, astonished. "Professor Liu? What information?"

"Beijing believes you know where to find him," Yao said. "They are using every means to find you. They know you are affiliated with Wuming."

"What do you care?" Ma asked. "Uyghur injustice is a low priority for the United States."

"And most Han," Yao said, nodding at Ma. "You know too well that these are issues of humankind, not ethnicity. But, to be honest, I work for the U.S. government, and we want to find Professor Liu as well."

"Why do you want him?" Medina asked.

"Honestly," Yao said, "we want to find him because Beijing is interested. We believe he has something to do with a missing submarine."

Medina lowered the pistol. "A Chinese submarine?"

"Correct," Yao said. "Now we really need to go. My friend is in trouble—"

Chavez's phone buzzed. Ma nodded for him to put it on speaker.

Yao nearly collapsed when Clark's voice came across, loud and clear, as if he were in the room beside them.

"You called?"

"No time to explain, John," Chavez said. "But I have Hala's mother here. She wants to say hello."

E asy, Jack," Adara said, cursing softly as Ryan drifted the van through a sweeping corner, chattering the rear tires.

"Sorry," he said, stomach in his throat. He'd adjusted the rearview mirror so he could keep an eye on what was happening in the back.

Covered in blood, Adara cradled Lisanne's shoulders in her lap, working frantically. She'd applied a SWAT-T Tourniquet first—essentially a long strip of rubber—as soon as they were in the van. It was small, always in her pocket, and handy, so it went on while Ryan was getting the bag. She'd put a windless tourniquet over that one by the time they hit the edge of town, twisting it tight enough to make Lisanne wince from the pain. People liked to argue tourniquets in the comfort of their living rooms, throwing out stats about lost limbs and less drastic alternatives. Rolling down a mountain road in the back of a van in a hostile country with blood squirting out a brachial artery—all such arguments were void. Lisanne could well lose her arm if circulation wasn't restored in the next few hours, but Adara had seconds to stop the bleeding.

"How . . ." Lisanne gave a hollow cough. It was weak, little more than a gagging click. "How . . . bad?"

"You're hanging on," Adara said. "And that is amazing."

"Don't . . . sugarcoat . . ." Lisanne said.

Ryan wiped away a tear with his forearm.

"We've stopped the bleeding in your arm," Adara said.

"Hurts like hell," Lisanne said. "What else?"

"Two shots to the abdomen," Adara said. "No exit wounds."

Lisanne arched her back, grimacing, and then fell limp.

Adara patted her cheek. "Hey, kiddo! Lisanne!" She put two fingers to Lisanne's neck, sighing in relief, sniffing back tears like she had a cold. "I have a pulse. It's fast as a runaway train from blood loss, but it's still there. The shots missed her lungs, but one of the bullets went in right where her spleen is."

Ryan glanced in the rearview mirror. He swallowed, straining to get the words out of his throat. "What . . . can you do?"

Adara shook her head. "If the bullet hit her spleen and she's bleeding internally . . . there's nothing I can do."

Ding's voice came over the net. "Jack, Jack, Ding. How's she holding up?"

"Not good," Ryan said. "We're coming into the village now . . ." He tapped his brakes, slowing to let a dark beater crew-cab pickup coming in from the west turn onto the road ahead of him.

"Tell me that's you," Chavez said.

Ryan flicked his brights on and off.

"Gotcha," Chavez said.

Ryan chanced a look over his shoulder. "How we doing?"

Adara shook her head. "Same. She's out, but still breathing on her own and I have a pulse. She's a tough lady."

"No kidding . . ."

Ahead, the little pickup truck's headlights went dark. Still well away from the docks, it stopped in the middle of the road.

Tell Jack to stand by," Yao said from the front seat of the Great Wall pickup. Ma drove. Chavez sat in the middle.

Medina and the two Uyghur men sat in the back. The men made no secret of the fact that if they suspected either intruder of treachery that would harm Medina, they would not hesitate to shoot.

Yao had to ask to borrow the night-vision goggles back from the young Uyghur, Perhat, who seemed particularly fascinated by it.

"Something isn't right," Yao said. "The skipper is supposed to be alone." He passed the NVGs to Ma.

"Alone?" Ma said, peering through the device. "This boat is very crowded at the moment."

Lisanne was awake again, whimpering softly, grimacing from the pain.

Yao came over the net, hollow. "We're blown," he said. "I don't know how, but there are people on the boat. I can't be certain, but I think it's the tall guy with the hat."

"We can't be blown," Ryan said. "We'll just have to take the boat back from them."

"Jack," Yao said. "I want to run down there and kill that son of a bitch. But they'd see us coming before we made it halfway down the pier."

"I don't care," Jack said. "Lisanne needs a doctor—"

"It's okay," Lisanne whispered from the back. "It's my fault anyway." She coughed again. "Should have paid better attention . . ."

Ryan pounded the steering wheel with both hands.

"We can't be blown!"

"Jack, really," Lisanne said, every breath like she was leaking air. "It's . . ." She licked her lips, summoning the effort for a few more words. "It's . . . not your fault . . ."

"Stand by," Yao said over the net. "Medina has an idea."

F u Bohai cursed himself for not telling his men to kill the woman straightaway. They had yet to answer his calls, and that had him worried. The woman's friends must have shown up. He had little doubt now that these tourists from Finland were the ones who had chartered this boat. There were cabins around the lake. Perhaps they had knowledge that Medina Tohti was hiding out at one of them. It was the only thing that made sense in a country with security cameras on virtually every light post. Yes. She must be hiding in the wilderness, possibly being supplied by the person with the boat whose ticket stubs the CIA officer spoke of. Fu and his men would simply wait, and then force them to disclose her location. With any luck, he would have the Uyghur bitch by morning.

He tried Qiu once more on the phone . . . What had the CIA officer in Albania called him? *Pukwudgie* . . . What an amusing word.

Again, there was no answer.

He slapped the chart table with his palm, causing his men to glance up from their phones and the boat captain to give a muffled yelp beneath the tape over his mouth.

Yang, who was seated at the dinette, perked up and peered out the window.

"Did you hear that?"

"I heard nothing," Fu said.

Then, far down the docks, a boat motor burbled to life.

Fu bolted to his feet, rushing out onto the deck to look

down the pier. Gray hulks bobbed side by side all the way down, barely visible against the ink-black water. The engines were running, as Medina and her fellow conspirators would expect them to be when they arrived—but he'd never expected to actually launch. The boat was still tied to its moorings.

Farther down, the engine burbled louder. Something thumped against the dock. A light flashed briefly across the water—getting their bearings—and then winked out at the same moment the engine opened up. In his peripheral vision, Fu watched a small cabin runabout disappear into the night.

He loosed a scream of rage, pounded the bulkhead by the rear door. "Which one of you can drive a boat?"

Neither answered quickly enough. Fu strode to the V-berth and hauled the skipper to his feet, ripping away the gray tape, then spinning him to reach his bindings. He opened his knife, pointing it at Yang.

"Untie the dock lines," he snapped, before cutting the skipper's hands free. "You will follow that other vessel," he said. "Catch it, and you will be greatly rewarded."

"Y-Yes," he stammered. "No problem. I will do that. Thank you." The skipper's head snapped up, looking out at the man pulling a line off the stern. "No, no, no," he said, walking to the open door. "You must cast off the bow or you will run us into—"

The skipper stepped out as if to finish his imperative bit of instruction—but instead leaped over the side into the black water.

"Stop him!" Fu Bohai roared, then turned to his man who was left inside. "Tell me you have driven a boat before! Any boat!"

"Yes, Boss," he stammered. "Though never one this large."

"You take the wheel," Fu said.

"Yes, Boss," the man said again, tentatively sitting down to familiarize himself with the controls.

The outside man stuck his head in the door, pistol in hand, panting after running from one end of the boat to the other.

"He is gone, Boss."

"I don't care about him," Fu snapped. "Are we untied?"

Yang nodded.

Fu began to pound against the seat next to the captain's chair. "Then go! Go! Go!"

The new driver pulled the twin throttle levers toward him, causing the boat to lurch backward, burbling in the water. Away from the dock, he cut the wheel hard left and eased the throttle forward, taking the boat into the blackness of the lake.

"I said, go," Fu snapped, and, reaching across the wheel, jammed the levers all the way to the firewall.

"Boss," the driver said, knuckles white on the wheel. "I could use some light . . ."

60

He's back there," Chavez said above the roar of the twin Tohatsu 150-horsepower outboards. "For sure. Lights just came on."

He stood at the rear of the cabin, watching the lights of the approaching vessel grow larger and larger with each passing minute. Ma had provided them with an SKS rifle, old and beaten half to death, but it was better than a pistol and Ding was glad to have it.

Yao was on deck, slumped beneath the edge of the transom to remain out of sight, making yet another call on the satellite phone.

Ma was at the helm of his boss's second boat, a thirty-five-foot day cruiser for use when they did not have enough customers for the *Eternal Peach*. Ding suspected it was also the boss's play boat, the one he used for personal fishing trips and wining and dining influential members of the Party when they visited the park.

Over a hundred and eighty meters at its deepest point, Kanas was shaped like a crescent moon, much longer than it was wide, and curving gradually to the east as they sped toward the Russian border—just ten miles from the north end of the lake.

Medina stood next to Ma, her hand on the back of the captain's chair. The glow of the radio illuminated her gaunt face. Outside, snow, stark and white against the backdrop of the water, shot by in the beam of the single halogen running light. Spray chattered along the hull of the boat as it skimmed across the glass-slick surface.

The three other members of the Wuming had stayed behind, helping to cast off, vowing to continue the fight against their oppressors if Ma did not return. Once Medina had agreed to help, there had been no argument.

Jack assisted Adara as best he could. They'd turned on the propane cabin heater and made Lisanne a bed on a cushioned vinyl passenger bench that ran along the starboard wall, wedging her in with life jackets and covering her with wool blankets they found in an aft storage locker. Beyond that, there was little to do but hold Lisanne's hand and try to comfort her. She drifted in and out of consciousness, which, Ding thought, was probably a blessing, since they had no morphine. Medina, who had apparently taken upon herself the responsibility of medic for the Wuming, brought a small kit containing a bag of saline and an IV catheter. The fluids helped some, but Lisanne needed blood—a lot of blood.

Yao finished his call and walked past Chavez, into the relative warmth of the cabin.

"We good?" Chavez asked.

Yao nodded and said "Yep," which sounded to Chavez to be slightly less than good.

With Yao out of the way, he aimed the rifle at the oncoming light. If he couldn't kill the son of a bitch in the felt hat, he could at least blind the boat, snuff out the light so they would be unable to follow.

"They're moving up fast," he yelled. "I'll pop them when they get a little closer. Make them keep their heads down."

Nine minutes from the time they left the docks, Ma eased back on the throttles.

The oncoming boat loomed closer now—less than a quarter-mile behind and closing fast.

"I'm sure I don't have to tell you this," Yao said over the engines, "but if they're in range, *we* are in range."

The beam of the approaching vessel flooded the cabin's interior, throwing distorted moving shadows around the walls as the boats bounced along on step.

Ma turned sharply to the right, nudging the throttles back even more. The roar of the engines fell dramatically. Their speed dropped by half.

Medina looked at him. "This is too soon!"

Yao checked the moving map on his phone and moved forward, grabbing handholds as he went to keep his feet. "We're not far enough." He held the screen down so Ma could see it, pointing at two respective spots. "We're here. You need to be here."

The other boat was almost on top of them now.

Ma gave a curt nod. Instead of speaking, he continued to turn the wheel to the right, pushing the throttles forward only when the other boat was almost on top of them.

Even at less than fifteen knots, the twin 150s were clearly outrunning the running lights. Snow and glare reduced navigational visibility to a few dozen yards.

Bullets from the pursuing vessel slapped the transom, narrowly missing the motors.

Chavez pushed open the door, firing the SKS at the most blinding point of light—to absolutely no effect. He fired again anyway, on the off chance he could force the pursuers to keep their heads down. Another volley thwacked the doorframe by his shoulder, chasing him inside the cabin.

"Any reason why we're letting these guys climb up our ass?"

Ma glanced over his shoulder. "Hold on!"

Downed trees, a line of bright grass, and jagged black rocks suddenly filled the windshield, caught in the glare of the single halogen light.

Ma jammed the throttles forward and cut the wheel hard left.

Fu Bohai's driver, being unfamiliar with the lake—and boats—focused with laser precision on the vessel ahead, mirroring its every turn. Clouds obscured even the hint of a moon. The incredibly bright running lamps were almost a hindrance in the driving snow and surface spray, making it easy to become confused.

"You must have struck a fuel line," the driver said when the fugitive boat began to slow. "Shall I ram them?"

"No!" Fu said, standing beside the captain's chair, one hand on the console, the other clutching an H&K rifle. "I do not want you to ram them. That would sink us both. Stay close. He may speed up again once he makes this turn—"

Fu glanced at the chart plotter mounted to the ceiling, surprised that the moving triangle that represented their vessel had not caught up with their actual location. Ma was clearly following Kanas Lake's dogleg bend to the right, but the plotter showed they were still at least three miles away.

The driver cursed.

Ahead, the fugitive vessel increased its speed and virtually stood on its side as it arced sharply to the left, cutting a deep C of froth in the water and heading back the way it had come, roaring down the port rail, almost close enough to touch.

"You fool!" Fu screamed. He dropped the rifle to brace himself with both hands. "Turn! Turn the boat!"

They hit the mud at over twenty knots, slamming everyone forward. The driver flew out of his seat, impacting the windscreen with the crown of his head and breaking his neck.

Fu was thrown sideways against the metal console, snapping his left arm in at least two places. Pain and nausea brought him to his knees. One of the engines still roared, grinding the exposed propeller against the mud and gravel. Fu felt certain the otherworldly whine would shatter every piece of glass on the boat. He dragged himself up with his good arm long enough to kill the engine, before collapsing again to the floor.

The motors were off, but battery-powered lights were still operative, for the time being at least. Cold air poured through the shattered windscreen. The smell of fuel permeated everything.

Fu coughed, bringing sharp pains to life deep inside his skull. Seething fury blurred his vision. A steady flow of blood dripping off his brow said he probably had a concussion as well. Yang fared little better with a shattered leg and jaw.

Fu didn't care how badly the man was hurt.

"Find me the phone!" The excruciating pain in his head made him gag when he shouted. He lowered his voice to a whispered hiss. "Now!"

The boat lay keeled over to port on her V-shaped hull, piling everyone and everything that wasn't fastened down on the left. Yang found the phone under a pile of orange life vests.

Concentrating to stay awake, Fu telephoned the Burqin Airport, sixty kilometers to the south. He invoked the name of Admiral Zheng of People's Liberation Army Naval Intelligence and demanded to speak to the XPCC 10th Division officer on duty. Fu was connected immediately and gave a hurried rundown of his urgent need to stop the escape of a valuable fugitive from the forest around Lake Kanas. The officer in charge, a youthful-sounding captain, was extremely cooperative but not especially helpful. Air assets this far north consisted of a handful of L-39 Czechoslovakian fighter jets for border patrols, and two helicopters, both of which were Harbin H425s, the civilian version of the Z-9W (or WZ-9) built in China for the PLA Air Force on a licensing agreement with Eurocopter. The colonel barked at a subordinate to get both birds in the air and then contact Xinjiang Corps Helicopter Brigade in Urumqi.

"But . . . the helicopters are generally used for search-and-rescue," the captain said. "They are both equipped with infrared cameras, but no weapons."

"That is fine," Fu said, feeling as though he might pass out. "Just send them. These fugitives should not be difficult to find. Their boat will be visible somewhere on the north end of the lake."

"Please excuse me." The captain broke off the conversation to speak with someone else on his end.

"Major," he said as he came back on the line. "A JY-14 radar station near our frontier with Kazakhstan and Russia reports numerous contacts less than ten kilometers across the border toward the Novosibirsk region of Russia. An unknown type of aircraft, but judging from the speed and varied course, they are believed to be rotary-wing."

"The Russians . . ." Fu mused, too light-headed to think. "Why would the Russians be involved . . . ?"

"Unknown, Major," the captain said. "But considering your situation, it seemed connected. The Russian border is a mere twenty-six kilometers from Kanas Lake."

"Yes," Fu said. His left eye would not stay open, no matter what he did. "That makes sense."

"Two of our L-39s will overfly you in approximately twenty minutes," the captain said. "Perhaps they will discourage the Russian aircraft from making any incursions into China. I have already notified my superiors of your fugitives as well as the radar contacts. Very soon, you should have all the resources you need to make your capture."

Fu leaned against the bulkhead, ending the call as he watched a steady trickle of blood drip from the driver's ear where he lay draped over the wheel. The dead did not bleed, meaning the man was still alive. Fu took a deep breath, steadying himself. There was little he could do. He would need all his wits and strength when it came time to strangle every last person who had helped Medina Tohti lead him on this ridiculous chase.

61

SKS in hand, Chavez watched out the back window for ten full minutes after Ma's last-second turn, fully expecting to see the larger boat appear at any moment.

The snow had abated to a few flakes here and there, but temperatures fell sharply, making Chavez wish he had a thicker hat.

Adam Yao ended another call out on deck, patting Chavez on the shoulder as he passed, coming in to get warm. His brow was furrowed, his jaw tense.

"Everything on track?" Chavez asked.

"All good," Yao said, just like before, sounding as if he didn't quite believe his own words. "They're five minutes out."

Medina gazed out the back window, an unfocused, thousand-yard stare. "Do you think they survived?"

"Wouldn't surprise me if none of them made it," Yao said. "A hard stop like that . . . It can be like falling off a roof." He stuffed the sat phone in Chavez's bag. Odd, but both were simple earth tone duffels. They were all running on fumes. It was an easy mistake to make—and Chavez didn't mind carrying a few extra ounces of weight.

"I hope it killed them all," Ma said. "For the sake of our people who remained behind."

He reduced power again, this time referring to the moving chart on the electronic plotter as he scanned the shore.

Yao pointed with an open hand at the darkness beyond the glow of the running light. "There," he said as a small cove materialized out of the black void. Two boulders the size of small cars guarded the entry to the cove, forcing him to hug the southern shoreline as he entered. Deadfall floated in the still water. Ma nosed the logs gently out of the way. The bank was relatively flat, rising gradually toward the tree line fifty meters away. Between water and trees lay a grassy meadow the size of a soccer field and braided with small streams flowing out of the Altay Mountains beyond.

Ma worked the twin Tohatsus in opposition, reversing the port engine while he nudged the starboard throttle forward, swinging the stern around so the starboard, or right side, of the vessel sidled up parallel to the shoreline.

Medina stood beside him as he worked, engaged in a deep and whispered conversation.

The others worked quickly, speaking little, grabbing what few bags they had and wrapping Lisanne in a blanket to get her ready for transport. They expected unfriendly company at any moment.

Even with Ma's expert parking job, they were still ten feet from the mossy bank. Chavez and Ryan bailed off the boat into knee-deep water while Yao and Adara worked quickly to pass Lisanne, swaddled like a baby, over the side to them.

Out on deck now, Medina stormed to the far side of the deck, staring out at the water again. Her hushed conversation with Ma had apparently reached a boiling point.

A low hum, like the sound of a distant lawnmower, carried through the trees.

"We have to go," Yao said. "Now."

Medina wheeled, refusing to budge from her spot. "They will kill him if he does not come with us."

"Ma?" Yao said, glancing to the Han man, who stood at the cabin door.

Ma gave a knowing nod. "They will see the boat. Someone needs to lead them away."

It was hard to argue, but Chavez waved him on anyway. "We're not even sure anyone's coming after us since you took care of those last guys."

"Oh," Ma said. "You are a professional. You know they will come—and you know I must stay. Now take her and get off my boat."

Medina shook her head, digging in. "I am not going."

Ma went to her, taking her gently by the shoulders. "There is no time. I will take the boat north, away from here—"

Her head snapped up, the sorrow clearly visible even in the scant amber glow of the single lamp on deck. "We sink it!"

"No." Ma shook his head. "They will surely spot it from the air. Someone *must* draw them away. I do not know what your secret is, but—"

"I do not know, either—"

"Whatever it is," Ma said, "it is dangerous for Beijing—and that is good for us. You know this."

Her chest shook, overcome with sobs. She nodded, unable to meet his eye.

"What will happen to the work?" she whispered. "The cause?"

Ma smiled softly. "I am not the only one," he said, already steering her by the shoulders toward Yao and the shore. "We are nameless, but we are many."

———

M edina Tohti stood on the bank until Mamut was out of sight, swallowed up by the darkness of Kanas Lake.

"You are fortunate you have my daughter," she said under her breath.

"She's not a hostage," Chavez reminded her. "We only wanted you to know she is safe."

Medina considered this for a moment, and then started up the bank without looking back. "You are fortunate none-theless."

Chavez motioned the group after her, wanting to vacate the area as soon as humanly possible.

The vague lawnmower hum suddenly grew louder, bursting into the clearing as a Hughes OH-6 Cayuse (Little Bird or Killer Egg), skimmed in at treetop level and descended toward the grass, thirty meters away. Commonly called a "Loach" for its designation as a Light Observation Helicopter, or LOH, in Vietnam, the egg-shaped chopper was completely blacked out with both pilots wearing NVGs. Absent the thumping roar of a normal helicopter, the Loach was so quiet that Chavez hadn't heard it at all until moments before its arrival. Even then, it had been impossible to tell from which direction it came until an instant before it cleared the trees. Closer inspection revealed it had several modifications from a regular Loach—an extra main rotor blade, four tail rotor blades instead of two, a large baffled muffler under the tail boom. An infrared camera the size of a bowling ball hung off the bird's nose, imperative for guiding the pilots as they navigated narrow canyons and craggy moun-tain passes with no running lights. This one, an MH-6 vari-ant, had two horizontal platforms resembling black boogie boards, one on each side at the base of the doors like stubby wings.

"Looks awfully small," Chavez said as they helped carry Lisanne's blanket roll across the grassy hummocks.

"There were supposed to be two," Yao said, floundering in the spring mud, grunting in his effort to keep his corner of Lisanne's blanket roll straight and level. "We brought them in on a C-130. That last phone call on the boat was to tell me one of them had crapped out after it was off-loaded, leaving us with limited space for an evacuation. I'm not sure what the problem was, but I thought I might have to see you guys off and then hoof it back to the village—blend in, adapt, overcome, that kind of shit."

Chavez chuckled despite the situation. "Two is one and one is none," he said—one of Clark's favorite quotes. "We'll fit. If these guys are like the Loach pilots I know, they'd strap us to the skids before they left one of us behind."

Yao turned as he walked, head to one side. "Hmmm. Don't be too sure. Their mission is to get Medina back. The rest of us are expendable."

The MH-6 copilot leaned out of the left-side door, waving them forward.

"Let's go! Let's go! Let's go!" He tapped his headset. "Multiple aircraft heading this way from the south at a high rate of speed. ETA eight minutes." He twisted in his seat, pointing east. "We need to be behind that mountain in six."

"Copy that!" Chavez helped feed Lisanne into the side door while he listened for further instructions.

"We took the seats out in the back, so you'll go four on the floor," the copilot continued. He pointed to Chavez and Ryan

with a knife hand. "You and you buckle in on the outside platforms for balance. There are a couple of parkas in the back to
keep you from freezing your asses off!"

The pilot took his left hand off the collective long enough
to wave it in a circle over his helmet. "Let's haul ass!"

Lisanne went in first, followed by Adara, who refused to
leave her side, and then Medina. Yao made sure they were har-
nessed in. Chavez did one last quick-check of his team before
turning and securing his own harness. The copilot watched like
a hawk, and the moment Chavez's buckle snapped into place,
he turned and gave a thumbs-up.

Chavez glanced at his watch as the Loach lifted off, pirouet-
ting as it rose to point its nose to the east. Less than four minutes to cross the trees and reach the shadow of the next valley.
As if the pilot read his mind, the chopper's engine grew louder
and its nose dipped, shooting forward toward the mountains.
Chavez looked back one last time, to see the feeble beam from
Mamut's boat moving north across the black void of Kanas Lake.

In addition to the other stealth components, this CIA Quiet
Loach also appeared to be covered with a rubberized, radar-
absorbing skin. Even so, the pilots were flying NOE—nap of
the earth—winding their way through valleys, mere feet above
the ground. They followed rivers when they could, grassland or
gravel, and rose just above the trees when they had to, always
maintaining their speed. Several times, Chavez felt freezing
spray from groundwater sting his skin or thought he might drag
his boots on a treetop—but the pilots kept him just out of
reach. He tried to turn and check on his friends, to see how
Lisanne was holding up, but bitter, hurricane-force winds forced
him to keep his head down, buried in the parka. Caught up in

the urgency of an immediate departure, he'd made the rookie mistake of forgetting to pull the zipper up as far as it would go before takeoff. Buffeted by the wind, the metal button on his collar began to slap him repeatedly in the ear—taking him back to the first time he'd flown on one of these birds, a loose strap on his ruck slapping him silly in the wind. He thought of his son and what that kid had in store for him—and for some reason, it made him feel very old.

As the crow flies, the Little Bird's point of departure at Kanas Lake was just over thirty miles from the Mongolian border. The pilots cheated northeast to stay below radar. It took them a mile out of the way through a pass that got them over the first line of snowcapped Altay peaks. At this point, the Mongolian border was only ten miles away. Instead of continuing east, the pilots took the little chopper south into a long valley, adding almost twenty miles to their trip, but avoiding a suspected radar site at the triple frontier where the borders of China, Russia, and Mongolia came together.

Twenty-five minutes after liftoff, the copilot reached down to where Chavez sat on the platform less than a foot away, and gave him a thumbs-up, signaling that they were out of Chinese airspace. Chavez breathed a sigh of relief, slumping against his harness. The mountains quickly gave way to steppe and the ground beneath was generally treeless and rolling. It was still bitter cold outside the chopper, but the clouds had cleared once they'd passed through the mountains, revealing why, once the sun came up, Mongolia would live up to its nickname of Land of the Eternal Blue Sky. Ten minutes after that, the MH-6 turned on its landing lights. Three large trucks were parked facing one another on a deserted gravel road with their headlights forming a makeshift landing zone. They looked like they might be Deuce and a Halfs, but Chavez's eyes teared so badly from the wind that he could hardly see.

Landing was anticlimactic, since they weren't quite as worried about someone trying to kill them.

A Mongolian military officer and two young men Chavez assumed were with CIA air ops helped everyone off the chopper except Lisanne and Adara. Two docs from the Mongolian military climbed in with the women. She was still in and out of consciousness, but alive—for now. The docs looked incredibly grim and pounded on the pilot's seat to get him to go.

One of the hazards of covert missions was that they often had to remain covert during rescue or medical emergencies. The circle of people who even saw the stealth helicopter was already too large and Yao was stretching the limits directing it to fly Lisanne toward the city of Khovd, a hundred and fifty miles to the east. A military ambulance was already on the road to intercept ten miles out of the city, where the two doctors would transfer the patient. A Hawker Air Ambulance would take her the remaining seven hundred miles from Khovd to Ulaanbaatar. It was a testament to how remote they truly were that absent a return to China, the nearest trauma hospital of consequence was nine hundred miles from where they now stood. Even with a cursory glance at her wounds, the surgeons were astounded that Lisanne had not already bled to death. If she did live, the odds were against her keeping the injured arm. Jack and Adara both wanted to go with her, but there was barely enough room for one with their medical equipment. Adara's training won out, and she remained on the chopper, cradling Lisanne's torso on her lap.

Jack, relieved of his duties with Lisanne, returned reluctantly but quickly to mission mode and helped Medina board the truck. Covered with canvas and heated with propane, the back was set up like a small war room with a folding table, chairs, and two lanterns.

"Mongolia," Chavez said to Yao, shaking his head as they stood by the lowered tailgate, waiting for Medina and Jack to climb aboard. He hooked a thumb over his shoulder toward the departing MH-6 Cayuse, as it was swallowed up in the night. "I thought all the Quiet Ones were destroyed or dismantled after Vietnam."

He'd wanted to ask earlier, but there had been no time.

The Quiet Ones, as the CIA called them, were two OH-6As specifically modified for stealth in an operation code-named MAINSTREET. The test flights were done at Area 51—giving rise to many a "black helicopter" conspiracy, and the ultra-quiet birds were handed over to CIA's front company, Air America. Many who were in the business of stealth felt that there was no modern helicopter as quiet as these MAIN-STREET Loaches had been.

Yao scoffed. "If you were the CIA and you'd developed the quietest chopper in history, would you toss it into the dung heap after a single secret mission into North Vietnam?"

"I suppose not," Chavez said.

"Anyway," Yao said, climbing into the truck, "my official answer is what black helicopter? I don't know about any black helicopter."

Before boarding one of the remaining trucks, the Mongolian military officer, a general named Baatar, welcomed the group to his country and gave a short speech about how Mongolia considered the United States its most important "Third Neighbor." He assured them that he was at their disposal, and then urged them to consider departing his country as quickly and quietly as possible—so as not to alert the dragon or the bear who were his actual neighbors.

62

I do not understand," Medina Tohti said when they were all seated around the table and the truck was moving—also toward the airport in the city of Khovd. Her face was flushed red with sleepy warmth after hours in the cold. Everyone was beyond exhausted. "How did the Chinese not see us when we flew out? I know you stayed low, but surely they were looking—"

"They were," Yao said. "But they were looking in the wrong place. Russia and Kazakhstan were less than twenty-five kilometers away from the lake. Mongolia was double that." Yao gave an impish smile. "And someone may have reported the son of a Russian politburo member who had gone missing out on a mountain adventure in the wilderness area north of the border. Chinese air assets would have seen the search-and-rescue efforts on radar and assumed they were there to assist in our escape."

Chavez put a hand flat on a blank yellow notepad in front of him. "They will, in fact, likely still assume that."

"I would like to speak to my daughter again," Medina said.

Chavez dug the satellite phone out of his duffel. Yao had obviously put it there when he thought he might be left behind. "Of course." Chavez slid the phone across the table to her and yawned. "Entirely up to you, but it is the middle of the night where she is, just like it is here. I'm sure she is sleeping."

Medina pushed the phone away. "Okay . . . then tell me what you want to know."

"It involves Professor Liu Wangshu," Yao said. "Why would Beijing be so determined to find you? What do you have to do with him?"

Chavez nodded. "That's our question. Why you?"

"I am sure I do not know," Medina said. "I was one of his engineering students for a time. I was what you would call his teaching assistant."

"Forgive me for being so blunt," Yao said. "But I know how the Han majority feel about Uyghur people. How were you able to attend university as a teaching assistant?"

"I am not offended," Medina said. "In western China there are two kinds of schools for Uyghur children. Schools where Uyghur children learn Mandarin and Han Chinese history with other Uyghur children—and schools where Uygur children are fully integrated into schools that are majority Han. My math and science scores were such that I attended the latter. Eventually, I was sent to university. Hala was very young, but she was even more skilled in gymnastics than I was at mathematics. The state took her away to train at a special school in the city. I believe they may have done this so I would go willingly to Huludao."

Ryan, who had said little up to this point, frowned. "Bastards."

"Yes," Medina said. "They are that—though they would assure the world that everything they do is for our good." She sighed, staring down at the table as she spoke. "I am sure I was the first Uyghur student to hold this position with Professor Liu. And I feel equally sure I was the first female Uyghur engineering student. I believe he truly respected me for my intellect, though . . ." Her voice trailed off, changing direction. "We worked on several different projects, all having to do with propulsion—submarine drives, propellers, for the most part." She glanced up. "Submarine propellers are often closely guarded secrets. Maybe this has something to do with that."

"Maybe," Yao said. "Were these projects all on paper, or did you have functional buildouts?"

"Paper designs," Medina said. "We built some models, but nothing functional. I was in the process of modifying one of Professor Liu's propeller designs when I was expelled. My husband was dead, my daughter taken by the same government that killed him. All I had was my mathematics, and that, too, was ripped from me. One day I was a respected student, fully integrated into the program, the next Party officials came into my room without knocking and ordered me to pack my belongings. I was to return immediately by train to Kashgar. I telephoned Professor Liu's private number from the train station, begging for an explanation. He assured me that this was all a misunderstanding, a mistake on the part of the government and that it would all work out. He said not to worry, that I was vital to his work . . .

"But I was not vital and it did not work out. Whatever the reason, it must have been far above Professor Liu's head. The government changed my mobile number and his, effectively putting a fence between us. They are very skilled at that. In any case, Hala was still a virtual prisoner at her gymnastics school. There was nothing for me in Kashgar. One of my childhood friends had joined the group you call Wuming. I contacted her and . . . you saw the rest." She looked back and forth between Chavez and Yao. "There is something you are not telling me."

"There is," Yao said.

Chavez gave a little shrug, exhaled sharply, and then nodded. They wouldn't get anywhere unless Medina learned at least some of what they knew, though it was classified above top secret.

"Our government has reason to believe," Yao said, "that a Chinese submarine is in trouble, stranded on the seabed, unable to surface or communicate. It's highly likely that Professor Liu is aboard this submarine and that it has been outfitted with a quiet gearless ring-propulsion drive the Chinese call—"

Medina finished his sentence. *"Hai shi shen lou*—Mirage."

"Was Mirage one of the projects you worked on with Liu?" Chavez asked.

"It was *my* project," she said. "I submitted it to the professor as an assignment. He told me there were too many flaws. He said that I should go . . . how do you say it . . . back to the drawing board, before he would accept it."

"Was he working on a similar project?" Chavez asked.

"He was," Medina said, eyes narrowing.

"Do you think it is possible the professor had you expelled so he could call the Mirage drive his invention?"

Medina shook her head in disbelief, though it was clear from the look in her eyes that this was exactly what she thought had happened. She reached for the notepad in front of Chavez. "May I?"

Yao scooted forward in his chair, looking at Chavez. "I may

need to go to Huludao and take a look through the professor's office."

Medina shook her head. "No," she said. "He kept everything important to him under the floorboards of his bedroom." She looked sheepishly at the men. "I did not . . . I mean to say . . . he was my superior. There was nothing . . ."

"Bastard," Ryan said again.

Yao patted the table. "We are not judging you for the actions of bad men. Now, do you believe he would have kept plans from his work in this secret spot?"

"I feel sure of it," Medina said, scribbling on the pad. "He stored little at the labs, fearing others would steal his work and take the credit for it." She got to her feet, carrying the pad as she walked, swaying with the motion of the truck to work off her anger, since there was no room in the back to pace.

"I must return to China," she said.

"Not a chance," Ding said. "We almost didn't get you out." He didn't say it out loud, but he couldn't help but think that Lisanne might well still lose her life on the mission to get Medina. He wasn't about to let her return and risk falling into Beijing's hands.

"Listen to me," Medina said. "I can retrieve the files."

"No," Ding said. "I'm confident the professor's home has already been ransacked by government agents a dozen times over."

"I doubt they could find his hiding place," Medina said. "He has an engineer's mind. He knows how to build clever things. I would pit his intellect against the idiots from the MSS any day."

"My friend is right," Yao said. "We just prevented you from falling into Beijing's hands. You are the key."

"No," Medina said. "The key is the plans for the Mirage propulsion drive, and that will be in Liu Wangshu's home. I am certain of it."

"Then we will go," Ding said. Resolute. "Or, at least, *I* will."

Medina looked stricken at the thought. "If anyone goes, it should be him." She nodded at Yao. "You look Chinese, so you might be able to walk around Huludao for a time without being questioned, but even you will still need me to get past Auntie Pei. She is the neighbor across the street."

"No," Chavez said. "And that's final. I may not be the person for the job, but you certainly aren't. We'll figure out another way to get around Auntie Pei."

Yao patted the table again, harder this time. "Wait," he said. "How long after you turned in your assignment with the design of the Mirage drive were you expelled?"

"That very evening," Medina said.

"Did Liu tell you what components of the project he wanted you to correct?"

She looked up from the notepad. "He did not."

"I don't think there was anything for you to correct," Yao said. "I expect he saw right away your plans were workable. If he'd needed your help with anything, he would have waited to have you kicked out."

Chavez was nodding now. "So if the professor is somehow incapacitated on that sub, and the Mirage drive is damaged, then they want Medina so she can help repair it."

"Could be," Yao said. "It is more likely that they want to destroy the existing one to keep it from falling into our hands. If they have Medina, they can re-create a new one."

Medina smiled. "And if Medina can re-create it for

Beijing . . ." She tapped the side of her head with her pencil and turned the notepad toward them. "Then she can re-create it for you."

Chavez thought for a moment, and then smiled at Yao, who walked to the back of the truck so he could get a good signal on the sat phone.

63

In the control room of the *Indiana*, Captain Condiff watched over Petty Officer Markette's shoulder at the green "waterfall" on his screen that turned sounds into pictures that only sonar technicians could read.

The *Indiana* was at full stop, rigged for ultraquiet. The loudest pumps had been taken off-line, even if they were slightly more efficient than the quieter ones. Everyone not on station was in their bunk, to keep accidents from happening. Everyone spoke in whispers, not so much because the other sub would be able to hear them, but because it reminded them of their condition.

A half-hour earlier, Markette had "spotted" the new contact—another sub—diesel-electric probably, quieter than a nuke, but for a squeaky bearing in one of the pumps.

"Bearing two-seven-zero," Markette said. "Two thousand meters. She's going back and forth, hunting."

"Captain," the USS *Indiana*'s communications tech said. "Incoming on Deep Siren."

The lead F-35 pilot's voice squawked over the radio in the *Healy*'s control room.

"I think your company's decided to RTB. We'll be on station for a bit if you need us."

Captain Rapoza chuckled. It wasn't surprising that the Chinese icebreaker's little Z-9 helicopter had decided to return to base with two American fighter jets paying the *Healy* a social call.

The *Healy* and the *Xue Long* found themselves in a standoff of sorts, both hove-to, facing each other, literally on thin ice. Open leads webbed the surface all around them. Drifting bergs bumped their hulls. A stiff wind blew in from the north, forcing both ships to work hard to keep from being pushed steadily southward with the broken pads of ice.

A second-class petty officer named Lilly came across the radio from the afterdeck. He was from outside New Orleans, and to Rapoza, he always sounded like he had a mouthful of food when he spoke.

"Communication buoy on the surface, Captain," he said.

The *Healy* had contacted *Indiana* via Deep Siren, the Raytheon low frequency tactical underwater paging system. Though not deployed fleet-wide, even on Navy vessels, it made sense to station such a device aboard one of the only ships in the U.S. inventory that ventured out on the ice where submarines lurked below. If the *Indiana* was down there, as Pacific Command said she would be, then he'd get the message and respond. He'd done just that, deploying a tethered device called an X-SUB Communication Buoy that allowed for two-way communication. The *Indiana*, knowing much more about *Healy*'s position than she knew about the sub's, sent the buoy up twenty yards to port off the afterdeck. It was barely visible above the water.

"Very well," Rapoza said, nodding at his XO. "Let's get Captain Condiff on the line."

The petty officer nodded. "Go ahead, Skipper."

"Captain Condiff," Rapoza said. "I am instructed to ask you to stand by for a call from the President of the United States."

P resident Zhao," Jack Ryan said. "May I speak freely?"

Silence on the line as an interpreter repeated everything in Mandarin.

"Of course, Mr. President," Zhao answered in perfect Oxford English.

The two men had a history, albeit a fiery one. It would cause Zhao to lose face if he admitted it, but Ryan and his people had averted a nearly successful assassination attempt on Zhao's life. Ryan did not bring it up. A Chinese leader without face was no leader at all. As the previous president had demonstrated when he took his own life. Zhao was proving to be increasingly belligerent as he consolidated his power, but the two men could still talk—so far at least. The czar you know . . .

"Mr. President," Ryan said. "I would appreciate it if you and I could speak . . . how shall I put this, off the record."

More translation, which, Ryan knew full well, was in place to give Zhao time to compose himself between each of Ryan's questions or statements. He had no trouble with the language.

"There are things," Ryan said, appealing to the man's ego, "that are not for the ears of underlings. I give you my word that I will send my people out of the room and speak to you alone. I ask you to do the same. It will keep me from making an error in front of someone and losing face. We can speak as men and keep our honor."

Ryan knew Zhao was already thinking through the request while the interpreter translated.

Zhao was smart enough to know that Ryan was giving him an out, to keep from losing face himself. Face, in China, was paramount. And ethics tended to hinge more on if one got caught than whether or not the original deed was right or wrong. If Zhao and Ryan spoke in private, neither man could be "caught" and both could retain their face.

"As you wish," Zhao said at length.

Ryan kept his end of the bargain and shooed everyone out of the Oval, including Mary Pat. Subterfuge was one thing, but his word meant something.

"I am alone," Zhao said two minutes later.

"Thank you for this, Mr. President," Ryan said. "Again, I ask your permission to speak freely."

"By all means."

Ryan spent the next five minutes going over what he knew about the submarine, conveniently leaving out any mention of Professor Liu. He commended the brave actions of Commander Wan, executive officer of the *880*—and the brave men who remained at the bottom of the sea.

"May I ask how you discovered them?" Zhao said. "As you know, my people were searching an area many miles from there."

"A fluke," Ryan said. "A science vessel dropped a test buoy almost on top of them and picked up noises of the accident."

"A fluke indeed," Zhao said. "So you were not shadowing the *880* with one of your *Virginia*-class fast-attacks? As you have said, it seems one was able to respond from quite close."

"No," Ryan said. "I wish we had been. We could have started a rescue much sooner."

"We will handle any rescue," Zhao said, an air of hostility creeping in, then fading just as quickly.

"And that is the reason I wanted to speak privately," Ryan said. "My people believe we should try to work with you to rescue your men in hopes of learning more about your technology."

"That cannot happen—"

"Please," Ryan said, "hear me out. You have been very open about the advancement in your quiet propulsion systems. I have a copy of your address to the Central Committee on my desk as we speak. Impressive. Seriously. The thing is, Mr. President, I know you want to save your men. I want you to save your men. But I also know that if I try to step in, you will be forced to protect your military secrets. Leaders must make these tough decisions."

"Mr. President," Zhao said. "I believe you may be stalling. For all I know, you are even now sending your Navy SEALs to board the *880*."

"Let me be blunt," Ryan said. "Having access to your ring propulsion drive would be nice, but it is not an imperative. Of course, we are always refining, learning, investing in new designs, but our submarines are already among the quietest and most deadly in the world. You had no idea our vessel was even there until I told you. In short, Mr. President, I wish you didn't have this propulsion system, but I don't need it. And it's certainly not worth the lives of all your brave submariners to keep it out of our hands."

"And Commander Wan?"

"We are happy to afford him medical care until he is ready to fly."

"I would prefer he come aboard the *Xue Long* as soon as possible."

"As you wish," Ryan said. "I want you to be free to rescue

your men. To that end, I am pulling my assets out of the area as soon as the commander is safely aboard your vessel."

"Just like that?" Zhao said.

"Just like that," Ryan said. "And you may even tell your people you forced me into it. God forbid there is ever a sea battle between our great nations, because many of our finest would die. This is not that time. The men on the *880* have taken no hostile action toward my country. So save them. Please."

64

Tim Meyer sent an emergency message to Dot, telling her he had to meet.

She told him to call her instead, on the burner he kept hidden in a fake pipe beside the garbage disposal. Most guys who went into law enforcement or counterintelligence wouldn't know jack shit about installing their own appliances. Meyer sure wouldn't. If they did ever search his home, they'd look right past it.

"They arrested Gretchen Pack," he said, feeling light-headed, elated that he'd temporarily escaped the mole hunters.

"That is fortunate," Dot said. "They will assume she is their only leak."

"I don't know about that," Meyer said. "I still want out. I mean, they're pretty serious about plugging any holes after your guys killed the people in Albania."

"I assure you I don't know what you're talking about," Dot said. She was careful that way, always worried that he was wearing a wire or recording their calls.

"Whatever," Meyer said. "Sorry. I shouldn't have said that over the line. But listen . . . Rask, the station chief in Tirana,

489

has gone dark. Disappeared. Did your guys . . . you know. Him, too?"

"I said I don't know, so let's leave it at that. I still look forward to any information you receive on CROSSTIE."

"Will that be enough to get me out?" Meyer said. "Seriously, I think my days are numbered. They're still polygraphing people. I'm not so much worried about that. It just means they're still hunting."

Dot paused for a long time. Meyer knew she was still there. He could hear her breathing.

"Yes," she finally said. "Find us CROSSTIE's identity and we will take care of you as you've requested. Also, I am supposed to ask you, have you heard any talk regarding a special submarine propulsion system?"

EIGHT DAYS LATER

Jack Ryan leaned back in his desk chair, fingers interlaced on top of his head. The trip to Alaska had been postponed indefinitely.

The Russians had provided the Chinese a submarine rescue vehicle to get the marooned crew off the *880*. The Mirage drive must have been so badly damaged that they did not try to take it off the vessel. Hours after the rescue, the departing *Indiana* picked up the sound of an explosion that they presumed to be the destruction of the *880*. PLAN officials announced that Liu Wangshu was in the hospital, recovering slowly. VICAR's Russian asset in China, however, confirmed that the professor had succumbed to a massive stroke.

"You think it's possible?"

Dr. Patti Moon thumbed through a file of schematics and line drawings of the Mirage propulsion system as designed by Medina Tohti.

"I'm not that kind of engineer," Moon said. "But as far as the sound goes, yes, your idea is certainly possible. I can work with the team that manufactures this to make sure it chirps periodically."

"But nobody could hear it without special equipment?"

"Right," Moon said. "We can calibrate something, preferably a hard surface instead of a belt—a bearing, tiny flywheel, some piece that seems integral to the design but really is only there for the chirp. To anyone else it would sound like a biologic."

"Like a whale or one of those farting cod you showed us in our first meeting."

"Exactly," Moon said. "We'll make it happen. This looks like it would be an extremely quiet mechanism. Absent your invisible chirp, I mean. It should be a simple task for our subs to track anything that has this installed. But the Chinese could never know to look or they'd simply track down the noise and fix it." She closed the file and set it flat on her lap. "I'd think it would be tough to get the plans into their hands, though, without them knowing, I mean."

"I have some really smart people working on that as well." Ryan sat forward in his chair, leaning on folded hands. "How does it feel to be part of our little conspiracy?"

THREE WEEKS LATER

Monica Hendricks gave her replacement on the China desk a file on a Uyghur woman named Medina Tohti, including a set of meticulously hand-drawn plans for "some kind of submarine system." Hendricks was on her way out, but suggested her replacement pass the file along to Odette Miller, the referent from the Counterintelligence Mission Center to the Central Asia desk. The issue for Miller had little to do with the plans themselves, and everything to do with the young Uyghur woman who had brought them forward. She was under CIA protection with her daughter for the time being, but Hendricks had a hunch there was a good chance she was a dangle for the Chinese, or possibly just attempting to make herself more valuable than she really was in order to gain asylum. Tohti had come out of China, but Miller handled Central Asia. Medina Tohti supposedly had family in Kazakhstan. Perhaps Miller could open a CI case and do some digging into the woman's background. See what she could find before the Navy invested any more time or money into something that was probably a scheme to get asylum. The Uyghur woman talked a good game, but one never knew. Anyway, it was worth a second look.

Monica's replacement locked the plans in a cabinet with the counterintelligence case file and left them there for Odette Miller to access. It took three days for Tim Meyer to hear about the information from Miller naturally, but only two hours for him to find a reason to sneak a camera into the restricted file room.

B ack at the ELISE station in Crystal City, Monica Hendricks thanked her team. Mary Pat Foley was present as well. Apart from a close circle around the President, the people in this room were the only ones who knew of the ruse.

"He was responsible for Leigh Murphy's murder," Mateo

said, almost in tears. "I understand why we have to do this, but I don't like it."

"SURVEYOR was responsible for more than one death," Hendricks said. She didn't even like to say his name. "It absolutely kills me to let him go."

Foley stepped up to the table. "It's a gut punch, I know," she said. "But I can promise you, we're not done here. The Bureau has their best surveillance teams up on SURVEYOR's handler now. She's very good at her job. Gretchen Pack hadn't given them anything too damning yet. In fact, much of what she handed over could have been found on the Internet if you knew where to look. But once she started giving them anything, she was trapped and she knew it. The President and I believe—and I imagine all of you do as well—that it would be worthwhile to keep ELISE up and running for at least another month. Sadly, Admiral Li has to leave us to return to his day job, but Chief Hendricks has agreed to deprive the private sector of her presence for a little while longer while we watch the illegal, see if anyone else contacts her. You found two. We have to work under the assumption that there are more."

65

Fu Bohai heard the chirp of the keycard outside his hotel room door when Talia arrived. She tried to open it, but it caught on the metal privacy bar.

"Dorogoy!" she called, breathless. "Why do you make me wait?"

He rolled off the bed to let her in, more excited to see her than he thought he would be. His head still hurt from the boat wreck, but not as badly as the humiliation of letting Medina Tohti escape. Unfortunately, the idiot police officers who responded to Lake Kanas had killed the Han traitor, Ma, before Fu could speak to him.

Admiral Zheng had been furious at first, but for reasons unknown to Fu, he'd been mollified of late. Even allowing Fu to take some leave and visit Moscow.

He opened the door a hair, peering through the crack before shutting it again to unlock the privacy bar.

The barbed Taser darts struck Fu in the groin and chest as soon as he opened the door. Paralyzed from the electric current running between them, he stiffened and fell backward, striking his head on the nightstand and knocking his hat to the floor.

Talia rushed past, kneeling by his side.

"I am sorry, my love," she said. "He has a gun. He is Chinese, too, perhaps you owe him money."

Fu did not recognize the man. He was young, very fit, and he'd traded the Taser for a small black pistol with a suppressor on the end. There was something about him that was different. The way he stood was . . .

The man motioned to Talia with the pistol. "Move away," he said in English.

That was it, Fu thought. "You are American?"

"I am," the man spat. "The young woman you drugged, tortured, and murdered in Albania was my friend."

Talia recoiled at that.

The pistol never wavered. Fu found himself wondering if he would have been so steady under such circumstances.

"I see," he said. "You are CIA . . . I suppose you want to know wh—"

"No, I've got all I need," the man said, and then shot Fu Bohai twice in the face.

The sun and sand and beach in Fiji were everything Tim Meyer thought they would be.

The tide was out, giving him enough beach for an evening run. He usually had it to himself this time of the evening, but there was an old dude behind him now, running, not jogging. *Way to go, old dude.* His wife was probably getting a pedicure or something. That's what the old ladies did when they came here. Got their nails done.

For a time, Meyer thought the Chinese would have him killed, and in truth, they might have, had he not given them the plans to their submarine drive. Even so, he continued to look over his shoulder.

Man, that guy behind him could run. He'd peter out soon. He had to. Meyer was getting tired and he was in shape . . .

The Chinese had kept their part of the bargain and got him the hell out of the country and set him up with a bank account containing just shy of two million bucks—something to do with the exchange rate, but it was close enough—and a small villa outside Savusavu.

It was rockier than he thought it would be, but he had the beach to run on at low tide, and a surprising number of the middle-aged women who came here on holiday from Australia and New Zealand were in the market for a fling with the mysterious American tech mogul who lived here year-round. He'd been on the island only two months, but they didn't need to know that.

He could hear the old dude now, chuffing up behind him like a freight train, like he was trying to win a race or something. The guy was barefoot and his feet made swooshing noises in the sand in time with his breathing. His stride was amazingly light.

"Hey," the guy called out. "On your left!"

Meyer chuckled to himself. This guy was going to pass him. He considered racing, but then thought it would be more fun to watch the old man stroke out farther up the beach. He moved a half step right into the moist sand.

He felt the sting in his hip at the same moment the guy ran past.

A wasp, maybe.

He stopped to check, suddenly feeling light-headed. He

looked out at the ocean, then at the old man who'd gone by, trying to get his bearings.

The man slowed and turned around to trot back, looking winded, but not nearly as winded as he'd sounded earlier.

"You okay?" he said. "You don't look so good."

Meyer found it difficult to open his mouth, like his jaw was locked. He fell sideways, smashing into the sand, paralyzed.

The old fellow squatted down beside him.

Meyer wanted to asked him if they'd met, but no words would come out.

The old man gave a slow shake of his head. "Relax, Tim," he said. "That was a shot of succinylcholine I gave you. Quite a bit, actually, because there was no way I was going to hit a vein on the run like that. It works a little slower in the muscle. Metabolizes quickly. Won't be any trace of it by the time they get you on a slab. I'd explain it all to you, but there's no need. I'm sure you already know why I'm here."

Meyer managed a small groan. Other than that, he couldn't even close his eyes. It was painless, but absolutely terrifying.

"Anyway," the old man said, giving him a friendly little pat on the shoulder before he stood up and walked away.

Jack Ryan, Jr., wanted to take the elevator, but Lisanne insisted on the stairs. She'd lost an arm, she reminded him, not her leg—and even then she'd have wanted to take the stairs as well, thank you very much.

Ryan could hear the chatter up above. The smell of lamb in the shepherd's pie made his mouth water.

He smiled at Lisanne as they turned at the landing to start

up again, taking it slow. It had been only a couple months. She was pale, sweating a little on that beautiful upper lip of hers. By all rights, she should have been dead. And she would have been, had she not had her spleen removed after a horseback-riding accident as a teenager. With no spleen to catch them, the bullets had proceeded through her body without clipping any major arteries but for the one in her arm. Adara had saved her life there, no question about it.

"You nervous?" Ryan said.

Lisanne looked at him with a mock scoff. "Why would I be nervous? Because this is our first date?"

"Not that," Ryan said as they topped the stairs and made the corner into the West Sitting Hall.

Cathy Ryan met them at the door to the private dining room, across from the master residence. She was dressed in jeans and a USMC sweatshirt, a dish towel thrown cavalierly over her shoulder. Ryan's old man came out behind her, carrying a copy of *The Wall Street Journal*.

"Mom, Dad," Ryan said. "I want to introduce you to Lisanne Robertson. A good friend from work."